Twisted Sister of Mine

Book Five of the Overworld Chronicles

John Corwin

ISBN- 13 978-0-9850181-5-3

Printed in the U.S.A.

little sister—BIG TROUBLE

Justin Slade is living on borrowed time.

The vampling curse is gnawing away at his body and his sanity. Because the cure might lie in his special kind of magic, Justin goes to Arcane University in a desperate attempt to unlock his powers.

When he runs into his little sister, Ivy, at the university, Justin realizes this might be his chance to convince her he's not evil. Even better, she might be able to cure him if her shape-shifting protector, Bigglesworth, doesn't eat him first.

Save his sister. Save the world. Save his life. With the clock ticking toward a future as a blood-sucking zombie, Justin has to make every second count.

Connect with John Corwin online:

Facebook: http://www.facebook.com/johnhcorwinauthor
Blog: http://blog.johncorwinauthor.com/
Twitter: http://twitter.com/#!/John_Corwin

Books by John Corwin:

Overworld Chronicles:

Sweet Blood of Mine
Dark Light of Mine
Fallen Angel of Mine
Dread Nemesis of Mine
Twisted Sister of Mine
Dearest Mother of Mine (12-2013)

Stand Alone Novels:

No Darker Fate
The Next Thing I Knew
Outsourced
Seventh

To my wonderful support group:

Alana Rock, Kayla Moore, Patrick Yates, Karen Stansbury, Dana Prestridge, Karla Ileana, Keren Hall, Nicole Passante, Anino, and Pat Owens

And my editors:
Annetta Ribken
Jennifer Wingard

Thanks so much for all your help and input!

Chapter 1

I stared at the scroll of antique parchment in my hand and felt my eyes widen with wonder. If a bearded giant on a flying motorcycle had just dropped from the skies and personally delivered this letter, I couldn't have been more surprised.

"What is it, Justin?" Elyssa asked, leaning her head against my shoulder.

I continued to stare at the paper. Words failed to break the jumble of emotions blocking my throat. All I could do was glare at the intricate script.

Dear Justin Slade,

Congratulations. You have hereby been accepted as a novice at Arcane University. Please see the attached schedule of required classes.

Unfortunately, due to the late nature of your application, we were unable to procure living quarters for you at the school. Your name has been added to the wait list, and you will be notified should the situation change.

Elyssa gasped. Took the acceptance letter from my limp fingers. "You're in!" She squeezed the breath out of me with a fierce hug then added a lip-smushing kiss.

"I'm in?" I said, stunned. It was like a dream come true for me. Months ago, I would have jumped at the chance. But now—now I couldn't, and the reason was very simple. Within a month or two, I'd probably be dead.

Elyssa seemed to sense my sudden mood shift. "The vampling curse?" she said, eyes worried.

I nodded, felt my shoulder sag. "What's the point? I won't have time to begin a semester, much less finish a degree."

"What in the hell is going on in here?" Shelton said, striding from his study and into the large room that might have passed for a family room in any normal house, had it not been part of a super-secret hideout buried beneath the Museum Tower in downtown Atlanta. He snatched the invitation from Elyssa's hand.

"Hey!" she said. "Didn't anyone ever teach you manners?"

Shelton burped and ignored her outburst. "Holy mother of a godless goat. My man came through."

"Your friend, Miles?" I asked. I remembered Shelton telling me he'd put in a good word with one of his former professors at the university, but he hadn't seemed too confident in the outcome.

"Yup," he said. "Took him long enough."

Shelton had asked Miles to look into it before the insanity with Maximus. Before I'd been bitten by a vampling and infected with a curse that would turn me into a member of the walking dead. I dropped into a chair, anger and self-pity slamming my heart back and forth like a volleyball. "Guess it's a moot point now," I said. "Since I'll be a mindless zombie in the next month or two."

Shelton screwed up his face like he'd just eaten a lemon. "Don't be so dramatic. In case you hadn't figured it out, going to school is about the only thing that could save your life."

"Are you auditioning for a role in an after-school special?" I said, scrunching my forehead. "How in the world will going to school keep me from turning into a zombie vampire?"

Bella, a petite Arcane-slash-dhampyr I'd met in Colombia during another of my adventures, sauntered in, arms full of grocery bags. She dropped the bags on the kitchen counter and gave us a concerned look. "Goodness. Is something the matter? Please don't tell me someone ate the rest of Harry's Lucky Charms. I do not wish to listen to him yell and curse about going to the grocery store on an empty tummy again."

Elyssa sighed. "Justin got into Arcane University."

"But I'm gonna die," I added, figuring I hadn't said it enough yet.

"Oh, well I suppose that's a little more serious than coming between Harry and his favorite cereal." She pursed her lips, face serious. "Justin, Harry and I have talked about this, and we think the cure to your condition might be through education."

I threw up my arms. "How is spending my final days in classes gonna beat the Grim Reaper?"

Bella and Shelton exchanged looks. Shelton grunted, which apparently meant he didn't want to explain it. She sighed, looking heavenward as if some greater power could ever make Harry Shelton do something he didn't want to.

"First, I have good news," she said, withdrawing a vial from her purse. "Meghan asked me to swing by because she and Nightliss concocted a potion that should slow the vampling curse."

"Slow?" I said, daring to feel a sliver of hope. "Like, how much slower?"

"Well, she made the potion using some of Nightliss's blood—"

"Her blood?" I said, aghast.

Bella shrugged. "The poor dear still isn't doing well after fighting Daelissa." She made a sad face. "Angels have a natural resistance to the curse. This potion should give you another year—we hope."

"And that's what leads us to the second point," Shelton said, walking into the kitchen and pouring a cup of coffee. "The angels made the vampling curse. Supposedly, they're immune to it, or they can heal themselves."

"Then why am I not healing?" I asked, looking down at my bare leg beneath the hem of my cargo shorts. Dark veins had spread from the wound in my calf, leaving the skin looking bruised.

"Because you haven't unlocked your angel magic," Bella said. "We've done our best to help you, Justin, but we haven't found the key. By going to Arcane University, you might discover that part of you and well"—she smiled hopefully—"heal yourself."

"That's wonderful," Elyssa said, tears glistening in her eyes. "Should he take the potion now?"

"Of course," Bella said, handing the vial to me.

"Just one dose?" I asked, looking at the dark amber liquid with suspicion.

Bella nodded. "Meghan said you'll need to take another one in six months."

Hope shone in Elyssa's eyes. Her lower lip trembled, and I could tell she was trying not to cry. This had been hard on me, but I knew it had been just as hard on her. To watch someone you love slowly waste away was probably even more torturous than being the one dying. I wanted to be with her for a long, long time. To love her, to marry her, and, if we were crazy enough, maybe even to have kids one day, like a gazillion years in the future when we were ready.

I popped the cork and drained the vial. It burned down my throat, leaving a trail of fire. All I could do was hope this worked.

"My college boyfriend," Elyssa said, playfully punching me in the arm. "I can't wait!"

Shelton snorted like a horse and took a sip of coffee. "Brings up fond memories."

"Oh, dear," Bella said. "I wonder if those on the receiving end of your memories remember them quite as fondly, Harry."

Shelton leaned over the kitchen counter and leered at her. "Now, what would you know about my college days?"

"The place abounds with rumors." She tapped a finger to her chin. "Not the least of which was assaulting sorority houses with spider bats."

"Spider bats?" I said, my skin crawling at the thought of what those things must look like. My phone buzzed in my pocket. I pulled it out to see another missed call from Vallaena Slade—my father's sister.

"Her again?" Elyssa said, looking at my phone.

"Yeah." Some of my newfound happiness faded.

Elyssa sighed. "She'll never give up, you know."

"Who won't give up?" Bella asked.

"Justin's Aunt Vallaena," Elyssa said. "She says she wants to protect him, but it's obviously Daemos politics. With Justin's father marrying Kassallandra Assad, other Daemos are looking for every political advantage they can wring out of it. The only saving grace is that not many know about Justin's existence."

My happy mood plummeted at the mention of my father's imminent marriage. "They can count me out of that brothel of incest and damnation."

Shelton choked on a gulp of coffee.

"So, what does Justin need to be ready for school?" Elyssa asked. "Maybe we need to do some school supply shopping."

"Get him a cute backpack," Bella said.

"How about a lunchbox while we're at it?" Shelton said with a roll of his eyes. "He doesn't need any school supplies. He'll take an assessment test for placement, buy some books, do a couple of panty raids on the female dorms—"

"If I find another girl's panties anywhere on you"—Elyssa pursed her lips and raised an eyebrow—"your college career might be cut short."

Since my girlfriend's ninja Templar training made her awfully handy with a katana, I didn't want to think about the cutting part. "Your panties are the only ones for me," I said with a wink.

"As I was saying," Shelton said, voice rising above our banter. "That's all there is to it."

"Sounds easy enough," I said, though the idea of an assessment exam made my stomach roil. "What happens if I fail the assessment?"

He laughed. "You don't pass or fail it. It determines your placement level."

I didn't want to think where that would put me.

Bella placed a comforting hand on my shoulder. "You'll do fine, Justin. It's nothing to worry about."

I'd heard that before, usually just before blowing something up. So far I hadn't proven to be very capable at the arcane arts. Then again, I wasn't exactly human. After Mom had saved me from certain death at the hands of Jeremiah Conroy, she'd told me how proud she was of me and how much she loved me—a sharp contrast to the previous time I'd seen her, when she told me she never wanted to see me again. And that had been the least of the surprises I'd discovered about her. Meghan Andretti, an Arcane healer, had come to the conclusion that my mom was, like Daelissa and Nightliss, an angel.

It meant the Conroys probably weren't my mom's parents, or my grandparents. It meant Ivy, my sister, wasn't related to them either. Knowing my heritage only raised more questions about the future. According to Shelton and Bella, it could also be my salvation from the vampling curse.

"Something wrong?" Elyssa said, snapping through my train of thought. "You look worried."

I forced a smile. "Peachy keen. I'm just thinking about all I need to do to prep for school."

Deep down, though, a troubling thought kept recurring. I wasn't fully Daemos, or angel—just a part of each. Even worse, it meant I didn't possess a shred of humanity. My close friends came from all sorts of supernatural groups—vampire, felycan, lycan, Arcane—but they all had one thing in common: their human genes. It made me feel disconnected. The only person in the world who shared my bizarre lineage was my sister, and she thought I was pure evil. She'd told me it was her duty to rid the world of me and had followed through by staging her kidnapping at the hands of Maximus. When I'd gone after the rogue vampire, he'd captured me in an ambush, and I'd very nearly ended up fueling his vampire revolution and quest for world domination with my unique blood.

A cold ache blossomed in my calf, sending tendrils of sub-zero chills throughout my leg, as if to remind me that even though the potion might have slowed it down, the vampling curse was still determined to eat me alive and cut my education short if it could.

Chapter 2

"I need new clothes," Elyssa said. "I don't have a single thing to wear to the university."

Shelton looked her up and down. "Looks like you're wearing something now." He blew out a breath. "Women and new clothes."

"Harry, you don't know a thing about women, do you?" Bella said, looking a bit miffed.

"Sure I do," he said. "They like to talk and spend men's money."

Bella made a little growling sound in the back of her throat and took Elyssa by the arm. "I'd love to help you shop for something cute." She took a step back, craning her neck to look my girlfriend up and down. "I'm thinking purple and slinky."

"I'm all for slinky," I said, my attitude brightening. Then again, Elyssa's athletic curves looked amazing no matter what she wore.

"At least Justin understands our needs," Bella said with a sniff, casting Shelton a look.

Shelton, for his part, grabbed his coffee mug and said, "Come on, kiddo, it's time for your lessons."

I checked the time and felt my forehead go all wrinkly. "But, I still have an hour!"

"Better get an early start. Let the lady folk go shopping."

"Oh, wait," Elyssa said, snapping her fingers and stopping to look at me. "Let's get Justin's measurements. He definitely needs new jeans." She looked at the cargo shorts I wore. "Something that doesn't make him look like he's on a jungle safari."

"How about a sky blue shirt with ruffles?" I said. "Or a yellow tuxedo?"

Bella brandished her wand, waved it in a familiar pattern, and a stream of white sparkles floated over me like pixie dust.

"Hold your arms out to the side, dear," Bella said. "I'm getting your measurements."

I did as she asked, and after a few seconds, the sparkles vanished, replaced by numbers floating in the air.

"There we go." Bella smiled and the two women practically skipped with joy out the door.

"Women really love their shopping," Shelton said, scratching his whiskers. He grunted and headed deeper into his secret lair.

We reached the gauntlet room, a large space Shelton shuffled into different configurations for whatever challenges he wanted to throw my way. I took a slender white rod about three inches long from a nearby table, squeezed it, and gave it a shake. The ends telescoped in both directions, and the girth thickened into a plain white practice staff a little taller than me.

Shelton extended his own staff and directed it at a haphazard stack of cinder blocks. An invisible force toppled them to the ground. "Pile 'em back up," he said.

I closed my eyes for an instant. When I reopened them, the tendrils of my incubus essence hovered before me. Magical energy—or aether as Arcanes called it—was an invisible force to most people. Somehow, a mixture of my incubus senses and angel heritage allowed me to see it. Aether took all sorts of shapes. As my eyes focused into incubus sight, I saw streaking white comets whizz past, swirling ultraviolet orbs, gray amorphous clouds drifting lazily, and galaxy-like swirls of white and ultraviolet mingling with each other. A network of glowing capillaries webbed the ground. Arcanes called them ley lines. Most of the ones near the surface were tiny but numerous. Deeper down, large arteries of aether thrummed through the earth.

I drew in a deep breath through my nose, drawing energy into my tendrils as if they were straws.

Shelton took out his arcphone—the Arcane equivalent of a normal smartphone—and flicked on an application to measure my performance.

I imagined ropes of energy wrapping around the cinder blocks and directed my will toward the effort. Glowing white lines formed around the targets. Holding out my staff, I imagined lifting the blocks. Out of the corner of my eye, I saw the power gauge on Shelton's app jump straight into red territory. I gritted my teeth, groaned, and shouted, "*Shoryuken*!" The cinder blocks jumped, jerked, bumped together, and finally slammed into a crooked teetering tower.

With a gasp, I released my will, and the ethereal ropes vanished. The cinder blocks wobbled uncertainly before finding a semblance of balance despite their precarious positioning.

"Sweet monkey butts," Shelton said, holding the screen of his arcphone so I could see the results. "You blew through more energy to move those cinder blocks than it'd take to stop a woman from shopping."

I sighed. "I don't know why."

"Neither do I." He sighed. "That's one of the reasons I think the university will be good for you."

"Are you sure the kind of magic angels use is the same as Arcanes?" I'd pondered that question a lot lately, but hadn't arrived at any conclusions.

"It's got to be," he said, scrolling through the stats on his phone. "You use aether like the rest of us." He tapped his chin in thought. "Although, I don't recall seeing Nightliss use a staff or wand for a focus. Hell, I don't even remember her using words."

Since the intent mattered more than the words used to activate most spells, I'd taken my words from video games. Shelton shamelessly stole his from sci-fi movies, proving he was almost as big a nerd as me.

My shoulders slumped. "Bottom line—I'm the worst angel ever."

Shelton clapped me on the shoulder. "Ah, don't get down on yourself, kid—er—man. I had almost zero potential when I went to Arcane University. Hell, they sent me to the Science Academy first because my parents didn't think I had the gift."

"Wait a minute," I said, raising an eyebrow. "The Overworld has a *Science* Academy?"

"Right across the valley from Arcane University." One corner of his mouth twitched into a smile, as if he'd just remembered something amusing. "If it hadn't been for one professor who thought I was worth a damn, I probably wouldn't be the man I am today."

"He must've been a real jackass," I said with a grin.

Shelton laughed. "Yep. Good old Miles."

"This is the guy who pushed my application through?"

"You got it."

A trickle of hope washed over my self-pity. "Do you really think going to school will help me with my issues?"

"Like I said, my parents thought I didn't have the gift." His lips twisted with obvious distaste. "They sent me for testing every year, but my potential pinged zero. So they sent me to Science Academy. I fit in with the techies just fine, but Miles saw Arcane potential in me when nobody else did." He shuddered, as if remembering something unpleasant.

"Something wrong?" I asked.

A gruff, uncaring mask slid over Shelton's face. "Nah. I think I had too much coffee."

I knew better than to probe him with questions once he got that look on his face. Bella, on the other hand, didn't seem to care, and usually pushed Shelton until he locked himself in his study and watched space movies at full volume.

"When do I need to take the assessment?" I asked.

"The sooner the better." He checked the calendar on his phone. "Looks like they open for business tomorrow. Might as well get it over with."

"Gee, it sounds wonderful when you put it like that."

He wrinkled his nose. "I hate standardized tests. They're the work of the devil."

I couldn't agree more.

After lunch, I spent the rest of the afternoon practicing. By late afternoon, exhaustion hung like lead to every limb, and nausea clawed at my throat. I made a beeline for the bathroom, gripped the sides of the sink, and heaved. It took deep breaths to keep lunch firmly in my stomach. This was, unfortunately, nothing new. Every so often I would draw in more energy than my inner reservoir—Arcanes called it a well—could hold, and it would stretch to accommodate more. This caused what was known as magic poisoning, and it sucked.

The mirror reflected the greenish tint to my face and my bloodshot eyes. I stared at my tired visage and wondered if all of this was for nothing. Something in the shadows seemed to move, stretching toward me. Fingers flexed on a shadowy clawed hand as it reached for my back—

Knuckles rapped on the door, startling me, and the shadowy image vanished. I splashed water on my face.

"You okay in there?" Shelton said from outside the closed door.

"Wonderful," I replied, rubbing my eyes and looking around. *Or maybe I'm just crazy.*

Shelton grunted. "If you barf, make sure to spray air freshener. The odor nearly caused me to hurl last time."

I rolled my eyes. "Thanks for your concern. You're the best friend a person could have."

"Hey, I'm just sayin'."

I heaved again. Nothing came out. I looked in the mirror. Something shrieked. Two clawed hands of black mist lunged from the shadows behind me, reaching for my throat. I yelled and spun to face whatever it was. And found…nothing.

I closed my eyes. Took deep breaths. *What the hell is wrong with me?* A rotten scent crawled up my nose, wrinkling it with disgust. Hot, dank air touched my neck. The rattling sigh of the undead chilled my spine. Shivering, I opened my eyes.

A vampling, its rotten eyes filled with pus, its toothless maw wide open, lunged for me.

I shrieked like a girl and punched at it. My fist connected with something hard. Backing into a corner to keep the monstrosity from biting me, I gripped the lid to the toilet reservoir and held it like a shield.

When I looked around the bathroom, the vampling was gone. "Crap," I said. I hissed out a breath between my teeth as logic and reason kicked my brain in the cerebellum. The vampling curse enjoyed playing tricks on my mind. Sometimes the hallucinations were mild. Other times, they terrified me. Once they started, it was as if my brain couldn't differentiate between illusion and reality. I noticed a fist-sized hole in the wall and grimaced. Shelton wouldn't be pleased. I took a painting of a starfish from the wall over the toilet, pulled out the hanger nail, and, careful not to bend it, used my supernatural strength to drive it into the wall above the hole. After wiping away some of the tell-tale drywall dust, I hung the picture and nodded in satisfaction. Maybe Shelton wouldn't notice.

The signature at the bottom of the picture caught my eye: *Martin S.* I wondered if Martin's last name was Shelton or something else that began with the same letter.

The front door opened and shut, announcing the return of Elyssa and Bella. I assumed an innocent look on my face and went into the den to greet them. The nausea, thankfully, was already fading away.

"You're going to love this," Elyssa said, removing a men's suit from a bag. "Now you can take me to nice places where they don't allow cargo pants." She opened the coat and twisted a button inside. The dark material shimmered, changing to a disgusting light blue. "Isn't it cool?"

"Awesome!" I said, refraining from asking why she'd purchased me a suit, of all things. Why couldn't she be happy with cargo pants and T-shirts? "How does it work?"

"Just twist the button, imagine the color, and"—the suit changed to purple—"it will turn any color you want."

"Her dress is made from the same material," Bella said, holding up a silky outfit.

"Let me try it on for you," Elyssa said, her eyes sparkling with excitement. She and Bella took their goods down the hallway and into a bedroom.

Shelton shook his head, a grin on his face. "Give a girl flowers and clothes, and you're set for life."

"I wish it was that simple," I said, thinking back to my nerdy days when I couldn't have bought a date with a roomful of flowers. At least until I'd met Elyssa.

My girlfriend appeared a moment later, striding down the hall in a curve-hugging purple dress, her raven hair shimmering like a curtain across one shoulder. A slit ran halfway up the creamy skin of her thigh. I felt my mouth drop open and my eyes go wide at the sight of her. "Justin like. Justin like a lot!"

"You've reduced him to speaking caveman," Bella said with a proud grin.

Just the sight of Elyssa in the dress sent pleasant tingles to all the right places. "Why don't you show me the other stuff you bought,"

I said, trying to be casual about it. I took my hottie by the hand and led her back toward the bedroom we shared. I heard Shelton chuckle, but ignored him.

We entered the bedroom. I knotted my fingers in Elyssa's hair, pulled it back, raising her face, and took one of her soft lips between mine, giving it a gentle tug.

She exhaled a slow breath, eyes half-lidded, and purred. "I take it you like the dress."

"The things I want to do to you right now…" I let the thought hang for a moment. "Maybe we can get our own place soon. It sucks having roommates."

She traced her lips up my neck and bit an earlobe. "Oh? And what would we do with our own place?"

I smiled. Pressed my face against her neck and inhaled the wonderful scent that was her. "Well, for one thing, we'd spend a lot of time in bed."

She made an appreciative moan. "I like sleeping in."

"Oh yeah, sleeping in, video games, monogrammed towels."

Elyssa laughed. "Sounds like an adventure already." She pecked me on the lips one last time before grinning with excitement and showing me the new outfits she'd gotten. Amazingly, they were all very girly and modern, despite her love for Victorian-era dresses and other Goth attire. After pulling out the last garment, her forehead creased with confusion.

"What the heck?" she said, reaching in and pulling out a slender gift-wrapped box.

"Jewelry?" I asked, even though it looked too wide for that.

"I didn't get this. I'll bet Bella got it and put it in the wrong bag."

We walked into the den where Bella was having tea and talking with Shelton. It was obvious to me she had a thing for Shelton. He, on the other hand, seemed intent on staying distant.

Trademark Shelton.

"Did you leave something in my bag?" Elyssa said, holding it out to Bella.

The Colombian gave the package a surprised look. "No."

"You sure?"

"I certainly don't remember buying a gift."

"May I?" I said, holding out my hand.

I tore open the packaging to reveal a lidded box, set it on the table, and removed the lid.

Inside lay what looked like a Barbie doll with olive skin. But that wasn't what made my forehead pinch tight. The doll had been decapitated and the head taped to its feet.

"What in the blazes?" Shelton said, finally taking notice.

"Justin," Elyssa said, "doesn't that doll look a lot like—"

"Nightliss," I finished.

Chapter 3

Beneath the doll, I noticed a folded piece of pink paper and reached toward it.

Shelton grabbed my wrist. "Are you crazy? What if that thing is booby trapped?" He cursed a few times, grabbing his wand and muttering an incantation under his breath. A translucent dome appeared over the box. He pulled his arcphone from a pocket and set it next to the dome. "Let me scan it before you do anything else. I hope it doesn't have a damned tracker on it."

"Were you followed?" I asked.

Elyssa shook her head. "You know how careful we are."

"Did you ever leave your bags unattended?"

She tapped her chin, eyes looking to the side. "I left them outside the changing room for a couple of minutes but Bella was there."

"Oh, dear," Bella said, an apologetic look on her face. "I wandered off to look at lingerie. I found a really cute set of lacy pink panties with bows on them, too."

Shelton's eyes went a bit wide. He cleared his throat a couple of times. "Oh, really?"

Bella's violet dhampyr eyes lit up, as if she'd suddenly struck gold. "Why, yes, Harry. Would you like to see them?"

He made a choking noise and shook his head like a wet dog. "Darn it, woman, I'm trying to make sure you weren't tracked here."

The Arcane reached down her shirt and brandished a shiny gold chain with a cross and the Cyrinthian symbol for "obfuscate" on it. "I doubt the tracker could overcome my charm," she said.

Shelton nodded and seemed mollified. "You ever make charms for these two?"

Bella sighed. "I simply haven't had the time."

The dome over the package blinked green. "Whew." Shelton flicked his wand, and the shield vanished. "Looks like Bella's charm fried the magical tracker on the package once she got in range of it. It's clean."

I breathed a sigh of relief along with the others. There was a reason we were staying with Shelton in his super-secret hideout. All sorts of nasties would love to get their hands on us—one I could think of in particular, Daelissa. I removed the doll and set it aside. With a slight tremble in my hand, I took out the pink paper. I saw writing on the other side and had a sinking suspicion I knew who had written it.

You shouldn't hang out with evil little Darklings, bro. I still owe you for messing up my spell and disappointing Bigdaddy. Peekaboo! I'm gonna find you. <3 Smoochies <3

Ivy

Shelton took out his phone, started to dial, and abruptly stopped with a grimace. "I don't think I should be the one to call Meghan."

Elyssa took out her phone, dialed.

I gave Shelton a cool look. "You need to clear the air with her. She still thinks you had a hand in letting Vadaemos eat her father's soul."

"How many times—" Shelton began.

"Meghan, hey this is Elyssa." My girlfriend smiled. "I'm great. Yeah, did some shopping with Bella. Got this really cute dress."

I made a hurry-up motion with my hands.

She gave me an apologetic look. "Say, is Nightliss still there?" Elyssa made an affirmative noise, a look of relief crossing her face. "Is she doing any better?" She frowned. "Okay, well, we got a suspicious package from Ivy." She described the doll.

I heard Meghan on the other end, but the Arcane healer was apparently using a muffle spell on her phone, because even with my super hearing, I couldn't make out a word of the gibberish coming from the speaker.

Elyssa hung up after speaking with Meghan for a few more minutes. "Nightliss is still feeling pretty sick, but she hasn't been attacked by any blonde girls."

"She still isn't back in the saddle, eh?" Shelton said.

"Whatever Daelissa did to her messed her up pretty bad," Elyssa replied. "When Nightliss cured Felicia of the vampling virus, it took everything she had. Meghan thinks she's getting worse."

"You realize if we don't unlock the angel inside you, we're screwed, right?" Shelton said looking squarely at me. "Without Nightliss, Daelissa and the Conroys are gonna crush us."

"No pressure, right?" I said, rolling my eyes. It felt like too much depended on me, and I was still a freaking teenager. Foreseeance 4311 indicated I was supposed to make some earth-shattering choice that could save or doom the world. I tried not to think about it, especially since the experts told me these prophecies weren't the most accurate things in the world. Then again, Bella had a foreseeance about me showing up in her two-horse town down in Colombia, and that had obviously come true.

So, I grasped for a silver lining. "At least my mom is on our side."

"Off doing god knows what," Shelton said. "She's proven we can't count on her."

"Do you think my grandparents are angels like her?" I asked.

Bella offered me a wary smile. "No matter what they are, they're extremely powerful in magic and politics."

"Do the Conroys run the Arcane Council?" I asked.

"Nah," Shelton said. "Old man Conroy doesn't seem to care for politics. Then again, he might own a few council members."

"He probably owns the Primus," Bella said with a grimace. "Jarrod Sager has been in power for decades. Nobody keeps a position for so long without becoming corrupt."

I knew from conversations with Bella that the Arcanus Primus was the leader of the Arcane Council, but Shelton usually avoided talking politics.

His lip curled into a sneer at the mention of Sager's name and just as quickly smoothed back down. "We should see if we can backtrace this doll," he said.

Bella was already running her wand over the plastic figure and the gift wrap I'd torn off. She stopped over a spot and peered closer. "Oh my."

"What?" I said, leaning over and focusing my super-sharp eyesight on the spot. I made out a tiny speck of white. Magnifying my vision further, I was able to see that it appeared to be a bit of slimy dough.

Bella extracted it in a tiny, clear bubble which spun for several seconds before spitting out a bunch of holographic images of various supernatural types in a rotating slideshow, reminding me of a slot machine. The images slowed before settling on the picture of an amorphous white blob.

"Mr. Bigglesworth," I said in a low growl. "I should've known Ivy's errand boy—thing—whatever the heck he is, would've been the one to plant this package on you." I'd never met such a disgusting freak of nature—or more correctly, a freak of super-nature. Bigglesworth could assume the shape of people he'd eaten, by absorbing them in his blob-like body. The few times I'd seen him in human shape, his skin had looked unnaturally doughy and slick, although Bella informed me he could look far more convincing if he chose. I had a sneaking suspicion Bigglesworth let his disguises falter so I would figure out it was him. He seemed to enjoy toying with me whenever he had a chance.

One day, I planned to roast Doughboy in the oven, feed him to hungry seagulls, and hope they pooped all over the Conroys' car.

"Get rid of that thing," Shelton said. "For all we know he can track pieces of his body."

Bella uttered a word and burned the speck to charred ash. "It's clean of other traces. There are no fingerprints."

My phone rang, startling us from our reverie. I glanced at the caller ID and groaned when I saw the name. I'd been ignoring her calls, but her persistence annoyed the crap out of me. I decided to answer if only to tell her once and for all to bug off.

"Hello, Auntie."

"I am glad you saw fit to finally answer my call, Justinius." Her voice, as usual, sounded low and seductive.

"I want you to stop calling me." I slashed the air with a hand. "You're worse than a telemarketer."

"Please hear me out, nephew. It's very important."

"Important for you or me? Look, I'm not gonna be your pawn."

Vallaena sighed. "I have no illusions about bringing your stubbornness under control. Surely, you realize the wedding between your father and Kassallandra is not far off?"

"Yes." I said in a flat voice.

"I hope you understand the sacrifice your father is making to secure this alliance."

"Oh, gee, you mean like sacrificing his marriage to my mom so he could marry that red-headed slut?"

I heard Elyssa gasp and cast a look her way as she regarded me, arms akimbo, with a stern look.

Vallaena tutted. "That is no way to speak of an Anae of House Assad. Especially not for someone of your newly acquired stature."

I wrinkled my forehead. "Stature? What are you talking about?"

"Your father somehow convinced the Paetros to raise your standing from Castratae to Cenae." She made a wondering sound. "I have no idea what he did. Rising from outcast to Denae is unheard of, but all the way to Cenae should have been impossible for anyone short of a prince like your father."

"A prince?" I asked.

"Justinius, this is the sort of thing you would know if only you would accept me as your teacher in all things Daemos." She sighed. "You know next to nothing of your own people, or of the powers you possess. Please, let me teach you."

"So you can use me? I don't think so."

"Nephew, you try my patience," Vallaena said, her voice terse. "Do you wish to gain powerful allies when a war of unimaginable destruction approaches?"

I sulked for a moment before answering between clenched teeth. "Yes, of course."

"Your father has given you the chance to earn those allies in accordance with Foreseeance Forty-Three Eleven. If you earn the respect and trust of House Slade, the other Daemos will fall in line. Our nation will be united and ready to face the Seraphim threat."

"Seraphim?" I asked, wondering if I had a new homicidal super-race to worry about.

"The angels," she said. "I have spent a great amount of time studying these adversaries. Our history with them is rather more extensive than I thought."

Her mention of history piqued my interest. Had she discovered information we didn't have? Despite my dislike of my demonic aunt and her political maneuvering, I had to admit her points about earning stature with the Daemos would help if the angels started a war. This history she mentioned might sweeten the pot.

"Tell me more," I said.

She laughed. "I think not. First, prove you are willing to commit to your studies. Promise to learn from me, and I will tell you what I know."

"What sorts of things do I need to learn?"

"Political protocol, of course. I'm sure you will find it boring, but necessary." She paused as if waiting for a snarky comment before continuing. "Then, of course, you must learn better control over your powers such as manifesting and summoning."

"Summoning?" I asked.

Shelton and Bella gave me sharp looks when I said it.

"Yes. Summoning creatures from the demon plane is very important, especially hellhounds."

I wrinkled my nose at the thought of massive black dogs with sickly yellow eyes and breath like brimstone. One of them had nearly killed my felycan friend, Stacey. Then again, Kassallandra's hounds had rescued me. As with normal dogs, they acted according to what their masters taught them. "Why in the hell would I want to summon those?"

"It's very simple, child." I could almost hear Vallaena smile on the other end. "Either you learn, or you die."

I couldn't argue her logic. Just like learning magic, I had to be in full control of my demonic abilities. I'd nearly killed Elyssa after manifesting into my full demon form, a huge beast without conscience or remorse—only the desire to consume and destroy.

A groan escaped my throat. "I'm going to Arcane University to study magic," I said. "It'll be hard to make time for you."

"On the contrary," my dear aunt said. "The university will provide the perfect setting for learning. Let me know what your schedule is, and I will gladly tutor you after classes."

After I ended the call, Vallaena's words echoed in my mind.

Learn or die.

This was going to be one hell of a semester.

Chapter 4

Shelton came into the kitchen the next morning, a pensive look on his face. "Check your email. I sent you directions to Miles's office for the assessment."

I paused with a spoonful of cereal halfway to my mouth. "You're not coming with me?"

He shook his head. "Nah, no need. You're all growed up, kid."

I'd faced giant leyworms in a cavern filled with life-leeching angel husks and shadow people. I'd fought hordes of vamplings. I'd even fought an army of vampires and nearly been killed by a raging demon spawn. But something about going to my first day of Arcane school made me feel like a shy, nervous kindergartener. "You can't abandon me, Shelton." A pleading tone came into my voice. "Come with me."

He made a harrumphing noise. "I'm sure you'll be fine with your girlfriend there to protect you."

As if on cue, Elyssa came into the kitchen, her face lit with excitement. "Guess what?" she said, practically dancing with excitement.

"What?" I said, feeling somewhat mollified that she'd be there to watch me make an idiot of myself at the assessment.

"Dad called. He said I'm ready to take the Cho'kai! Can you believe it?"

It took a moment for me to remember what the heck that was. "You mean the trial to become a full Templar?"

She gripped me in a tight hug, let go, and clapped her hands like a little girl. "Yes! I've been studying battle strategy, perfecting my killing strikes, and I even achieved proficiency merits for three different forms of sword mastery. I thought, with all that's happened in the past few months, my father would make me go back to basics and start over."

"Welcome to the Girl Scouts," Shelton said with a shake of his head.

I ignored the comment. "He changed his mind?"

She nodded. "Now I have the chance to pass it in time to be the youngest person granted full Templar status."

"What are they doing about the whole, um, Divinity issue?" I asked. We'd recently discovered Daelissa was, in fact, the Templar Divinity—the one who blessed new Templars and gave them their supernatural strength and healing, among other things. Since she was a crazy angel with a taste for world domination, having her in control of the Templars seemed like a bad idea. Thomas Borathen and other Templar legions had broken from the Synod. I hated to think what that might mean in the future—a Templar civil war, maybe.

"Supposedly, Daelissa is still helping the Templars who sided with the Synod." Her lip curled in anger. "Even though we're no longer allied with them, we're inducting new members. Unfortunately, without Daelissa, it means those who don't already have supernatural abilities or immunity to certain curses won't get any."

"Is the Cho'kai the same thing as the ceremony Daelissa used to perform?"

"No," she said, shaking her head. "It's a test of courage and ability. If you pass it, then you go through the initiation." She quirked her lips. "I don't know what they plan to replace it with."

We'd discovered Daelissa wiped the minds of Templars after giving them their superpowers. She'd wiped Elyssa's mind of me in an attempt to turn her against me. "When does the trial start?"

"They don't assign a date. Half the time you don't even know you're taking the Cho'kai until you're halfway into it." She dipped a banana in yogurt and ate it, excitement dancing in her eyes. "It's always different too. It might take a couple of days, or weeks. This one guy—" Her smile abruptly fell.

"What is it?" I asked, wondering if I'd ruined the moment with bad BO or something.

"The Cho'kai might take too long," she said. "I—I don't want to spend time apart from you."

I narrowed my eyes. "In case I don't unlock my inner angel?"

"I don't want to risk missing—" she choked up. "If the potion doesn't work. If you don't unlock your powers, I don't want to lose a single precious moment with you." A tear trickled down her cheek.

I didn't even want to consider Meghan's potion not working, but knew it was a risk. "The Cho'kai is so important to you," I said. "It's your dream to become the youngest Templar ever."

She shook her head. "No. My dream is a long life with you, Justin. Nothing else is more important."

I wiped the tear from her cheek. "Listen to me, Elyssa. I love you. I want you to be happy. If you don't take the trial just because of me, it'll make me really, really sad. I *want* you to go forth and kick ass." I smiled. "Besides, Meghan's potion will give me plenty of time to unlock my angel powers."

Uncertainty clouded her eyes. "I don't want to take the chance. What if—"

"It's going to work," I said, smiling. "I know it is." A tingle of bitter cold bit my calf as if the vampling curse was calling a bluff.

"Look, it doesn't matter if I'm the youngest ever," Elyssa said. "It's no big deal. I'll tell them to wait."

"Don't put your future on hold for me," I said, the thought of her giving up her dreams weighing me down with guilt.

"How many times do I have to say that you're an important part of my future?" Elyssa said. "Don't you get it? You're more important to me than breaking some stupid record. I've thought about this a lot, and I think it all boils down to me wanting to make my father proud. But you're more important to me than that."

"I understand," I said, starting to feel a little frustrated. "But, you've given up a lot to be with me, Elyssa. I want you to do this for you."

"But—"

I put a finger on her lips. "We'll beat this," I said. "I know we will. And now that we have more time, I want you to seize this moment and make it yours, babe. Don't do it for your dad, or for me. Do it for you."

She blurred toward me, pressing her lips against mine so fast, I hardly had time to think. When she pulled away, her eyes glistened. "When you say things like that, it reminds me why I love you," she said.

"My cheery attitude?"

A smile lit her face. "You just always seem to know what I'm thinking. You help me realize that it's okay to do things for myself. Of course, knowing the potion gives us time..." her voice trailed off. "I would never leave you for a minute otherwise."

"Not even when I have to use the potty?"

She snorted. "Oh, babe, you're too much sometimes."

I kissed her. "Don't you need to go practice or something?"

"Yes." She pecked my lips. "I'll see you for supper."

The moment she was gone, my grin faltered, faded, and fell. I'd really wanted her to come with me this morning. But it felt like I'd done the right thing, supporting her even if I missed her like crazy. And I sure as heck didn't want her thinking the potion might not work. She deserved her chance at the Cho'kai after pouring her heart and soul into the Templars for so long.

"Aw, geez, you have to go and look like a freaking puppy who just crapped the bed," Shelton said, grabbing his duster and slapping a brimmed hat atop his head. "Fine. I'll go."

He wasn't Elyssa, but at least I wouldn't be alone. "Thanks, Shelton."

"C'mon," he huffed, and grabbed his car keys.

Shelton drove us to the Grotto and parked next to a pink Ferrari with fluffy yellow seats. As we walked toward the ticket booth to purchase a ticket for the Obsidian Arch, I noticed what looked like an undulating jellyfish circling the parking lot. I'd seen such a creature before in Bogota, Colombia at the Obsidian Arch way station at La Casona.

"Minders," I said, with a shudder. "What the heck are those doing here?" The creatures looked like something out of a nightmare and, considering they fed on people's thoughts and could make people see whatever they wanted, maybe that was true. I'd never seen them on guard duty in the Grotto before.

"No idea," Shelton said, walking up to the ticket booth. A surly man with heavy jowls sat in the small square building behind a window made of the same liquid glass utilized by buildings inside the Grotto. He looked the two of us up and down. "Yeah?"

"Service with a smile," Shelton said, rolling his eyes. "Two tickets for Queens Gate with return."

"That'll be four hundred tinsel," the man said, gazing steadily at Shelton.

"I'm a Triple-A member." Shelton slid a card through the seamless glass, though I noted it stopped his fingers from passing through. The card bore the logo of a staff with a fireball coalesced on the end and the words "Arcane Academics Association" imprinted on it.

The man shoved it back without looking. "No discounts."

"What the hell do you mean, no discounts?" Shelton said, his eyes going hard.

"Conclave ruled it was unfair the Arcanes got discounts while others paid full price." A grunt. "Take it up with them if you don't like it."

"Four hundred tinsel is a rip-off!"

The man shrugged. Picked up an arctablet—the Arcane equivalent of touch-screen tablet—and resumed playing a puzzle game.

"Uh, how much is that in dollars?" I asked Shelton.

Shelton fumed for a moment before answering. "The exchange rate sucks right now. One tinsel is worth about two bucks." He glowered at the ticket agent. "Son of a bull-licking ba—"

"We have money," I said, pulling Shelton away from the ticket booth before he said something to piss off the ticket agent. My father had apparently left Shelton with access to one of his secret bank accounts. It wasn't a million bucks, but it definitely took care of the basics.

"It ain't the money, man; it's the principle of the matter. I've always gotten an Arcane discount, and now some stupid Conclave law comes along and ruins it!"

I shrugged. "Well, it's definitely a rip-off, but I don't think we have a choice." I checked the time, wondering when the assessments started. "Let's just buy the tickets and go."

He narrowed his eyes at me. "You realize you'll have to use this arch pretty regularly if you want to see your girlfriend, right? You'll be halfway across the world while she's over here earning her ninja merit badge. Four hundred tinsel a pop ain't gonna be cheap, and the money your dad gave us isn't gonna stretch that far."

I imagined not seeing Elyssa for weeks at a time. She was one of the few people who'd kept me sane and alive since discovering I was more than a mild-mannered nerd with a penchant for live-action role playing. We'd work something out. Shelton and Bella were right—unlocking my angel powers would not only heal me, but give us a fighting chance to beat Daelissa.

"Can't I earn frequent flyer miles?" I said in a plaintive voice. "How about a student discount?"

Shelton's gaze softened, and he made a grumbling noise. "I know it's tough. Damned women, falling in love and all that crap." He swatted the air. "That's why I don't get involved."

"Not even with Bella?"

He squirmed under my question, tugging at the collar of his T-shirt as if it had grown too tight. "You gotta be kidding. She's like hundreds of years older than me. That woman would—"

"Be more than you can handle?" I smiled.

Shelton grinned. "Ain't that the truth about all women?" His grin faltered, and a look of pure disgust twisted his lips. "Women are poison."

My eyebrows pinched at that statement. When he didn't elaborate, I said, "I think the right woman is just enough to handle. Enough to keep you interested and coming back for more. You don't want someone who bores you."

He huffed out a breath. "Poison, man." A shrug. "Don't get me wrong. Bella ain't bad. Sometimes she scares the hell out of me, and I don't even know why." He flinched. Looked at me. "Don't you dare tell a soul I just admitted that."

"That you're intimidated by a woman?" I laughed. "Elyssa intimidates the crap out of me sometimes, dude. And I'm not ashamed to admit it."

"How in the world did you drag us into talking about relationships and feelings?" He shuddered. "Someone must've slipped estrogen in the damned coffee this morning."

I sighed. "Well, I don't think it's any secret Bella digs you. Either that, or she's a masochist for hanging out with you and your grumpy self this long."

Shelton gave me a hurt look. "Hey, I ain't grumpy. Just antisocial. But you know, maybe Bella—"

Thirty feet away, the doors leading inside the Grotto opened, and a young blonde girl stepped out, skipping merrily along in front of a matronly woman with long, silvery hair. A shock of cold fear drowned out Shelton's words.

Self-preservation claimed my reflexes and triggered a panic event racing from my brain all the way to my toes. I gripped Shelton and jerked him behind the ticket booth, cutting him off mid-sentence. Sheer terror commanded me to flee this place at top speed. I glanced at Shelton's pickup truck, some hundred yards and a million miles away in the parking lot. We'd never make it without being seen.

"What the hell?" Shelton grumbled.

I peeked around the corner. Shelton peered in the same direction. I didn't know the silver-haired woman from sight, but judging from the company she kept, I could take a good guess.

"You afraid of that kid?" Shelton said.

I trembled as I pressed my back against the ticket booth and said in a low whisper, "That girl is my sister."

Chapter 5

Shelton's mouth dropped open a fraction. "That's Ivy?"

I nodded.

"She's the one who almost wiped out every vampire in Maximus's compound with a spell too powerful for most Arcanes to even dream about pulling off?"

I nodded again.

He let out a low whistle. "Hoo-boy. I just recognized the woman with her. It's old lady Conroy. Man, I wouldn't mess with that woman if you gave me an army of ninjas and pirates with laser guns."

"Jeremiah tried to kill me the first and last time I saw him. I have no doubt Eliza wouldn't hesitate to finish the job." I risked another peek and took a good long look at the woman who I'd once thought was my grandmother. Shaking off the horrific feeling, I took note of where my sister and Eliza were headed—not toward the parking lot, but the stable. Instead of walking inside, however, they veered toward the back of the long, wooden structure where it sat against the rocky cavern wall. I frowned. "Where are they going?"

Shelton moved to the back corner of the ticket booth and looked. "They ain't going to pick up an elephant, that's for sure."

A man wearing yellow-and-black-striped Arcane robes appeared at the rear corner of the stable and gave Eliza a deep bow. He said something I couldn't make out over the noise of the menagerie housed in the stable and motioned for Ivy and her grandmother to follow.

"Dude looks like a bumble bee," I said, snickering.

"That's a utility Arcane," Shelton said, narrowing his eyes.

"Utility?"

He nodded. "Arcanes who perform public works like aether power, arch maintenance, and all that jazz wear those clown suits."

With the threat to my existence out of sight, I took a deep breath. Swallowed the knot of panic in my chest and fought down the urge to flee. This was a golden opportunity to spy on my beloved relatives, but mustering the courage proved harder than I thought.

You have to find out what they're up to. The fate of the world depends on it.

When my subconscious put it like that, it felt like I had no choice. I sighed. Steeled myself with the knowledge I could run really, really fast if necessary and said, "Let's go."

I headed toward the stable. Shelton headed toward the parking lot.

We stopped, turned, and looked at each other.

"Are you out of your mind, kid?" Shelton's forehead wrinkled with the kind of expression he probably reserved for the mentally insane.

"I have to find out what they're up to," I said. "You go. Tell the others what I'm doing in case they catch me and kill me."

He clenched his teeth and forced a storm of curses through them, swirling his long, leather duster as he spun a hundred eighty degrees and stalked my way. "If Elyssa and Bella find out I left you to do something this idiotic, they'd cut my tommy-knockers off and boil them in acid."

For an instant, I felt bad for putting Shelton in the situation but remembered the time he'd tried to kidnap me and my dad, and the guilty feeling evaporated. Sometimes, a little coercion was the best way to make Shelton do the right thing. I looked toward the stable for a moment to be sure my murderous relatives hadn't reversed course and trotted toward it.

"G'day, guvnah!" shouted the cheery looking pooper-scooper boy as he appeared from within the stalls.

I almost screamed at the unexpected declaration of good cheer. My heart did its level best to implode through a black hole of its own creation. I choked back a shout, pressing a hand to my chest and glaring at the young boy whose only function in this place seemed to be cleaning animal dung from the stable.

"Holy mother of beef burgers," Shelton said, giving the kid an affectionate pat on the head. "You about scared the crap out of me, Oliver."

The boy grinned. "Can I be of service, Harry?"

Shelton gave him a sly look. "Maybe." He produced a couple of silvery bills I recognized as tinsel, the official currency of the Overworld. "A woman and girl just went behind the stables. Do you know what's back there?"

The boy gave Shelton an innocent look, though the proffered bills vanished so fast, I thought I might have imagined the boy's fingers snatching them. "Oh, sir, I wouldn't know anything about a hidden control room or anything like that."

"What a shame," Shelton said. "Well, is there anything else you can't tell me about it?"

"I wish I could tell you about an air vent with an illusion covering it so it looks like part of the cave wall." He walked behind the stable, leading us down the narrow alley between it and the smooth-hewn cave wall behind it, trailing his fingers along the rock at waist level until, at one point, they went through it. He pushed something. It clicked, and a thin, mesh-like spider web detached from inside. Oliver rolled it up and stowed it inside the fake wall.

"What was that?" I said in a hushed voice.

"It keeps out bugs and stuff," Shelton said. "Like an air filter."

The boy pointed toward a section of wall several hundred feet away. "The main entrance."

Shelton gave him a couple more bills. "Thanks, Oliver."

The boy gave Shelton a grave look. "I don't mean to pry, but are you on another investigation?"

"You two know each other?" I asked.

Shelton shrugged. "Oliver assists me from time to time."

"I helped him pull a bounty on a rogue fader a few months ago," the boy said proudly.

"A what?" I asked.

"A dream leecher," Shelton said. He regarded Oliver for a moment. "Ever been inside the control room?"

"I've looked inside from the air passage a few times. It's quite large." Concern welled inside his large eyes. "They ward the floor against non-authorized personnel. I let a cat run loose in there once, and it set off an alarm."

"Did the cat explode?" Shelton asked.

The boy shook his head.

Shelton ducked and poked his head through the illusionary wall. Pulled it out. "The duct is big enough for us," he told me. "Let's go see what there is to see."

Taking a deep breath to allay the knot in my stomach, I followed Shelton through the fake wall. Invisible from the inside, I clearly saw Oliver and the back of the stable. The sounds of elephants, birds, and other creatures within the structure provided audio camouflage. Shelton squatted in the vent and duck-walked. I followed his lead. We arrived at a ninety-degree turn about ten feet away, turned, and stopped at the lip of the passage where it ended in another of the spider-web type filters. Shelton detached it and set it aside after rolling it up to reveal a massive room straight out of my memories.

If I hadn't known better, I would have sworn I was back beneath Thunder Rock, an abandoned angel relic infested with all sorts of horrors that tried to kill me the first and only time I'd been there. I could almost see the oily black forms of infantile cherubs toddling from dark corners, arms outstretched, and rictus-shaped orifices crying, "Dah-nah" as they tried to suck the life out of me. I remembered running for my life. I remembered somehow activating one of the smaller arches and taking it for a terrifying ride which dropped me into the middle of El Dorado, another city of nightmares.

A hand tightened on my bicep, and I snapped out of my trance.

Shelton's concerned gaze greeted me. "Don't lose it now, kid," he said in a low hiss.

I nodded and gave him a thumbs-up. He released a long sigh.

Running my eyes across the room, I noted the familiar features. Arches just large enough to accommodate a person lined one side of the room, each one embedded on a platter of shiny onyx and ringed by silver—a safety measure I likened to the one around the much larger Obsidian Arch in the Grotto way station. The silver ring prevented the magical energy field from spilling outside and fracturing reality. Those cracks usually led to the Gloom, a place I didn't care to visit.

These arches seemed intact, whereas the majority of the ones in Thunder Rock looked as though they'd been blasted with dynamite. But something else seemed different here. Something I couldn't quite place my finger on. I looked up and down the rows for a moment, before it occurred to me what was missing. In the center of the room beneath Thunder Rock stood a snowy-white arch veined with obsidian. I remembered that arch taking up far more real estate than the smaller arches—maybe three or four times more. This room didn't have that arch.

Shelton nudged me and motioned toward the far side of the room.

A map of the world towered over the bee-robed Arcane where he stood talking to Ivy and Eliza. Cyrinthian symbols lined the wall to the left of the map, each one linked to dozens of dully glowing stars dotting the map. The landmasses on the map only vaguely resembled the continents I knew. In my spare time, I'd looked over maps depicting the evolution of the world and realized whoever made the map in this room had most likely done so before humans had ever walked the earth.

That simple fact stirred up a million questions, but a star in the approximate location of Atlanta began to brighten and fade in syncopation with a star in South Africa, distracting me like squirrel darting across a dog's path. The Arcane held up a finger to Eliza as a glowing white orb lifted from a pedestal centered before the map. He placed a hand atop it, and a steady hum rumbled through the room. Brilliant motes of light arced from one star to the other, alternating black and white as a klaxon blared from the Grotto way station housing the Obsidian Arch. A network of arches just like the one here spanned the globe, if the stars on the map were any indication.

The crackling hum throbbed, building in volume, echoing in the huge cavern, and sending a vibration through my body. As the sound built, the light connecting the two stars pulsed faster and faster, until with a thunderous boom, it solidified into a sparkling beam of energy, no thicker than a pencil. Equal parts ultraviolet and brilliant white, it arched across the map from one point and down to meet the other.

I watched in open-mouthed fascination as miniature silhouettes, some human-shaped, others much larger, streaked through the arced beam. They traversed it so quickly, only my supernatural sight allowed me to make them out. Once the last figure left the beam, the Arcane released the orb. The connecting beam flickered off, and the control sphere sank back onto the pedestal, looking like nothing more than head-sized gray marble. The stars in South Africa and Atlanta dimmed to match the sullen glow of the other stars on the map.

As my eyes readjusted to the relative dimness of the yellow glow illuminating the rest of the room, they turned upon Ivy and Eliza, who stood watching the operator. He turned back to them. His mouth moved. Turning my head ever so slightly and focusing my ear, I barely made out some of his words.

"…will be dangerous even going there." He pointed toward a row of black arches, which stood marginally taller than the others in the room, and shook his head. Unfortunately, the bellows and brays of pack mules, horses, camels, and the rest of the noisy menagerie in the stable located across the narrow alley from the vent colluded with the distance between me and the speakers to block out what they were saying.

Ivy stood on her tiptoes and fiddled with the symbols on the side of the map. One of the arches sparked to life, sending shards of black and white energy arcing on the silver circle around it. Eliza waggled a finger at her, and she stopped.

"Damn shame what they did to that little girl's mind," Shelton said, his mouth curved down in distaste.

"Wish I could hear what they were saying, but those stupid animals are making a ruckus," I said.

Shelton took out his wand, made a circular motion toward the opposite end of the duct, and the sounds from the stable cut off, leaving only the ambient noises in the control room to deal with. "Can you hear them now?"

Eliza Conroy spoke in a southern genteel drawl, her voice loud and pompous enough to carry across the distance. "Jeremiah won't be pleased to hear this. We plan for our associates to use this site as a staging ground." She crossed her arms. "We would take it rather badly if you and the other workers don't assist them with a smile and a spring in your step."

The arch operator bobbed his head, a frightened look on his face. "I promise it won't be a problem."

"A problem what?" Eliza said back, one eyebrow arching.

"A problem, ma'am?" the Arcane replied, his tone more of a cautious question than a statement.

"I do declare, nobody teaches young folks manners these days," she said, shaking her head. "Mr. Tuttle, our associates will declare themselves as Darkwater employees. You are not to interfere in any way, or I suwanee, I will tan your hide. Do you understand?"

The man continued bowing and nodding affirmatively while Ivy quirked her mouth into an amused grin and waggled her finger while her poser grandmother's back was still to her.

Eliza shook her head and threw up her hands. "Heavens to Betsy, but the Conclave must be out of their cotton-picking minds forcing Arcanes to pay these *ridiculous* gate fees!"

Mr. Tuttle kept right on nodding. Magnifying the scene with my enhanced sight, I saw beads of sweat on his pale, gaunt face.

Eliza took Ivy by the hand, as my sister squatted to peer underneath a console, and admonished her. "Young ladies do not squat in dresses." She made an exasperated noise. "I suwanee!" Then she and Ivy strode for the door to their right, while Mr. Tuttle stood wiping his forehead with the sleeve of his robe.

"What the heck does 'suwanee' mean?" I whispered.

"Some kind of crazy southern swear word," Shelton said.

"I suwanee, those two scare the crap out of me," I said, testing out the new phrase.

Shelton rolled his eyes. He put the web filter back in place, turned, and motioned me toward the stables. The animal sounds returned as his sound barrier dropped.

I heard the clack of hard shoe soles on the polished rock floor and barred Shelton from taking another step with my arm. I saw Ivy and Eliza from the chest down as they started to pass the vent.

About halfway across, Ivy gasped. Stopped and tugged her grandmother's arm. "Did you hear that, Bigmomma?"

Shelton and I froze. Sweat dampened my armpits. If she saw us, it was over. My little sister had once executed a spell that would have killed hundreds of vampires in one fell swoop had I not altered it. In other words, she had skillz with a 'z' and could probably take the two of us out without much effort.

"I do declare, child, you nearly pulled your poor Bigmomma's arm right out of the socket." She leaned over Ivy, her voice changing from strict, to doting and affectionate. "Now what did my little darlin' hear?"

Ivy drew in a sharp breath as something trumpeted in the distance. "You hear that? It's an elephant! Someone must have just ridden one in through the arch. Can we go see it, please?" She hopped up and down, holding her hands together as if in prayer. "Please, please, please?"

Eliza gave her an affectionate smile. "Oh, child, I'm afraid there isn't enough time. We need to get home."

Ivy slumped, and her pretty but sad face appeared in profile at the end of the vent. "But I never get to do anything fun."

"Once this is all over, we'll take you to the zoo. How's that?"

My sister clapped her hands. "Really? Can I see a koala?"

Eliza's hand straightened Ivy's golden locks. "We'll even take you to a zoo in Australia. Won't that be fun?"

Ivy jumped. "Yes, yes, yes!" When she landed, I saw her face again. The big smile she wore reminded me so much of our mother, I felt a pang in my heart at how twisted and bent this little girl's mind was all thanks to the damned Conroys.

"How long is it going to take, Bigmomma?" She sighed. "When is Bigdaddy finally gonna get that rune?"

"Now, don't you worry, young lady. He knows what he's doing. In fact, he'll be at your school for a while." She pinched Ivy's cheek. "Won't that be wonderful?"

Ivy straightened. "He'll be at my school? He can see how well I'm doing?"

"You bet your pretty face, sugah. Now, let's get going. He'll be back later tonight, and I want to have a special dinner waiting for him." Eliza took the young girl's hand and led her away, the clomp of their shoes fading with distance.

Shelton let out a long shuddering breath. "Holy crap, man. I almost lost it there for a second."

"No lie," I replied, feeling the tension ease in my entire body. "I suwanee!"

Shelton groaned. "Will you stop it with that heinous word?"

We made our way out of the duct. I sneaked to the corner of the stable, peeked around it in time to watch Ivy and "Bigmomma" get into the back of a waiting black sedan. A part of me considered trying to follow them. I was probably fast enough to keep pace. But before I could work up the courage to enact my bold plan, the original sedan split, popping apart into two identical cars. The two cars split into four. As I watched, each replica divided into more. By then, I'd hopelessly lost track of the original car, and a stream of identical sedans were already filing out of the cavernous chamber and up the ramp to the exit.

"Son of a monkey's third cousin," Shelton said, aiming his wand at the line of cars. "I can't even figure out which ones are the fakes."

"They can't possibly know we're here," I said. "Why would they go through the trouble to create all those illusions?"

"I've seen high-level diplomats who use that kind of illusion as a precaution." Shelton tucked his wand into the inside pocket on his leather duster. "I think I know why they have minders guarding this place."

"Because of the Conroys?" I asked.

"Because of this little side project they got going on here." A sly grin stretched his lips. "And I just figured out how we can get a five-fingered discount on arch travel."

I gave him a blank look.

"It means we can steal a ride—take the arch for free."

I raised an eyebrow. "For free? Did I miss something?"

He chuckled and motioned me toward the door leading into the control room. "Say hello to Darkwater's newest employees."

Chapter 6

I didn't have time to decide if Shelton's idea scared the padooky out of me or made me happy before he reached the part of the wall where Oliver had indicated the control room door should be. After running his hands along the seamless rock wall, Shelton said, "Aha!" and twisted his hand. A latch clicked, and he vanished through the rock. I followed, noting a thick, metal door which he'd opened into the control room.

Tuttle stood at a table, the holographic image of plain-dressed man hovering above the surface of an arctablet.

"She said what?" the man said to Tuttle. "That's insane."

Tuttle nodded, his eyes wide. "Yeah, and we have to bend over backwards to help. I swear, my union rep better have some advice. Working for the Conroys is going to give me a coronary."

Shelton strode across the control room, and I followed, the global map towering to our right. He cleared his throat, and Tuttle shrieked, jumped back, and threw out his hands in a defensive gesture. The holographic image of the other man gave us a startled look and disappeared in a blink. Tuttle peered at us. Dropped his arms to his sides and coughed nervously.

"Can I help you?" he asked, his face scrunched in almost comical confusion, the absurd worker-bee coloring of his cloak only adding to the comedy.

"Tuttle, my associate and I are with Darkwater." Shelton said. "We need a connection to Queens Gate. Ms. Conroy said—"

"Oh yes, of course!" Tuttle said. "One moment, please." He hurried to the large gray sphere and ran his finger across its surface. As he did, a trail of stars on the map brightened perceptibly. He stopped as a star in the southern part of Great Britain lit and made a flicking motion with his finger. The star dimmed and brightened in time with the star in Atlanta. Tuttle turned to us. "Queens Gate will confirm in a moment. Are there any others in your party?"

Shelton shook his head. "Nah. Do the folks at Queens Gate know to accommodate us when we need to return?"

"I'll be sure to notify them," Tuttle said.

"Do you have to wait for confirmation from the other side before opening a connection?" I asked.

The worker-bee Arcane shook his head. "No, not at all. If there's already an open connection the nodule blinks red to indicate it's busy. If I wanted, I could place my palm atop the modulus and raise it to open the connection."

I walked up to the big gray orb—the modulus, I guessed—and looked at it. "You establish a connection by running your finger across it until the proper star—nodule—lights up, then flick it to establish a connection?"

"Exactly. The operator at the other end will initiate the final sequence by raising his modulus." Tuttle shrugged. "It prevents accidents, you know—in case someone at the other end just exited the gate, we wouldn't want to start it back up while they're still inside the traversion zone."

"That's the area inside the big circle?" I said.

"Yes." He nodded approvingly. "You're familiar with traversion arches, then?"

More than I want to be, buddy. The terrifying journey from a broken arch in Thunder Rock across what appeared to be several alternate realities and ending up in the dead city of El Dorado came to mind. "A little. I think it's interesting."

The modulus blazed to life, and a thin beam of light sparked and pulsed from Atlanta to Queens Gate. Tuttle glanced up. "Better get ready to travel."

"Thanks, pal," Shelton said, and we trotted outside and across the black-and-yellow-striped caution circle to step inside the traversion zone. The space in the middle of the Obsidian Arch flickered white, black, and gray, blinking faster and faster in time with the thrum of energy that seemed to vibrate the very air itself. A clap of thunder rolled across the chamber. The area inside the arch shimmered to clarity, revealing a similar chamber on the other side.

I'd been through the Grotto arch before, though it'd been on official Templar business for Bogota, Colombia, but the experience never failed to amaze me.

"This is so cool!" I said as we stepped through the opening. The scenery ahead blurred, warping like the inside of a fishbowl, and popped back to normal within an instant.

As we left the arch behind, the air next to me cracked like glass on the verge of shattering.

Shelton's eyes went wide. "Run!"

Because I couldn't remember a time when someone screaming that word meant anything but horrific death if I paused to ask questions or scratch my head like a dimwit, I snatched Shelton under one arm without so much as blinking. I sprinted for the edge of the silver circle. A cracking noise grated my ears. I felt a blast of freezing air hit my back an instant before an invisible force washed against my body like the outgoing ocean tide, pulling me backward. I strained, but my feet slipped little-by-little on the smooth surface. The edge of the circle was only inches away. I strained with everything I had, but it wasn't enough. I glanced over my shoulder and felt my eyes widen in horror. Multiple fractures lined the space around the arch. One shattered, leaving a gaping hole to a gray void. I knew without asking exactly what it was.

The Gloom.

Shelton shouted something, but I couldn't hear him over the roar of wind…and something else. A voice. I turned my ear toward it. It spoke in low rumbling tones. The meaning of its words hovered at the tip of my brain, but I couldn't understand them. Something primal within urged me to seek out that voice. To answer its call. I slowed my struggle. Shelton yelled something incoherent, wriggling, but unable to move his arms since I'd pinned them to his sides when I grabbed him.

The voice called again. I turned toward the void. My feet skidded across the floor, squeaking as the rubber soles resisted.

Something stung my arm. I looked and saw Shelton biting my arm. He said, "What the hell are you doing?"

I looked from Shelton to the void, and my brain *freaked.* "What the hell am I doing?" I shouted.

The voice from the other side spoke again, faster, more urgent. I spun away from it and back toward the outer ring. Once past that line, we would be safe. But it was further away now, maybe twenty feet. I leaned forward against the tremendous roar of wind and strained with everything I had to move my foot forward. Lifting my foot, I soon found, was futile. The moment I picked it up off the floor, the gale-force wind jerked back, and I was barely able to get it back down again.

"My friggin wand!" Shelton yelled.

I adjusted my hold to free his arms. The extra wind drag was all it took. The air current jerked my feet out from under me. My chin cracked against the floor. I dropped Shelton, and we slid toward the gaping portal of doom.

Shelton rolled onto his back and struggled to extract his wand from his inside jacket pocket. But at the rate we were sliding, I didn't see what he could do to stop us in time. Panic throttled me. Casting my gaze around for something, anything to grab hold of, I spotted the arch to our left. In my peripheral vision, I saw a worker-bee Arcane desperately flicking his wand at us with no effect.

The arch remained too far away for me to grab, and besides, it was too thick to wrap my arms around. The floor of polished obsidian was too slick to find a handhold. I briefly gave thought to manifesting my demon form and clawing into the floor. But that would take time, and I had no control once fully spawned. For all I knew, I'd kill Shelton and, if I escaped, kill anyone else who got in my way.

If only I had a rope!

The answer hit me like a cinder block. Thinking back to my lessons, I quickly settled on the arch as my best solution. I blinked my eyes. My vision flickered to incubus mode, revealing a glowing maelstrom of aether swirling around me as the Gloom rift sucked it in.

I sucked in a breath and drew in magic. Concentrating on the arch, I shouted, "*Shoryuken!*" Glowing strands of power jetted from my fingertips, wrapping around the base of the arch like spider webs. Twisting my fingers into a fist, I caught the strands, flung out my other hand, and grabbed the collar of Shelton's leather duster. We jerked to a stop barely a foot away from the rift. Shelton fumbled his wand and shouted a word.

A large blob of energy coalesced at the end of his wand, undulating like water in zero gravity. He flicked the rod, and the mass floated lazily toward the rift, seeming to ignore the incredible suction. It splatted against one edge, creeping over the glasslike cracks in the air, clogging the portal. With a high-pitched whistle, the last hole closed. The inexorable drag vanished. Shelton pumped a fist in the air and whooped.

I heard another cracking noise. My eyes flicked toward the noise in time to see another of the fractures straining the fabric of reality. Without another thought, I released the glowing strands from my fist, scooped Shelton under my arm, and blurred out of the ring, nearly plowing into a group of spectators who were snapping photos and taking videos of the event with their arcphones.

I set Shelton down and bent over, panting like dying dog while the tremendous hum of the Obsidian Arch wound down. As it powered off, the fractures mended, sealing themselves until nothing remained but clear air.

"Are you okay?" said a utility Arcane.

I nodded even as my knees buckled.

"Holy bulls in a blender," Shelton said, straightening and wiping at his forehead. "Good thinking, kid."

"Good thinking?" said an older man in a long gray robe, his accent that of a proper British gentleman. "I'd say that was exceptional." He tilted his head and regarded me. "Which academy did you graduate from, young man?"

Technically, I hadn't even graduated from high school, much less an arcane academy. I hadn't even been back to school for months after Maximus's attempts to draft high school students into the vampire corps had turned several into the zombie-like vamplings and incited a bloodbath that had claimed the principal, football coach, and other unsavory characters. "I haven't graduated," I said, wincing.

"Ah, of course, you're coming to the university for orientation or a prep course, aren't you?"

"I'm here for the assessment," I said.

Shelton's upper lip curled in distaste as he took in the man. "He's a bloomer."

The man's eyes narrowed. "Surely, you're joking."

My friend made a non-committal gesture. "Nope. The kid hasn't had any formal training, but he's pretty good, isn't he?"

At this, the man's attitude changed completely. "I believe you'll find there's no place for his kind at the university."

Shelton's lips curled into a feral grin. "Yeah? Well, tough, buddy. 'Cause he's already in."

"Perhaps you don't recognize me," the man said, raising his nose to lofty heights. He directed a severe gaze down its length at Shelton. "I am Andrew Buckley, Dean of Admissions, and I am the judge of who we admit and who we don't."

"Oh, so that's why lycans and other supernaturals can attend the university?" Shelton said. He snapped his fingers. "Oh, yeah, that's right. The Overworld Conclave found the exclusion of others in violation of the Covenant."

Dean Buckley's jaw tightened. "The filth should stay at the Science Academy where they belong." He spun on his heel and strode toward a set of large ornate doors which presumably led into the pocket dimension of Queens Gate.

A mob of people with signs stood in a roped-off area to the right of the doors, shouting slogans and waving at a long line of people who appeared to be waiting for admittance through the doors. The dean strode past the line and the shouting mob without looking. Two men in what looked like the big puffy hats and red uniforms of Buckingham Palace guards opened the door for him. Beyond lay a shimmering green vista with snow-topped mountains. The guards closed the doors and took up positions again.

The arch operator asked us a dozen more times if we were okay and begged us not to tell Eliza Conroy about the incident. "I've never seen so many Gloom fractures," he said, staring with disbelief at the quiet arch. "We might have to shut down operations until we find out what went wrong."

The people at the front of the departures line groaned when they heard the operator's words. One man demanded they let him through the arch so he'd be home in time for dinner. The operator held up his hands and waved them at the line of disgruntled travelers. From the corner of my eye, I saw a minder drifting our way. I turned and saw several more on approach, their ghostly tentacles flailing with what looked like excitement.

Shelton's lips curled. He grabbed my sleeve and pulled me well away from the creepy mind twisters.

"I take it you don't like Dean Buckley?" I asked.

He chuckled. "That jackass is not only in charge of educating kids, but he's one of the old bigots on the Arcane Council."

Thinking of Dean Buckley reminded me of the term Shelton had used to turn the dean from an admirer into a total hater. "What, pray tell, is a bloomer, besides an old style of women's underwear?"

Shelton gave me a sideways glance. "It means something different to everybody, but to the elitists, it means you never had formal training and came into your powers late." He shrugged. "There are plenty of nom kids in the world who have abilities, but don't even know it."

"Uh, I don't mean to be nitpicky, but I'm not human, so I was never a nom at any point in my life." It felt strange to say that aloud, but it was true. Supers called normal humans "noms", not only because of their normality, but because to supers like vampires, normal humans were nom-noms—self-aware snack packs.

"Yeah, well there's a reason I told him that."

"Because you want me to be an outcast?"

He shook his head. "I don't want people like him getting their hooks into you, or taking an interest." Shelton's eyes narrowed. "Believe me, when those kind of people are interested in you, it's usually gonna end up bad."

I rolled my eyes. "You're one of the most anti-social, anti-establishment people I have ever met."

"If you knew about my past, you'd understand."

My curiosity lit up like a beacon. "I'd love to hear that story."

He snorted. "Maybe someday."

Judging from how my every day went, I'd likely be dead before someday ever arrived.

Chapter 7

I took in the scene near the door to Queens Gate—the dwindling line of people entering and the roped-off crowd to the right. I read one of the signs someone waved in the air. "We have the right!" it exclaimed in red letters. Another read, "Arcanes Don't Own Queens Gate!"

"What in the world is this about?" I said as Shelton and I stopped next to the rat maze of ropes designed to herd people through the line to the entrance. Thankfully, the line had shrunk considerably since our arrival. A man in a dark suit inspected papers given to him by an older gentleman. He ran his wand along the older man, grunted, and tapped the wand to the papers before waving the man toward the doors.

The man in the suit looked us up and down. Raised an eyebrow. "You have business here?"

Shelton's jaw went tight. "Yeah. What's it to you?"

The man's eyebrow went up a notch. "The Arcane Council is restricting access to all relics dominated by Arcane school zones. As you may or may not know"—he sniffed as if we were complete idiots—"vampires attacked two novice schools." He held up a wand. "Therefore, you must be screened and approved for entry."

"You've got to be kidding me," Shelton said. "Why not set up an automated screening ward outside the entrance?"

The man shrugged. "The council plans to, but the Overworld Conclave is balking." He sighed and looked at the crowd of protesters. "The bloody vampires think they own the place."

I thought back to the last time I'd actually walked the cobblestoned streets of the Grotto. I'd seen plenty of vampires there, though I hadn't been through any of the Arcane school zones. I assumed they considered the entirety of Queens Gate a school zone. "So you're not letting any vampires through at all?"

"No. We're not taking any chances." He held up his wand. "Who's first?"

I shrugged. "Me, I guess."

The man said a magic phrase sounding suspiciously like "Scabadee Scoo" and ran the wand up and down my body. He frowned as results floated in the air before us. "You're spawn."

"Daemos," I said, deciding I'd suffered enough discrimination for the day.

He tutted. "Yes, yes, whatever." His nose wrinkled, but apparently there was no edict preventing my kind from entering. "There's something very strange about these readings," he said, looking back at them. I suspected it had to do with the big red word blinking at him beneath the breakdown of my supernatural lineage. Even though the words floated in the air in reverse before the man, I read *Daemos, UNKNOWN, AP-ERROR*.

"It doesn't say vampire, does it?"

He grudgingly shook his head. "I suppose not." The man looked at Shelton. "And now for you."

Shelton seemed to go through a fistfight with his conscience before growling assent. "Fine."

This time, the results came back as *Human, AP-17*. The security officer's eyes flashed wide. He looked Shelton up and down and muttered, "Unbelievable." After a long-suffering sigh, he gave a signal to the guards and motioned us inside. "Please enjoy your visit." His tone seemed to indicate he actually hoped otherwise.

If we ran into more bungholes like him and Dean Buckley, our visit certainly would suck.

"What's the 'AP' stand for?" I asked Shelton as the guards closed the doors behind us.

"Just some classification crap they like to throw around."

I guessed Shelton didn't care much for being classified, and I had to admit it was a bit hard to pin him with any designation except the "jackass who likes to keep everybody guessing."

We stood on a wide yellow brick road which wound its way toward a city nestled in a valley between two towering mountains. An adorable little cottage sat to one side of the yellow brick road, and something that looked like a shiny rocket ship from a nineteen fifties sci-fi movie sat to our right.

I took in the steep rocky summits on either side of the town. The base of each mountain started as gentle green slopes which gave the valley a bowl shape. A cityscape like something from Victorian-era London stretched between the two mountains. Tudor-style houses dotted the green landscape up to the perimeter of the city where lines of antiquated row-houses stretched the expanse. A huge clock tower rose above the rest of the city, flanked on either side by the tops of domed buildings.

At the edge of the valley bowl, mountainsides turned to craggy cliffs tufted with bits of grass and tenacious bushes, climbing toward the sky until they ended in plateaus, with one mountain terminating slightly higher than the other. At the other end of the valley, I saw where the mountains joined into one steep cliff.

"Amazing," I breathed.

"It's a sight, all right," Shelton said.

"Is the university up there?" I asked.

"Yep. We'll take the sky car," Shelton said, pointing toward the cottage. He led me around the side to a bright red cable car sitting atop a slab of polished obsidian.

I looked up the steep cliffs to either side of us and glanced back. The doors from the archway station were built into a solid rock wall which rose at a ninety-degree angle from the floor of the valley. It seemed hewn from the side of another mountain, which joined with the others to box in the valley. I gazed at the plateaus atop the mountains, but the university and academy were hidden from sight. Another thing I did not see was a single cable designed to allow a cable car to ascend those heights.

Then again, who needed cables when you had magic? "What's up with the rocket ship?" I asked.

Shelton grinned and led me to it. "The techies take this to Science Academy." He opened a hatch on the side of the vessel. Inside were shiny chrome bench seats occupied by several students—a young man with a backpack, a girl with geek chic glasses playing on an arctablet, and several others who looked like any other college students I'd ever seen.

A chrome-plated robot with a clear glass globe for a head stood at the front of the ship. Its torso pivoted a hundred and eighty degrees to face us. "Greetings, Earthlings," it said in a robotic monotone while multi-colored lights in the shape of a mouth blinked with each word. "Please take a seat if you are bound for the academy. We will depart momentarily."

I looked around the cabin and whistled. "It's like a budget science fiction film."

Shelton laughed. "Yeah. I'll say this for the techies—they have style."

We closed the hatch and headed back for the cottage with the cable car. A moment later, the rocket ship rumbled. Long flames licked from the nacelles, though I noted they didn't burn the grass.

"Fake flames?" I asked.

Shelton nodded. "That thing's way past using rocket propulsion. It's got some anti-grav stuff."

"What?" The sheer shock in my voice seemed to surprise Shelton. "You mean advanced scientific locomotion? Why don't the noms have this technology?"

Shelton shook his head. "Firstly, the Arcane Council would never want noms having access to this stuff, and secondly, because the Overworld Conclave forbids it."

"But think of the good it could do society! Anti-gravity cars would be so wicked."

He snorted. "Yeah, and I'd bet noms would love commuting on flying carpets. Never gonna happen."

"Stupid politics," I said, grumbling.

"There are a lot more noms than there are supers. If they had access to magic and our mad science, they'd have the edge, and Overworld politicians don't like that." Shelton shrugged. "They even have an entire division devoted to sabotaging nom scientists and recruiting those who are the most promising."

"Didn't stop them from making nukes or digital watches," I said.

He snorted.

An announcement for the departure of the cable car to the university interrupted my thoughts. We hurried aboard just before it lifted. I realized an instant later why it didn't need cables. "This is a slider, isn't it?"

"Yup." Shelton stared out the window as the spires of a castle rose into view.

I watched as a girl wearing a pink arcane robe played a game on an arcphone. Some kid in a brown robe across from her glanced up from an old book and frowned. "You're on the wrong shuttle, techie."

She wrinkled her forehead and gave him an unsure look, as if wondering if he'd spoken to her and not one of the many other students aboard. After meeting his stern gaze, she seemed to decide he was, indeed, talking to her. "The handbook said arcphones are allowed now." She shrugged. "Don't see how they can ban them anyways. Everybody has one." She looked around the cabin, as if searching for someone else to support her logic.

The guy sneered. "If you suck at magic you might need one."

"Kid, you might wanna join the real world," Shelton said. "'Cause I can think of a half-dozen things an arcphone can do better than a human brain and a staff." He pulled his phone out as though for emphasis. "It's a focus, just like a wand or staff, except it ain't made of wood, and it gives you a heck of a lot more computing power for complex spells."

"Oh, please," the guy said.

"Well, you sure as heck can't play Unicorns versus Zombies on your staff," the girl said, stuck out her tongue, and went back to playing.

The student glared at Shelton. "A real Arcane doesn't need that garbage to do magic."

"You're a lost cause," Shelton said, dismissing him with a wave of his hand. "Then again, you'll probably never amount to more than a magician."

A chorus of "Oohs" went up from the other students, some of them grinning at the argument while others held out their phones, probably recording everything.

The student's jaw dropped open, and his eyes filled with rage. "Do you know who I am?"

A burst of laughter from the crowd only enraged him even more, just as the cable car, now a dizzying height above the valley below, thumped down in a landing zone.

"Please tell me you did not just drop the 'I'm a big deal' card," the girl said. "That's just sad."

"I am William Vanderbilt," the guy said. "And my father—"

"I'm sure you're a real good magician," Shelton said, before the student could finish. "Maybe I'll buy you a top hat for graduation and come see you in Vegas." He threaded his way through snickering students and left the car.

I squeezed through the crowd as William hurled obscenities at our backs.

I knew Arcanes really hated terms like sorcerer, wizard, and warlock, but magician was apparently the lowest of the low.

The landing zone sat atop a bluff overlooking the valley on one side and the plateau on the other. A long stone path led down a gentle slope. Trees dotted the verdant terrain. Narrow stone paths led to quaint cottages, and fields bordered by low stone walls held flocks of bleating sheep and goats. It reminded me of a setting from rural Ireland or Britain except for one thing.

Arcane University.

The sprawling campus looked like something straight out of the Middle Ages. A massive castle and several other mansion-sized outbuildings stretched across the terrain from one end to the other. A snow-blanketed mountain peak towered behind the university, its slopes covered by thick forest.

The castle dominated the center of the complex, its walls composed of white stone bordered by gray and lined with arched windows. Soaring spires reached for the sky atop huge round towers that rose from all four corners, each one boasting intricate stone designs around the edges and windows. A long oval building of white stone with a transparent dome glittered like diamonds to the right of the castle, and something that looked like the Coliseum in Rome, only ten times bigger loomed behind it. Romanesque buildings that appeared to be housing facilities crowded the left side of the complex. A riot of colors bordered the east and west sides of the university—gardens, apparently.

"What's that for?" I asked Shelton, pointing at the giant stadium.

"That's where they hold the Grand Melee," he said.

"The what?"

Shelton gave me a surprised look. "That's right, I never told you, did I?" He grinned. "Imagine this: robots fighting golems in gladiator battles."

"Ooh," I said. "That sounds cool."

"Yeah, now imagine a giant robot from outer space fighting a golem the same size, shooting fire and laser beams at each other."

My eyes went wide, and my mouth hung open. I might have even drooled.

Shelton's grin grew wider.

"That's the Grand Melee?" I asked.

"In a nutshell." He headed out on the stone path toward the looming castle. "They have team fights with man-sized robots and golems, followed by middle-weights, and then by colossi."

"Is it a competition between the Science Academy and Arcane University?"

He nodded. "After Science Academy was built, the first dean kept bragging that science would replace magic and claimed it was more powerful and flexible. Things got pretty nasty between the two schools until an arbitration panel came up with the idea of letting the two schools duke it out by proxy."

"With the Grand Melee," I guessed.

"Yep. They hold it the last weekend of the first month of school."

"At the end of this month?" I asked.

He gave me a sly look. "Wanna go?"

"Are you kidding me?" I said, barely able to contain my excitement. "Heck yeah!"

Shelton laughed. "This place is gonna get crazy. People come from all over the world to see it."

"Who could blame them?" I replied, fantasizing about laser beams and monstrous gladiators.

As we neared the castle, several flying carpets streaked past, followed by a girl on a flying broom, and a guy on—I did a double take—a flying *mop*. "What the heck?" I said, following the strange sight with my eyes until the fliers vanished around the far end of the complex.

"Get used to it," Shelton said.

We reached the entrance to the castle, a massive stone arch, and stepped inside a cavernous hallway.

The girl in pink robes passed us. She beamed a smile at Shelton. "Thanks for the help with that jerk on the sky car."

Shelton snorted. "My pleasure, cupcake."

The girl turned down a different hallway, walking backward as she did, and blew Shelton a kiss before spinning around and continuing on to her destination.

"Damn, I miss those college girls," Shelton said, taking off his hat and running a hand through his thick hair.

"Aren't you kind of old for them now?"

He pshawed. "Man, I'm still in my twenties."

"Early or late?"

He didn't answer.

"That's what I thought," I said, grinning.

We walked down a carpeted hallway, took a spiral staircase up a few flights, and then took so many twists and turns I didn't know where we were anymore. At long last we reached a doorway with a placard outside that said "Miles Chamberlain, MhD."

"Are you ready to start the assessment?" Shelton said, voice serious.

I swallowed a ball of nerves and nodded. "Let's do this."

Chapter 8

Shelton stepped inside and rapped on the open wooden door.

"Harry Shelton, as I live and breathe," said a baritone voice in a proper British accent. "Come on in!"

I followed Shelton inside and saw a short man with curly graying hair, round spectacles, and what looked like a tweed robe.

"Hey, Professor," Shelton said, a smile on his face that looked way too friendly to be the rough-edged Arcane I knew.

"Have a seat," Miles said, gesturing toward a chair. He looked at me. "And this is the young man you spoke of?"

Shelton nodded. "Yep."

I shook the professor's hand. "I'm Justin Slade." It still felt strange calling myself that instead of Case, the fake last name my parents had used to hide from their respective families.

"He's here for the assessment," Shelton said.

"Absolutely," Miles said. He withdrew a wand from a desk drawer. "Let's head on down to a gauntlet room."

Miles led us through a warren of corridors, down some stairs, and into a large circular space that reminded me a lot of Shelton's gauntlet room.

"Wow, it's still here," Shelton said, looking at a particularly big black burn mark on the ceiling directly overhead. "Man, I remember when I did that."

"You made that mark?" I asked, looking at Shelton.

Shelton shrugged. "Trying to impress a girl. I ended up nearly burning my clothes off, and the blast propelled me into the ceiling."

I snorted with laughter. "Why is it all your stories about impressing girls end up going horribly wrong?"

"I think that's just the way it is with guys trying to impress girls." He grinned. "You might know a thing or two about that."

I recalled trying to impress Katie Johnson with my live-action role playing skills, complete with foam sword and shield, and ended up getting my entire squad killed by the enemy team. "You know, I think you're onto one of those universal truths with that one."

"I remember a time or two where my attempts to impress a girl went awry," Miles said while cleaning his glasses on a handkerchief. "I once tried summoning a demon, but instead brought forth a minor non-sentient entity called a skruk that defecated all over the floor and urinated all over Clarissa Dickson's boyfriend before I was able to banish it." He chuckled. "Oh, you should have seen her face after that." He sighed and looked into the distance. "She never did talk to me again."

I stared in horror at Miles, wondering what in the world ever made summoning a demon a good idea. "That's terrible."

He sighed. "Yes, I know. It's not very nice to ignore someone like that." Miles clapped his hands and rubbed them together. "Well, shall we get started?" He hummed to himself as he pointed his wand at a candle and sent it floating to a table sitting in an area configured like a target range. "Light that candle, if you don't mind, Justin."

I'd done this sort of thing plenty of times, though it usually ended up with a molten pile of wax and a blazing table afterward. I looked at Shelton. He winked, nodded his head. I knew from doing this drill over and over that I didn't need to draw in any aether, since it only took precise focus and concentration to pull off. I was as precise as a bulldozer. I stared at the candle. Drawing upon my well, I pointed my practice wand at the candle and whispered, "*Hadouken*."

A fireball the size and shape of my fist blasted toward the candle. It zipped through the air in a streak of flame, brushing the top of the candle, and splashing against the stone wall behind the table with a *whoosh*. I clenched my teeth, ready to curse my ineptitude, when I noticed the candle burning despite missing an inch of wax near the top.

"Hmm," Miles said and made a note on a scrap of parchment. "Now, Justin, blow out the candle."

I was tempted to use my supernatural lung capacity to do the trick, but figured Miles wouldn't go for it. Narrowing my eyes at the flickering flame, I drew on my well, focused my will, and pointed my wand at the candle while whispering, "*Ventus*." A gust of wind knocked the table over and sent the candle flipping end-over-end to land on the floor ten feet away from its original position.

Again, Miles made a thoughtful sound and marked something down on his parchment. I imagined, at this point, his words described the hopelessness of my magical education.

Over the next hour, he asked me to do things which, on the surface, seemed simple, but in reality were anything but. Most of them, I flat out didn't know how to do. Shelton and Bella hadn't gotten that far with me, so I only stood there with a constipated look on my face while I tried to levitate a feather and later tried to animate a stick figure made of toothpicks. By the time it was all over, I was sweating like a pregnant yak and ready to run screaming from the room.

We followed Miles to his office where he ran his wand over me, quirked an eyebrow as a similarly ambiguous readout floated in the air before him as it had for the security guard at the doors to Queens Gate.

"How odd," he said and made some notes. "You are Daemos?"

I nodded. "And part human. My mom is an Arcane." I didn't dare tell him the truth of the matter.

"I see." He stared at the parchment with his notes, most of which probably declared me magically incompetent and of questionable lineage, to boot. After a few minutes, he finally spoke. "Harry was quite right, my boy. You are gifted, but lack control in any sense of the word." He delivered the evaluation without a hint of condescension or derisiveness in his voice. "I suggest remediation for the time being, and we'll check on your progress by the end of the semester." He laid the parchment on the table and looked at Shelton. "Do you agree, Harry?"

Shelton shrugged. "You hit the nail on the head."

"Indeed." The professor looked at the parchment again. "His usage is well above ordinary. I would go so far as to say it is extraordinary, but he simply uses far too much for small tasks."

"What about all the stuff I couldn't do?" I said. "The feather, that stick figure…" I trailed off, not really wanting to review the complete roster of tasks I'd been unable to perform.

Miles smiled. "Most new students barely complete half the tests unless they attended other academies before coming here."

His words made me feel somewhat better. At least I wasn't the only failure. "Is everyone here my age and older?"

He chuckled. "This is an Arcane institution and quite unlike the nom educational equivalent. We admit students as early as age ten, depending on their potential. There are many basic skills students must learn before ever attempting magic, and, in most cases, young Arcanes don't even exhibit talent until age eleven or twelve."

"They couldn't find him a dorm room, Professor," Shelton said, his tone unusually respectful toward the man. "You wouldn't happen to know of any openings, would you?"

Miles frowned thoughtfully and pulled a large book from a shelf behind his desk. He set it on the table and looked at it for a moment before shaking his head. "This book is linked to the primary dorm roster, and I'm afraid it's showing everything is quite full." He sighed. "I would offer Justin lodging at my house, but the administration frowns on such things unless it's for family members." Another sigh. "A shame really. They assigned me such a roomy house, one which my family hardly fills."

"You could adopt me," I said with a hopeful grin.

He laughed. "Yes, well, as your advisor, I will keep a keen eye on the roster and let you know of any openings in housing. I will also have your schedule ready on the morn." He held out his hand.

I gripped it and received a firm shake.

"Congratulations, Justin. You're officially a student at Arcane University."

After leaving Miles, Shelton and I headed toward the sky car.

"So, I actually did okay?" I asked him. "I thought I sucked."

He chuckled. "I'm proud of you. It was a little hairy there, but you did more than most beginners." He kicked a loose stone with his boot. "I think going through remedial classes is just what you need. Maybe by reviewing them in a formal setting, you'll pick up on something Bella and I overlooked."

I thought back to high school and how well I'd done in my classes. Maybe there was something to be said about being squeezed through the same educational process as everyone else that would put my brain back on track. On the other hand, ice throbbed through the veins in my leg, and it was all I could do not to limp. I chalked up the pain to being so tired, but a stab of fear took me in the chest as I wondered if the vampling curse was fighting the potion.

We reached the sky car shuttle back to the valley and jumped in just as the doors slid shut behind us. Two men in black Arcane robes stood to our right, scrutinizing us as we took seats on the opposite end. As the vehicle shifted into motion, the motion caused the men to sway to the sides, briefly revealing a man in clothing that looked like a cross between a business suit and a robe.

I felt Shelton stiffen next to me the same moment I saw the other man's eyes widen.

"Oh, crap," Shelton said, his knuckles turning white from the grip he had on the armrest.

The other man stood, walked between his bodyguards. "Harry?"

Shelton took a deep breath. Sighed. Looked up at the other man and snarled, "Hey, Dad."

Chapter 9

I felt my mouth hang open as those words hit my ears. The two men looked almost nothing alike. "You have a dad?" I said, the words tumbling from my lips.

Shelton gave me a look. "What kind of dumbass question is that? Everyone has a dad." He stood and gave the other man a stony look. "What brings you to the university?"

The other man looked at Shelton, as if trying to divine what emotions lay behind his son's rigid exterior. "Work. I'm making a tour of the schools, to assure everyone the council is doing everything in its power to keep kids safe, especially with the Grand Melee coming. The vampires have left us no choice but to prepare for any eventuality." He looked at me and held out a hand. "I'm Jarrod Sager."

I stood, feeling even more confusion frazzle my brain. "The Arcanus Primus?"

"Yeah, he's a big shot," Shelton said with a shrug.

I shook the man's hand. "But your last names are different."

"Long story," Shelton said, giving me a narrow-eyed look, clearly indicating I should just shut my mouth.

"Uh, I'm Justin," I said, trying to think up a new fake last name in case he asked. The name Slade was too well known.

Jarrod's eyes shined with recognition anyway. "Justin Slade." His voice was even and neutral, but I could sense something else behind it. "I've wanted to meet you for a while. But after what happened here and in Colombia, you dropped off the map."

"Uh, what makes you think I'm Justin Slade?"

He offered a practiced smile. "Your name and appearance has gained some infamy in Overworld politics. Why, in the last Conclave meeting, the vampires tried to ram through a vote removing Thomas

Borathen as commander of the Templars and calling for your arrest for crimes against super-humanity."

"The Conclave can't do squat to the Templars," Shelton said. "Choosing their leaders is an internal matter. And Justin did what the vampires didn't have the balls to do to Maximus."

The Primus folded his arms. "The Daemos are about the only supernatural nation keeping quiet about you. Then again, they prefer subtle manipulations."

"What about the Arcanes?" I said, doing my level best to keep my voice steady and neutral even though I'd never heard anyone summarize the consequences of being me in such a methodical fashion. "What do they have to say about me?"

"Some want to give you a medal for what you did to Maximus. They think it's pretty clear Maximus's organization, Blood Rush, committed the massacres at our schools, not the Red Syndicate." His lips pressed together in a tight line for a moment. "Then again, there are hawks who favor war with the vampires. They claim there's no evidence Maximus had anything to do with the massacres. In fact, they think he was a scapegoat and you were a willing accomplice of the Red Syndicate to frame him."

"They just want blood, pure and simple," Shelton said. "It ain't about justice. It's about revenge."

The Red Syndicate governed the vampire nation. During the Maximus conflict, their ambassador had approached Elyssa, asking her to put him in touch with me. "Do they want me arrested?"

Jarrod shrugged. "It's not clear what they want. But it appears they waited too long to decide."

I pinched my eyebrows. "How so?"

"The Daemos," Shelton said with a sense of grim satisfaction. "The Conclave can't do jack crap to you because you're considered part of the Daemos nation now that your dad had you raised from Castratae to Cenae."

Jarrod made an appreciative sound. "Very good, Harry. I guess you do have political savvy beneath that rough exterior."

"I'm not a snake like you," Shelton growled. "Maybe old man Conroy will finally decide he wants your post. He might be an evil old bastard, but at least he's honest about it."

"Would it make you happy to see me out of office?" his father said.

Shelton's voice went cold. "I don't know that anything would make me happy at this point."

The family drama tightened my stomach like drum. I prayed the sky car would land soon. "Do the Conroys participate in politics?" I asked, hoping to keep Shelton from inflaming the situation.

"No, your grandfather and I have always been at odds," Sager said.

He obviously didn't know my mom was an angel if he thought Jeremiah was my grandfather, but I played along. "Is there anything you don't know about me?"

"Plenty." He cast a sideways glance at his son and turned back to me. "I'd like to sit down with you in a formal setting very soon. We need details on the Vadaemos and Maximus incidents, and we'd like to talk to you about your mother, Alice. She's been seen with the Conroys, but nobody has been in contact with her."

"What do you want with my mom?"

"First of all, she's a very powerful and respected member of the arcane community, but secondly—"

"He's not gonna sit down and give you guys an interview," Shelton said. "So buzz off."

I'd been thinking along similar lines as Shelton but in slightly more diplomatic tones.

"You never learn, do you?" Jarrod said, turning to his son. "You think having a big mouth and a gut full of bravado is going to get you through life, but it's not, boy. You need to use—"

"Manipulation?" Shelton said with a snort. "My attitude's gotten me this far."

His father made a scoffing laugh. "Into your thirties? That's not far."

"I'm twenty-six, *Dad*." Shelton said the last word with what seemed to be unholy hatred. "But if I make it into my thirties, I'll be more than happy to invite you to my next birthday party. We can wear party hats and watch family movies. Me and you and Mom and Martin—oh wait, that's right. Martin is dead. Guess my brother won't be able to make it after all."

I felt my eyebrows rise. *Guess I'm not the only one with daddy issues.*

Sager's face went pale at the mention of the name. I remembered the signature on the painting in Shelton's bathroom. Martin must be—have been—Shelton's brother.

The sky car bumped onto the ground, and the doors opened. Shelton grabbed me by the sleeve and literally dragged me after him while his dad stood there in white-faced anger, or shock. I couldn't tell which and didn't want to know. My own mind had gone numb at his words. In the last ten minutes I'd learned more about Shelton than I had in the past several months.

Shelton released my sleeve and walked in brooding silence to the doors leading back to the arch chamber. When we entered, it was obvious something was wrong. A group of grim-faced people stood inside the silver band circling the traversion zone of the Obsidian Arch. The arch appeared to be off, but a very familiar crack in the fabric of reality glowed within. Two women, staffs planted firmly on the polished floor, held hands and directed beams of light from the tips of their staffs into the rift. It appeared the light acted as a clamp to hold the rift open.

Wind howled inside the zone, whipping at the Arcanes' hair and robes. The other people inside appeared to be Templars wearing the skin-tight armor they usually favored, though it was bright red instead of the customary black. They formed a human chain, connected by what looked like diamond fiber rope tied to a huge anvil-shaped chunk of metal which apparently kept them anchored.

Unable to look away, despite knowing Shelton's father was probably standing somewhere behind us, I watched as a large gloved hand gripping the rope emerged from the rift. The other Templars hauled on the line. Seconds stretched to minutes, and finally the Templars helped a large man climb out of the rift, a young boy strapped to his back. Moments later, another Templar emerged with a woman strapped down to her back.

The Arcanes rapped their staffs against the floor, and the beams of light vanished. The sides of the rift collapsed with a thunderous boom.

"Oh, that was bloody close," muttered someone nearby.

I turned and saw the vampires with their protest signs watching the drama unfold, their protests forgotten for the moment.

A man shouted in joy and rushed inside the silver circle, gripping the woman and boy in tight hugs after the Templars unstrapped them. His tears glistened in the light. The security man who'd questioned me and Shelton earlier eclipsed the happy reunion by standing in front of the crowd and holding out his hands for silence.

"Until the cause of the Gloom rifts can be determined, the arch is closed," he said.

A chorus of groans went up from the crowd, and a few people shouted angry comments.

"I'm sorry," the man said. "But the risk is too high." He made eye contact with me and Shelton. "As I'm sure you are aware."

Shelton and I growled in unison.

I was dying to see Elyssa after the hard day, and to top things off, neither of us had packed a suitcase. At the very least, I wanted clean underwear and a toothbrush. I stepped away from the crowd and took out my arcphone. "Nookli, dial Elyssa."

"Dialing," my phone replied in a mellifluous voice.

It rang several times before she answered and said in a low whisper. "Justin, I can't talk. The trial started, and I'm in a very serious situation right now."

"Sorry," I whispered back. "I'm stuck at Queens Gate. I just—"

"Are you okay?" she said, her whisper sounding concerned. "The virus isn't—"

"No, I'm fine, sweetie. Um, kick ass, okay?"

"You're sure? I'll abandon this and come right now if you want me to."

"No, don't!" I said. "Really, everything is great."

I heard shouts in her background and a tremendous roar. "Uh-oh," Elyssa said. "Guess they heard me." She made a smooching noise. "I love you, Justin. Call me immediately if you need me." Another roar sounded, and the line went dead.

A frantic knot of worry bowled up my throat. What the hell had roared at her? What terrible things were the Templars doing to her? I took deep breaths, somehow managing to quell my rising panic. Elyssa was a total badass. She could take care of herself—I hoped.

"Well ain't this dandy," Shelton said. "Guess we're stuck here."

To keep myself from pouting about Elyssa, I forced myself to think about something else. "I wonder what's causing these Gloom cracks to appear all of a sudden."

Shelton looked toward the stables. The layout of Queens Gate station looked very similar to the one at the Grotto, so I knew what he was thinking before he even said anything.

"The operator might know," I said.

Shelton nodded. "I wonder if it has something to do with this Darkwater project of the Conroys."

We headed toward the control room, passing by the Templars and Arcanes who'd rescued the mother and son from the Gloom, and headed around the back of the stables. The control room door here at Queens Gate was hidden in about the same spot as the one in the Grotto. Shelton opened it and found two operators immersed in an intense conversation.

"I'm with Darkwater," Shelton said without preamble. "Mind telling me what the hell is going on with the arches?"

I had to admire how ballsy Shelton was with this subterfuge. Then again, he probably used it all the time with his bounty hunting.

The two operators glanced over at Shelton. One of them spoke. "I explained matters to Mr. Conroy. These sorts of anomalies are to be expected. We haven't used these arches in centuries because they're unstable," he said, waving a hand toward the rows of smaller black arches identical to the ones I'd seen at the Grotto.

The other man stepped forward. "We told him there must be damage at the other end. Thunder Rock was abandoned for a reason and trying to use one of these arches to get there might be more dangerous than sending an expedition in a more conventional manner."

My chest went cold at the thought of anyone wanting to wade through the horrors lurking in the water and caves in that accursed place, but I held back the next question begging to escape my lips, namely, why in the world did Jeremiah Conroy want to go to Thunder

Rock? If I asked such a question, the operators would know we had nothing to do with Darkwater.

Shelton was a step ahead of me already. "What I don't get is what the old man expects once we get there."

The operators paused, glancing at each other as if wondering how we wouldn't know. They seemed to shrug off the doubt, though, and one of them spoke. "All he told us was there's a special arch there that he wants the arcane engineers to get working." The operator shrugged. "He won't tell us anything else."

"The long and short of this bloody mess is this," the second man said. "Something is breaching the traversion tunnels created by the arches. This means anyone who goes through one of these arches could drop out in a completely random place—maybe another realm, maybe the Gloom." He threw up his hands. "I have no bloody idea. The other problem is these cracks in the traversion tunnel are wreaking havoc with the Obsidian Arch network. We still don't fully understand the magic behind these things even though our people have studied them for centuries."

I thought back to the tunnels of light depicted on the global map in the control room while an arch was in use. The magical pipes carried people from one point to another. If one had leaks in it—my mind flashed to the terrifying journey I'd taken from the small arch in Thunder Rock to El Dorado. It had dropped me into several different places, some of which were most definitely not of this earth before depositing me where I'd wanted to go. At the time, I'd been trying to get back to Elyssa after cherubs had separated us in the depths of Thunder Rock. But a strange bubble in reality had prevented me from reaching her, and I'd been sucked back in and dropped through a broken arch in the dead city of El Dorado in the far southern reaches of Colombia.

The operator's explanation shed new light on what exactly had happened to me. The arch I'd taken must have malfunctioned for some reason, leaving cracks in the traversion tunnel and allowing me to fall into different realities for a span of seconds before sucking me back in and finally depositing me at the other end. I'd been very lucky. Otherwise, I might have been trapped forever in a hellish nightmare of a realm. One of them had been filled with cherubs. It wouldn't have taken long before they'd sucked me dry and turned me into a shadow person.

"A special arch?" Shelton said, ignoring the man's concerns about the tunnels. "I wasn't told anything about that."

"Probably because you're there to secure the area, not work on sensitive magical equipment," the first operator said, his nose elevating to a condescending angle.

"I know that, but securing the area means I gotta know the layout. I need to know what's high priority and where we can fall back if things get ugly."

The second operator sighed. "Battle mages think they're such badasses."

Shelton smirked. "We do our job just like you do yours. Now, you want to be safe, or do you want to keep things from me and make my job more difficult?"

The first operator considered it for a moment and shrugged. "The layout of the control room is supposedly very similar to this one with one major exception."

"And that is?" Shelton prodded.

"The special arch we're supposed to work on looks like a half-sized version of an Obsidian Arch, except that,well"—he looked at the other operator—"it's white and black."

My mind flashed back to the information Miles had given us. The arch the Seraphim had used to invade our realm the last time was the same exact color combination.

Jeremiah Conroy intended to fix it.

Chapter 10

Shelton and I exchanged troubled glances, before he recovered and turned back to the man. "I'll need a diagram with the layout of the control room."

The men exchanged confused looks. "We don't have one," the first said. "Nobody's ever documented it to the best of our knowledge."

"Then how does Jeremiah Conroy know there's even control room there, much less this special arch?"

"How does he know anything?" the man replied, as if it were the stupidest question he'd ever heard.

"I hear he has demons who work for him," the second said in a conspiratorial whisper. "And not the small ones either."

"He's insanely powerful," the first said, nodding his head vigorously.

"He told us to expect a similar layout to this one, but that's about it, other than our engineers will be working on the white and black arch."

"What the hell?" Shelton said. "What does an arch like that do?"

The operators shrugged in unison.

Shelton leaned forward. "It's important I know."

The first operator shook his head. "He didn't tell us. His engineering crew was supposed to be here tonight to help us with the arches."

"With the Obsidian Arch shut down, how are they gonna get here?"

"He might have to fly them over the old-fashioned way," the first said.

"All right." Shelton motioned me to follow him. "We're gonna look around and base our information off this room. If you find out anything else, let us know."

We walked down the rows of small arches. Each one stood about ten feet tall with a silver ring embedded in polished obsidian at the base. Straight aisles ran between the arches, wide enough for several people to walk abreast of each other. Shelton ran his hand along the twisting architecture of one arch, his brow wrinkling.

"What is this stuff anyway?" He shook his head. "It feels like rock, but it doesn't."

I touched the slick surface, my hand following the odd spiraling design. "No idea."

"Tell me again how you used the arch in Thunder Rock."

Looking around the room, I spotted a row of arches separated from the others by a slightly wider aisle and led Shelton there. From here we could see the travel map on the wall. I pointed out the symbols next to the map and the symbols on the floor in front of some of the other arches.

"At the time, I didn't know enough about Cyrinthian to have a clue what those meant. Now I know those are numbers, each one corresponding to an arch. You touch the button, the arch lights up. Then I think you select a destination from the map, step through, and end up at the corresponding arch at your destination."

"That easy, huh?"

I shrugged. "It's just a guess. A cherub was trying to devour my soul at the time, so I only had a few pants-wetting minutes to figure out how the arches worked."

"But from what you told us, it didn't go down like that." Shelton nodded at the symbols on the floor in front of the separate row of arches. Each one consisted of a circle with multiple lines crisscrossing it, each line extending past the edges.

"Yeah, most of the numbered arches were broken, and the cherubs cornered me at an arch like this one." I knelt and touched the symbol on the floor. "I looked that symbol up the first chance I had. It means *omni*."

"Like omnidirectional?"

"More precisely, it means all." I rubbed a hand over the slick metallic substance. "I didn't need to indicate on the map where I wanted to go. I just closed the circle and willed it to take me home."

"And we saw how that turned out," Shelton said with a wry chuckle.

"I get the feeling these arches are more advanced. Like maybe these were added separately from the others." I stood up. "Just look at the layout."

Shelton stood back and looked at the room. "I think you're right. Notice how the map is centered on the other arches, but this row juts out to the side?"

I followed his gaze and saw what he meant. "When I thought of home, the arch flashed through the images of a bunch of places—my old house was one of those—before finding Elyssa. But you want to know what's really strange about it, now that I think back?"

Shelton snorted. "Everything?"

I shook my head. "No, the arch seemed ready to take me to a location where there was no corresponding exit arch."

He took in a breath. "It could take you anywhere, no other arch required? Do you know what that would mean for travel?"

"It would be almost as advanced as the Key of Juranthemon."

"Yeah." Shelton nodded. "It'd be a close second."

The Key of Juranthemon coupled with the Map of Juranthemon allowed the user to create instantaneous travel portals between any doors, at least according to Underborn. Unfortunately, the notorious assassin now had both of those relics, having forced me to choose between saving Felicia's life, or giving him the map and key.

I inspected the omni-arch. The piano-black material was triangular where it met the polished black floor. It twisted like a vine from there, somehow gaining more angles and sides, though my eyes had trouble finding where exactly the changes in geometry took place. The linked arches, by comparison, remained triangular from one end to the other, even though they twisted en route. "The angels must have been working on a new kind of arch before the Grand Nexus blew up."

"Maybe they never got them operational." Shelton walked a circle around the arch. "Because something went wrong when you tried to use it."

I told him my theory about the cracked traversion tunnel. "It's like I fell out, but the tunnel sucked me back in."

"And you end up coming out at a broken arch in El Dorado." He braced his chin on his knuckles, eyes lost in thought. "Maybe the destruction of the Grand Nexus broke the arches."

"I'm going with that answer for now," I said. "Maybe we should give one of these a test and see if it works."

Shelton shook his head, eyes wide. "Hell no, kid. I ain't taking the chance of ending up in angel central. Let's look around more and see if anything else sticks out. Then I got more questions for those operators."

I couldn't blame Shelton for his caution. For all I knew, trying to power an omni-arch could cause a catastrophe. The way my luck had run, it was likely. We looked around for a while, and Shelton interrogated the operators, but they had little more to offer than they had earlier, so we left and headed back toward the door leading to Queens Gate.

The vampire protestors were back at it again, I noticed, and we had to wait in line since the security guard who'd screened us earlier was still intent on harassing everyone. I just hoped he didn't do body cavity searches. The line remained long as ever, thanks to the broken arch preventing people from departing and forcing them to seek a place to stay in Queens Gate.

"You've got to be kidding me," Shelton said, his lips curling into a snarl when it was our turn. He scowled at the guard. "We just passed through here a little while ago, and the arch is shut down, so it's not like anyone else could've come in."

"People come in from London all the time," the man replied, raising a haughty eyebrow as if daring Shelton to challenge his logic.

"But you remembered us when we came in!" he said.

The guard, however, was more or less like a honey badger. He just didn't give a damn.

After clearing us for reentry, the man turned to the next in line, his wand ready to violate their every secret.

Shelton grumbled under his breath.

"He's just doing his job," I said, though my heart wasn't really into defending the guard. I just wanted Shelton to shut up before he got us into trouble.

"Look at the moron, lording it over everyone like he runs the place." Shelton pshawed. "Give someone a little bit of power, and they abuse the hell out of it."

I glanced back as a man with a bright red bowler perched atop his bald head bypassed the line of people and sauntered up to the gatekeeper. He said a word or two, and the gatekeeper motioned him past. "Man, this place really lets the elites get away with anything."

Shelton had apparently seen it, too. "It's all about politics." He took out his arcphone, flicked the screen and looked at it for a moment. "Sweet."

"What is it?" I asked.

"I got some buddies up at the Science Academy," Shelton said. "I texted one, and he got us access to an empty dorm room for the night."

"There's our silver lining," I said, trying not to think about Elyssa. I noticed most of the people who'd come back were headed down the yellow brick road to Queens Gate proper for lodging.

We turned toward the rocket ship, boarding it with a group of frustrated adults dragging along tired kids who looked about elementary school age. I almost asked Shelton why such young kids were here, but remembered what Miles had told me about the schools accepting kids as young as ten.

Even though the rocket was the size of a subway train car, people occupied more than half of the bench seats stretching lengthwise along the curved hull of the transport, with room to stand in the center. Shelton and I took spots near the middle. The man with the god-awful red bowler stepped inside a moment later. He glanced at us, making eye contact with me for a second before sitting on the bench opposite us in the front. I found it hard to stop staring at the man's gaudy, red polyester suit and his shiny, white shoes. A red polka-dotted shirt with a lacy collar attempted to murder my eyes from beneath the polyester jacket.

"Isn't that a crime against humanity?" I said, motioning my head toward the man.

Shelton sputtered with laughter, not even trying to conceal the object of our mutual derision. "Man, that can't be for real." He touched his chin in thought for a moment. "Although I do remember one of my teachers at the university who loved to wear robes with fake fur on them." He shuddered. "There's no accounting for taste."

Turning my eyes away from the bizarrely dressed man, I said to Shelton, "Tell me again why there's a science academy in the Overworld. Isn't that more of a nom thing?"

He chuckled. "You know movies with mad scientists?"

"Like Frankenstein?" I asked.

"Yeah, kinda like that." He motioned toward the robot with the fishbowl head and blinking lights as it greeted everyone and announced departure in a robotic monotone. "Just look around, man. Think of robotic spiders, flying saucers, and levitating skateboards. Science Academy is every nerd's wet dream."

I couldn't deny that. "I take it the Arcanes and techies don't get along?"

Shelton gave me an *are you serious?* look. "In case you failed to notice, they're purists at the university. Hell, they only just allowed arcphones, and that's because so many parents complained to the council about having to write letters instead of being able to text or call their kids."

I had difficulty getting it all straight in my head. "But don't arcphones mix science and magic?"

Shelton took off his hat and brushed it against his side. "The School of Magical and Scientific Synergy is the part of Science Academy that deals with mixing the two, but most of the other departments deal in pure science."

I felt my forehead wrinkle more than usual. "I don't get why the university and academy can't just get along. Arcphones are freaking sweet."

He chuckled. "One word: elitism. Arcphones allow those with less inherent arcane talent to compete on a level playing field with powerful naturals. The naturals don't like that. That's one reason the Arcane Tourney is limited to non-technological foci, like staffs and wands without built-in generators."

From the perspective of pure ego, it made sense, even if it was all wrong. "Are the techies as stuck up as the Arcanes?"

He waggled a hand in a so-so fashion. "The Grand Experimental Expo is sort of like the Arcane Tourney, except it's about inventing the craziest stuff possible."

"Sounds like a grown-up version of a science fair."

He nodded. "It's a heck of a lot more entertaining than the stupid Arcane Tourney, I'll tell you that much."

I stared out the window as the top of the mountain loomed closer. "It would be so cool if they'd share with noms." I shrugged. "I just don't get why it has to be so top secret. We could have spaceships and travel the universe."

"Didn't you hear what I said earlier?" Shelton said, his voice gruff. "Elitists like my dad will never let that happen. Why would you allow the noms to have that kind of power?" He narrowed his eyes. "And before you get any bright ideas about giving arcphones to your high school buddies, you should know giving Overworld technology or magic to noms is a capital offense."

I gave him a wounded look. "I know it's all hush-hush, geez."

"Yeah, well the penalty is death or eternal banishment to the Gloom. I still don't know which is worse." He shuddered. "I had to fulfill a bounty on someone I knew. I didn't know at the time they'd broken that particular law, or maybe I would have turned it down."

"Wow, Shelton. You cashed in a contract on a friend?" I shook my head. "Now, that's low."

He stared at me with narrowed eyes for a moment. "She wasn't my friend. Just someone I went to school with."

I didn't know whether to admire Shelton for doing his job despite the circumstances, or to despise him for doing his job *because* of them. I tried not to judge the man, but it was hard. One minute he could be a complete butt muncher, and the next, he could be rescuing my butt from a bad situation. He'd allegedly been involved with Vadaemos, the same demon spawn who'd killed Meghan Andretti's father. He'd also tried to kidnap me and my father for a bounty. Shelton was either a very complicated person or a complete schizoid—and I didn't know which.

The episode with his father and revelation about his brother made me all the more curious. But it nothing short of a nuclear bomb seemed capable of penetrating Shelton's protective armor.

I decided to abandon the subject for the time being as the rocket climbed toward the mountain where Science Academy awaited.

The rocket bumped down on a landing pad. The robot pilot swiveled at the waist and said in a robotic monotone, "We have arrived, Earthlings."

We stepped outside onto a sidewalk made of a strange material that looked almost like liquid mercury, though not as shiny. The moment our feet touched down, the material surged beneath us. I yelped in surprise, much to the amusement of a group of geeks just behind us. The pathway carried us into a large tunnel. A white glow suffused the corridor, gleaming off the polished chrome-like material on the walls. Beams of red light scanned us as we went through and, at the end, a hulking robot with giant cylindrical guns on the arms strode our way on legs bent backwards like those of a kangaroo.

"Identify," it said in a cybernetic voice.

"Oh, for crying out loud," Shelton said. "Doesn't this joke ever get old?"

The gun barrels whirred to life, rotating so fast they were a blur, and a single red eye in the center of its chrome body blazed to life. "Identify."

"Ignore it," Shelton said and headed toward another moving pathway.

Staring at the spinning guns, I sidled up to Shelton, placing him squarely between me and the robot, even though I noticed the other passengers from the rocket were ignoring the contraption as well. The man with the red bowler paused at the end of the branching path, his eyes locking onto mine. He tipped his bowler at me, winked and smiled, then took the opposite path away from us.

Before I had a chance to wonder about the odd man, Shelton drew my attention back to the lethal-looking robot, dismissing it with a wave of his hand. "If the scans don't recognize someone, that thing comes out to make you crap your drawers."

"Well, it works," I said.

He sniffed the air. "Whew, guess it did."

I poked him with an elbow. "Ha, ha. Laugh it up, buddy."

He did.

The moving pathway took us past a long building, all curves and organic grace, with a silvery sheen visible by the white ambient light glowing from an unseen source around it. The same liquid glass I'd seen in use at the MagicSoft and Orange stores in the Grotto seemed to be in use here, judging from the gentle undulations of the windows. I gawked at the beauty and cutting-edge aesthetics with unabashed admiration.

Shelton held a hand to the left as we came to a fork in the moving pathway, and the surface shifted us left toward a three-story building that looked as though it might belong to an outpost on Mars. "Those are the dorms. My friend left me with a passkey."

Something overhead flashed by so fast, I wondered if I had imagined it. Two more streaks blurred toward the building, followed by a slower-moving flying saucer which stopped to hover for a moment, casting a blinding dome of light on the two of us. I almost expected to be abducted by aliens before the rotating ship resumed course and whirred onward to the building.

"Where can I get one of those?" I asked, certain I was already drooling.

Shelton laughed and pressed his thumb against a biometric reader on the building door. It slid open with a *whoosh*, and we stepped inside. The interior of the dorm looked normal, almost like a hotel, but with no carpeting or front desk. Our room was a small affair with a bunk bed against one wall and two empty desks against the other.

"I call top," I said, grabbing some folded sheets off the bare mattress and spreading them out.

"I don't think so," Shelton replied.

I looked at him over my shoulder. "Want to arm wrestle for it?"

He blew out a breath. "Fine. Keep the stupid top. I didn't really want it anyway." He paced around the room impatiently, stopping at the window, after a minute, and looking at the lights outside. "Man, I'm starving. Let's head to the food court."

My stomach rumbled in agreement. "What do they have to eat here?"

Shelton ran through a list as we made our way back outside. About halfway between the dorms and another group of buildings he identified as the food court, the moving pathway abruptly stopped. I staggered forward a couple feet before regaining my balance.

"What the hell?" Shelton rubbed his boot against the liquid-looking metal. He knelt down and rapped on it. "Step off for a sec," he said, moving onto the grass bordering the pathway. I followed suit. "Alright, now get back on."

I did, but nothing happened.

"Huh." He jumped up and down on it. Cursed. "Well, I guess this thing still breaks down all the time."

"Uh, does the rocket ship ever break down?" I asked, thinking back to the terrifying height of the mountain and imagining the ship malfunctioning before it reached the top.

He shook his head. "Nah, hardly ever."

"Hardly ever?"

"It has a backup system anyway." He started walking toward the distant food court. "C'mon."

I took a step and heard a thud. I paused, looking around, and saw nothing. Took another step. The ground vibrated ever so slightly beneath my feet.

Shelton spun to look at me. "What the hell?" His eyes narrowed. "Okay, now they're going too damned far."

I followed his gaze and spotted the robot from the entrance standing about thirty yards away, the red light in the center of its body glowing. "Hello, Your Majesy," it said in a cockney accent. "I'd like to personally welcome you to our lovely academy." With that, the huge cylindrical guns on either arm spun up, whining like twin jet engines, and spewed forth jagged bolts of death.

Chapter 11

I dove, shoving Shelton out of the way of a burst of white-hot energy, and rolled to my feet several yards away.

"Please do not move," the robot said, cockney accent gone and replaced with a calm, male robotic voice as it continued to blast away. "If you move, I will likely miss."

Shelton rolled across the ground as the death beams charred the grass around him to ash. In one fluid movement, he whipped out his staff rod, squeezed it, and popped it out to full length. He shouted a word, and an incandescent nimbus sprung up in a partial sphere around him. The beams speared into the shield, spreading across it with a dull red glow. Shelton's feet skidded back across the grass from the force of impact.

"I apologize," the robot said in a calm tone. "My weaponry appears to be failing for some reason. I will adjust." With a mechanical whirring sound, a rack of missiles sprang from the back of the robot, swiveled, and aimed at Shelton.

He cursed. "I don't know if I can hold out against that!"

I jumped up and down. "Hey, robot! Over here, you stupid thing."

Its torso swiveled. "It is unkind to call me stupid." With that pronouncement, it fired a red-tipped missile right at me.

I blurred out of its path, and the missile shot past. "How about you stop shooting at us?" I said.

"Justin, watch out," Shelton shouted, pointing wildly behind me.

I turned in time to see the missile arc lazily upward like a brilliant star against the night sky and curve back down toward me. "Oh, crap." Thinking back to all the science fiction movies I'd seen, I immediately knew what to do and how to stop this madness. I waited for the missile to level out about ten feet off the ground and streak toward me. Mustering all my speed, I ran straight at the robot.

Let's see how he likes a taste of his own medicine. "Prepare to die!" I shouted triumphantly.

About two seconds into my victory charge, I realized a serious flaw in my plan when the robot's twin guns whirred to life and spewed death rays. I shouted in dismay, dodged left, and narrowly missed plowing through a sapling some thoughtful gardener had planted there as lasers splintered the tree and set it on fire. My foot found a muddy spot where the same thoughtful gardener had apparently overwatered the area around the tree. At my high speed, the lost traction sent me sprawling like a greased midget in a mud wrestling match.

As I slid on my back through wet earth, I saw the missile on approach. It looked about the same size as the homemade rocket kit my dad and I had put together and fired off at a park once, although the tip looked sharp enough to spit me like a pig. Afterward, the explosion would spread me like confetti and, no doubt, really tick off the gardener.

Shelton roared a word, and a jagged beam of light speared from his wand even as he held his staff and its glowing shield to the side. His shot missed the missile. I scrambled for purchase, clawing my way back to my feet. But it was too late. An invisible force yanked my feet out from under me, reversing my course as though someone had lassoed my feet and pulled me with a horse. An instant later, the ground where I'd been exploded in a shower of hot mud and grass.

I screamed as the hot blast lifted me off the ground. The force hurled me away from the explosion, tumbling end over end. When I hit the ground, it felt like my spleen ricocheted off my liver and plowed into my stomach.

"Resistance is futile," the robot said. "Please submit to your doom."

"Screw you," Shelton said as a sphere of boiling light the size of his head gathered at the tip of his staff. He swung his staff like a golf club, catapulting the ball of energy toward the metal monstrosity. The robot swiveled, dodging with uncanny grace, though not quite fast enough, and the projectile boiled through the robot's left arm, melting the metal to useless slag.

The robot staggered to the side, reoriented, and fired a missile at Shelton.

By now, I'd regained my feet, watching in horror as my friend looked death in the eye. He brought his shield up, but I knew the explosion would probably fling him like a rag doll and break every bone in his body. I grabbed the tree toppled by the robot's death beams and wrenched it the rest of the way out of the ground. With a grunt of effort, I flung it like a spear. But my aim was off—way off—and it missed the missile by a mile. I saw Shelton running toward a large stone statue. I knew he'd never make it in time.

In an instant, the thought of my fight with Amanda, one of Maximus's evil minions flashed into my head. Something instinctual in me had reacted when Amanda had tossed a pack of explosives at Adam Nosti's feet, allowing me to protect him from the brunt of the killing force. Somewhere, lurking inside me, I knew I had the power. I had only seconds to figure it out.

Letting go of my surroundings, I withdrew into myself. My incubus senses took over my vision, and the glow of magical energy suffused the scene like an impressionist painting. Shelton's aura glowed like a beacon, white flames encircling him. The robot, I noticed, also had a glow around it. My friend's eyes looked to me as he stopped running, planted his staff in the ground, and reinforced his shield. I knew it was a look of hopelessness. Focusing on the air in front of his shield, I imagined it as solid as a wall. Nothing happened.

I clenched my fist and shouted, "Barrier!"

Something blurry appeared in the air, several feet in front of Shelton's own shield. I'd done it! I was about to shout with jubilation when the missile went right through it. It slammed against Shelton's shield.

"No!" I shouted in unison with Shelton.

I waited for the BOOM.

The missile plunked to the ground, fizzling like a dud bottle rocket. Shelton stared at it with confusion for a moment before using the chance to run his butt off toward the large statue of a man surrounded by shrubbery, diving behind it like a frightened squirrel.

"How odd," the robot said. It fired another missile at Shelton's position, swiveled, and fired one at me.

I'd had enough. Fury growled in my chest like a ravenous bear awakening after hibernation. Icy cold tendrils swarmed up my leg, and my knee buckled. I fell to the ground. Throwing up my hand in a last-ditch effort I tried to raise the barrier I'd managed a minute ago. But nothing happened this time.

Pain pierced my skull like ice picks, and I felt the demon shift coming over me. My skin pressed tight against my clothing, and a snarl of rage roared from my throat.

"No!" I shouted, my voice sounding monstrous. "Stop it!" I fought the rage, somehow darting from the missile path on all fours as it whizzed past at terminal velocity. If I manifested to full demon form, I would kill or destroy anything in my path like a mindless beast.

"Perhaps one is not sufficient," I heard the robot say, as though down a long tunnel.

This asshole is really getting on my nerves.

I looked up in time to see every missile in the robot's arsenal launch toward me in a volley of white smoke and orange flame. Its one remaining gun spun to life and spat jagged beams of energy.

With a roar, I rolled to the side, somehow fighting off the mindless beast trying to tear its way free of my sanity. Claws grew from my fingers; my skin turned dark blue. I galloped on all fours beneath a wave of death rays and skidded to the right, avoiding the swarm of missiles. The robot rotated to face me. A dazzling ball of energy flew from Shelton's hiding place and melted the end of the robot's one remaining gun as it spun up to fire again. I heard Shelton roar something at me.

Rage brawled with my remaining shreds of humanity. I focused on Elyssa's image. Remembered her laugh, her smile. She kept me sane. She was the only one who could tame the demon within. And even if she wasn't physically here, she was always with me.

The beast roared and slammed against the bars of its cage, but somehow, I kept the door from flying open.

"You are very uncooperative," the robot said.

I snarled. Leapt at my enemy. On instinct, my head lowered and, with a ringing clang of horn on metal, crashed into the robot. My vision blurred for an instant. Regained focus. The robot lay on the ground, struggling to right itself. I roared. Gripped one of its arms and tore it off. Pounded the metal torso.

"Justin, watch out!" I heard Shelton shout from somewhere to the side.

The rage didn't want to watch out. It wanted to mangle, kill, destroy.

Thankfully, one shred of sanity remained in my addled mind, and I dove away.

"Oh dear," the robot said an instant before the missiles struck where I'd been.

The explosion drove into my back like a giant club, batting me across the lawn. I plowed through shrubs sculpted into the shapes of planets, and my face plowed into the dirt. I struck something immovable, and my rear end flew up and smacked into something hard before dropping back to earth.

I tried to groan, but dirt filled my mouth, my nose. I tried to move, but nothing responded. Hands gripped my shoulder and jerked me to the side. I sputtered as my face came free of the dirt and mud, sucking in a breath and coughing violently.

"Holy dog balls in a hand basket," Shelton said. I felt his hands wiping at my face, and then I could see.

"Can't move," I said, my voice still sounding deep and guttural.

"You've got shrapnel sticking out of your back," Shelton said in a strange tone I'd never heard from him before. He almost sounded…concerned. "Oh, man. Hang on."

My body felt went numb, and I wondered if it meant I was dying. I felt a tug at my back. A rush of pins and needles raced along my skin followed shortly by intense agonizing pain. I screamed.

Shelton squeezed my shoulder. "This is gonna hurt like a bitch, man. So hang in there."

I gritted my teeth and squeezed my eyes shut as he jerked more shrapnel from my back. Each piece burned like serrated agony through muscle and flesh. I must have passed out at some point because, when I came to, I saw the ground, a pair of booted feet walking, and what was probably Shelton's butt.

"Gug," I said.

"Taking you back to the dorm," he replied.

"Wait. Walk." I tried to move my arms. They responded feebly.

Shelton leaned over to plant me on my feet. My knees wobbled but somehow held, probably because he slung my arm over his shoulder.

"Man, you're gonna need more clothes." He looked me in the eyes. "You ok to stand?"

I nodded even though every inch of my body hurt. "How long?"

"Were you out?" He mused the question for a moment. "Twenty minutes, maybe." He pointed ahead to the dorms. "Let's get inside, get you cleaned up. We gotta talk."

After drinking copious amounts of water and taking a shower, I felt somewhat better. My back was healing on its own, though slower than its usual speedy rate. I had a nasty feeling the vampling virus had something to do with it. As I slid on sweat pants and a T-shirt Shelton had pilfered from the laundry room, someone knocked on the door. He answered it and took delivery of a pizza.

I grabbed a piece and gobbled it, hardly pausing to breathe. Even as my food stomach filled, my demonic appetite made itself more apparent with a clawing sensation inside my belly.

"So, about the robot," Shelton said, taking a piece of pizza and blowing on it, "the one that attacked us ain't the same one from the entrance."

I paused mid-bite and raised an eyebrow. "Not the same one? But it looked—"

"Identical, I know." His phone projected a three-dimensional holographic image of the killer robot. Even though the missiles had blown it open, I noticed the torso was devoid of electronics or mechanical gear necessary for a robot to function.

"Um, where's the sciencey stuff?"

"For one thing, this wasn't a robot."

I paused in the middle of another bite and spoke with my mouth full from the last one. "It wasn't?"

"Nope." He displayed the image of one of the half-melted guns from the arm. "This was a golem someone went through a lot of trouble to make look like a robot. Specifically like the one at the entrance."

"A golem?" It seemed inconceivable anyone would go through the trouble. Then again, I probably didn't understand the meaning of the word. So many inconceivable things had happened to me over the last few months, I spent more time trying to figure out the next improbable way someone could kill me than I did choosing which cereal I wanted from the grocery store.

"Those gray men who tried to kill you are only one form of golem," Shelton said. "Hell, you can animate just about anything into a golem—stick figures, rocks, clay."

"Yeah, but why make it look like a robot?"

Shelton magnified the image on the gun, revealing an array of splintered sticks inside. "Those are wands, each one specifically spelled to cast death curses."

"But they looked like lasers."

"Death curses come in lots of forms." He went to an image of a missile. "These were basically charmed like flying brooms with potion bombs in the tips."

I peered at the missile, recognizing it as the one that had fizzled out. Greenish liquid dripped from the tip. "Potions—like witches brew?"

He nodded. "More or less. It's a form of magic people with less inherent power like to pursue, but whoever made these, was a master. I've never seen such a tiny amount of potion do so much damage."

"Why did that missile not explode?"

"That's a damned good question." Shelton braced his chin with a hand and pondered it for a moment. "You put up a barrier of some kind, but it wasn't physical. It could be you somehow threw up some kind of energy that defused the spell, or maybe we just got plain lucky."

"Well, since luck is never with us, I'd almost say it was my barrier, but knowing how terrible my magic skills are, it makes me want to say it was luck."

He laughed. "Well, it saved my ass."

I polished off my fourth—or was it fifth?—piece of pizza, and my stomach growled. "I need to feed."

Shelton turned off his phone and leaned back in his chair. "I was afraid you might need to."

Times like this really made Elyssa's absence painful. She understood my need to feed because she needed blood for her dhampyr side, although she could easily get blood packs, while I couldn't just as easily obtain bottled soul essence.

In other words, I needed a woman. Feeding off males was nearly impossible for me unless they were in a specific frame of mind. Women, on the other hand, could be doing laundry and still give me enough of an emotional vibe to feed on.

"Well, good thing we know someone," Shelton said. He checked the time on his phone.

I wrinkled my brow. "We do?"

He nodded. "Well, I don't personally know her, but I put in a call to Bella, and she said she knew someone going to school here who could help you out."

"Good thinking," I said.

He nodded and tapped his temple. "Brains. Not just for zombies anymore."

I laughed, even though the thought of Bella choosing someone to help me was a bit worrying. "So, uh, who—"

A knuckle rapped against the door.

"Come in," Shelton said.

The door opened, and a woman in a short purple skirt with a tight white T-shirt stepped inside. Her skin was the color of caramel, and her hair fell in long black waves over her shoulders. Chocolate brown eyes looked over an aquiline nose. She was every bit as lovely as the last time I'd seen her.

"Hello, Justin," Lina Romero said with a smile.

Chapter 12

Lina crossed the space before I could respond, squeezing me in a hug that sent pain racing up my ravaged back. I made a sound between a grunt and a whimper and feebly returned the hug. She felt very warm, very soft, and very curvy against my body. I jerked away as the demon in my pants took notice.

Lina gave me a knowing smile. "So, you are in trouble again?"

"It's a habit with this guy," Shelton said, trying to act nonchalant, though his roaming eyes and smirk told me he was enjoying the sight of the pretty girl.

"A golem robot thingy tried to blow us up," I said.

"Shrapnel in the back," Shelton added.

Lina's eyes grew wide. "Oh, no. I must look." Before I could protest, she was tugging the T-shirt off my back. She gasped. "Justin, this is terrible!" Her Colombian accent was lighter than the last time I'd heard it, but thickened with her distress. "It is so good I came to you."

"Why are you here at the academy?" I asked, still a bit off balance by her appearance.

"I'm attending A.U." She smiled. "I'm finally a college girl."

Shelton leaned back in his chair, still munching on pizza. "Well, she's here and willing. Go ahead and do what you need to do."

I liked Lina. She was smart, pretty, and feisty. But she'd also wanted to be more than friends when we first met. At the time, Elyssa had lost her memories of me, and I'd all but given up on her ever remembering me or loving me again. Lina had helped me out quite a bit in my time of need—and no, not in the naughty way either. But she'd wanted more than I could give. My heart belonged to Elyssa then and now.

"You're concerned about what happened last time," she said, giving me a sober look.

Shelton leaned forward. "And what was that?"

"Uh—" I started, unsure what to say, if anything.

Lina smiled. "I had a crush on Justin."

"Bah." Shelton leaned back in his chair. "Man, I thought it'd be something interesting, not high school romance."

She rolled her eyes, the smile never leaving her face. "Bella told me about you, Harry. Maybe you should look into this high school romance stuff a little more. She could probably teach you something."

He chuckled. "Man, I'll bet she could teach me things that would—" He cut off abruptly, giving us each uncomfortable glances. "Ah, forget it. Just feed already, I'm sick of hearing the kid groan."

Lina brown eyes met mine. "It's okay, Justin. No more girly crushes."

I took a deep breath and regarded her for a moment before deciding I was just too damned hungry to care. I extended my incubus senses, and Lina's halo, a glowing nimbus around her body, flared to life. I latched a tendril of my essence into her gently swirling aura. Emotions flooded through the connection, but I filtered the noise and evened out my own emotional state to match the ones that were most benign. I was constantly improving my technique, though to any older Daemos, I probably looked like a toddler with applesauce smeared all over his mouth and cake in his hair.

Energy trickled down the connection and into my psythus—the spiritual belly which housed the energy my demonic side used for many of my supernatural abilities.

Lina sighed. "It is so fascinating being connected like this."

Shelton leaned forward again. "Does it feel sexual?"

I blew out a breath. "Don't be a perv, man."

"I'm not." He gave me a wounded look. "You're a friggin incubus, so naturally I'd think it's sexual."

"It's more of a pleasant sensation, like when you drink a glass of wine and have a fuzzy glow," Lina said. "Or like enjoying time with a good book while curled up next to a fire."

"I'm focusing on those pleasant emotions," I said. "If I didn't, it would naturally gravitate to sexual."

She pursed her full lips and raised an eyebrow. "Oh? Are you saying that you could make any woman want sex?"

I shrugged. "Well, like Shelton said, I am an incubus."

"Hmm." Her accent gave a sultry flavor to the sound. "How interesting."

Shelton shook his head. "Man, oh, man, what fun it would be to have that ability."

"And yet, he saves his love for one woman." Lina sighed. "How sweet."

"I guess I'm a romantic at heart." I thought back to the opportunities I'd had when first discovering my abilities and how many temptations I'd forced myself to overcome, including Katie Johnson, my crush at the time. But I'd wanted my first time to be special, and boy had it! I thought of that time with Elyssa, her questing lips, her heaving breasts, the way her hips—

"Oh, my!" Lina said with a little gasp, dropped into a chair, her face glowing red. "Justin, what are you thinking about?" Her breathing grew heavy, and she bit her lip as a little moan escaped.

"Holy crap!" I jerked back from reminiscing about Elyssa and forced my emotional state back down to non-naughty levels. "Lina, I'm really sorry. Guess I got to thinking about—"

"Elyssa." Her smile didn't quite reach her eyes.

I nodded.

Lina grabbed a bottle of water from her purse and took a long gulp. She paced for a moment. "You are a dangerous man, Justin Slade."

Shelton rocked back with laughter.

A knock sounded on the door. Shelton's laugh died, and we exchanged worried glances.

"Expecting someone else?" I asked.

He shook his head as he pulled out his wand. He waved it through a pattern, and a ball of energy glowed at the end. Lina stood, muttered something under her breath, and twin balls of white flame formed in her hands.

I jumped back. "Whoa, when did you learn to do that?"

Shelton gave her a confused look. "Wait, how are you—ah, the bracelets."

I noticed the way the jewels on her bracelets had folded into the palms of her hands, forming a focus for her magic to work through. Lina gave Shelton a grin. "It is a trick Bella taught me."

Another knock sounded on the door, followed by a calm voice. "Justin, I forgot to identify myself after the first knock. Many apologies. This is Cinder. Please do not destroy me."

"Who is Cinder?" Lina asked, the spheres of energy in her hands casting an eerie glow on her face.

The light at the end of Shelton's wand winked out. "Ah, he's mostly harmless."

I opened the door. A man in a gray suit stood outside. He looked ordinary, aside from his unnaturally gray skin, although there was something different about his appearance from the last time I'd seen him.

"Hello, Justin," he said in a nearly monotone voice. "It is good to see you again."

I held out my hand. He took mine and shook it. "You're getting better," I said, motioning him inside. "Something about you is different."

"Hey, you dyed your hair black," Shelton said, slapping the golem on the back. "I like it."

Cinder paused, no doubt uncertain how to respond, before saying, "I believe it makes me look more human than the silver color." He tilted his head. "Was the strike on the back an act of aggression or one of fondness?"

Shelton groaned. "Man, you have a lot to learn."

"I don't mean to be rude," Lina said, "but what's wrong with your skin?"

"He's a golem," I replied.

"A golem?" Her eyes widened in surprise. "But, he looks so…real."

"Maximus's top Arcane, Dash Armstrong, was experimenting on gray men." I briefly explained about the gray men, how they'd attacked me and Elyssa, and that we suspected another angel I'd nicknamed Mr. Gray was the creator of the things. "Somehow, Cinder became a free man," I finished.

"He's not just an automaton anymore?" Lina walked around the golem, touching his skin. "My goodness, he feels so real."

"Thank you," Cinder said in his gentle tone. "I am working on improving all aspects of my appearance and texture."

"He wants to be a real boy," Shelton said.

Lina covered her mouth with a hand, and a sad look came into her eyes. After a moment's hesitation, she said, "Justin, you meet the most interesting…people."

"Why are you here, Cinder?" I asked as my mind finally got over the surprise of seeing him.

"As you know, I wish to improve myself." He looked around the room in a slightly robotic manner, probably in an attempt to mimic human expressions like making eye contact. "Since Science Academy and Arcane University deal in advanced applications of robotics and golems, I decided it would be an ideal location to seek out answers and meaning."

"Sounds reasonable," Shelton said. "But don't you have problems with professors wanting to take you apart to see how you work?"

Cinder nodded, and his mouth stretched into a plastic smile. "Indeed. One professor attempted to kidnap me."

"What did you do?" Lina asked.

"I ran."

Shelton snickered, covering his mouth with his hand in a vain attempt to cover it up.

Cinder tilted his head like a curious puppy. "I appear to have made a joke without realizing it, Harry. Would you explain what is funny so I may have the information for future reference?"

I dropped into my chair and realized my back wasn't nearly as sore as it had been moments ago. My feeding session with Lina had apparently helped.

As Shelton fumbled with explaining what he found funny about Cinder's statement, I looked the golem up and down. He still looked very much the same, though the black hair lent a more realistic quality to him. I wondered if it was possible to make his skin a little pinker, though. His gray, pallid "flesh" had a morbid look to it, as though he was on the verge of death.

Even though I felt the golem was being honest about his presence here, I still had some doubt. What if this wasn't the real Cinder? Whoever had disguised the other golem as a killer robot knew what they were doing. It might have even been planted by Mr. Gray. I had to be sure this Cinder was the one I knew. "How did you know we were here, Cinder?" I asked, interrupting Shelton's long-winded explanation about humor.

Cinder looked at me. "At this dormitory, or the school?"

"Both."

"I attempted to call you earlier this evening, however, you never answered. I called Bella, and she told me you were here." He touched his chin thoughtfully in the same way Shelton was touching his and continued. "It seemed to be a very interesting coincidence that you were here, so I came over."

I went to the singed and torn mess that had been my jeans before the attack by the golem and found my arcphone inside the pocket. It was magically toughened, and it didn't have a scratch. Flicking it on, I navigated to the calls screen and saw a missed call from Cinder. Katie and I had taken him to the Grotto to get his own phone when he announced his imminent journey of self-discovery, so unless someone had kidnapped Cinder, replaced him with an identical golem, and sent the clone after me, this guy was the original.

"Are you trying to determine my authenticity?" Cinder asked.

I nodded. "I'm sorry, but after what happened earlier, I can't take any chances."

"Would it help if I recounted the events of our first meeting and subsequent escape with our mutual friend Katie?"

"I think he's the real deal," Shelton said. "Can you imagine trying to recreate Cinder's deadpan personality?"

I chuckled. "No." Then again, I'd never heard another gray man talk. Either Mr. Gray didn't want them to have a personality, or it was impossible. I needed people—and golems—I could trust. We had to find out who'd sent that robot and why. Then again, whoever had sent the robot sure had given it a strange personality. What kind of robot spoke with a cockney—"Oh, crap," I said as I realized where I'd heard a voice like that. "Mr. Bigglesworth sent that robot golem doohickey. And I'd be willing to bet he was the man with the red suit."

"Fits his M.O.," Shelton agreed. "He likes to hide in plain sight."

"This is one reason I called you, Justin." Cinder regarded me with his flat gray eyes.

"Because of Bigglesworth?"

"Not precisely. He is, however, connected to a group of individuals who wish you harm. I have seen members of this group not only here, but also at Arcane University." He offered a robotic shrug. "Since I consider you my friend, I determined it wise to notify you of their"—he paused, head tilted as if searching for something—"nefarious activities."

Shelton snorted with laughter.

Before Cinder could question him about humor again, I snapped my fingers to hold his attention. "Who exactly have you seen here?"

"Your sister, Ivy, and your grandfather, Jeremiah Conroy. Although I attempted to discover their purpose, the only determination I made was they are looking for something specific in order to repair an arch."

Shelton and I exchanged glances. "Did they say what kind of arch?"

Cinder shook his head in the first natural movement I'd seen from him. "My apologies, Justin, but I was only able to overhear one of their conversations. Although I desired to learn ninja stealth techniques from Elyssa, she was unwilling to spend time helping me."

My girlfriend still had trouble trusting the golem, despite my assurances. Then again, she was a Templar, and they weren't the most trusting people in the world. "Tell us everything you heard," I said.

Cinder began to recite what he'd heard. "Ivy said, 'Why is it here, Bigdaddy?' Jeremiah replied, 'Because it was a safe place to put it.' Ivy then replied, 'If we fix the Alabaster Arch, will you take me to the zoo? Please? You promised after Maximus you would.' Jeremiah then said, 'But that didn't work out so well, did it sugar?' Ivy replied, 'It wasn't my fault. It was my evil big brother's fault.'" Cinder halted his recitation.

"Don't take up an acting career anytime soon," Shelton with an amused expression.

I raised an eyebrow at him then turned to Cinder. "Is that it?"

He nodded. "At that point, they left the building and headed for the transport to the Queens Gate arch station. I determined it too risky to follow them."

"Why don't we just take Ivy to the damned zoo?" Shelton said. "Might get her on our side."

"Your sister thinks you're evil?" Lina said, horror in her eyes. "What have your grandparents been saying about you?"

That was a can of worms I didn't feel like opening, but I told her in brief how Ivy had attempted to kill all the vampires at Maximus's Atlanta compound, and how I'd somehow managed to tweak the spell so it simply removed their vampirism instead.

"How powerful are you?" she asked, brown eyes wide. "How powerful is your sister?"

"I suck at magic right now," I said. "I came here to learn. Looks like someone doesn't think that's a good idea."

"Oh, it's a lot deeper than that," Shelton said, his eyes glowing with the kind of fervor he usually reserved for his arcane detective work. "Think about it. They want to activate the special arch in Thunder Rock, but guess what? It's not working because someone sabotaged it. They figure the missing piece is here somewhere. Then they see you here, assume you probably know about their plans, and send Bigglesworth to kill you."

"Back up a minute," I said. "They still haven't gotten those smaller arches to work yet, according to the operator at the Grotto. That means they haven't gone to Thunder Rock. So how would they know there's something missing from the special arch there?"

"Maybe Daelissa visited Thunder Rock and found out it wasn't working." Shelton shrugged. "I mean, hell, remember when your mom saved you from Jeremiah? Remember how she seemed to teleport away? For all we know, the angels can do that kind of stuff all day long."

That was something I hadn't even considered. "Pretend I'm stupid, Shelton, and tell me where you're going with this."

He snorted. "Not hard to do that."

"Hey, now!"

He held up his hands. "I kid. I kid." He removed his hat, scratched his head, eyes lost in thought for a moment. "The problem is, we don't know enough about this Alabaster Arch. We don't know if there's just the one in Thunder Rock, or more of them scattered around the world."

"Well, we could ask Arcanes at other Obsidian Arch way stations whether their control rooms are identical."

He nodded. "But I have a feeling our Darkwater credentials are only gonna last so long, especially if we start asking sensitive questions."

"They are very secretive about those arch stations," Lina said. "One of the operators nearly took my hair off when I asked about seeing one."

"He nearly took your head off," Shelton said with a smirk. "Not hair."

"Such violence seems an overwhelming response to such a question." Cinder regarded Lina. "It is good you escaped without major damage."

"You are so cute!" Lina said, smiling.

I wrenched the topic back on course. "Shelton, do you know anyone who could ask about the control rooms, or maybe tell us about them?"

His jaw tightened. "Yeah, unfortunately." He looked at the floor. "My father."

Chapter 13

"Your dad?" I asked. "There's no other way?" I wasn't looking forward to another Shelton family reunion, or whatever his real last name was—a question best kept for another time.

"Oh, I'm sure there are plenty of other ways. But none would be faster than me asking Pops about the four-one-one on the control rooms." Shelton absentmindedly twirled his wand on the table. "Hell, he might even know off the top of his head."

"How much do you know about this Alabaster Arch?" Lina asked, looking at me.

I told her the little I knew about the one I'd seen in Thunder Rock. Another memory sparked to life, and something useful bubbled to the top. "You know, I actually activated that arch while I was there."

Shelton's eyes widened. "You activated it?"

"Yeah, there was a symbol for it, so I pressed it."

He leaned forward on his elbows. "What happened?"

"Well, there was a deep bellowing sound, like an alarm, and it flashed black and white for a minute, just like the others do. I remember looking at the world map and realizing the arch didn't light up any of the stars, so I decided not to take it."

Lina touched my hand. "It is good you didn't. Otherwise, we never would have met."

"And you'd probably be angel food," Shelton added.

I grimaced. "Yeah, well, it certainly looked like the arch was working, but I never saw it actually connect with a location on the other side. Then again, I didn't stick around to watch, because a cherub grabbed my leg."

"Well, let's assume there's something bugged with it," Shelton said. "Otherwise Conroy wouldn't be hunting for this mystery piece."

I considered that for a moment, and a question I'd asked myself earlier returned to mind. "I wonder if the arch has something to do with the Grand Nexus. If it goes back to the Seraphim plane of reality—"

Shelton snapped his fingers. "Exactly. This Grand Nexus is just like Grand Central Station. It's the place all the angels came into our world. When it went kaplooey, all the angels nearby turned into husks."

"But there are husks at El Dorado," Lina said. "Wouldn't that mean—"

Shelton snapped his fingers again. "There was another arch there."

Cinder tried to snap his fingers, though it took him a couple of tries to meet success. "This gesture means I have made a startling discovery?" he asked.

Lina put a hand over her heart and gave him an *oh-he's-so-adorable, squeee!* look. "Something like that, yes."

"The Grand Nexus might not be one place," Shelton continued, ignoring the exchange, "but several interlinked places. Unless the husks somehow managed to take those smaller arches from Thunder Rock to El Dorado, I'd bet good money another Alabaster Arch exists in Colombia."

I pictured both places in my head. Both were abandoned relics. Both had the creepy cherubs—far too many to explain them having migrated there through any other means. It meant both places must have an Alabaster Arch or some other connection to Thunder Rock. "Okay, this is what we need to do. We need to research this Alabaster Arch and see if it shows up in either of these schools' histories. Maybe cross-reference Thunder Rock and El Dorado for starters." I turned to Lina. "I'll send you some pictures of my grandparents. Maybe you can keep an eye out for them."

"There are pictures of the Conroys in the main hall," Lina said. "They apparently donated lots of tinsel to the university. But, I would like a picture of Ivy."

"I don't actually have one of her." I no longer had pictures of anyone in my family. The thought made my breath hitch in my chest.

Why did I even bother? Everything seemed so futile. As if to underscore the fact, icy cold veins throbbed through my entire leg.

Lina suddenly squeezed me in a tight hug and kissed me on the top of my head. "Everything will be okay, Justin."

I hugged her back and felt the hot sting of tears trying to break free. I let go and smiled, trying desperately not to lose it in front of everyone. "You bet!" I said, my voice brimming with fake enthusiasm. I hopped up from my chair. "I'll go to the library stacks tomorrow and hunt around for clues to the Alabaster Arch."

"I'll hunt down dear old daddy of mine," Shelton said. "I'm sure he's still trapped here with the rest of us."

"Just try not to get into any fist fights," I said.

"Pshht," Shelton said, dismissing my words with a roll of his eyes. "He ain't worth the energy."

"Who, exactly, is your father, Harry?" Lina asked.

His eyes met hers. "That's a damned good question." He stood, slapped his hat atop his head, and gathered his wand from the table. "I'm gonna take a walk. This room is stuffy." Without another word, he left.

"I should head back to the university," Lina said. "I really need to work on my elementals, but the overflow list for gauntlet rooms is so long I had to wait two hours for my turn today."

"Really?" I said. But school hasn't even started."

"Some students are here on scholarship like me," she said with a sigh. "If we don't keep a high grade average, we lose the money. Elementals are my weakest subject, so I have to practice as much as possible."

"You can't practice outside?" I said. "Looks like there's tons of open ground around the university."

She shook her head. "They don't allow it for safety reasons." Lina rolled one of her bracelets on her wrist. "To make it even harder, the elite students who participate in the Arcane Tourney have priority on gauntlet rooms."

"The more I learn about Arcane University, the more it sounds like every other nom school." My hand balled into a fist at the thought of the bullying I'd suffered in high school. "Elitists think they own the place and everyone in it."

Lina touched my hand and smiled. "It's not so bad. I'm sorry for complaining."

I smiled. "Thank you for, uh, helping me."

"It was my pleasure." She regarded me with her big brown eyes. "It was really good to see you again, Justin." Lina leaned forward and pecked me on the cheek.

I smiled. "You, too."

Cinder watched her go and turned to me. "Where is Elyssa, Justin? I do not ever recall seeing you without her nearby, except, of course, when we were captives of Maximus."

"Taking her Templar graduation test." I glanced at the bunk beds and felt a pang of regret. I was missing her something awful already.

"I remember her mentioning the Cho'kai on many occasions. Perhaps once she is on active duty, you will see her even less." He tried to smile, though it looked more like a maniacal leer than anything else.

"Uh, that's not something you smile after telling me," I said, frowning. "It's a bad thing for me, not good."

He considered it for a moment—at least how I interpreted his silence. "Advancement for your mate is not a good thing?"

"Not when you put it the way you did." A yawn took me by surprise, and I suddenly realized just how exhausted I felt.

"Shelton once told me when he yawns and stretches in my presence, it is a cue he wishes me to leave him in peace so he can sleep." The golem tilted his head slightly. "Am I correct in assuming that is why you yawned?"

"No." I chuckled. "I am tired though, so I think I'm gonna hit the sack."

"Very well," Cinder said. "Rest well, and dream of large women."

I felt my eyes go wide and a large grin stretch my lips. "Where did you hear that?"

"Bella told me it would be appropriate to say such a thing the next time Shelton yawned in my presence." He paused. "Was she correct?"

I nodded. "It's perfect. Why don't you get some rest and dream of large women as well?"

"I do not require sleep, though I must admit I am curious to understand why dreaming of large women is desirable."

It took all my effort not to laugh.

The next morning, I awoke to an empty room and someone knocking on the door. The sheets on Shelton's bunk lay folded and unused. My back felt a little sore, but other than a ravenous hunger demanding breakfast, I felt great. I jumped up and answered the door to find a robot that looked like a shiny white trashcan on wheels with a domed lid for a head. It looked suspiciously like one I'd seen in a movie.

"Package for Mr. Slade," the robot said in a calm tone then whistled robotic noises while handing me a large suitcase.

"Uh, who sent this?" I asked.

"The sender is one Bella last name unknown via overnight shipping from Atlanta, Georgia."

I took the suitcase. "Thanks."

"Sign, please," the robot said.

I swirled my signature with a finger on the proffered arctablet.

"Thank you." The robot spun and zipped down the hallway toward the exit.

The suitcase brimmed with fresh clothes. "God bless you, Bella," I said with a grin and grabbed clean underwear.

After a shower, I felt more than wonderful—I felt fabutastic. When I entered the room, I saw Shelton sorting through the clean clothes. "Where were you last night?" I asked.

"None of your business, Dad," Shelton said without turning around. He gathered some clothes under an arm and settled his wide-brimmed hat atop his head. As he headed toward the door, I noticed something off about his face.

I gripped his arm and looked. "What the hell happened to your face?" One eye was swollen almost shut, and his lip was split.

He jerked his arm away. Strode for the door. "Fell down some stairs."

I blurred to the door and braced my back against it. "Spit it out Shelton. What happened?"

"Don't make me—"

"What, curse at me? Shoot me with your fancy magic wand?" I crossed my arms. "I found out yesterday your father happens to be the Arcane head honcho. Not only that, but his last name is different from yours. Then you vanish all night and come back looking like this. I want answers, Shelton, and I want them now."

He clenched his jaw. "There ain't much to tell."

"Good, because I'm hungry."

He continued to look at me. "Let's save it for later. We have a big day ahead of us."

I shook my head. "Knowing the way my days go, I might not have another chance." An exasperated breath escaped me. "This isn't the first time you've been all weird. Remember Colombia? You said you'd help and vanished. After everything was over, I found out you'd turned tail and run home because of something from your past."

"That was different." He shrugged. "I've made some enemies in my life. Everyone does. You, of all people, should know that."

Boy, did I ever. "Did your past beat the crap out of you? I need your help, Shelton. You can't just vanish on me." I leaned forward and spoke in a low tone. "What the hell is going on?"

His fists clenched, and his face screwed up in something like disgust or anger. Then he turned and hurled his clothes across the room where they fluttered to the floor in a heap. He jerked off his hat and tossed it on the table. "Fine, but this stays between you and me. Nobody else hears this, not even your girlfriend. Promise?"

"Why—"

"Do you promise?" he shouted, eyes full of anger.

I nodded. "Yes."

He dropped into a chair. Sighed. "Man, oh man, oh man." His eyes squeezed shut, and he pounded a fist on the table.

I kept quiet, doing my best to be patient. I'd never seen him so worked up.

Shelton took a deep breath. "I'm adopted." His hand trembled. He gripped the side of the table. "My real parents weren't exactly model citizens. The council tried to arrest them a long time ago, but they escaped and left me in my crib." His eyes met mine. A cauldron of emotions steeled his gaze. "Jarrod Sager took me in and adopted me. He and his wife had another kid, Martin, when I was about three. I, of course, had no idea. I didn't know why they treated me differently. Why Martin got everything, and I was left out." A smile broke through his façade. "He treated me like a real brother. He shared with me, he helped me through some dark times."

"Like a best friend," I said.

Shelton nodded and took a deep breath. "To make things worse, I was a late bloomer with magic. The Sagers took me to a healer every year to have me checked out, but it looked like I wasn't ever gonna develop skills. Martin, though, he was as talented as his dad. I, of course, had no idea at the time Sager wasn't really my dad. It wasn't until my real parents tried to reclaim me that I found out the hard truth." A haunted look clouded his eyes. "The reason Jarrod Sager adopted me was so he could draw my real parents out of hiding."

"He used you as bait?" I said, horrified.

"Yeah." Shelton chewed on his lower lip. "I guess he and my dad used to be best buds in college. Then my dad tried to kill him."

"Why?"

He shook his head. "Even I don't know the whole story. Suffice it to say Sager became obsessed with taking down my dad. He used me for that purpose, and it worked. Before my dad died, he told me the truth." Shelton's red rimmed eyes grew unfocused. "I just wish I knew for sure."

I waited for him to finish the thought, but it didn't look like he was going to. "Knew what for sure?" I asked.

Shelton flinched, like I'd woken him from a dream. "Whether my parents were really evil or not." He rubbed his eyes. "I know the official story, but the winner writes the history books, and I guess we know who won that battle."

I didn't know what to say. Sager had to be absolutely heartless to use a child in such a way. I also understood the need to know. Plenty of people thought I was evil just because I was part demon spawn. "Maybe we can find the truth," I said.

Shelton shook his head. "Let the dead rest, man." He drew in a long breath and sighed it back out. "Sager's wife didn't know about his plan. Neither did Martin. It wasn't long after that when Martin died. Sager tried to make amends with me, but I told him what he could do with apologies."

I didn't know what to say. My emotions toward my father churned with anger, betrayal, but also a longing to have him back. To have my whole family back together, living in the house I grew up in with my little sister. I had a terrible premonition my fantasy would never come true.

"That was when I went to Science Academy. I met Miles Chamberlain, and he turned my life around. Gave me a second chance." Shelton's face went tight. "Guess I blew that, too." He looked at me. "I went into bounty hunting and made nothing but enemies."

"How did you get involved with Vadaemos?" I asked. "Were you somehow involved with the death of Meghan's father?"

Shelton ran a hand down his face, eyes miserable. "I had nothing to do with her dad." He stood and picked up the clothes he'd thrown. "I'm going to clean up."

"You're evading the question," I said.

"Look, we can go our separate ways anytime you want." Shelton locked eyes with me. "I was a lot happier before I met you."

I returned his challenging stare. "You're more than welcome to go your own way Shelton. I'm thankful to you for giving us a place to stay, for teaching me magic. But you're a closed book to everyone. I'm not the one to forgive you or judge you for your past. But I need to know I can trust you."

He nodded. "Yeah. Can't blame you there." Shelton snatched clean underwear—a pair of boxers with dancing cats on it—from the suitcase. "Well, I'm going to clean up. Maybe after, we can go grab some breakfast."

After he left for the shower, I dropped into a chair. Ran my fingers through my hair. Was it a good sign Shelton had opened up? Or should I cut and run before his history caught up to him at a critical moment? I'd learned a few things since my brutal initiation into the Overworld, but one stood out more than the others in this case.

What I didn't know could kill me.

Chapter 14

After breakfast, Shelton and I went back to Arcane University via a rocket shuttle that went back and forth between the schools. On the way over, a flying stagecoach passed us going the other way—no doubt the university's shuttle. I was only mildly disappointed it didn't have flying horses pulling it. Looking out the windows was preferable to looking at the floor since some clever engineer had used liquid glass to offer a terrifying experience for anyone with acrophobia. Looking down only reminded me of Shelton's earlier story about the possibility of rocket failure.

A raised voice emanated from within Miles's office when we reached drew near.

"I demand you change me to Professor Oldham's class," a familiar male voice said.

"I'm afraid his class is full," Miles replied. "I will not have someone removed from his class simply so you can attend it."

"You'll hear from my father on this," the other person said in a furious voice and stormed from the office. The jerk from the shuttle who'd argued with Shelton appeared from the doorway. His lips curled into a sneer when he saw us. "Well, if it isn't Harry Shelton and his pet demon spawn," William Vanderbilt spat. His sneer turned to a smirk. "That's right, Shelton. I've heard all about how your parents betrayed the council. Personally, I can't believe the Primus hasn't disowned you yet."

"Turns out I know a little about you too, kid," Shelton said, returning the smirk. "Better practice a lot more for the tourney this year. I guess you didn't do so well last year, did you?"

William's handsome face went livid. "Want to try me, old man? I'll show you how good I am."

Shelton made a raspberry sound with his lips. "Out of my way, pipsqueak." He shoved past the enraged student and headed to Miles's office without a backward glance.

William clenched a fist around his wand and aimed it at Shelton's back. I gripped his wrist and gave it a little squeeze. He squealed and dropped his wand. I picked it up and threw it far down the hall. "Fetch," I said. "If you're still standing here when I count to ten, I'm going to break your hand."

The speed with which he departed was quite the testament to William's bravery—or lack thereof.

"William Vanderbilt—Billy as they call him—is quite the ruddy ass," Miles said with a grimace as he handed over my schedule. "I suppose his father will use his clout to remove someone from Oldham's class so he can have a slot."

"Are the Vanderbilts bigwigs?" I asked.

"Council hot shots." Shelton blew out a disgusted breath.

"Indeed," Miles said. "I had a rather interesting conversation with Dean Buckley today as well. He wanted me to revoke your admission."

Alarm widened my eyes. "Can he do that?"

"No, not without cause," Miles said.

Shelton gave me a look. "So don't go giving them a reason."

Since trouble had a way of finding me, that seemed a tall order.

"I wouldn't overly trouble yourself, my boy," Miles said with a jovial grin. "You are a member of House Slade, and the Daemos are not without influence."

The last people I wanted to rely on were my demonic relatives, but I said nothing about my misgivings.

"I'm going to visit Sager," Shelton said after we left Miles. "You should go buy your books."

After a rat's maze of hallways, we eventually emerged into a huge circular area, which appeared to be located within one of the spired towers I'd seen from the outside. The sounds of paper rustling, pens on parchment, and the thump and close of filing cabinets lent a decidedly bureaucratic feel the atmosphere. People walked about with scrolls, stacks of parchment, and books. They hurried up carpeted stairways leading higher into the tower and through the grid of corridors lined with cubicles and desks. I walked to the center of the foyer, looked up, and felt a wave of vertigo at the vast distance between the floor and the peak of the vaulted ceiling far above. The administration tower appeared slightly crooked, though it might have been the way the marble balustrade wrapped around the interior for a seemingly infinite number of floors.

Shelton stopped a man who huffed in irritation at the interruption and asked him if he'd seen the Primus. The man told him the Primus was meeting with the Chancellor and hurried away.

"This is gonna be fun," Shelton said, his face looking a bit paler than usual.

I raised an eyebrow. "You okay to do this?"

He nodded. "Yeah. It's hard to even look at the man after...well, you know. It's been years now, but still." His voice trailed off, and his eyes lost focus. He snapped his head suddenly. "Yeah, yeah, I'm fine."

"Maybe I should come with you."

Shelton's eyes locked onto me. "I'll talk to him alone."

"But—"

"Having you around is only gonna make it harder." He drew in a deep breath. "Please."

I looked at him for a moment before responding. "You realize how important this is, right? If you insult him, he's not going to help. Be nice."

He gave me a pained look. "Hey, I can turn on the honey when I need to." He blew out a breath. "I didn't get good at bounty hunting by being a complete jackass."

"I'd beg to differ," I said, showing the hint of a smile. "You—"

I didn't have time to finish the sentence before Shelton's arm shoved me back against the wall of a nearby stairwell. I suppressed the natural reflex to push back and shut my mouth. Following Shelton's gaze, I settled my eyes on a man in a top hat and old-fashioned suit. He stood next to the marble balustrade bordering the second floor where it overlooked the first. Next to him stood the man in the red polyester suit and red bowler hat. I zoomed my vision on his face. He looked a little pale, but not doughy like Bigglesworth. Still, I knew the shape shifter could make his flesh look realistic if he wanted to.

I recognized the man in the top hat as Jeremiah Conroy. He wore a long, neatly combed goatee and his spectacles perched on a large nose.

"Do you see Ivy?" I whispered to Shelton.

He shook his head.

"I need to hear what they're saying."

Shelton gave me the crazy eye. "You need to keep hidden."

"They know I'm here already," I said. "Remember the killer golem robot? Plus, I doubt they'll kill me in front of everyone."

"I wouldn't put anything past old man Conroy," he grumbled.

Before I could put my ninja skills to the test, the man I suspected was Bigglesworth tipped his bowler hat and walked away. Jeremiah twirled his cane once and headed toward the Chancellor's office. I glanced back and forth between the two men.

"Look, I'll tail Conroy and see what he's up to," Shelton said. "You can follow Bigglesworth if you want, but you'd better be damned careful." He pulled out his arcphone. "Lemme see yours." I took out mine. We bumped phones. "Linkup."

My phone, Nookli, lit up. "Do you authorize, Justin?"

"Yes," I replied.

"Link activated," Nookli said.

An overhead map of the school appeared on the screen. Two blips indicated our respective locations. I nodded, slipped my phone into my pocket, and skulked after Bigglesworth. He took the knight hall back toward the busted wall but turned away from the two passages on either side of it, choosing a spiral staircase, and taking it down. I followed as closely as I dared, hoping he wouldn't vanish around a corner down below. After counting to five, I crept down the stairs and peeked through the first doorway into a long carpeted hall. Nobody there. I moved further down, paused at the next doorway. Still nothing. My chest tightened with apprehension. Had I lost him?

Whistling echoed up the stone stairs. It had to be him. I walked down, down, down the staircase until cool, damp air indicated I must be underground. The stairwell ended in a solid iron door with a thick bar across it, secured by an equally thick padlock. I stopped and listened for the whistling. The last hallway had been at least fifty steps back. Had he exited the stairwell? I inspected the door, but unless there was some trick involved, I didn't see how he could bar and padlock the door behind him.

A hoarse cry of pain echoed from far away. The sound didn't come from upstairs. It came from behind the door. I knelt, tried to peer beneath the one-inch crack between the floor and the bottom of the door. It was then I noticed bits and pieces of white material on the stone tiles. I suddenly knew with great certainty the man in red was Bigglesworth and also how he'd gone through a locked door. He'd simply flowed through the bottom crack.

Another scream reached my ears. The hairs on the back of my neck stood on end. Bigglesworth was doing something terrible to someone. I checked the padlock. Thankfully, it wasn't constructed of nearly indestructible diamond fiber. I gripped the lock and pulled. It groaned and screeched. My muscles strained. The padlock popped loose, and I nearly toppled over backwards.

I lifted the bar. Opened the door. The hallway beyond showed no signs of life. I walked left to the end of the hall, some thirty yards away. A dark hallway lay on my right. My night vision flickered on, and I saw what looked like a thick iron portcullis with a ragged hole cut through the center. Drops of molten metal on the stone floor and at the tips of the bars gave evidence of the quick, messy job someone had done to get through. I had a feeling Bigglesworth might have done it.

Another scream sounded from back the way I'd come. Then again, maybe he hadn't. I tip-toed down the hall, grateful for my soft tennis shoes, noting the widely spaced doors along either wall and the blank wall at the far end of the hallway.

"Surely, your worshipfulness knows more than that," Bigglesworth said from one of the rooms ahead. "Your people took all the records. Where did they put them?"

"I bloody told you all I know, you right bastard," a hoarse, but defiant voice replied. "The records are gone—destroyed."

"Another bloody lie, eh?" Bigglesworth chuckled. "How does this suit your fancy?"

I stopped outside the door as the other man screamed himself raw. Risking a glance, I peeked around the doorframe. A man who looked perhaps thirty strained hard against straps binding him to a chair, his profile to me. The veins in his neck bulged, and his skin glowed beet red. Bigglesworth stood over the other man, doughy white fingers touching his captive's forehead.

Attacking the shape changer head-on seemed the wrong approach. True, I might be strong and fast, but this guy wasn't exactly solid. If he could inflict pain through touch, he could probably incapacitate me. Bella had told me his kind ate people. I shuddered at the thought. She'd never found out much more about Bigglesworth's species. Knowing his weaknesses would have been dandy right about now. As usual, I had no choice but to improvise.

"So, guvnah, what's it gonna be?" Bigglesworth's mouth stretched inhumanly wide. "More pain, or will you tell me and let me go on my merry way?"

The other man shuddered violently, coughs racking his body.

As Bigglesworth chided and threatened the man, I thought furiously about how to get rid of the shape shifter once and for all. The only destructive spell I knew wasn't really supposed to be destructive—it was supposed to light a candle. Instead, I usually ended up launching fireballs. I had to pretend Bigglesworth was a candle and see what happened. It sounded simple enough in my head. All it required was a bit of focus.

With Doughboy's attention solely on his captive, I switched to incubus sight and drew in magic. I flinched as the energy swelled against my reservoir, stretching it. I pressed my lips together, glared at Bigglesworth, and imagined him as the biggest, nastiest candle I'd ever seen. I pulled out the practice staff Shelton had given me, clasped it in both hands, and with a concentrated effort of will, flicked the knobby end toward my target and shouted, "*Hadouken!*"

A ball of blue flame the size of my head streaked from the wand like a comet. Bigglesworth looked up in surprise at my shout and flung up a hand as flames engulfed him.

"Yes!" I shouted, pumping a fist.

The flames washed over the shape shifter and splashed against the wall behind him. Cherry-red lava dribbled down the wall, puddled at the bottom. Bigglesworth didn't have a mark on him.

"If it ain't me old buddy, Justin," he said in his Cockney accent. He smiled. "I'm almost glad that ruddy golem didn't blow you up, mate." His lips stretched grotesquely wide. "I'm gonna enjoy tearing you to little bits meself."

Chapter 15

I stared in stunned silence at the undamaged Bigglesworth.

"You look surprised, guvnah." The shape shifter didn't walk so much as he flowed across the space between us in an instant, his feet slithering along the floor like snakes. His arm stretched like rubber, flashing toward my neck.

I leapt away. My back slammed against the wall opposite the door. His fist nicked my face and crushed the stone next to my ear like a sledgehammer. I blurred right to avoid him. He glided into the hallway.

I tried to bind him with the same ethereal bindings I'd used to save me and Shelton from the Gloom and flung my hands toward the shifter. Glowing lines swept toward Bigglesworth, wrapping around his form. The moment they touched him, the magical bonds melted to nothing.

"What the hell?" I shouted.

Bigglesworth gave me an evil grin, his mouth stretching horrifically wide and displaying a mouthful of razor-sharp teeth. "I'm gonna enjoy eating you, mate. I'll bet you're just chock full of vitamins and minerals."

"Yeah, right, Doughboy." I shot back. "I'm gonna go Betty Crocker on your doughy ass." I summoned more energy and flung another fireball at him.

The shifter didn't even flinch as it washed over him. "You ain't too bright, guvnah." He stalked toward me, arms stretching wide to block the hallway. "Or maybe you ain't figured out magic don't affect me."

"Say what?" I backed away, clueless about what to do next.

Bigglesworth giggled like a schoolboy. "Ain't too many who knows about my kind. A fact I find very useful."

I glanced behind me as he spoke. The dead end loomed closer. Unlike the opposite end of the hall, this one had no portcullis, or way out. An open door to my left appeared to lead into a room similar to the one where Bigglesworth kept his victim. Somehow, I had to get past this thing. I dashed toward him. Feinted left. Dodged right. The flesh on his arms splayed like nets, completely blocking the hall. I smacked into the trap, the fleshy material stretching against my body. Fiery agony erupted in every cell where my skin touched his.

Before I could twist free, the netted flesh snapped shut like a Venus fly trap. I cried out in desperation, summoned all my energy, and directed a blast of fire. The fireball passed through him without harm and blasted into the ceiling. Molten stone splashed down. I was sure some of it landed on me, but the volume of pain inflicted by Bigglesworth overwhelmed everything else.

The shifter suddenly wailed in an inhuman voice. He writhed and twisted, slinging me away. I slid down the hallway and slammed against a wall. Dazed, but desperate not to be the creature's next meal, I staggered to my feet. Where the molten rock had landed on Bigglesworth, his flesh smoked and steamed.

He snarled. His body melted like a wax figurine, forming a white, featureless puddle of goo. The doughy mass flowed toward me, cresting like a wave and blocking the entire hallway. A huge mouth formed in the center, chomping and biting like a rabid dog straining to break through a pair of sheer yoga pants. My back pressed to the wall. I couldn't run. Magic wouldn't work. Punching wouldn't do a thing.

I was doomed.

And then I remembered the molten rock. It had hurt him, or at least made him really mad. Magic might not *directly* hurt Bigglesworth, but what about indirectly? I clenched my fists. Focused and drew in more energy—or tried to. As my incubus senses took in my surroundings, all the magical energy dried up like morning mist under a hot sun. Even with the thrum of major ley lines pulsing beneath the castle, every time I tried to draw energy toward me, it vaporized.

My gut instinct told me the shifter was somehow doing it. I had no idea how full my fuel tank remained. At this point, it didn't matter. I had to use whatever was left. Flicking my staff toward the floor in front of the shifter, I unleashed another fireball. It exploded, spraying red-hot magma into the wall of flesh. The gaping mouth in the undulating wave screamed, but didn't stop coming. I shot another fireball and another. One exploded on the left wall, the other on the right. Bigglesworth cringed from the spray of molten stone, but he couldn't avoid the splashes. Despite the damage, he still came, relentless as a vampling. Panic raced through me. My heart jackhammered against my chest. I didn't want to think about what would happen if this monster engulfed me like a Justin burrito.

Sweat dripped into my eyes and exhaustion sucked the energy right out of me. I knew then I must have burned through my magical reserves. I might have one more burst left, and that was it. But how in the hell could I focus more damage on him? I'd practically made him wade through molten rock. And then it hit me. I would have face palmed at my stupidity, but didn't have time. Bigglesworth was less than ten feet away.

Drawing every last reserved of strength, I shouted, "*Hadouken!*" with as many exclamation marks after it as possible and slashed the staff at the ceiling just in front of the charging wave of flesh. Globules of red-hot rain spilled down, some of it hitting my clothes and exposed skin. A sizzling blob splashed right into Bigglesworth's mouth.

The flesh crackled and blackened, creating a nearly indescribable stench, like burning hair mixed with sewage and lavender soap. The only thing that could have made it worse was Old Spice.

The shifter flinched away from the superheated stone. The chomping jaws melded into a giant pair of lips and screamed at such a high pitch I had to cover my ears. My body trembled. My knees demanded I drop to the floor in exhaustion. But now was not the time. I glanced at a section of roasted Bigglesworth. It looked like a burnt pancake. With savage anger, I stomped it. It made a satisfying crunch beneath my shoe.

Then I ran my ass off. I passed the mass of goopy, screaming yuck where it twisted from the floor like a tornado with teeth, praying the shifter didn't try to engulf me in that horrific maw, and made a beeline for the room with the captive inside. The diamond fiber straps securing the man parted when touched, and he slumped forward. Summoning my incubus strength to bolster my reserves, I tossed him over my shoulder and took off.

A tendril of white flesh snapped at my ankle the moment I stepped outside the room. I flicked my staff at the ceiling. A teensy tiny little fireball swerved crazily through the air like a released balloon expelling the air from an open end, whistled weakly, and popped into a pathetic display of sparkles. Even though I would have been lucky to singe a fly with what was left of my magical energy, Bigglesworth hadn't known I was tapped out.

His tendril flinched the moment I flicked my staff, freeing my ankle. And then I did what I usually did best in such situations. I ran.

I blurred up the stairs, losing count of the hallways I passed in blind panic, and swerved through a doorway into a milling crowd of students in the hallway just outside a large room lined with tables. The sounds of clinking silverware and dinnerware drifted out. I'd apparently stumbled upon the cafeteria, or whatever people called the squat-n-gobble in an institution of higher magical learning.

A girl who looked middle school age gasped, looking straight at the unconscious man slung over my shoulder. Murmurs went up from the crowd as they saw me. Someone screamed. Students dashed off in all directions, panicking like spooked deer. By the time the stampede finished, only a couple of students remained, one of them quite familiar.

Lina, her mouth quirked into an amused expression, said, "You know how to handle a crowd, Justin."

I would have shrugged but for the dead weight on my shoulder and a tide of exhaustion sweeping over my muscles. "Guess I need to change deodorant."

"What happened to Professor MacLean?" she said, walking around behind me, inspecting him. Lina stepped back around, tilting her head slightly to the side. "He didn't assign you too much homework did he?"

"Uh, classes haven't started yet, have they?" I tried to shrug again and failed. MacLean's body felt like a lead weight burrowing into my shoulder. "Is the nurse's office around here somewhere?"

"You mean healer," she said, with a smile. "Oh, Justin, you know how to keep things interesting." She suddenly yawned, and I noticed dark rings under her eyes.

"Are you okay?" I asked. "My feeding didn't overtire you did it?"

"No, no," she said. "A friend found an old abandoned gauntlet room in the Burrows, and I stayed up late last night practicing."

"Oh. You look exhausted."

She yawned again. "So, what happened to the professor?"

"Bigglesworth," I said. "But don't say anything to the healer."

She looked confused. "The shape shifter you mentioned?"

"Yeah. I can fill you in on the way."

Lina waved me to follow her down the hall, and I gave her a quick summary of my Bigglesworth encounters. Thankfully, the healer station wasn't too far down the hall.

The healer, a red-headed woman with freckles, looked up with a shocked expression. "Is that Professor MacLean?" She regarded Lina and me with a suspicious expression.

"I found him injured at the bottom of a flight of stairs," I said. "I think he might have fallen." Telling her he'd been tortured by a shape-shifting maniac with a Cockney accent would only land me in trouble, I figured.

She motioned me into a ward filled with beds and had me deposit the meaty figure on one. "Please take a seat in the waiting area, and I'll be right out."

Lina sat beside me. "This is the second time he's tried to kill you in two days." She gripped me hand. "If he's immune to magic, I don't know what you can do to protect yourself."

"He has a weakness," I said with more confidence than I felt.

"Justin, I'm worried about you." Her large brown eyes looked even sadder than usual above the dark rings under her eyes.

"I'll be fine," I said. "Why don't you go rest, and I'll fill you in later?"

She sighed. "Do you trust Shelton to watch your back?"

I forced a sure grin. "Heck yeah."

Her eyes narrowed. "If you say so." She leaned forward, kissed me on the cheek. "Text me later. Let me know you're okay."

"I will."

"Promise me, Justin."

I held up my fingers in a dubious imitation of an honor sign. "Promise."

Lina gave me one last troubled look before pulling her hand away from mine and leaving.

I turned my gaze toward the ward. A sudden wave of nausea climbed up my throat as magic poisoning from my recent exertions paid me an unpleasant visit. The healer emerged from the back room and raised an eyebrow. She reached into an old wooden desk, pulled out a pill, and tossed it to me.

"Swallow that. It'll help." She filled a cup with water and handed it to me, then bent down and held open my eyelids so she could look into my eyes. "Looks like you've been through this a few times before. And what happened to your clothes?" She stood back, eyes darting to the myriad burn marks.

My mind fumbled for something. "Oh, just the latest fashion," I said.

"I see." Her nose wrinkled. "Guess I'll never understand the allure of wearing clothes that look like they came from a trash bin."

I returned to her previous comment. "How did you know I had magic poisoning?"

She stood upright and chuckled. "Are you kidding me? This is a place where kids learn magic. Naturally, they're going to stretch their limits and puke their brains out." She walked around the desk and took a seat. "Then again, most kids get over it once they hit full potential around sixteen. Only late bloomers still have to deal with it at your age."

"Guess that's me," I said, trying to smile, but even with the pill attacking the nausea, all I wanted to do at this point was sleep.

The healer sat at her desk, leaned on her elbows, and gave me a shrewd look. "What really happened to Professor MacLean?" A wand appeared in her hand, and it looked like she knew how to use it. "He doesn't have any bruising that would come from falling down stairs. In fact, the only trauma I found was from microscopic abrasions in his skin pores."

"Abrasions?"

She nodded. "The only reason I haven't called security to haul you away is because I don't know how you could have given them to him. Perhaps they could be magically induced, but I've never seen injuries like that before. It's almost as if something was trying to consume him one cell at a time."

I gulped. Thinking about my close call with Bigglesworth didn't help with my receding nausea.

The healer raised both eyebrows. "Well? The truth, or security?"

"You might not believe me."

"You'd be surprised at what I'd believe, young man."

I had a feeling my life story would stretch the belief of even the most gullible person. I took in a deep breath to bolster myself as weariness weighed down my limbs and gave her some of the truth. "I'm new here, and I got lost trying to find my way from Administration over to the cafeteria. I ended up going too far down some stairs and was about to turn around when I heard screaming. So, I went down there and found some kind of blob creature trying to eat the professor."

"A blob?"

"I've never seen anything like it before."

She held up a glass vial with an undulating bit of doughy Bigglesworth. "Like this?"

I shuddered and felt my back press hard against the chair. Even with my leaden limbs, I felt like I could sprint away. "I don't think it's a good idea for you to keep that."

"You're telling me this is a small part of a larger being?" she said, seemingly unconcerned.

"What I'm telling you is the monster it belongs to can probably sense where this bit of it is and find it." I couldn't mask the disgust I felt just looking at it. "Where did you find that?"

"It fell off your shoe after you set MacLean down."

I jumped up like spiders were crawling on me, pulling off my shoes, and shaking them out. If I hadn't been in front of her, I probably would have pulled off my clothes and burned them even more. Thankfully, no other bits of Bigglesworth fell off me. I thought back to the fight and remembered stomping that burnt chunk of him. Maybe there'd been some living tissue still on my shoe.

The healer watched me with a bemused expression and then shook her head. "This isn't a part of some new experimental golem for the Grand Melee is it?"

"I don't even know how to make a stick figure walk, much less animate a blob of goo," I said, staring at the bit of Bigglesworth squirming in the vial like a worm seeking escape. "But please, for the love of all that is holy, burn that thing."

She watched the thing for a moment. "If this is an undiscovered form of supernatural creature, it needs studying." She opened a wooden case on her desk and placed the vial inside, locking it. "This bio-hazard lockbox is warded to isolate anything inside. Even if this creature could sense and track a part of its body, it won't be able to through this."

I wrinkled my forehead. "For your sake, lady, I sure hope so." I nodded at the door into the infirmary. "How's the patient?"

"He'll wake up soon. I was able to repair the damage. Thankfully, it was limited to his hands and face." She stood and walked over to me, wand in hand. "Did the creature harm you?"

I nodded.

She ran the wand up and down my body. "Goodness. You're already healing remarkably fast." She grunted. "Ah. Daemos."

"Yes, I'm a big bad demon."

She laughed. "Oh, don't be melodramatic. I'm not biased against your kind one way or the other." Her hand with the wand abruptly stopped as she stared at the holographic numbers hovering above. "Hmm, must be something wrong with my spell."

I looked at the numbers and saw a statistic that looked like the ones the security arcane at Queens Gate had registered when scanning me and Shelton. "What does AP forty-one mean?"

"It's a measure of arcane potential," she replied, giving me a confused look. "But forty-one is impossible. The highest ever recorded is twenty."

Chapter 16

My potential was more than double that of the most powerful Arcane in history? Not only that, but Shelton had scored a seventeen when the security screener took it at Queens Gate. He was a lot stronger than he'd let on.

"Yeah, it must be wrong," I said, knowing the truth would only freak her out.

She flicked the wand with an annoyed look, and the numbers vanished. "Clearly it doesn't measure Daemos accurately."

"Can I see the patient?"

She narrowed her eyes. "I suppose. Perhaps he can clear this up."

We walked into the back. I noticed two young kids, faces pale, eyes sunken. "What's wrong with them?" I asked.

She shook her head. "A very good question. Their dorm resident assistant found them passed out. He said they'd been practicing non-stop in the hopes of making it into the Arcane Tourney junior division. I'd assumed they overworked themselves, but…" she trailed off.

"But what?"

A troubled look crossed her face. "Nothing I do is helping them. It's like the most severe case of magic poisoning I've seen."

"Oi, what a blasted headache," said a man in a distinct Scottish brogue from a bed across the room.

The healer and I flicked our gaze to see Professor MacLean rising unsteadily, a hand pressed to his temple.

"Feels like the mornin' after a bit of fun went a wee bit too far." He looked at the two of us. "So what the bloody hell am I doing here? Did you find me passed out with an empty bottle of spirits?"

My heart sank. He didn't remember?

The healer studied him for a moment. "We think you were attacked by something."

"Attacked? I should bloody hope not. This is a school, for heaven's sake."

She held her palms out to him in a calming gesture. "You're fine though. Are you sure you don't remember anything?"

He shook his head. "I'm afraid not, Healer Hutchins." MacLean headed for the door.

"Wait," Miss Hutchins called. "You'll need to talk to someone in security. We don't want this happening to anyone else."

MacLean turned and gave her a steady look. "If I remember anything, I'll be certain to tell them. Now, if you'll excuse me, I really must get to work." He left.

I gave Miss Hutchins an apologetic look. "I gotta go." The exhaustion plaguing my body had all but vanished. "Thanks for the pill. I'm feeling a lot better now." Before she could get out another word, I dashed into the hallway and followed MacLean.

While I wasn't exactly a walking lie detector, something in the man's eyes told me he wasn't being completely truthful about his memories. I couldn't put my finger on why I thought so, but my gut feeling was too strong to ignore. I also had another reason for following him. Bigglesworth would probably try to kidnap the man again. A spike of helplessness stabbed my stomach. The shifter could flow through cracks and crevices in his liquid form. For all I knew, he could fit anywhere water could.

How do you protect yourself from something like that?

The Scottish man eventually entered a tall, arched doorway adorned with stained glass and fiendish looking gargoyles guarding either side. I peeked inside and a library of epic proportions unfolded before me. MacLean headed down an aisle between rows upon rows of tables. I stepped into the library and stopped in slack-jawed amazement. The walls stretched high above, curving into a sparkling glass dome. A shaft of golden sunlight streamed through the crystalline roof. Staircases spiraled up the walls, leading to landings lined with countless bookcases. Just beneath the glass dome far above, people scurried about like ants.

Animal-shaped chandeliers floated serenely around like giant parade balloons, some of them orbiting beneath the crystal dome, positioned to catch sunlight and refract it to every corner of the library. Smaller animal light fixtures hovered above the rows upon rows of tables where industrious students worked, preparing—I supposed—in advance for classes.

Duty aroused me from my stupor. I looked ahead as MacLean vanished into one of many rectangular wings jutting off the main dome, each one lined with bookcases several stories tall. I jogged toward his last position. People glided about the towering bookshelves on flying carpets of all shapes and designs. A bin at the end of the shelf overflowed with them. Patrons grabbed a rug, stood on it, and soared to the level they wanted. I'd just passed the bin when I saw MacLean gliding down the aisle on one, disappearing around a corner. I tried to blur after him, but even with the pill to make me feel better, I still hadn't regained enough energy. So, I grabbed a rug that looked like a sheep, tossed it on the floor and stood on it.

Nothing happened.

I imagined it going up.

Still nothing.

A dude nearby must have sensed my noobishness because he walked to me and said, "These rugs are so basic, you need to verbally tell them where you want to go."

"Up," I said and the rug lifted from the floor. I gave the guy a thumbs-up. "Thanks!"

Since I was at the far end of the aisle from where MacLean had vanished, I scooted back to the main row and went around the side. No sign of him. I continued gliding past aisles, looking down each row for some sign of him. My super vision still worked okay, thankfully, or I would've had to roam up and down each of the monstrous rows. The experience reminded me of the time I'd gotten separated from Mom at a grocery store and spent twenty minutes hunting the aisles before finding her in the meat department, talking to Bertha Jankowski about sausage recipes.

I'd gone halfway down the chamber when I spotted my target flit from behind a bookshelf ahead and ascend into the main dome. "Up. Way, up," I told my flying rug. It responded sluggishly, building speed as it went. "Follow that rug." I pointed at MacLean's, and the rug shifted course to follow. It might be a basic rug, but it seemed pretty good at following instructions.

My quarry approached the topmost level in the dome and vanished into the maze of bookshelves on the landing. I urged my faithful steed faster and reached the same landing a few seconds behind. After dropping the rug in a nearby bin, I jogged down the narrow aisle. Here, the bookshelves stood normal height, and the glass dome hovered close overhead. I didn't even want to look over the balustrade at the long drop to the floor below. After following a rat's maze of shelves, I hit a dead end. No MacLean. I retraced my steps, taking another branch I'd skipped, and ended up at another dead end. Still no dice.

I walked back to the beginning of the shelves, examining every twist and turn, before deciding I couldn't have missed him. But where else could he have gone? I went to the first dead end and examined the books. Glowing sconces lit the way every other shelf. I tried moving each one in a variety of ways, but no secret passages opened. I ran my fingers along the books, testing to see if one seemed odd or out of place. It took several minutes just to check one shelf. At that rate it would take forever and a day to examine all these books unless I simply tore them all off the shelves. I tugged at one of the shelves to see if a secret passage lurked behind but, in my de-energized state, only managed to shake it a bit.

The only thing left to do was sit and wait for MacLean to reappear. On the bright side, it was evident the man was up to something and definitely knew more than he'd let on. If I were some innocent dude who'd been kidnapped and tortured by a shape shifter, I'd be freaking out, calling the supernatural cops, and anything else I could think of to make me safe. Instead, he'd shunned help and vanished behind a bookshelf somewhere.

In the meantime, I desperately needed to feed. I closed my eyes and reopened them in incubus feed mode. Reaching out with my senses, I searched for a female presence. The first thing I bumped into was male. He was furious. Fear bubbled beneath his fury. I was just about to move on when it occurred to me that nobody should be feeling that in a library. Not unless they'd just narrowly escaped a torture chamber or felt unholy hatred toward a particular book.

Normally, I wouldn't be able to sense a lot from a male unless his emotions were strong. Concentrating on these emotions, I circled back around the shelves. The sensation weakened until I headed toward the other dead end. The sensation grew stronger than ever. I still couldn't tell how far away the source lay. The emotions began to fade. Was the person calming down, or physically moving away from me?

Abandoning decorum, I swept books off the shelves, heedless of the mess. Within minutes, the shelves were clear and not a one of them had opened a hidden passage. I twisted, pulled, and levered all the sconces. Nothing. Ready to roar in frustration, I threw back my head and growled. One of the unusual chandeliers floated above my head. From the side, it looked like a bronze platypus with a unicorn horn. From the underside, however, I noticed something different engraved in the bottom—a circle with a triangle inside it. The outline of an eye complete with an iris and pupil stared from within the triangle. Unless someone stood right underneath the light fixture, they probably wouldn't notice the symbol. Something about the symbol tickled my brain. I'd seen it somewhere before, but couldn't pin it down.

Unfortunately, the lamp was a bit too far overhead to reach without a nice super jump. The solution, thankfully, didn't take long to kick me in the brain. I jogged back to the bin, grabbed my magic rug, and laid it beneath the eye symbol. "Up, up, and away," I said, and the rug rose dutifully into the air. I told it to halt when the fixture was within reach. Gripping each side with a hand, I tugged down on the chandelier. Unlike the ones noms used in their buildings, this one didn't have a chain or wires connecting it to anything, and my tug simply made it float a little lower before hovering back to its previous level.

None of the bookshelves opened.

This was really starting to tinkle me off. I examined the symbol, running my fingers along it, and then, on a hunch, decided to poke a finger in the eye. One of the bookshelves slid soundlessly back into the wall and to the side.

"Bada-bing, bada-boom!" I said, high-fiving myself and feeling slightly better about my mental capacity for logical reasoning. I landed the rug and hurried through the super-secret entrance. The bookshelf closed behind me. A big red button on the wall, however, offered a way out.

Before me lay a curving corridor of granite about wide enough for two people to walk side-by-side. Something stinky tickled my nose. Looking down, I spotted a crushed cigarette. At least now I knew why MacLean had stopped.

He probably wanted a nicotine hit to calm his nerves.

I followed the curve of the passage until I reached a door with yet another of the circle-triangle-eyeball symbols, though this one wasn't an engraving but an actual three-dimensional hunk of metal embedded in the iron of the door. An eyelid covered the eye. I stepped to the door and gripped the handle. The eye blinked open with a metallic click, revealing a faceted green gem with a black stone centered where a pupil should be. I nearly screamed and wet my pants all at the same time. I tried to back away, but my hand was stuck to the handle. In fact, my entire body froze in place, as though an electric current incapacitated me.

The eye blinked again, rotating up and down as if examining me. It gazed at my eyes for a long moment before the iris flashed red, nearly blinding me. My body unfroze. Before I could topple backwards, a wall of steel sprang up from the stone floor behind, blocking the corridor. Even at full strength, breaking through the wall or the formidable steel door didn't seem likely.

I reached out with my senses and tried to draw in magic. I might as well have been trying to suck a watermelon up my nose. Nausea swelled inside my stomach, and I gagged. I knew from experience, trying to absorb aether so soon after magic poisoning wasn't pleasant.

"What the bloody 'ell," said a familiar Scottish accent from behind the door. The eye blinked in a very humanlike way. "Who the bloody hell are you, and how did you get in here?"

I gave up on my attempts to energize and took deep breaths to ward off the sick feeling in my guts. "I'm the guy who saved you from Bigglesworth," I said. "My name is Justin."

"Who are you with?"

"Nobody. It's just me."

MacLean sighed, and the gemstone eye narrowed. "Bloody shame."

"That I saved you?" I leaned closer to the eye. "Look, I know you're probably proud of your super-secret hideout and all, but these things are a dime a dozen to me. My friend Shelton has a gazillion of these—"

"Who did you say?"

"Shelton?"

"Harry Shelton." His voice went flat.

"Um…yeah?" I remembered Shelton's split lip and his propensity for making enemies and quite suddenly realized mentioning him might have been a horrible mistake. "But—"

The eye clicked shut. The light in the corridor winked out. And the sound of crushing death grated against the stone floor.

Chapter 17

For the second time in a short while, I wanted to scream bloody murder. A light appeared as the iron door before me flung open and the huge frame of MacLean stood there.

"Well, why didn't you say you were with Harry?" he said in a booming jovial voice. His ham hand gripped mine and shook it until my bones rattled. "Paul MacLean. Pleased to meet you, Justin."

"Y-you like Shelton?" I was genuinely surprised.

He released my hand and shrugged. "Well, 'like' is such a strong term with Harry." He laughed and motioned me forward. "Come on in. Welcome to my secret abode." He waved a hand around the small stone room. A bunk bed stood in a corner and a table in the middle of the room.

I spotted a hallway leading away from the room and figured the entire library must be riddled with them.

MacLean reached into a box and pulled out a brown bottle with cold vapors steaming from it. He popped the top with a thumb, settled into a chair, and propped his boots atop the table. "Grab an ale if you'd like, lad. It's brewed on campus by the best potion masters." He took a long draw and sighed. "Bloody hell, I really needed one of these."

"Why did Bigglesworth kidnap you?" I asked, ignoring his offer of alcohol.

MacLean smiled. "Direct and to the point, eh?" He narrowed his eyes. "How do you know about the Flark?"

My left eye twitched. "The what?"

"That's what Bigglesworth—the nasty bugger—is."

"A Flark?" I narrowed my eyes. "Did you just make that up?"

He chuckled. "Nope. Don't know who did. Personally, I'd rather just call him a bugger and be done with it."

"You're avoiding my question. Why did he kidnap you?"

"You're ignoring mine, lad." He folded an arm across his stomach and took another draw of ale.

After a moment of silence, I huffed. "Fine. I know him because he works for the Conroys, and they want me dead."

MacLean nearly dropped his ale. Sliding his boots off the table, he leaned toward me, lips pursed. "You're bloody Justin Slade, aren't you?"

A sigh escaped me. "Yes. Will you answer my question?"

"But you're with the Templars, aren't you? Working for the Borathens."

I was about to answer when shadows crept from the corners of the room. Deep cold bit into my leg. A shadow skull stretched from a corner behind MacLean. "Eat," it whispered in a raspy susurrus, seductive and demanding. "Devour. Consume." The cold in my leg intensified, and hunger like no other I had felt before hollowed my insides. MacLean's veins seemed to pulse and glow as my eyes settled on him. I smelled his blood. I wanted to bite his throat. Tear it out. Drink—

"What the hell is happening to me?" I said balling my fists. More shadow skulls formed, taunting, talking, telling me to feed, their fanged mouths diving at MacLean's neck.

The world flashed white for a brief instant, and my back slammed against stone. The shadows vanished like smoke, and the cold receded. MacLean towered over me.

"They gone?" he asked.

I flexed my jaw to make sure it wasn't broken. He reached down and pulled me to my feet.

"You saw the shadows?" I asked, my head still reeling from his sucker punch.

The large man downed the rest of his ale in a long gulp and grabbed another. "It's my bloody curse and gift." He sighed and dropped into the chair. "It's why the Flark wanted me."

"You can read minds?"

He laughed. "If only 'twas that simple. I have the Dark Sight. The ability to see the world within the world."

I blinked. "Say what?"

He shrugged. "I can see the psychic impact of events in the world around me. For example, if someone is killed, you can see the blood spatter, the body. But what I can see with the Dark Sight is the trauma left from the murder. The negative stain left on the aura of that place." He looked at my leg. "When you froze up, I viewed you. Your leg pulses with a black curse. The shadows came from inside you."

"A vampling infected me," I said, my stomach lurching with fear and regret.

His nose wrinkled. "Something inside you is fighting it. Unfortunately, it seems trapped."

My inner angel? I hoped that was the case. "Can I free it?"

He shrugged. "I don't have the answer to that. The sight doesn't always provide answers. Sometimes it only makes for more blasted questions."

"How is this sight useful to Bigglesworth?"

MacLean took a drink of ale, crossed his arms, and stared at me for a long moment. "First, you need to tell me more. I've heard of you, true, but I don't know you, lad."

"Can Shelton vouch for me?"

A laugh boomed from him. "Are you bloody kidding me? Aye, Harry was a bloody good friend, but I haven't seen him in years and, from what I've heard, he ain't the sort of man to trust these days."

I puffed out a sigh. "Can't argue with you there, I guess."

He nodded. "So, Justin Slade. Tell me about yourself."

"Oh, brother. Do you know how many times I've had to repeat my life story? Maybe I should just write a freaking memoir and get it over with."

He laughed, one hand still gripping the ale.

I noticed a symbol carved into the table, virtually identical to the circle-triangle-eye symbol on the door and the chandelier. The meaning suddenly kicked me in the head. I pulled Nookli, my faithful arcphone, from my pocket and ran a quick search. The answer flashed before my eyes.

"What are you doing?" MacLean asked, giving me a suspicious look.

I flicked my gaze back to him. "You're Illuminati."

His mouth dropped open a fraction. "That's rubbish."

"Dude, everything leading here has Illuminati symbols—the door, the chandelier, this table." I jabbed a finger on the carving. "Besides, any nerd worth his salt knows what that symbol means. I just had to run a quick search to be sure."

His face fell. "Really?"

I showed him my phone. He took it and sighed. "Bloody internet."

"Well, maybe if you guys changed it up every once in a while." I squinted at the symbol. "I dunno, maybe instead of an eye, you could use a skull and crossbones with a lightning bolt going through it."

"Do you know how many symbols we'd have to redo? And some members have tattoos." He sighed. "Just drop it for now, and tell me your story."

I gave him the highlights of my supernatural career, skipping the small stuff. When I finished, I asked him, "Shouldn't the Illuminati know all this?"

MacLean gave me a steady look. "Not these days. The organization has gone to hell." He sighed, snapped his fingers as if remembering something, and reached back to pull a rough-bound book stuffed with yellowed parchment from a shelf. He turned the pages, humming to himself, until he jabbed a forefinger onto the page. "Ah, here's that foreseeance you were talking about." He turned the book to face me.

Upon the page I saw the words supposedly spelling out my future—Foreseeance 4311.

> *In the year of plague comes the Unmaking or the Remaking. The half-damned will make a choice. Each will ally with a harbinger. Should the light prevail, all will be cast in shadow. But should one light the flame in the dark, the shadow may not rise. With either choice comes the end.*

"Do you have any idea what it means?" I asked.

"It means this is the year all bloody hell breaks loose," he said. "I don't suppose you've heard about the mysterious plague sweeping villages and small towns across the world?"

I raised an eyebrow. "Not a thing." I shrugged. "Then again, I haven't exactly been watching the news."

"I'm surprised your Templar friends haven't told you." His lip curled a bit at the mention of the organization. "Their special services people—the Custodians—have been working overtime to control vampling outbreaks."

I recalled Elyssa mentioning something about it. "Is it really that bad?"

"Aye. Maximus had recruiters everywhere. Some of the fools tried to make their own little vampire cults and unleashed the vampling curse instead." He blew out an explosive breath. "It's worse than the Templars are letting on, but if I'm not mistaken, that means this is the year of plague, because I sure don't remember it ever being this bad."

I thought back to my first encounter with those relentless vampire zombies. Maybe he was right. "It's September," I said. "That means the end of the world is a lot closer than I thought."

He nodded. "And the harbingers? Already here."

"Huh?" I asked, feeling my eyebrows pinch.

"Your Darkling friend, Nightliss, is obviously allied with you—"

"And Ivy has Daelissa," I said.

"Aye, and read this corollary foreseeance," he said, pointing to another paragraph beneath Foreseeance 4311.

> *As the alliance splinters into factions, so come the destroyers. None shall be strong enough alone to withstand their might. For they once ruled here and once again shall they rule. Unless the half-damned soul reunites the dissolution, all shall once again descend into the shadow of the light.*

After I read it, MacLean said, "The Overworld Conclave—the alliance—is splintering. Vampires fighting Arcanes, the Templars divided and on the verge of civil war, and my people, the Illuminati, are barely a shadow of what they once were." He stared mournfully at the symbol on the table. "We used to fight the Templars, you know.

The Seraphim created the organization—well, Daelissa did. It was all to protect herself while she was vulnerable."

"You don't fight them anymore?" I asked.

"No need. The organization took on a life of its own and became too large for her to control." He snorted. "She lost to bureaucracy."

"According to this foreseeance, I need to reunite the alliance," I said. "Somehow make the Arcanes, vampires, and Templars all one big happy family again."

"Or your sister does." His eyebrow rose. "If she does, it wouldn't bode well." His finger moved to another passage.

> *I see not one, but two half-damned upon this plane. One is wreathed in the dark, the other in the light. Both gather their armies for the fight. In the end, two choices will be decided, but only one will matter. And the sacrifice must be made.*

"Both sides are gathering armies," he said. "I think Daelissa wants to bring the vampires to her side. If your sister unites them, we'll be left without much of an army at all."

My stomach clenched at the thought of the Conroys in control of everything.

"There's more," MacLean said, pursing his lips. "We know of at least four Seraphim still alive and kicking." He counted them off on his fingers. "Daelissa, Alysea, Fjoeruss, and one whose name we do not know."

"Wait a minute," I said, "Alysea—"

His lips curled into a smile. "Your mother's true name, lad."

My heart skipped a beat. I had almost forgiven Mom after she'd saved me from Jeremiah in Maximus's compound, but why hadn't she told me more? Why had she left me to feel my way blindly through a maze of glass and daggers?

"What else do you know about her?" I asked, eager to know.

"I'm sorry, lad, but not much. The Illuminati didn't find out about her until a century or so ago when the Conroys came into power." He looked up at me. "Even then we didn't realize she wasn't human right away."

"Are the Conroys Seraphim?"

"No." MacLean gave a firm shake of his head. "Of that, we're bloody sure. We think Alysea was still incredibly weak from the Desecration—that's what the Seraphim call the destruction of the Grand Nexus." He scratched the back of his neck. "The Conroys must have nursed her to health somehow. She might have suffered from extreme memory loss, so they could have made her believe anything, I suppose." He spread his hands. "Even so, there's a huge chunk of time in her life we can't account for, considering this whole bloody mess started in Biblical times."

I blinked as the information soaked in. *How old are you, Mom?* "I think Daelissa did something to her while she was vulnerable." I had to believe Mom wouldn't help the evil bitch.

"Aye, perhaps. Unfortunately, the detailed records vanished a long time ago. All I know is the Darklings, Daemos, and humans united; they fought the Brightlings and barely won. They couldn't beat the Brightlings by force, so they disabled the portal the Seraphim used to travel to this world—the Grand Nexus—by removing a vital component called the Cyrinthian Rune. When they removed the rune, it caused a tremendous backlash that husked all the humans, angels, and Daemos anywhere near the nexus or the network of Alabaster Arches connecting them."

I shuddered at the thought of husks, the nasty little infantile creatures. I'd faced hundreds of them beneath Thunder Rock and El Dorado. "Did it destroy the Grand Nexus for good?" I asked.

He shook his head. "It's possible returning the rune to the nexus will repair it. For centuries, Arcanes passed down the responsibility of hiding the rune, and it eventually fell into the hands of Ezzek Moore, the father of modern Arcanes."

A puzzle piece clicked in my brain. "The Conroys are looking for the rune."

"Exactly, lad. They need it and think I'm the only one who can find it."

Chapter 18

The confusing conversation I'd overheard between Ivy and dear old Grandma suddenly made a lot more sense. I knew why Jeremiah was here and why Bigglesworth didn't want me breathing. They probably thought I knew something about the rune and was playing the part of meddling kid. Well, they had that part right. I was a proven meddler even though I'd learned the hard way just how hazardous it was for my health. I zoned back into reality from my wandering thoughts and caught MacLean's eye. "When did they figure out Daelissa was still alive?"

"That happened near the end of the Roman Empire," he said. "Daelissa posed as a woman named Lissa and became Ezzek Moore's lover during his struggle to unite Arcanes under the Council of Seven and build Arcane University. She nearly tricked him into revealing where the rune was before he discovered the ruse."

"Talk about a crazy girlfriend," I said, shuddering.

"Aye. She killed Moore's favorite apprentice and several of his close friends before they drove her away." His lips curled. "They were bloody lucky she wasn't anywhere near the strength she is now, or she would've killed them all." He paused for a swig of ale. "Ezzek realized they needed a much better way to hide the rune. He took his most trusted people and formed a secret organization to protect it and fight the Templar army Daelissa was creating."

"The Illuminati," I said.

"Exactly, lad."

"So, where's the rune?"

He shrugged. "We lost that secret centuries ago. The only thing I know for certain is it's somewhere in Queens Gate." He gestured vaguely around the room. "Could be here at the university, over at the academy, or maybe down in the valley somewhere. Bigglesworth somehow found out about my ability and figured I could spot the disturbance the rune has on the world around it."

"How large is the rune?" I asked.

MacLean shrugged. "Maybe the size of an acorn." He made a circle with his thumb and forefinger to illustrate.

"Talk about a needle in a haystack," I groaned. Ice shivered down my spine as I remembered the towering murals of the angels in El Dorado. They depicted human sacrifice and all sorts of horrors. If Daelissa and her peeps took over and resumed using humans as food and live entertainment, there were no limits to the horrors they could commit. Humans didn't throw spears and rocks at each other anymore. They used jets, bullets, and nuclear weapons.

"My god, they could annihilate us." I shook away the thoughts. "Can you find the rune?" I asked. "And if so, can it be destroyed?"

He gave me a shrewd look. "If Ezzek could have eradicated it, he probably would have. In all likelihood, he probably worried destroying it might cause another light-draining shockwave and husk even more people."

"We need to find it." I stood and paced, thinking. "We can leave it where it is, but it's vital we know for sure Daelissa doesn't have it." I leaned against a wall as my mind raced. "Where exactly is the Grand Nexus? Is it in Thunder Rock?"

MacLean shook his head. "No. But Ezzek discovered even without the rune, the Alabaster Arches still work to a certain extent. If you take any of them, they all lead to one place."

"The Grand Nexus," I said.

"Bright lad. His surviving journals don't say where the true nexus is, but you could find out easily enough."

I laughed. "Easily? I'd have to wade through husks and shadow people to get to one of those arches." I'd already told him the details of my adventure at Thunder Rock and how I'd tested the Alabaster Arch there. "The Conroys are trying to repair the smaller arches in the normal control rooms so they can take one through to Thunder Rock. At least now I know why."

MacLean leaned back, ran both hands through his thick hair. "That wily old bastard, Jeremiah."

"Look, I know it's best if the rune stays hidden, but we need to know where it is. What if Jeremiah or Bigglesworth figures out another way to find it, and we don't know until another blast wave wipes out half the planet again?" The thought sent a shudder through me. "Do we even know for sure how many Alabaster Arches there are? Or how many people would be affected by another blast wave?"

"I believe there are five, including the Grand Nexus." MacLean shrugged. "I know for sure Thunder Rock and El Dorado have them. If only our records hadn't been destroyed." His fists tightened. "One is in Australia, but I don't know the location. And the other, maybe China."

"Gee, that really narrows it down," I said, pulling up a map on my phone and scrolling. "We don't have much of a choice, then. Looks like Thunder Rock or El Dorado would be the best places to go."

"Agreed."

I rubbed my tight forehead. I was well on my way to getting premature wrinkles if my stress levels stayed this high. "If I can do something about Bigglesworth, would you be willing to track down the rune? You can save all the little children in the world."

"Can't stand the little buggers." His lips peeled back in a grimace.

"Then why the hell are you a teacher?"

"I was assigned here by my organization."

"Wow, your boss must hate you." I exchanged phone numbers with him. "I've got to go figure out a way to get rid of Bigglesworth. Call me if you need anything."

"Take care, lad." MacLean paused. "And thanks for the rescue. I owe you one." Before I could answer, he closed the door.

I retraced my steps to the library, grabbed a flying rug, and swooped over the balustrade toward the main floor far below. My head spun with new information. Illuminati. Cyrinthian Rune. Ezzek Moore and Daelissa getting it on—*gross!*

The rug jerked to a halt. Unprepared, I tumbled over the side, my cry of terror cut short as I hit the floor. My thoughts had so absorbed me, I hadn't been paying attention. The breath slammed out of me. As I lay gasping on the cold marble floor, someone giggled.

"Why, bro-bro, what are you doing here?" asked my dear little sister, Ivy.

Chapter 19

Even as I gasped for breath, I frantically rolled to the side before Ivy could do anything horrible to me. She only grinned with amusement.

"Don't be silly," she said. "I'm not going to do anything bad to you in front of all these nice people."

I noticed students staring at me, the nerdy ones giving me stern looks, while others stifled laughter. "Laugh it up," I grumbled, glaring at the hovering rug. I climbed to my feet. "You stopped my ride, didn't you?"

Ivy giggled again. "It was pretty funny."

My jaw went tight. "There's nothing funny about trying to kill someone, much less your own flesh and blood, Ivy."

"But, you're evil," she said, batting eyelashes over large innocent eyes.

"And I don't appreciate the little gift you left for Elyssa."

"Oh, Mr. Bigglesworth got the doll to her?" She clapped her hands. "I'll bet Nightliss was so shocked."

"She didn't see it." A mix of frustration and anger tightened around my shoulders in an iron grip, spreading up my neck and into my forehead. My sister was so messed up. Was she beyond hope?

Ivy's mouth fell open, and her eyes went wide with disbelief. "But, why? I worked so hard on that." She narrowed her eyes. "Are you lying to me? She really saw it, right? I'll bet she freaked."

"No, she didn't," I growled. "It's not nice to threaten people."

"She's not a person." Ivy crossed her arms and gave me a stern look. "She's a Darkling."

"Yeah, yeah, a horrible agent of darkness." I held my hands out like a ghost and moaned. "Better watch out, the sweet little angel is going to get you."

My sister's blue eyes went hard. "You are beyond hope, Justin."

"You're the one beyond hope," I shot back. "And your Bigdaddy tried to suffocate me to death in Maximus's underground lair. Who's the evil one now?"

"He did?" For the first time, she seemed a bit unsure.

"Your doughboy pal Bigglesworth tried to kill me today, too. Stick that in your pipe and smoke it."

Ivy quirked her mouth and raised a blonde eyebrow in a *yeah right!* look. "I'm sure you did something to deserve it."

I resisted the urge to grab her by both arms and shake her, instead leaning in, a snarl on my face. "Nobody deserves cold-blooded murder, especially not family."

She flinched away, and I noticed a pink glow coming from her hand. An orb of energy coalesced in her palm. "Don't come at me, bro. I will hurt you."

My anger transformed into acute sadness, like a blade in my throat. I fought back sudden moisture and backed away from her. "You've already hurt me, Ivy." I wiped my eyes. "You think I'm evil, and you think killing me is okay." Drawing in a deep breath to ward off the pain, I gave my sister one last look, turned, and walked away.

"Where are you going?" she said, her voice full of surprise. She ran ahead of me and held out a hand. "Justin, come with me. Come talk with Bigdaddy. Maybe he can forgive you, and we can fix you. Mommy is there, and I'll be there, and you can be a part of a happy family again."

"I can't."

She squeezed her hands together in supplication. "Please? Pretty please with sugar and ice cream and your fave berries on top? I just know if you talk to Bigdaddy he can convince you. I promise we're the good guys."

"You're not," I said simply. "Daelissa is using you to take over the world."

"No, no, no, the Brightlings are good, Justin." She grabbed my hand. "Please, come. I promise you'll see!"

I actually considered it for a moment. Maybe talking to Jeremiah would help me understand why in the world they thought helping Daelissa was a good thing. Had she brainwashed them? Promised them power? I couldn't think of any other reason why they'd want the Seraphim to rule again. "Ivy, do you know what Daelissa and her people did the last time they ruled this world?"

"Oh, they didn't rule it," she replied. "The Darklings invaded and almost killed everyone, but then the Brightlings fought back and almost won, but the Darklings tried to kill everyone by blowing up the Grand Nexus."

"No, it's the other way around," I said.

"Says who?"

"Nightliss."

"Of course she'd tell you that, silly." My sister flashed a grin. "She wants you to help in *her* quest for world domination."

Suppressing a groan, I said, "Ivy, I promise you that's not what happened. Daelissa is lying to you."

"No, she's not. Besides, she's not the only one who says it's true."

I sighed. "You realize your grandparents are going to say it's true because Daelissa told them. That's called circular logic."

"No, my grandparents believe it because another angel told them."

Had Mom fed her these lies? "And which angel is that?" I asked in a tight voice.

"Graeme." She sighed like a lovesick girl. "He's so beautiful. I've only met him a few times, but he's so sweet, too." A girlish giggle erupted. "He brought me a puppy once."

"That's…nice," I said, wondering if Graeme was the fourth and unnamed angel MacLean had mentioned. "What's your puppy's name?"

Her face fell. "Oh, Bigdaddy wouldn't let me keep him. He said Jumpy would distract me from my studies."

I almost made a remark about how evil it was to deprive a little girl of her puppy, but held back. I felt so close to making a connection with her. Heck, maybe if I promised to take her to the zoo this moment, she'd rethink her position. If I could only insert a sliver of doubt—no matter how tiny—between her and the lies Daelissa burned into her impressionable little brain. I just had to figure out how. "Would you like to meet Nightliss and ask her questions?" I said. "If you do that, I'll talk to"—I almost gagged on the word—"Bigdaddy."

Her eyes narrowed. "Are you trying to trick me? You know Nightliss will only capture and torture me."

"I won't let her." I held up my hand palm out. "Promise."

She mulled it over. "I don't know, Justin. How can I trust you?"

"How about if I bring her to you someplace you'll be safe?"

"Well—" her lips pursed. "Maybe that would work, but I wouldn't want Bigdaddy or the others to know, because they'd get really mad."

My heart leapt, and I fought to keep from sounding too enthusiastic. "Sure, just tell me where."

She mulled it over for a moment. "I don't know where."

I couldn't help but notice how adorable Ivy looked when she was deep in thought. Or how much she reminded me of Mom. It was almost torturous to have her so close at hand and not be able to talk to her like a normal human being. The end of the world might be near, but I felt like I might do anything to have her trust me.

"How about this," I said, resisting the urge to touch her shoulder the way a brother or even a friend might. "Let's forget all this end of the world stuff. Do you feel safe with me on campus?"

A blonde eyebrow lifted as she regarded me. "I guess."

"I saw a gelato shop down the hall from the cafeteria. Why don't we get some ice cream and just talk about normal stuff?"

A grin broke on her lips. "Are you buying?"

Her smile infected me, and I grinned back. "Of course."

She looked around. "Well, I kind of sneaked away for some alone time. They're always telling me what I can and can't do, and I'm tired of it."

"I know the feeling," I said. "So, is that a yes?"

Her smile brightened. "Yes!" She giggled and clapped her hands.

We wove through the crowded hallway. Students stopped what they were doing as we passed, some of them staring at Ivy as though she might blow them up with a look. She strode blithely past them, talking to me about her puppy, Jumpy.

"I only had him for a couple of days," she said, lips pouting. "If they trust me with big things, why not little things?"

I nodded in agreement. "Adults can be really stupid," I said.

"Totes!" she said, eyes wide with sincerity.

We entered the gelato shop. Ivy ordered a double scoop combo of Fairy Frost with Mango Unicorn, while I tried the potion master special flavor of the day, Gumper's Concoction Number 101. Even though I couldn't readily identify what it tasted like, it was delicious.

"Where did you go to school before this?" I asked Ivy after we found a seat in the crowded shop.

"The Ezzek Moore Arcane Academy for the Gifted," she said, somehow licking her gelato in between words without pausing. "I didn't know about, well"—she leaned close, a conspiratorial gleam in her eye—"about Mom being an angel." She straightened, licked a dribble of melted gelato from the side of the cone. "I just thought I was really talented."

"I never had that problem," I said. I stopped myself before blurting out how terrible I was with magic. If I ever had to fight her, I didn't want her to know how easy she would have it.

"You went to a nom school?" she asked, her blue eyes bright with curiosity.

"Yeah." I sighed, thinking back to those simple days. "I was a chubby overweight nerd. I didn't know anything about Mom or Dad. I thought I was just a normal human."

"Really?" she asked, ignoring a stream of melted gelato as it ran across her fingers. "What was it like being normal?"

I shrugged. "Pretty normal, I guess."

We shared a laugh.

I told her about the live-action role-playing game, Kings and Castles. I told her about my crush on Katie Johnson, how I'd met Elyssa and Stacey.

"You fell in love?" she asked, blue eyes brimming with curiosity. "Does it feel wonderful?"

"It can be wonderful and scary all at the same time," I said, unsure how in-depth I really wanted to go about it.

"It must be nice having another person who's gooey for you," she said and let out a little sigh before resuming the attack on her gelato.

I continued my story, telling her about the bullying from football players and how I'd finally discovered what I was.

"Football?" she asked. "That's a game?"

"Yeah, you carry a ball shaped like this"—I formed the oval shape with my fingers and thumbs—"and you have to get it into the other team's end zone."

"Weird," she said, eyebrows rising in unison. "People make games out of anything."

I chuckled. "Yeah."

"It makes me really mad that the football players beat you up," she said, her eyes soft with sympathy. "I hate how big people think they can walk all over the little ones."

Ivy looked little, but with her powers, she was anything but. "Yeah, it was rough," I said. "But even having super powers didn't solve everything."

She quirked her lips into cute expression of agreement. "At my gifted school, the strong kids would bully the others. This one guy, Billy Vanderbilt, would make the little kids do everything he said. If they didn't, he'd do terrible things, like make them eat toads, or levitate them upside down, or even make their clothes vanish."

My jaw tightened at the mention of his name. "I've seen him around. He's definitely a mean guy."

Ivy nodded. "He and his group of bullies used to pick on us all the time. One day I got so mad, I cursed them."

I got the impression she wasn't talking about swear words. "What did you do?"

"I made them hungry for bugs. Every time they saw one, they'd get so hungry they had to eat it."

I gagged. "Like spiders and cockroaches?"

An impish grin spread across her face. "Yeah. I even spawned a nest of locusts in their dorm room." She giggled. "They got so sick."

I couldn't help but laugh myself despite how insanely gross it sounded. "Did they know you did it?"

Her expression sobered. "Yeah. I got in huge trouble with Bigdaddy and Bigmomma. Daelissa thought it was funny, but she told me not to do it again."

"Yeah, when I finally beat up Nathan, I only got myself in more trouble." I told her how I'd been blackmailed into playing football and how horribly that had ended up, with the slaughter of all those people. Technically, it hadn't been my fault—it had been Brad Nichols, driven insane by the vampling curse, who'd killed those people.

Ivy took it all in with wide eyes. "Even though we have magic, the noms sound a lot like us," she said and polished off the last bit of her cone.

"We're all human," I agreed.

Ivy giggled. "Not really."

I snorted. "Yeah, sorry. I'm still new to this whole angel and demon thing."

My sister reached a hand across to mine and touched it. "I like you, Justin."

Moisture gathered behind my eyes at this simple statement. I put my other hand over hers. "I like you, Ivy. I like having a little sister."

A tear gathered in the corner of her eye and trickled down. "Maybe we can have a talk like you said, and maybe you'll agree with us."

"I want to have our family back together," I said. "Me, you, Mom, Dad—"

Her hand abruptly jerked from mine. "No, not him."

"Not Dad?"

She shook her head, wiped the tear away. "He's a demon, Justin. You can't make him good."

"But—" the next words died on my lips. If I tried to explain that we were both half and half, it might further alienate her. I didn't know what to say. It was hard enough getting her to accept me. Besides, Dad had more or less abandoned Mom to marry Kassallandra.

Her forehead wrinkled. "Besides, I don't think he's our real dad. He can't be." Her statement sounded like pure denial. Ivy checked the time on her arcphone. "I need to go. Bigdaddy will already be mad at me for sneaking off."

I nodded. "Let's figure out a time and place to have our talks," I said. "I've really enjoyed spending time with you. Can we do it again soon?"

The corners of her mouth curved up. "I'd like that."

"Maybe we could go to a zoo one day."

Her eyes brightened. "Oh, I'd love that so much." Her face fell. "But, I can't. Not until we figure things out." She offered an apologetic grin. "Okay?"

I nodded. "Fair enough." I walked her back to the library.

"I should go on by myself," she said when we reached the entrance. "Just in case, you know."

"I understand," I said.

She suddenly threw herself against me, squeezing me in a tight hug. I returned the hug and felt a surge of joy. There might be hope for her yet.

Ivy let go, gave me a shy smile, and wandered away into the library, vanishing around a corner. I turned a moment later and nearly rammed into a man right behind me.

"Excuse me," I said and tried to walk around him.

He blocked my way, a leer on his face. "Well, well, if it ain't my old buddy, Justin," he said in a cockney accent.

It was Bigglesworth.

Chapter 20

I shuddered, backed away from the creature that had tried to kill me hours before. Bigglesworth sported a sky blue polyester suit and wide-collared shirt imprinted with the photo-realistic image of a forest on it. I choked back my initial desire to snarl and cuss him out, instead, somehow finding the will to keep my mouth shut.

"Cat got your tongue, mate?" He grinned.

"You smell slightly burnt," I said, making a show of sniffing. "Flark."

A shocked look flicked across his face. "I'd like to know how you found out what I am," he said.

I tapped my temple. "I have my resources." Changing subjects, I said, "What did you want with that man you were torturing?"

"A matter for my mistress. Nothing you need concern yourself with." He stepped closer.

I took an involuntary step back as my body flinched at the memory of how painful his touch had been. "Why are you helping Daelissa?"

He tilted his head slightly. "If you knew anything about Flarks, perhaps you'd know the answer to that question."

"You could just tell me."

He chuckled. "Why ruin the fun, mate?" He stepped closer.

I didn't back away this time.

Bigglesworth lowered his voice. "And it's gonna be so much fun killing a ruddy wanker like you."

"Justin, it is nice to see you."

Bigglesworth and I looked toward the source of the voice.

Cinder attempted a grin, instead managing a leer that teetered somewhere between maniacal and psychotic. "I am researching."

"What the bloody—" Bigglesworth tilted his head to the side. "You've gotta be kidding me." His eyes drifted to me, the orbs shifting to an unsettling shiny black color. "Methuselah. Makes sense now."

I almost asked him who the heck he was talking about, when Cinder went stock still, his eyes locked onto Bigglesworth. "Are you in danger, Justin?"

"That remains to be seen," I replied.

His gaze flicked to me. "Shall I battle the creature for you?"

I shook my head. "We were just having a nice talk." I turned to Bigglesworth. "So, Methuselah surprised you, didn't he?"

The shifter's black eyes resumed normal coloring. "He only cares about balance. Don't think you've won anything, mate." Bigglesworth tipped his bowler. "Until we meet again."

Cinder stared after the Flark for a moment and turned to me. "I am sorry, Justin. If I had known this was the shifter you'd told us about, I would not have—" He broke off, going absolutely still for a moment. "—opened my wide mouth."

"Big mouth," I said.

"Ah. I do not understand the exact difference but—"

"Do you recognize the name Methuselah?"

"It seems to have triggered a memory in me." He tilted his head. "I believe some entities referred to my creator as Methuselah."

"In other words, Mr. Gray," I said.

"And Bigglesworth believes my creator is interfering by sending me when, in fact, I am here for completely different reasons." He blinked. "How interesting. Perhaps—"

I waved off his next words. "Look, let's worry about this later. Bigger issues have come up, and we need to brainstorm."

Cinder stared at me with a blank unblinking expression.

I sighed. "It's an idiom that means we need to think hard about how to solve a problem. So let's get out of here before Bigglesworth has a chance to set up an ambush outside."

He raised a hand and snapped his fingers in a robotic motion. "Twenty-three skidoo."

I blinked at him a couple of times before deciding I didn't want to know what the heck a skidoo was. "Um, come on."

We left the library the same way I'd entered while Cinder talked my ear off about his study of golems and the latest innovative designs.

"Nothing current comes close to my own design," he said as a simple statement of fact.

"The robot golem that attacked me and Shelton seemed pretty smart."

"It was merely given a spark with specific attributes. My spark is more flexible, adaptive." His gray eyes scanned the hallway ahead. "I took the liberty of retrieving pertinent parts of the golem and studied them, thinking perhaps they were built by my creator."

I stopped and considered the hallway before us, unsure which way to go. "Do you know how to get out of here and back to the transports?"

"Of course." Cinder led me at a brisk walk until we were outside the huge castle.

It occurred to me I hadn't heard anything from Shelton. In fact, between my encounters with Ivy and Bigglesworth, I'd completely forgotten to see if he was okay. I pulled out my phone and texted him. *Are you still alive?*

"Hold on, Cinder." I said, stopping.

He turned, hands out at the ready to grasp something.

"That's another idiom," I said before he asked me. "It means wait."

He lowered his hands and nodded. "I will file it away for future reference. I have found the students here use a number of idioms which do not logically correlate to the meanings behind them. One referred to another student's freeze spell as 'sick' even though the spell did not induce sickness."

I held up a hand. "One problem at a time, please." Shelton still hadn't replied, and I felt a cold weight lodge in my gut. Something felt wrong. I remembered the linkup Shelton had performed with my phone earlier and opened the tracking app. The blip indicating Shelton's position wasn't anywhere in the castle. It appeared to be in the forest behind the school.

I ran toward the direction, but my legs didn't want to cooperate with super speed, instead limiting me to a strictly non-supernatural pace. Even though Healer Hutchins's pill made me feel better, it hadn't done anything to feed my incubus tummy. Oddly, I wasn't starving like I should have been, and I wondered if her pill also muted the clawing agony of starvation.

Shelton still hadn't responded. For all I knew, he lay dead in the forest. Jeremiah Conroy could have killed him and dumped the body. Or he might be dying and running out of time. I cursed.

"W-w-will you go to the dance with me, Belinda?" a nearby student stammered.

I looked at the source of the voice. A short, plump student with thick spectacles was literally quaking in his boots as he looked hopefully at an attractive blonde girl flanked by her two pretty friends. He reminded me a lot of my pre-incubus self, though I had to admit he had bigger nuggets than I'd had back then to ask out such a daunting target.

A tall, good-looking guy stood next to the nerd, nudging him with an elbow.

The girl sniffed. "Oh, please." She looked at the handsome guy. "Is this your idea of a joke, Kevin?"

The tall guy burst into laughter. The sad nerd drooped.

I glanced at Shelton's blip again and gritted my teeth.

"What is the matter, Justin?" Cinder asked.

"Shelton might be in big trouble." Shelton's blip moved in an erratic pattern. I had to get to him fast, but an empty incubus tank wasn't going to do the trick. I looked at the students again and groaned. I needed fueling fast. Doing so might incite unpleasant side effects in my victim. I flicked on my incubus senses, and the glowing auras of the females flared to life.

"You are a hopeless, creepy nerd," Belinda said to her crushed suitor. Her friends burst into laughter.

I suddenly didn't care what my feeding did to these people. Three tendrils of essence shot from me, each one latching into the halo of a female. The girls stiffened in shock as I opened myself completely to them. Their eyes locked onto mine, desire and lust burning within. I extended the tendrils from them into the hapless nerd. Their attentions flicked from me to him. Before he could say "Twenty-three skidoo" the girls lunged at him, smothering him in kisses.

"Oh, Godwin!" Belinda cried out as she ran kisses up his earlobe.

Kevin's jaw dropped, and I could've sworn I saw a blood vessel pop in his head.

Energy flooded into me as the nerd steadily lost the fight to keep his clothes on. My skin flushed with heat. I wasn't sure how full I was, but had no more time to waste. Withdrawing from my targets as carefully as possible so as not to damage their psyches, I released them.

By now, the nerd lay on the ground beneath a heap of panting girls. Kevin—the handsome bastard—looked nauseated, his face a sickly shade of green.

I gripped Cinder's arm. "Let's jet." Figuring he'd get the gist of my words, I blurred away toward the forest.

Chapter 21

Cinder and I plunged through thick trees. Underbrush snagged at my clothes, tearing my fashionably charred shirt, slowing my pace. The dense canopy dimmed the surroundings to a creepy twilight. Stopping to consult my phone for Shelton's location, I saw he shouldn't be too far—

A brilliant bolt of blue energy splintered a tree some twenty yards away.

"Get your ass out here, you lying bastard!" a very angry man shouted.

I spotted Shelton crouching behind a tree just to the left of the splintered one. A shadow moved a few yards behind him. Another dark figure moved to his left and another in front of him.

"Come out, little mousy," said someone in a mocking voice. "We'll make this nice and quick."

I pulled Cinder into a crouch. "Take out the man behind Shelton. I'll nab the one in front of him. Hopefully Shelton can handle the third guy."

Cinder nodded.

"Go," I whispered and blurred through the trees toward my target.

He stood about Shelton's height and wore a gray cloak which blended with the dim light in the forest. Unfortunately, the price of speed was a lot of noise. My target's head jerked toward me. I'd hoped to close the space faster, but the choking underbrush pulled at my clothes. The man cursed, aimed a staff at me, and a shaft of blue energy speared inches from my shoulder.

I dodged, nearly slamming into a thick oak as I did. The energy blew a smoking hole through the trunk of another thick tree. I felt a flare of heat, and the blast sent me stumbling sideways. I hit a tree full on and bounced off it, slamming onto my back.

"Acworth, get your ass out here!" my target yelled. "He's got friends!"

As I lay stunned in the underbrush, hopefully hidden from another attack, I heard a deep growl soon joined by another and the crack of leaves and twigs accompanied by sniffing. Another rumbling growl sounded, much closer this time, and I crouched, ready to dodge whatever made the sound. Two saplings bent away from each other, and glowing eyes filled the dark space between. A large furry muzzle poked through followed by a ginormous wolf. Another wolf—undoubtedly a lycan—joined the first. The monstrous werewolf let out a blood-chilling howl.

"Hear that, Shelton?" my target shouted. "Doesn't matter how much help you have, you're mine."

I braced myself for an assault and shouted, "Can't we settle this peacefully?"

The man laughed. "Peacefully? Peacefully? You must be kidding me. He took my girlfriend!"

I mentally face-palmed. Shelton had stolen a guy's girlfriend? "Look, I know it's bad to steal someone's girlfriend, but killing is a bit much."

"Stole her? Ha! He only wishes." The night lit with another brilliant blue lance. "He turned her in for a bounty!"

"She was a criminal, you moron!" Shelton yelled.

Apparently, diplomacy was off the table.

Acworth, the giant wolf, I presumed, lunged at me. My hands gripped his muzzle inches from my face. His weight and power strained at my muscles, making it very obvious I was nowhere near full strength. Otherwise, I might have been able to shove him off. I growled with effort.

His teeth pressed closer to my face. Saliva drooled onto my cheek. I shifted into my incubus senses. Aether hung like a heavy mist in the forest, light and dark swirls painting the air. But drawing in the ethereal substance was like trying to drink water through a bent straw. I tensed, pulling at the elusive energy with all my might. Out of the corner of my eye I saw the other lycan draw closer, its tongue lolling as it watched its mutant buddy try to eat me. And then I saw the bright sensual aura drifting around the smaller wolf. It was a female. Lashing out with my essence, I caught the female's halo and let her have the full brunt of my sexual super powers.

Her bright blue eyes caught mine. Lifting her head to sky, she howled. Struggling to keep Acworth from biting my head off, I gritted my teeth and extended my essence from the female to him. Her attention shifted. She howled again. Acworth's ears twitched, and he gave her a sideways glance even as he pressed harder against my hands.

The sound of someone tromping through the underbrush neared me, and the gray-cloaked form of Shelton's accuser appeared, aiming his staff at my head.

He glanced around, eyes bright with anger. "We've got your friend, Shelton. Give yourself up, and we'll let him go."

Silence.

The man chuckled. "Yeah. I didn't think so." He leaned over me. "Harry Shelton doesn't have friends. He's a user. He's filth. I'm not going to kill you, but I'm gonna give you a reminder about how important it is for you to choose your friends wisely."

The female wolf howled again, the sound followed by popping bones and shifting muscle. The Arcane's brow wrinkled as he noticed the naked woman panting and staring lustfully at the big wolf looming over me. Acworth made a whimpering sound that almost sounded like a surprised human saying, "Huh?"

Strength coursed into me from the bond with the woman. "Go play with your chew toys, bitch." I clamped the huge wolf's muzzle shut with both hands, planted my feet on his belly, and kicked. Acworth flew back several feet, slamming into a tree with a yelp. I amplified the connection between him and the female. Lust flared in the stunned wolf's eyes. He began shifting back to human. The Arcane shouted at Acworth. He aimed his staff at my head, and blue energy coalesced around it.

I rolled away as a pulse of heat baked a mud pie in the earth where my head had been. He fired again, and I wasn't quite fast enough to avoid a searing wave of heat across my infected leg. Intense cold raced through my calf, my thigh, and crawled into my groin. Anger surged through me like a shockwave. I felt my skin ripple, muscles bulge, and bones creak. A guttural roar burst from my throat as a gray-clad figure burst through the trees. Shelton appeared right behind him, his staff rippling with energy.

Shelton's accuser screamed in terror as my body grew to tower over him. Agony in my head tore at my consciousness, and the rage of my inner demon tried to snuff out lucidity. I gripped a nearby sapling and squeezed. Felt the satisfying crunch of bark and wood beneath my huge hands.

"No!" I roared. "Stop!" Fighting back with everything I had, I forced myself to stagger backward, away from the people. I saw Acworth and the woman, my connection with them gone, as they stared in horror at the beast consuming me.

Shadows crept from the forest, silent wraiths with faces I recognized. Maximus. Dash. Brad Nichols, his face consumed with rot from the vampling curse, and right behind him Mortimer, his head dangling at a grotesque angle, eyes pleading for mercy.

Feed. Drink. Devour. The voices in my head grew in volume until I could hardly hear my own defiant roars. The curse was waging a war in my mind, and I was losing.

Elyssa, I need you!

The cold in my body strained to expand my rage, my bloodlust. I couldn't let it happen. I'd rampage. I would murder everyone in sight. I thought back to the first time Elyssa and I had made love. I remembered when she'd died in my arms after I'd drained her life. "No, no, no!" I cried in a guttural voice. I reared back my head and howled in anguish. Tears sizzled in my eyes, burnt to steam by soul flames.

I dropped to my knees in supplication. Elyssa was my anchor. My solace. And suddenly, the anger evaporated. My muscles contracted, and my bones shrunk. After a moment, I stood panting, my stretched and ripped clothes hanging loose around my frame. My shoes were little more than strips of material hanging to my bare toes. I definitely couldn't pass this look off as the latest in fashion. A hand settled onto my back, and I looked up into Shelton's concerned eyes.

"You okay, buddy?"

I almost laughed at the understatement.

Instead, I nodded even as my body shivered from the cold pulsing in my leg. I felt the tendrils spreading across my crotch, reaching toward my stomach. Despite the potion, the curse was spreading. My body had been through tremendous trauma in the past few hours—golem robots, evil shape shifters, angry Arcanes, and their drooling lycan buddies. Was that causing the curse to accelerate its spread?

I looked up and saw Shelton aiming his staff at Acworth, the female, his accuser, and two other men with gray cloaks who looked like Arcanes. Cinder stood behind them, his gray eyes keeping a constant watch.

Trembling, I rose to my feet.

"Damn it, Zagg. Why the hell can't you just let it go?" Shelton glared at his accuser.

"Because I love her you heartless piece of sh—"

"What crime did she commit?" I asked, in a croaking voice.

"Illegally selling magic items to noms," Shelton said. "She's lucky she didn't get the death penalty."

"It was a setup!" the female cried, hands crossed over her bare chest. "Kayla would never do that! I know my sister better than anyone. She would never break the covenant."

"Doesn't matter what you think, Natalie" Shelton said. "She broke the rules. She's paying the price."

"She's innocent!" Zagg screamed. "And you took her away from me, you bastard."

I couldn't help but feel terrible for the guy, but didn't know what I could do except tell him and his buddies to leave us alone. On the other hand, the negative impact of Shelton's past had morphed from annoying to beyond ridiculous. Who else had a vendetta against him? Would I be dodging spells my entire educational career?

I bit back a curse. "Look, I know some higher-ups in the Templars. Maybe I can get someone to investigate her case and get back to me. If she's really innocent, maybe they can get her out. In return, you have to promise not to try to kill me or my friends." My request sounded so ridiculous, I shook my head in disbelief.

Zagg looked at me with such pain and hope in his eyes, I had to look away. "Who do you know?" he asked in the voice of someone daring to believe.

"My girlfriend is Elyssa Borathen."

He sucked in a breath. "You know Thomas Borathen?"

"He's a legend," Natalie said. "If he can prove her innocence, nobody would doubt it."

"I'm not promising Thomas himself will look into it, but someone will," I said. "I want your word."

Zagg jumped up, and Shelton looked like he was about to fry him with whatever he had cooking at the tip of his staff before he stopped himself at the last minute. Zagg shook my hand.

"You have my word. If you can free my Kayla—" He choked up. "We were supposed to get married, and then…" He trailed off, looking with pure hatred at Shelton.

Shelton held up a hand in surrender. "For crying out loud, man, I was just doing my job."

Acworth and the other group members regarded me with suspicious expressions. Natalie, however seemed to believe me, if her expression was anything to go by.

"Cinder," I said. "Can you give her your suit jacket, please? It's kind of cold out here."

"Of course, Justin." He handed it to the girl, who wasted no time in covering up. "Shall I give her my pants as well? I do not think the cold will affect my genitalia in the same manner as—"

I quickly waved him off. "No, that's not necessary. I'm sure they have clothes nearby."

Acworth nodded. Even in human form he was a big man, thicker and taller than even the meaty MacLean. "We do." His voice was a low rumble. "Why should we trust you, spawn?" He spat the last word like a bad taste.

"Look, I may be demon spawn, but I'm still…a nice guy." I shrugged. "I mean, would Elyssa Borathen date a creep?"

He regarded me with narrow eyes for a moment. "I don't personally know her, but I know from my Templar friends the Borathens are honorable people who won't stand for corruption. But don't think their honor gives *you* a free pass, spawn."

Natalie gripped his big arm and whispered something. He looked at her, his eyes going from rock hard to gentle in an instant, and nodded.

"Alrighty, then," I said, rubbing my hands together. "Why don't we get out of here and back to civilization?"

A basso roar sounded from somewhere in the forest, and the sound of trees bending and breaking reached my ears. An alarmed look flashed across Zagg's face.

"Just great," Shelton said. "All that noise attracted the tragon."

"The what?" I said as the crunch of vegetation grew louder by the second.

"Everybody run!" shouted one of the other Arcanes, jumping to his feet and plunging with abandon back in the direction of the castle. The other Arcane screamed, leapt to his feet, and followed the first one.

Acworth and the girl shifted back into wolf form and loped away while Zagg hurried after them, fear blazing in his eyes.

"Judging from the reactions of the others, I recommend we do as suggested and run," Cinder said.

"Okay." I tilted my head at Shelton. "Cinder, throw the slowpoke over your shoulder and carry him back."

Before Shelton could let out a cry of surprise, Cinder slung the Arcane over his shoulder and ran through the forest.

A deep rumbling growl reached my ears. I glanced behind me as the hairs on the back of my neck rose to full attention. A Tyrannosaurus Rex regarded me with glowing red eyes. Correction—it looked like the dinosaur, but its forelimbs were longer, its scales glistened red, and dinky little wings flapped on its back. The creature blinked. Then it bellowed and shot a jet of fire from its mouth. A tree to my right burst into flame. I yelped and ran. The monster roared and gave chase, plowing through underbrush and tree alike as though they were made of paper. Even as I blurred through the forest, underbrush snagging my torn clothes, I knew I'd be lucky to get away.

A blast of bright yellow light hit the thing square in the eyes. It stumbled to the side, breaking a swath of trees. A cloud of what looked like giant spiders with bat wings screeched and took flight. I looked ahead and saw Shelton bumping along on Cinder's shoulder, somehow managing to aim his staff at the tragon. Cinder burst from the trees and into daylight ahead. Using his path instead of blazing my own, I swerved around a large tree and toward the edge of the forest.

Something caught my foot. I flipped through the air, glanced off a tree, and rolled to a stop in the grass a few feet outside the forest.

Before I could scramble to my feet, the tragon, less than ten yards away, lunged for me.

I was dead meat.

Chapter 22

The air a foot away from my nose shimmered blue, rippling like water as the tragon's snout struck it. Rending jaws with more teeth than a pool full of sharks snapped at me, but missed, slipping harmlessly off the blue dome. The tragon's maw opened wide. Flames jetted from its throat. I flinched back, even as the fire clouded the shield without penetrating it. At first, I thought Shelton had saved me with a defensive spell, but then I noticed how far the rippling shield extended. Even he couldn't manage one so large.

"Ha!" Shelton said, whooping. "Saved by the fricking shield again!" He laughed maniacally, panting like he'd been the one to run from the forest and not Cinder. "Oh, man, that reminds me of the good old days." He clapped a hand around mine and pulled me to my feet.

"This shield is normally here?" I asked.

He nodded. "Yeah. All sorts of creepy crawlers live in the forest, man. It's like a nature preserve for nearly extinct animals. They sure as hell don't want any getting loose and gobbling up the students."

"Any unicorns?"

He snorted. "No, but plenty of spider bats. I used to make a hole in the shield so they could terrorize Greek Row." He laughed again. "C'mon, let's get back to the academy."

"Whose bright idea was it to crossbreed a T. Rex and a dragon?" I said.

"Science Academy nerds."

They really are mad scientists.

Cinder, Shelton, and I headed toward the shuttles bound for Science Academy.

"I need to call Elyssa," I said and sighed as I remembered her unavailability. "Or someone."

"About Kayla?" Shelton said. He snorted. "Waste of time."

I wrinkled my forehead and gave him a look of disbelief.

He held up a hand to ward me off. "Look, I appreciate what you did, but they practically caught her red-handed."

"But not literally," I replied.

"Yeah, that too." He huffed. "The girl is guilty, and I guarantee you Thomas Borathen won't do a thing to help her. He'll take one look at the evidence and blow you off."

He was probably right. Thomas and I were on better terms now that he'd accepted I wasn't evil incarnate, but we were far from being buddies. Elyssa would help me in a heartbeat, but she was in the middle of her Templar tests. I went through a mental list, but the only other Templars I knew who might help were Ryland and Elyssa's brother, Michael. I put Michael in a similar boat with Thomas. He accepted my relationship with Elyssa, but only barely. I had a feeling it was less about being demon spawn and more about being a guy who was dating his little sister. What Michael and Thomas conveniently overlooked was Elyssa's ability to kick my ass anytime she wanted. She didn't need protection from me. If anything, I'd need protection from her if I tried to do something she didn't want me to do.

"Michael," Shelton said out of the blue.

"Huh?"

"He'll help you. He won't like it, but he will."

I narrowed my eyes. "What makes you think he will?"

"He knows Kayla and Zagg from when he attended the university."

I stopped dead in my tracks. Cinder nearly ran into me. "Michael Borathen went to Arcane University? He doesn't even know magic."

"That wasn't why he went. A lot of Templar candidates attend to learn defense against magic." Shelton shrugged. "Even your girlfriend probably went when she was younger. In case you hadn't noticed, there are other supers here. The university caters to a lot more than just Arcanes."

The thought had never occurred to me. "They should change the name to Supernatural Academy then."

"Yeah, well I ain't on the naming committee." He resumed walking. "Anyway, ask Michael. It's still a waste of time, but at least it'll keep Zagg and his merry band of idiots off our butts for the time being."

I matched his pace. "Who else do we need to worry about, Shelton? Did Zagg give you the split lip, or was that someone else?"

"Well, aside from a couple of professors, most of the people I pissed off don't go to school here. Zagg and his bunch are grad students, I guess. I didn't expect him to be here." Shelton wiped a clump of muddy grass off his leather duster. "I was following Jeremiah and literally ran into Zagg when I came around a corner. He was with the other two Arcanes I don't know, and they chased me down. I tried to get to the shuttle, but I guess he'd already called Acworth and Natalie to cut me off."

"So you ran into a forest with a tragon." I shook my head. "I'm surprised someone didn't get eaten sooner."

He chuckled. "Guess my plan worked out okay in the end."

"It might not the next time." I gripped his upper arm and stopped him. "You need to tell me right this minute if I need to worry about more of your past acquaintances trying to kill us."

Shelton regarded me for a long moment before nodding. "The guys who split my lip wanted money. Thankfully, I was able to take care of that. Like I said, there's bad blood between me and a couple of professors, but they pissed me off when I went to school here, so I got back at them after I graduated." His eyes went distant for a brief period as if trying to remember anything else. "Otherwise, I can't think of anything."

"I am curious about this bad blood you mention," Cinder said. "Is the blood defective? Whose blood is it?"

"It's slang," I said in an exasperated voice. I sighed. "Let's go. I'm bushed."

"Yes," Cinder said, picking twigs from his shirt. "I also have bits of bushes on me from the forest."

Shelton barked a laugh.

"I take it you never had the chance to talk to your dad about the arches, did you?" I asked.

Shelton shook his head. "Nah, between stalking Conroy and Zagg ambushing me, I forgot about it."

"Well, it might not be necessary now." I told him about MacLean.

"Holy dog balls in a turtle shell," Shelton said, shaking his head in wonder. "Talk about a blast from the past." He chuckled. "MacLean always loved watching spider bats chase terrorized coeds."

When we arrived back at Science Academy, I took a long shower, put on clean clothes, and braced myself to talk to Michael. A huge guy, Elyssa's brother possessed the same ninja-quick reflexes as his sister and also like Elyssa, was a dhampyr. I'd only recently discovered he was working—or had been working—for Underborn, the most notorious assassin in the Overworld, not to mention a lying slime-ball who'd manipulated me and Elyssa every chance he had. Why Michael had worked for the man was beyond me.

After mulling over the past for a good five minutes, I realized I was stalling and dialed him.

"What is it?" said a deep voice from the other end after two rings.

"Hello to you, too," I said in a cheery voice.

Silence.

When he still said nothing else, I cleared my throat and told him about Kayla.

"You want me to help Shelton out of a mess," he said in a tone indicating it wasn't a question.

"I know you don't care for Shelton or me," I said. "But if there's a chance Kayla is innocent—"

"Okay, I'll do it."

"Uh, really?"

"On one condition."

I tensed. *Here it comes.* "And that would be?"

"Help me with Elyssa." For a moment, his low voice almost—*almost*—bore a sign of emotion.

"She's still ticked about Underborn," I said.

"Yes."

"You know I can't make her do anything, right?" I tried to keep the crack of fear out of my voice. "Even bringing up the subject is like telling her I want to eat puppies for breakfast."

"I know, but that's my price."

Holy hell. I wondered how in the world I could ask Elyssa to mend fences with Michael and decided that he was only asking me to help, not to actually perform a miracle. "I'll help. But I can't promise you she'll listen."

"I can't promise you Kayla is innocent. But I'll look into it." He went silent again, not even breathing loud enough to be heard over the phone. *The man has ninja skills for sure.*

I decided to risk asking another question since it related to his problem. "Are you still working for Underborn?"

"I'm out of his game." He paused. "Underborn isn't on anyone's side, but I thought I could protect Elyssa better from the middle. It worked out in some ways, but not in others. Underborn wanted her to know I was working with him. That's why he brought me along to see Elyssa that day. By the time I figured out who we were going to see, it was too late for me to leave."

"Why would he want Elyssa to know?" I asked.

"To show me who was in control. To show me he knew I was trying to manipulate his plans with regards to Elyssa." Michael hissed out a sigh, the first sign of emotion I'd heard. "I thought I was smart enough to avoid his traps and to turn them back on him. I was wrong."

I didn't know what to say to that. If someone as capable as Michael couldn't outthink the assassin even when it knew it was coming, I had no hope of avoiding Underborn's traps when he blindsided me. "Thanks for being honest. I think that's what Elyssa really needs. She loves you and trusted you. Seeing you work with someone like Underborn destroyed that trust. If you're being completely honest with me, then it's obvious you wanted to protect her. You knew bad stuff was coming, and you did what you could to shield her."

"Yes."

"I'd do anything to protect her," I replied. "Maybe that's not the same as being her brother but—"

"I think you understand. I'll look into your issue."

The line went dead.

"That went better than expected," I said to myself since Shelton had gone out for food, and Cinder was off doing whatever golems did when they had nothing better to do.

I dropped into a chair at one of the desks in the room and spotted the class schedule Miles had given me. Beneath the schedule, he'd listed the books I would need in a neatly quilled scrawl. A nervous cramp gripped my stomach. I'd almost forgotten about classes and hadn't even thought to buy books. I texted Lina and asked her where I could buy books. While I waited for a response, I lay down on the bed and looked at pictures of me and Elyssa.

Most of them were selfies, with me holding the phone out and snapping the picture with one hand. Elyssa crossed her eyes in one and kissed my cheek in another. My heart felt like a chunk was missing, and it hurt. I hoped her trials were going well, but the selfish part of me wished she'd just hurry the hell up and come give me a kiss.

I woke up with a start. Looked around the room in confusion. Checked the time. It was almost seven-thirty, an ungodly hour to even think about waking up. I closed my eyes, but something nagged at me. After a moment, I grunted and sat up. A sheet of parchment slid off my chest, and my brain made the connection between what was nagging me and the time. My first class started at eight.

"Crap!" I said and jumped out of bed.

Shelton, snoozing on the bottom bunk, mumbled something about me shutting up, and rolled over to face the wall.

My mind ran a quick calculation on how long it would take me to shower, dress, cross over to the university in the shuttle, and possibly eat along the way. I was pretty good at math, so it only took a moment to realize I had to cut something out of that list. Since I wasn't about to traipse around the school emitting a ripe odor, I decided against cutting a shower from the list. I slid on my flip-flops, wrapped a towel around my waist, and ran into the shared bathroom. Steam filled the tiled space, and all the shower stalls looked occupied. Time ticked on as I waited. To save time, I brushed my teeth and shaved. I heard a curtain slide open and cut off another guy as he made a beeline for it.

"Sorry," I said in response to his exclamation of surprise.

After showering at supernatural speed, I rushed back down the hall, nearly busting it on the slick tile floors thanks to my wet flip-flops, and got dressed. I made it to the shuttle station and watched as it drifted away from the platform, jam-packed with students. I knew from yesterday that the Arcane University flying stagecoach had just left from across the valley.

I checked the time. Fifteen minutes to go. Another stressful thought kicked me in the stomach. I had no idea how to get to class. I checked my notifications and saw an unread text from Lina.

Download the University guide app on your phone. It'll tell you where everything is.

Thanking the heavens, I went on the Arc Store and downloaded the app she recommended. I searched for where to buy books, and it traced a winding route that led to the university book store. Then I searched for my first class, Elementary Magic. By the time the coach arrived, I knew I'd have no time to buy books and also make my class in time.

I piled into the coach along with the other students, my nerves taut and a cold sweat breaking out. This was not the way I wanted to start my college career. The second the shuttle set down on the other side, I jumped off and followed the outlined route. When I reached the end, I looked at the sign outside the closed door and realized it was not Elementary Magic, but Elementary Enchantment. Chest tight, I scanned the nearby rooms and finally spotted the right one. Apparently the app wasn't completely accurate, but it had at least brought me to the right area.

I eased open the door. It betrayed me with a loud creak. A thin-faced woman with a stern face glared at me as she wrote something in the air with her wand. I gulped and stepped inside.

"Well, well. The late addition arrives late." She looked me up and down. "This will be your one and only tardy allowance, Mr. Slade. Do you understand me?"

"Yes, ma'am. I'm sorry."

Giggles erupted from the class. I stepped past a partition blocking my view into the room and horror washed over me. The classroom sign hadn't been kidding. This was elementary all right. Miles had put me in a class with little kids.

Chapter 23

Humiliation must have turned my face fifty shades of red as I hunted for a desk sized for an adult and failed. Every one of them was built for a munchkin, not a teenager.

"Find a seat now," the teacher said.

"But—"

"Sit!" she said, pointing to an empty desk in the last row. A girl with odd silvery hair sat in the far back corner, isolated by empty desks to either side of her.

I took the desk to the girl's right, wedging myself into the ridiculously small seat. My knees bowed out to either side, and I had to slump.

"Very good," the teacher said and turned back to her writing.

I glanced up at the writing and saw her name. Ms. Crab. *What an appropriate name.*

"Now, I want everyone to turn to page ten in their textbooks," Ms. Crab said. Her eyes fixed on me. "Mr. Slade, please read the first paragraph."

Every head swiveled my way.

I cleared my throat and glanced helplessly at my empty desk. "I, uh, don't have a book yet."

Her eyes narrowed. "Stop mumbling and speak clearly, young man."

"I don't have a book, Ms. Crab."

She nodded, as if that statement told me everything she needed to know. "I think it's obvious what sort of student you are, Mr. Slade."

"Please, I'm usually a lot better—"

"I did not say you could speak," she said in a deadly quiet tone. Her eyes went to the other students. "What is the punishment for being lazy, class?"

"The dummy cap!" they all shouted at once.

I almost opened my mouth to ask what they were talking about when a rainbow-colored cap with a spinning propeller atop it floated through the air and landed on my head. My hands automatically went to pull it off, but Ms. Crab flicked her wand, and my hands slapped atop the surface of the desk. Try as I might, I couldn't move them an inch.

"You, Mr. Slade, are a lazy boy. Until you prove otherwise, you will wear the dummy cap. If you do not have your book tomorrow, or if you show up late, you will wear the cap again." She narrowed her eyes to laser focus. "Do I make myself clear?"

I gulped and nodded. "Yes, ma'am."

"Yes, Ms. Crab," she said in the slow tone someone usually reserved for a particularly dim-witted student.

"Yes, Ms. Crab," I said, forcing the words between clenched teeth as anger simmered in my blood.

"Do not use that tone of voice with me, young man, or I will evict you from this class in a heartbeat."

I drew in a deep breath, reaching hard for the happy place hiding inside me, and with a fake smile, said, "I'm sorry, Ms. Crab. It won't happen again."

She gave me a look indicating she didn't believe a word out of my mouth, turned back to the class, and commanded someone else to read the paragraph.

The girl sitting next to me gave me a shy smile and angled her book so I could read from it, even with my hands still glued to the desk. By the end of class, I wanted to kill Miles. And Shelton. And probably Ms. Crab, too. The class revolved around defining magic, how to use it safely, and that one should always ask permission from their parents before spell casting. I estimated the educational level to be about fifth grade, judging from the ages of my classmates.

After class ended, Ms. Crab waited until everyone else had filed out before flicking her wand and releasing my hands. "I only allowed you in here because Miles told me you have exceptional potential, young man. But if you think for an instant I'll allow insubordination or tardiness, you had better adjust your attitude." She flicked her wand again and the dummy cap flew from my head and landed neatly on a hat rack in the back corner of the room.

"Yes, Ms. Crab," I said, resisting the urge to defend myself, curse at her, or pick her up and break her over my knee. The woman's wrinkled facc looked tough as old leather—a perfect match for her attitude.

I shuffled out of the classroom, head hanging low. *What a horrible start to the school year.*

I checked the schedule and saw my next class, Elementary Meditation, started in five minutes, which meant I still couldn't go to the book store. Thankfully, the room was just down the hall. Bracing myself, I stepped through the door and into a room reeking of incense. Instead of desks, rugs of various shapes, sizes, and designs lay at regular intervals on the floor.

A hand touched my arm. "Oh, you must be the Slade boy," said a middle-aged woman wearing what looked like a sari. She pushed back curly rings of brown hair from her face and looked me over with bright blue eyes. "Miles told me all about you." Her voice was soft and dreamy, but excited all at the same time.

"Nice to meet you, Professor."

"Belinda, please," she said smiling. "Here, let's get you a foundation and a totem." Before I could say another word, she led me to the wall where even more rugs hung. "Close your eyes, and let the universe guide you, Justin."

"Uh—"

"Close your eyes," she repeated in the voice a hypnotist might use and slid her hand across my eyelids. "Now, let the universe tell you which is the right foundation. Hold out your arm."

"Like this?" I said, keeping my eyes closed and extending an arm straight out in front.

"Exactly." She turned me around once. "Now walk forward and find your foundation."

I took two steps, tripped on something, and stumbled forward, barely catching myself on the wall.

Belinda exhaled a pleased sigh. "Open your eyes, and claim your foundation."

I followed her instructions and found myself leaning against a black rug with pink cats frolicking on it. "This one?"

She nodded. "And grab a token from the barrel next to the door without looking inside."

I pulled the rug from the rack on the wall and walked to the barrel. Avoiding the temptation to look inside, I reached in a hand and pulled out a plastic cat.

What is it with me and cats? I couldn't help but think of Stacey and Nightliss.

"How interesting," she said. "Now, please find a place for your foundation, take off your shoes, and relax."

I saw familiar faces in the room and realized it was the same group from first period. I set my rug next to the silver-haired girl in the back corner of the room. Again, I noticed the clear space around her.

"I'm Justin," I said, holding out my hand.

"Hi, Justin," she said, in a quiet voice, glancing at my hand, but not shaking it. "I'm Morgana."

I knew I was probably freaking her out, thanks to the huge age difference. I realized how Barry Papadopoulos must have felt back in grade school, and not because his name looked impossible to pronounce. He'd been homeschooled for years, but apparently his education hadn't been up to par. Instead of fifth grade, he'd been stuck all the way back in first grade with my group.

To us, he'd practically looked like a grownup, and we used to ask him all the hard questions: Where's the best place to buy candy? Which superhero has the coolest outfit? Why are girls so dumb?

I had a feeling these kids wouldn't be asking me for advice, especially after my humiliating first impression in Ms. Crab's class.

Once class started, it only got weirder. Belinda told us to stop, listen, and feel Gaia. It seemed more like a new age class than anything about magic. About the only feeling I got from Gaia was a cramp in my left butt cheek from sitting on the floor too long.

Arcane History came next. When I entered the room, the teacher looked up from a textbook and did a double take. My chest tightened. It was Zagg.

He narrowed his eyes and came over to me. "You have news?"

I nodded. "But that's not why I'm here."

"Wait a minute." Zagg's eyes went wide. He shuffled through a stack of papers and pulled out one with my name on it. "You're the late addition?"

My face heated up. "Yeah."

His eyebrows rose. "Sorry, but this is just, well, pathetic. What's someone your age doing taking Elementary Arcane History?"

"I don't know, but I'm sure my advisor had a good reason." If he didn't, I was going to kill him.

Zagg looked at the desks around the room, took one look at how tall I was, and shook his head. "There's an empty classroom just down the hall with adult desks."

I thanked him and went down the hall to grab one, moving an empty midget desk in the back row to make room. By the time I returned, my classmates filled the room, buzzing with chatter. I saw Morgana sitting in her usual back corner. She seemed to be the only person not talking.

The bell rang, and Zagg closed the classroom door. "Who's the founder?" he said in a loud, exuberant voice.

"Ezzek Moore!" everyone shouted.

"What was his favorite color?"

Shouts ranging from gray to pink went up from the kids.

Zagg laughed. "Did he like chocolate?"

Kids giggled and looked around at each other, obviously unsure of the answer.

Zagg regarded them with an amused look for a moment and then said, "Of course he loved chocolate. Who doesn't?"

What did chocolate have to do with anything? Screw this elementary education. What was next on the menu—hand puppets?

Zagg leapt atop his desk, a staff gripped in his hand. "Today you're going to hear about Ezzek's fight with Giuseppe Garibaldi. Can anyone tell me who Giuseppe was?"

A boy in front shot his hand up ahead of several other classmates and answered when Zagg nodded. "He was a bad man who didn't want Ezzek to make a united council of Arcanes."

Zagg's staff bloomed into light. "That's right!"

The next thing I knew, Zagg was playing both sides of an epic battle between Moore and Garibaldi, harmless lights zapping back and forth while students watched in rapt attention. Before I knew it, class was over, and Zagg left us hanging on the outcome of the fight. I wasn't the only one saying, "Aww," when he told us we'd find out what happened next tomorrow.

After the students filed out, I told Zagg that Michael was looking into Kayla's case.

Relief swept into his eyes, and he gripped my hand with both of his, shaking it vigorously. "Thank you so much."

"He isn't promising a happy outcome," I warned him.

"I know. I know." He released my hand. "But it's better than her rotting away in prison with no hope at all." Zagg dropped onto a stool and wiped sweat from his forehead. Apparently, his teaching method took quite a bit of energy. "Sometimes, hope is all we have, you know?"

His little truth hit close to home. I nodded. "Yeah. Sometimes it is."

Lunch came next, according to my schedule. I left the classroom and followed the path the university app gave me to the cafeteria. The delicious odor of roasted chicken drifted into my nose, and I dared dream the food here might be better than the slop served at my former high school.

The cafeteria looked more like a grand dining hall with rows of wooden tables lining the room and giant candelabras hanging overhead. Students of all ages occupied the tables, though I noticed the age groups didn't seem to mingle. I looked around the room and failed to find a serving line staffed by uncaring lunchroom ladies. I glanced at a nearby table and noticed everyone had a plate with fresh veggies and a juicy chicken leg. My mouth watered.

As I cast about the room for the elusive lunch line, I spotted Ivy sitting alone at one of the tables. In fact, even the tables near her were empty. I noticed other students looking at her, some of them with what looked like fear.

"Ivy?"

"Justin!" she said, eyes lighting up.

"I didn't know we had lunch at the same time."

She gave me a conspiratorial grin. "They don't usually let me eat lunch in here."

"Who, your grandparents?"

"Bigmomma makes my lunches, but today I sneaked in here." She sighed. "I don't like being alone."

I took a seat. A golem appeared a moment later, a covered plate in hand. The creator had painted a face and clothes onto the server, giving it an almost surreal appearance, as though it had leapt from the pages of a fairy tale and ended up with a rather mundane job in a school cafeteria. With a flourish, it set the plate on the table, uncovered it, and departed.

"It's good," Ivy said, picking at her food.

I resisted the urge to pepper her with questions about the Conroys, Daelissa, or the impending end of the world, and opted to keep things away from business. *If I can become her friend, maybe I can win her trust.* Although that wasn't my only motivation. "Don't you have friends you could sit with?" I asked, digging into the roasted chicken.

Her eyes looked sad. "I don't make a lot of friends. I think they're jealous of how strong I am."

I could see that. "Have you tried talking to anyone?"

She took a carving knife and jabbed it into the chicken, as if killing it. "I tried. But they call me names." Her eyes went hard and cold. "It makes me really angry when they do that." She stared intently at the chicken, lips pursed, eyebrows pinched.

"Are you okay?" I asked.

Ivy jerked as if woken from a dream. "Yeah." She took a bite of the chicken, but it didn't look like she was enjoying it.

I spotted a flash of bright silver hair and saw Morgana sitting alone at a table. "I'll be right back," I said, and walked over to the other girl. She looked up at me, eyes worried, her face set in something resembling resignation. "Would you like to join me and my sister for lunch?" I asked, nodding my head toward Ivy.

"Really?" she asked, her face masked with disbelief. "That's your sister?"

I smiled. "Yes, really."

"And you want me to sit with you?"

"I sure do."

She bit her lower lip. Nodded. "Okay."

I helped her with her tray, and we joined Ivy. I introduced them to each other.

"Hello, Ivy," Morgana said. "You have a pretty dress."

Ivy stared at the young girl for a long moment, her eyes flicking back and forth between me and her. A smile quirked her lip. "What happened to your hair?"

Morgana looked down at her plate. "It—it's always been like that."

Ivy chewed on a piece of chicken. "Looks weird."

"Ivy!" I said. "That's not nice."

"Well, it does," she said, wrinkling her forehead.

"I think her hair is pretty," I said. "It's unique. Do you see anyone else with silver hair in here?"

Ivy scanned the room. "No, but that doesn't mean—"

"You said you don't like it when people call you names. Telling someone their hair is weird is not nice." I looked and saw a big tear rolling down Morgana's cheek as she stared disconsolately at her food. I felt absolutely horrible. This had been a mistake. I'd thought Ivy was somewhat normal, but instead, she was just cruel.

"I'm sorry," Ivy said, surprising me and reaching her hand across to touch Morgana's. "I didn't mean to make you cry."

Morgana wiped away tears. "It's okay. The others do it all the time."

Ivy's face went hard. "They do it to me, too."

"They do? But you're Ivy Conroy." A look of reverence overcame Morgana's face. "You're the smartest girl here."

My sister's face brightened. "You really think so?"

Morgana nodded. "I wish I was strong like you."

Ivy looked at Morgana's shimmering locks of silver hair. "Justin, you're right. Her hair is very pretty."

A wave of relief spread through me at Ivy's shift from cruel to nice. Maybe she just didn't know any better. Miraculously, we managed to carry on a somewhat normal conversation about hair colors for several minutes before a bell clanged in the distance.

Ivy's face fell. "Well, I guess lunch is over."

"Will you be here tomorrow?" I asked.

She shrugged. "Maybe. Sometimes I can't sneak away." She pushed away from the table and stood, leaned over and gave me a hug. "I'm glad we got to see each other," she whispered.

"Me too," I said. Before I could rise and give her a proper hug, she vanished into the crowd.

"I wish I was like your sister," Morgana said.

A part of me realized she already was. Neither of them seemed to have any friends, and they both seemed too sad to be so young. "Why do you sit alone?" I asked.

She nibbled on a cookie as a sea of students flowed past, leaving for the exits, some laughing, others carrying on serious conversations, and most of them regarding Morgana with strange looks. I wondered if it was because of her hair, or if there might be more.

But the young girl never answered my question.

When I looked past the silver hair, I noticed dark circles under her eyes and the pale cast of her skin. Whatever problems she had were probably affecting her sleep. I decided not to pry. Sometimes there were things I just couldn't fix no matter how much I wanted to. I had to hope my sister wasn't one of those things.

After lunch, I had two more classes. The first was Reading and Writing Cyrinthian with Miss Quinn, a prim and proper older woman who seemed the exact opposite of Belinda. Magical Safety came next, taught by Mr. Rivers, a grumpy old man with a huge, bald head and wide, horn-rimmed glasses. If anything, it reminded me of shop class. The day's lesson consisted of holding a wand by the correct end and how to stop, drop, and roll should someone catch on fire when holding the business end of the wand toward their body when they cast a spell. I nearly fell asleep.

In both classes, Morgana and I sat in our usual spots in the back corner of the room. I took notice of other students as they kept wary eyes on the girl, and curiosity urged me to ask her more questions. But after class, she vanished into the crowd. Before I could track her down, a stick figure golem with round, articulated joints and a basketball-shaped head walked up to me and handed me a folded bit of parchment with a wax seal on it. A stamp beneath the seal said, "University Mail System". I broke the seal and opened the letter to find a brief note in neatly penned ink.

Your dear aunt requests the pleasure of your company at the fountain in the rear gardens at two thirty.

Vallaena had arrived.

Chapter 24

I followed a route recommended by the handy-dandy university app to the rear gardens. It took me through winding halls, past a huge gymnasium where students played what looked like basketball on flying carpets, and out the east side of the castle where a stone path led toward one of the exquisitely manicured gardens I'd noticed from the bluff where the shuttles landed.

Flowers of all colors and sizes bloomed from shrubs grown to resemble giant mushrooms, candy canes, and more, like a scene straight from Candy Land. As I walked across a rubbery licorice bridge and gazed at the bubbling brook of chocolate beneath, I wondered if it would actually be safe to eat anything here. If so, I imagined an obesity epidemic rampaging through school.

A wide, stone path between the garden and the castle complex led to the huge stadium I'd seen earlier. In the distance, I heard rumbling, like the low thunder of an earthquake. Checking the time, I saw I still had fifteen minutes to meet Vallaena, so I detoured toward the stadium. The walkway, lined by flags imprinted with the names of champions from years prior, bordered the stadium. A portcullis guarded an entrance designed to admit giants at the front of the structure. The metal grate hung several feet off the ground, so I walked beneath it just as the ground shook beneath my feet. I followed a cavernous tunnel toward a grassy field.

My jaw dropped the moment I emerged. Two gargantuan creatures lumbered up and down the field, each one something out of my wildest nerd fantasies. One of the three-story creatures looked cobbled together from stone. The other looked like animated earth, comprised of mud, twigs, and other natural debris. Even though their forms bore a humanoid resemblance, they had no faces. Two Arcanes whooped from the sidelines, high-fiving each other as the golems raced up and down the field, churning up earth with their massive feet.

The mud golem made another turn, and ran back toward the Arcanes, every lumbering step sending a shockwave through the earth. It suddenly froze in mid-stride, one of its thick legs crumbling. The creature slammed against the ground, sending mud and bits of debris flying everywhere. The shrapnel bounced harmlessly off a shield around the inner perimeter of the track.

"No!" shouted the two men.

One of them waved a staff toward the stone golem, and it stopped in place, towering over everything like a humanoid mountain. If these were the kinds of golems they used for the Grand Melee, there was no way in the world I wanted to miss it.

I could have stared at the spectacle all day, but duty called. I jogged back to the candy gardens and found Vallaena sitting on a stone bench. Behind her, the statue of a female arcane held aloft a staff fountaining red liquid. My aunt wore a dark blue dress, knee-length, with matching flats. The plain ensemble did nothing to detract from her classic beauty, her straight narrow nose, full lips, the graceful curves of her body. In fact, the demure look only seemed to highlight just how hot she was.

Gross, dude, she's your aunt!

I felt a flush creep up my neck.

"Hello, Justinius," Vallaena said, smiling sweetly as a gentle breeze picked at her blonde locks.

Resolving to be as nice as possible despite the lack of trust I felt toward this woman, I put on a smile of my own. "Hello, Vallaena." I sat next to her. "What's up?"

Her blue eyes looked me up and down. "You've grown since I last saw you."

"Puberty," I said.

She shook her head. "No, it's something more than that." She peered into my eyes with uncomfortable intensity. "You are no longer the confused boy I first met, but a young man. A leader. Your father would be proud."

I stiffened at the mention of my dad and looked away.

"Though I see you aren't yet ready to accept some realities." Vallaena touched the top of my hand. "Duty weighs heavily on your father, Justinius. Do not hate him for the choices he must make."

"Call me Justin," I said, trying not to acknowledge her statement or allow it to make me feel guilty. "What do I need to learn first?"

"Protocol. It is extremely important to Daemos." She stood, brushing a lock of blonde hair from her face as a breeze ruffled it. "Once I feel you are adequately versed, you will learn summoning."

"Like hellhounds and demons?" I asked, still sitting on the bench.

She nodded. "Yes, but it goes deeper." She held out a hand. "Take my hand."

I regarded the fair skin of her hand with suspicion before taking it, wondering if Daemos protocol meant I had to kiss her knuckles or something. A surprised yelp escaped my throat when she yanked me to my feet like I weighed nothing. It was easy to underestimate someone's strength when they looked like Vallaena.

An amused smile crossed her face.

I suppressed a snarky comment.

Still holding my hand, she led me through the gardens, past pools of bubbling fudge, chocolate-brown bunny rabbits nibbling on green licorice grass, and all sorts of candy-themed plants, trees, and animals. I touched a flower on one of the trees. It felt like normal vegetation.

"None of this is candy," Vallaena said, as if reading my thoughts. "The animals are real, though they wear illusions to make them appear edible."

"They're still edible," I said.

She laughed. "True, though the gardeners would likely be very unhappy with you."

We passed out of the garden, took the walkway past the stadium, and cut across the wide green field between the school and the dark forest where my new best buddy, the tragon, lived.

"Why are we coming out here?" I asked, gazing at her with narrowed eyes.

"I know you don't trust me," Vallaena said. "Please believe I only have your best interests at heart."

"More like *your* best interests," I said.

"What is good for you is good for all our people," she said. "I am here to teach you, nothing more."

I stopped and said, "Before we get into all that protocol stuff, I want you to tell me more about manifesting."

She raised an eyebrow. "Manifesting is related to summoning and banishment."

My forehead scrunched. "Huh?"

"We summon a part of ourselves when we manifest, and banish it again to return to normal," Vallaena replied.

Her explanation made sense. It certainly felt as if I were summoning a demon when I manifested, though lately the vampling curse made it feel like the demon was banishing me instead. "I've been having issues," I said, after a moment's hesitation. Despite my misgivings, I knew she was the only one who could probably help me in this area. I told her about my issues, the curse, and how I'd nearly lost control during the battle with Zagg.

Her eyes went wide at the mention of the vampling curse, and for the first time, worry clouded her face. She put a hand to her chin as she thought. "This is not good." She paced for a moment. "We do not possess immunity to Seraphim curses."

My stomach went cold. "Is there a cure?"

Vallaena stopped, gave me a look which bordered on sorrow. "I am unsure."

I waved off the subject. "It doesn't matter." Meghan's potion gave me time, and I had to hope I could unlock my Seraphim side and heal myself. "I need to know how to control the manifestation, especially with the curse trying to take over."

She gave me a sad look. "I can explain part of your problems. Spontaneous manifestation is a problem young Daemos males face during puberty. Females can control the urge, but males cannot help themselves."

I groaned. "Gee, that sounds familiar."

"Indeed." A smile flashed across her face. "The vampling curse may be a trigger, but even without it, your hormonal urges would also trigger manifestation, especially under stressful situations."

"The curse is definitely stressing me out." I ran a hand through my hair. "What can I do to stop it?"

"I can teach you how to properly summon your demon form."

"I'm listening," I said.

Vallaena continued. "We are not morphs—not in the way lycans and other shifters are."

"Or like Flarks?"

Alarm showed in her eyes. "There are Flarks in the game now?"

Apocalyptic problems were hardly a game, but I didn't feel like bringing that up with her. "There's one. Do you know about them?"

Her upper lip curled with distaste. "In my studies, I learned Flarks are creatures from the Seraphim world. They are the devoted servants of the angels."

I remembered what Mr. Bigglesworth had said. If I knew anything about Flarks, then I'd know why he was helping Daelissa. "Devoted servants," I said. "Their loyalty lies foremost to the angels."

"Naturally," Vallaena said with a shrug.

In other words, Bigglesworth was only helping the Conroys because Daelissa wanted him to. Maybe he felt loyalty toward Ivy because she was part angel. Maybe he regarded her as an abomination. With Daelissa holding his reins, he was a danger to my sister. As for the Conroys—they weren't even relatives, just power-hungry Arcanes who'd kidnapped my sister and had now imprisoned my mother. Bigglesworth could eat them, for all I cared.

"You are not telling me something," Vallaena said.

I quirked an eyebrow. "Are you kidding me? There's a lot I'm not telling you."

A nod. "Very well. Perhaps I will earn your trust. I am here to help, after all."

"Great, you can start by helping me control my spontaneous manifestation issue first." I sighed. "It's really embarrassing."

She smiled. "I understand." Her eyes scanned me up and down. "I think you should strip before we begin." She slid the strap of her dress off one shoulder, and reached for the other.

I grabbed her arm. "Whoa, whoa, wait! I'm not getting naked with you. What are you doing?"

Her forehead wrinkled in surprise, as if I'd just asked her why grass didn't scream when you walked on it. "Your clothes will be ruined if you leave them on. I can, of course, control my manifestation, but I also wished to show you my full form. I just purchased this dress on sale, and am not about to ruin it."

I could only stare incredulously at her.

She returned an indignant glare. "Just because I have money doesn't mean I spend it foolishly. I refuse to feel guilty for bargain hunting." She motioned at my clothes. "At the very least, strip down to your underwear. I know how smitten you are with that Templar girl of yours, and how brainwashed you are by human values of love and sex. I will respect your corrupted notions."

Since I'd already wrecked a perfectly good pair of jeans and one of my favorite shirts in the fight with Bigglesworth and subsequent spontaneous manifestation against Zagg, I relented, and stripped to my boxer briefs.

Vallaena removed every last stitch of her clothing and folded it neatly into her purse. She pulled a pair of yoga pants and a sports bra from within, slipping them on. They hung loose from her frame, though I figured it was by design.

She knelt, examining the black stain on my calf where the vampling fangs had penetrated the skin. The wounds still looked puckered and fresh. I noticed a scrape on my leg I must have sustained the night before. It wasn't severe, but I usually healed within minutes of an injury. The blood seemed to have clotted, but my blighted skin wasn't healing. Blackened veins ran up through my thigh, vanishing past the hem of my boxer-briefs. Either the potion wasn't working, or trauma accelerated the curse's spread.

Vallaena traced the dark veins up my leg with a fingernail.

"Hey, now," I said, dancing back. "No touching, please."

She shook her head. "How could the foreseeance be wrong?"

I realized she was talking about Foreseeance 4311. "Foreseeances can be wrong," I said.

Vallaena gave me a sad panda face. "Justin, at the rate the curse is spreading, you will not survive the month."

My heart seemed to stop dead. My back muscles knotted. It took a moment before I could speak, and even then my words sounded hoarse with tension. "Guess I'd better learn fast then." She had to be wrong. But what if she wasn't?

My aunt murmured something to herself, and shook her head. Looking up at me, she said, "There may be one cure."

A little flutter of hope started my heartbeat again. "Are you trying to give me a heart attack? Why didn't you say something earlier?"

She stood, looking me in the eye. "Because it is next to impossible to find."

I didn't like the sound of that. "How hard?"

Vallaena took both of my hands, and squeezed them. "Justin, you must eat the heart of an angel."

Chapter 25

I nearly choked on my own tongue. "Eat the heart of a freaking angel? How am I supposed to do that?"

"As I said, it is nearly impossible."

Jerking my hands from hers, I backed up a step. "Okay, let's say I kidnap Daelissa, cut out her heart, and eat it. What makes you think it'll cure anything? It might just give me indigestion."

She pressed a hand to her chest. "Our hearts are where we store our powers, our emotions, our very core."

"No, all that stuff comes from our brains. And I don't think I could eat any kind of brains, not even from an animal." I made a gagging noise. "That's just gross."

"True," she said with a nod. "Our brains process what we do, but it all passes through the heart. When our kind feeds, we channel essence through our hearts. Angels feed in much the same way, though they winnow the essence into purer forms, dissecting the spectrum between dark and light."

"How does this mean eating a heart would cure me?" I asked.

Vallaena steepled her fingers. "Because Brightlings created the vampling curse, they are immune to it. Eating a heart would channel their pure essence into you and cleanse you."

"Are you sure this isn't a crazy myth?" I said, shaking my head. "Angel hearts sound like something you'd find in the canned pasta aisle in a grocery store, for crying out loud."

"Let me give you a history lesson, nephew," Vallaena said. "Many eons ago, our people joined with the Darklings to combat the Brightlings. The enemy used curses against us, some more terrible than the vampling curse. Though the Darklings had some defense against these attacks, the Daemos had no such immunity. One of our infected warriors embarked on a suicide mission to kill a Seraphim. He succeeded. As he lay dying from his wounds and a curse, he ate the angel heart as a final insult."

Gross! I shuddered at the thought of eating a raw heart.

Vallaena continued. "According to the legend, it healed him completely, mind, body, and soul." She gave me a pointed look. "If this story is not simply legend, it means an angel heart could cure you. And you are our last hope, Justin."

I scratched my chin. "Gee, that sounds like a line from a movie."

She scowled. "Do not make light of this. If you die, our chances for defeating Daelissa and the Brightlings dims considerably. They will enslave mortals and Daemos alike."

And take away the power you crave. I threw up my hands. "No pressure, huh, Vallaena? Good lord, you're going to give me anxiety attacks with talk like that." I blew out a breath. "Look, you may be right. If I happen to get my hands on Daelissa, I'll be sure to eat her heart, okay?"

"There is another possibility." Her eyes narrowed. "The one they call Nightliss."

"Oh, hell no, woman. If you think for a minute I'd hurt her, you need your head examined."

"But what if she were to sacrifice herself for you?" Vallaena said. "She could save you. Save us all."

I slashed the air with my hand. "End. Of. Discussion." I really hated to separate all my words with a period but my dear aunt needed to receive the message loud and clear. "I will die before I do anything to harm her."

Vallaena sighed long and deep. "You're so melodramatic at times."

"And you're bat-poo crazy sometimes." I offered her a tight smile. "Now, can we get back to demonology one-oh-one?"

Her typical cool demeanor returned. "Very well. Let us begin."

Then she punched me in the stomach.

I doubled over, and felt the air rush from my lungs as my legs left the ground. I flew backward through the air, landing on a jagged rock that cut into my bare skin. I cried out in pain. Rage flushed my skin with heat. Vallaena was on top of me before I could get up, her body a blur of motion. She punched me on the bridge of my nose. Stars burst into my eyes. When they cleared, I saw Vallaena leap to her feet, a sneer on her face.

I managed to climb to my feet. "What the hell you stupid—" I forgot my next words.

My aunt's skin shifted to a cold shade of blue. Beneath it, coils of muscle writhed, bulged, and grew. She went from average height to over six feet, as curving ebony horns grew from her head like plants growing in a time-lapse video, blonde hair lengthening until it hung halfway down her back. Instead of turning into a monstrous clawed creature of death, she stopped. Her breasts bulged against the athletic bra, while her hips and bottom filled out the yoga pants with tantalizing curves. She looked every inch like a seductive queen of pain.

"I will tear out your heart," she said, baring white teeth, and growling before lunging at me.

I ducked under her first thrust, and punched her stomach. She grabbed me by the neck, and slammed me to earth with a solid thud. In a blur, she straddled me. Gripped my underwear with one hand. "You won't even want your puny girlfriend after I'm done having my way with you."

The awe and fear at her unexpected attack melted in an instant. "Nobody but Elyssa will ever experience that," I said and let the rage burn through my veins. The demon burst from its cage. I roared in pain as I felt that part of me claw its way free. My body shuddered, muscles swelled. Pinpoints of pressure in my forehead exploded in pure agony as horns burst from my skull.

"And, hold it there!" Vallaena said, abruptly leaping from my chest and jerking me to my feet by my hand.

I lost my hold on the rage as confusion sucker-punched me in the brain. "What?" I said, my voice a mix of its usual timbre and menacing, guttural depth. I stood slightly taller than my aunt. Blue and peach tones splotched my skin. My right leg bulged with muscles while the other wasn't quite as pumped up, causing me to stand a little lopsided, and my right arm looked just as scrawny by comparison. The demonic force inside me pressed and fought against my will, demanding I let it break free. I pushed back, against the pain, barely managing to hold it off.

"I would apologize for the attack," Vallaena said, "but it was the fastest way to make you lose control and release your spirit."

"You wanted to make me angry." I staggered as my demon side surged against my will.

She shook her head. "We exist in two worlds, Justin. We are corporeal, but we are also spiritual. That part of us exists in the demon realm. When you lose your temper, you lose control over your spirit. This is one reason why you manifest without wanting to."

"We're possessed by demons?"

"No, we are the demon, and the demon is us. We are one and the same, but coexisting in two different realms. It is both our strength and our weakness. Our physical bodies require food. Our spiritual nature requires essence from other living beings." She took my hand, and turned it palm up.

I looked at my hand, at the blue skin, the black fingernails. It remained human in shape, but huge.

"One part of your spirit wants to be free to do as it wishes. The other part understands control and restraint, Justin. It has a conscience. This is the first step in learning to control that dual nature."

"Brings a whole new meaning to free spirited," I said, looking at my half-morphed form. "But I'm a bit off kilter."

She smiled, her perfect white teeth contrasting with her blue skin. "You will learn."

And then the lessons began in earnest. For the next couple of hours, she forced me to lose control again and again, stopping me just before I went completely berzerk. Thankfully, it didn't involve grabbing my underwear.

After practice, I went back to the dorm room. I saw Shelton munching on a large pizza while Cinder observed him from a seat. I grabbed a piece and inhaled it. "Man, that is so good," I moaned.

Cinder's eyes met mine. "I think it would be interesting to eat food."

"You don't need to eat at all?" I asked.

"I require neither food nor sleep, though I can process food if I wish. But I only sense the textures, and none of the flavor, so it is a wasted exercise. I believe the emotion I feel at this inability would be called depression."

"This is the part where you sigh," I told him, and demonstrated a sad sigh.

Cinder mimicked me almost perfectly but still didn't come across in a very convincing manner. I grabbed another piece, and let out another moan of pleasure.

"Justin," Cinder said, retrieving his phone from the inner pocket of his gray suit jacket. "When you were whining the other day—"

"Whining? I don't whine."

Cinder tilted his head ever so slightly. "Is not whining a nasal or complaining sound? Or to snivel and complain in a peevish self-pitying way?"

Shelton laughed. "He's got a point."

I pursed my lips and gave Cinder a dirty look.

He stared back without blinking.

"Yes, fine, okay, I guess I do whine sometimes." I took a bite of pizza and spoke with my mouth full. "What was your point?"

"As I was saying, when you were whining the other day about how often you are forced to repeat your history, I decided it might be appropriate to make a transcript. I took the liberty of recording your words with my phone, and transcribed it into a document." He pushed his phone across to me, and I skimmed over the text. It was dry and to the point, but was, essentially, a synopsis of my crazy life since discovering I was an incubus.

"This is why I love you, Cinder," I said, scrolling down the document.

Cinder cocked his head slightly. "Do you feel romantically toward me, or is this an indication of agape love?" he asked, his voice never wavering in pitch.

Shelton's drink sprayed from his mouth.

I woke up extra early the next morning and purchased my school books. Even with a book and most of my mental faculties intact, Ms. Crab still treated me like a moron. The remaining classes were much the same as before, with Zagg's class being my favorite. The man had a way of telling stories, like a bard with a magic staff. Ivy wasn't at lunch, much to my disappointment, so I joined Morgana and made small talk, trying to figure out why she avoided other students. My gentle prying yielded nothing but her shrinking further into a shell.

After classes, I met with Vallaena again for a daily dose of Demonic 101. By the time I ate supper, I was ready for night-night beddy-bye time. I checked my phone for the umpteenth time that day, hoping Elyssa had finally messaged me. Instead, I found only a little stab of disappointment at the blank notification screen.

The rest of the week rolled by, each day absolutely stuffed to the gills with instructional work and even homework. I kept an eye out for my sister, but didn't see her once. I wondered if she'd gotten in trouble for going to lunch that one day, and worried about her. Morgana asked about her every day, never failing to look sad when she didn't show.

When Friday afternoon arrived, a buoyant sense of relief lightened my heart at the thought of a free weekend. Even Vallaena's attempts to make me lose control had less effect than usual. After my lessons with her, I practically skipped back to the dorm. The usual exhaustion had melted away in the face of the immense amount of chill time I planned to enjoy.

My phone buzzed with a message, and my heart danced. I nearly dropped the phone trying to view the message. But it wasn't from Elyssa. It was from Meghan.

Justin, Nightliss wants to see you. She's not doing well.

Worry shattered the relief, and weighed my heart like lead. I showed Shelton the message, and his eye twitched.

"You're telling me the main weapon in our arsenal is still sick?" he said.

I nodded. "Sounds like it."

We took the shuttle down to the arch station the next morning. Apparently, the Gloom cracks weren't a public menace anymore, because people lined up to take the Obsidian Arch. Shelton saw the line and groaned. He motioned me to follow him, and we made our way around to the control room where we found the Arcane operators. Using our fake Darkwater story, we convinced the operator to let us go through next.

"So I hear you guys got the small arch back at the Grotto working," the operator said as he escorted us outside.

I almost let surprise show on my face before catching it, and nodding. Shelton never missed a beat, giving the man a calm shrug.

"What exactly did you hear about it?" he asked, a look of suspicion on his face.

The operator's face creased in concern. "Uh, just that it was working, but they hadn't sent anyone live through it yet."

Shelton nodded. "Might be best kept to yourself." He waved his hand between him and me. "We're around to make sure info doesn't leak. You come to us with anything else. And don't tell anyone about us. Understand?"

"Y-yes sir." The operator bobbed his head up and down. "I don't want to get anyone in trouble."

Shelton clapped him on the back. "Hey, no problem. We're not as bad as the old man, if you know what I mean. If we can warn people to stay quiet before you-know-who finds out, then everyone is better off."

The man seemed to breathe a sigh of relief. "Good." He went to open the door, and hesitated. "I did hear one other thing from an operator back at the Grotto. He said the Gloom fractures were caused by the work they were doing on the smaller arch, but they think they figured out how to keep it from happening again."

"That is definitely something you want to keep on the down-low," Shelton said, giving the man a sly wink. "The public would freak if they knew."

"I will. And I'll be sure to let you know if I hear anything else."

"Tell the others, too." He gave the man his number, and we left.

"Being a fake Darkwater employee has benefits," I said as we waltzed directly to the arch, waited for it to flicker on, and stepped through to the Grotto.

Shelton and I emerged on the other side, both of us braced to combat any Gloom fractures the moment we set foot on the polished stone floor. Thankfully, the operator's theory about the Gloom fractures seemed to hold true. Minders still patrolled the perimeter around the arch, their creepy forms drifting uncomfortably close as we left the striped safety zone line around the arch.

We found Shelton's car still in its parking slot, and took it to Meghan's house.

"I'm so glad you're here," the Arcane healer said, a tired note in her voice. She brushed a lock of blonde hair from her face and waved us to follow her in.

The moment I stepped inside, I smelled something. The odor wasn't unpleasant exactly, but it reminded me of an old-folks home and baby powder. My insides tightened at the thought. Meghan showed us to a bedroom where a small form lay beneath heavy blankets. I walked up to the bed, disbelief warring with sorrow as I looked upon the gaunt face surrounded by tangles of black hair streaked with gray.

Meghan took my hand, and looked me in the eye. "Justin, she's dying. I don't think she has much longer."

Chapter 26

"Nightliss?" I said, my voice cracking with pain. Her cheeks looked hollow, and her eyes sunken.

The angel's eyelids fluttered open, and blinked a few times before her eyes found me. "Justin?" She struggled to pull an arm from beneath the covers.

I pulled back the cover to help, and gasped when I saw the loose skin and bones of her arm. "What's wrong with her?" I asked Meghan, my voice sounding plaintive.

"Daelissa's curse," Meghan said from the doorway. "I thought I'd removed it all, but apparently it was beyond my ability. I only gave her a slow wasting away instead of a fast death."

"It is okay," Nightliss said, her voice sounding like an old lady's. She smiled, but her bony, protruding cheeks looked gruesome. She made the poster child for anorexia look fleshy by comparison.

"Oh, god," I said. "What can we do? There must be something."

"Only Daelissa or another Brightling could cure me," the little angel said.

"My mom can!" I jumped up, mind racing to think of how I could possibly contact her. All I had to do was figure out where the Conroys lived. "I'll ask Ivy."

"No," Nightliss rasped. "Too dangerous."

Meghan stepped inside the room, and stood near me. "While you're here, I wanted to check on your leg."

"Is it worse?" Nightliss asked.

"Don't worry about me," I said, standing up. "Worry about Nightliss."

"I have to worry about you," Meghan said. "Even if I can't do anything, about it, I want to make sure the potion is working."

"Justin, I can help." Nightliss motioned to me with just her fingers since she apparently couldn't move her arm very much.

I thought of her blood in the potion. "You've done too much already," I said. I didn't want her overextending.

"Vallaena told me—"

I sprang to my feet. "What?"

Sorrow creased the angel's brow. "My heart, Justin."

I took deep breaths to combat the rage roiling through my blood at the thought of Vallaena coming here and telling Nightliss about our conversation. I spun to Meghan. "How the hell did Vallaena find out where Nightliss was?"

The healer shrugged. "She called, and said she needed to see Nightliss on your behalf. I assumed—"

"That lying little…" I swallowed my next words, and ground my teeth as the desire to punch a wall wrestled with my rational mind.

"Justin!" Nightliss must have used all her strength to shout my name, because she sank even deeper into her pillow after doing it, eyelids fluttering.

I sat on the edge of the bed, taking her hand in mind as the anger fled, replaced by pain. "What is it?"

She swallowed, grimacing. Took in a breath. "My heart is yours. Take it, please. The world needs you."

I looked away as hot tears sprang into my eyes. "No. I won't do it."

"I am dying. Make my life count."

"Your life already counts," I said. "And it's going to keep on counting, damn it." I couldn't hold back the flood and felt tears running down my cheeks. "I won't let you die."

"It's too late for that," she said, her breathing growing shallow. Her eyes closed, and her arm went limp.

"No!" I shouted, pressing a hand to her neck, looking for a pulse.

Meghan pushed me aside, running her wand along the small angel's body. She breathed in relief. "She lives." Her red-rimmed eyes met mine. "Justin, I don't think she has more than a week left, and even that estimate might be generous." The healer gripped my hand and led me into the den where Shelton sat drinking coffee.

He looked up at me with a bloodshot gaze. "We're screwed, aren't we? Nightliss is dying. The vampling curse is eating you alive." Pressing the heels of his hands into his eyes, he groaned. "Guess I'd better enjoy the free life while it's still around."

"Shelton, shut up," Meghan said, a scowl on her face. She handed me a tissue. "Is it true about Nightliss's heart?"

I wiped my eyes, and blew my nose. Shrugged. "Vallaena seems to think so. All she has to go on is some Daemos legend from the war with the Brightlings." I told her the story.

"It could be true," Meghan said. "It's also true Nightliss may die soon, and your chance of a cure may die with her."

"She isn't going to die," I growled. Knuckles cracked as my hands balled into fists. "I won't let her."

"How, exactly, do you propose to do that?" Meghan asked.

"My mom." I strode back into Nightliss's room, and choked back the pain of seeing her in such a state. She'd always been so full of life. So beautiful. So sweet. That Daelissa could do such a thing to so selfless a person made me sick. I leaned down and kissed her on the forehead. "I'm here for you," I murmured. "I'm your friend, and I love you. I will cure you." I kissed her hand, and tucked it back under the blanket.

Shelton looked up from the table, his face miserable. I gave him a curt wave. "Come on. We're going."

"Where?" he asked.

"Back to the school. Somehow, I'm going to convince Ivy to tell me where Mom is so she can cure Nightliss." I stopped in my tracks, mind racing through possibilities. *Can Ivy cure Nightliss?* It was probably ridiculous to think Ivy might help. Would she even help me with Mom?

"Look, Justin, I don't think you need me there anymore," Shelton said.

"You're abandoning me?" I said, my voice sounding more hurt than I thought it should.

He looked away. "You're taking classes, you'rc all set. Why do you need me hanging around?"

"To help me find the Cyrinthian Rune. To watch my back if Bigglesworth or the Conroys try anything. To help me find my mom." I sighed and rubbed my forehead, trying to calm my breathing. Why did everyone always end up leaving me? Mom, Dad, Elyssa, and now Shelton? *Stop feeling sorry for yourself.* "You know what? Mission accomplished. Go home. Cinder can watch my back."

"I feel like I did more harm than good," he said, still not looking at me. "With Zagg and that mess."

"Yeah, you made mistakes. They came back to haunt you. Big deal." I shook my head and walked toward the door. "Guess it's easier to hide from the past than it is to fix the present." I heard Shelton say something, but opened the door and slammed it behind me. Once outside, I realized we'd come in Shelton's car, and he had the keys. So much for a dramatic exit. Then again, I didn't need a stinking car. I could just run, though it might be tricky in broad daylight.

I heard the rumbling of a powerful engine in the near distance, and saw Shelton's souped-up pickup truck round the curve and screech to a halt in front of Meghan's. Bella hopped down from the tall cab, and smiled when she saw me.

"Justin!" She hurried over and gave me a hug. "Meghan told me you two were here. I take it the arch at Queens Gate is working again?"

"Yeah," I said in a mumble.

Her smiled faded, and a concerned look came over her face. "What's wrong?"

"Nightliss is dying, and she wants me to eat her heart to cure my vampling curse."

The petite dhampyr's eyes went wide. "Oh, dear." She paused, her eyes examining my lips. "You didn't take her up on the offer, did you?"

I blew out a breath. "Of course not. Can I have the keys to Shelton's truck?" I held out a hand. "I need to get back to the Grotto."

She quirked an eyebrow. "Why isn't Harry driving you?"

"He's done reliving the college experience."

Bella pursed her lips. "He's giving up, isn't he?"

"I guess. Can I have the keys?"

Bella squeezed my hand. "I'll talk to him, Justin. He's just being an old mule."

I shook my head. "No. I'd prefer it if you didn't. I don't want him around if he doesn't want to be."

"But, you need someone to watch your back." Her violet eyes grew wide.

"If I have to beg him to come, what's the point?"

Bella put a finger to her chin. "Did Lina find you?"

I nodded.

"She's a sweet girl, and her training is coming along marvelously from what her grandfather told me." The dhampyr flashed a grin. "I'll ask her to help."

"I don't know if that's a good idea."

Bella waved away my concern. "It's a wonderful idea. I'm sure Elyssa will be done with her Templar duties soon, and she'll be along to save the day." She paused, eyes lighting up as if some new idea had jabbed an electrical current directly into her brain. "In fact, you know what?"

I felt my concern deepen. "What?"

"I'm coming, too."

"Um, but where will you stay?"

"In the dorm, of course." She smiled, and pinched my cheek. "This will be so much fun. I really miss college." She gave the house a sideways glance. "Well, let's go. Do you want to drive?"

"Aren't you going inside Meghan's house?" I asked. "Don't you want to say hi to Shelton?"

Bella shook her head, violet eyes turning serious. "I'm sorry, but Harry has disappointed me too many times. I'm so angry with him right now, I might do something bad to him."

"You don't look that angry."

She grinned. "Centuries of practice, young man."

We hopped in the truck. A quick twist of the key in the ignition and it rumbled to life. I pulled out from the curb, casting one last glance at Meghan's house. Maybe I expected to see a healthy Nightliss waving goodbye. Maybe I expected to see Shelton run out at the last minute, and tell me he really wanted to come, or at the very least get his favorite vehicle back. Instead, all I saw was a closed door. Heart heavy, I pressed the accelerator and left.

Bella had me swing by Shelton's hideout so she could pack. It took her all of ten minutes to throw everything inside a large suitcase, which had to be a world record in terms of women packing anything. I put the suitcase in the truck, and we headed out to the Grotto, leaving it in the long-term parking section. After a few words with the Arcane operator, he bumped us to the front of the queue, and we stepped through the arch into Queens Gate.

After a long wait in line to enter the pocket dimension, the surly security Arcane scanned us. Bella's dhampyr classification appeared, along with an arcane potential of eight.

"Are you a sympathizer?" the man asked, narrowing his eyes at Bella, and pointing a thumb over his shoulder at the group of protesting vampires.

"Young man, I am now and always have been against supernatural profiling." She sniffed. "Besides, I am almost certain Maximus's people were behind the massacres at the Arcane schools, and you can thank this brave young Daemos here for bringing the criminal to justice."

The man's forehead wrinkled, and he looked at the admission papers he'd given me and Shelton the first time we'd passed through his screening. "Justin Slade?"

"Can we just go in now?" I asked, eager to avoid a spectacle.

The man touched his wand to my papers, and handed Bella her papers. "I suppose so." He gave us one last suspicious look before turning his penetrating gaze on the next poor sap in line. "Next!"

"I can't believe the Conclave stands for this rubbish," Bella said as we stepped through the doors into Queens Gate.

We took the shuttle up to Science Academy and headed to the dorm. Once we arrived at the building, we headed up the stairs, and down the passage toward the room. Male students wandered the halls, many of them casting curious glances at Bella as we walked by. One guy stepped out of the bathroom with only a towel around his waist and yelped when he saw her.

Bella smiled. "Aren't you just adorable," she cooed.

"You're sounding like an old woman again," I chided her.

"I *am* an old woman," she replied with a wink.

As we rounded the corner to my hallway, I spotted a young man fiddling with the door to my room. At first, I thought it might be Bigglesworth, but realized the Flark could easily slide beneath the door. Conroy obviously had other people working for him. I jogged down the hall, suitcase in one hand, and Bella running close behind.

"What do you think you're doing?" I asked, noticing Bella had drawn her wand, and feeling better about my chances should this guy decide to fight.

He glared at me. "What do I think I'm doing? I'm the RA—the resident assistant—for this dorm." He looked at Bella and then at her suitcase, his mouth hanging open slightly. "Who's she, and what is she doing here at this hour?"

"I'm Bella," she replied, as if that should answer all his questions.

"Do you know how many complaints I've had about this room since you moved in?" He pulled out an arctablet and read from it. "Loud noises late at night, people coming and going at all hours, females at non-visitation hours"—at this point he glared at Bella. "And now you are apparently moving in your girlfriend." He shook his head. "Dude, you can't do this. Number one, this isn't a coed dorm, and two, you can't just move anyone you want into your room even if it was coed." He sighed. "I've got no choice but to evict."

"But where am I gonna stay?" I asked.

He shrugged. "I don't know. I don't care. All I know is you can't stay here."

Bella put away her wand. "Not even for one more night?" Her violet eyes went huge, and her forehead crinkled in sadness. "We have nowhere else to go."

"No, I—I can't," the man said, his voice faltering under the weight of those big sad eyes.

"Just one night?" The pitch of Bella's voice sounded heavy with desperation. "I'm so cold and hungry."

The RA made a groaning sound. "Fine, fine." He looked away from the dhampyr. "Just for tonight. I could get in big trouble for this."

A tear sparkled down Bella's cheek. She stood on tiptoe and kissed the man on the cheek. "Thank you so much."

He blushed. Stammered. "S-sure. Okay, bye." He walked briskly down the hall, never looking back.

I gave Bella two raised eyebrows. "Remind me to never cross you. You're more dangerous than I thought."

She grinned.

We went inside, and I sucked in a sharp breath.

Ivy smiled back at me.

Chapter 27

"What—how did you get—never mind. Stupid question."

"I'm not really here," Ivy said, flashing another grin. "I'm projecting." She looked at Bella. "Who's that?"

"I'm Bella," the dhampyr said. "You must be Ivy. I've heard so much about you."

"Has Justin been talking about me?" my sister replied, a mischievous smirk playing on her lips.

"Only the good stuff," I said. "Why haven't I seen you at lunch again?"

She made duck lips. "They've been keeping a close eye on me, so it's harder to sneak away. Bigmomma figured out I went to the dining hall the other day."

"How?" I asked.

"People were talking about it." She sighed. "Now Mr. Bigglesworth won't let me go anywhere alone."

"I guess that means we can't get together for ice cream again?"

Her forehead pinched into a sad expression. "I want to, Justin. I'll try. I just wanted to say hi, and tell you—well, tell you that I missed seeing you."

"I miss seeing you, too," I said, holding out a hand.

She reached for mine, but the projection passed through me.

Should I ask her about Mom, or would that be pushing it? "Maybe Mom can help you sneak out." It felt like a thinly veiled ploy, but somehow I had to get in touch with Mom.

"They put her in an astral prison," she said. A tear trickled down her cheek.

A lump of ice slid down my throat and into my chest where it played pinball with my heart and stomach. "What do you mean, astral prison?"

"Daelissa told me Mom did something bad, so she imprisoned her until they can have a talk." Her eyes looked downcast. "I don't understand how Mom could betray us."

The news of Mom's imprisonment sent a double shock of pain to me. The Conroys evidently knew about her extracurricular activities. She might be in mortal danger, or they might simply think they could change her mind somehow. But the second part meant I had no hope of helping Nightliss unless I could free Mom. I forced my face to remain neutral while my insides churned.

What am I going to do?

Ivy's head jerked to the side as if she'd just seen or heard something. "Someone's coming. I've gotta go," she whispered and blew me a kiss as her image puffed into a girl-shaped cloud of pink vapor.

"Am I mistaken, or does it sound like your sister actually likes you now?" Bella asked, a bemused expression on her face.

I shrugged. "Maybe. We had time to connect." I told her about the gelato and lunch.

"You don't think she's trying to trick you again, do you? Remember when she faked her kidnapping so you'd rescue her from Maximus, but it turned out to be a lie?"

Pain clenched my heart at the memory of that betrayal. "I don't know," I admitted. "Maybe she is, or maybe she's really coming around." I threw up my hands and huffed out an exasperated breath. "Why can't something be simple for once?"

Bella touched my shoulder. "I hope you're reaching her, Justin, I really do." She pulled a bottle of red wine from her suitcase along with two glasses, and set them on the table. "Goodness, I can tell Harry's been eating here. This table is a mess." She poured two glasses of wine, and motioned me to join her at the table.

I sat down, held up the glass of wine. "To good friends who don't abandon you in your time of need," I said.

She rolled her eyes. "To friends." Clinked her glass against mine.

I looked around the room and sighed. "What am I gonna do when they boot us out of the dorm tomorrow?"

"I wish I could help you, but I'm not as connected as Harry," Bella said. "I can call—"

"No." I gave a vehement shake of my head. "He wants out, he's out. I'll figure this out on my own."

She sighed. "Men are so mule-headed sometimes."

Bella had a point, but I was too stubborn to admit it. I knew practically nobody on campus. I texted MacLean, asking him if he'd considered helping me find the rune, and, coincidentally, if he happened to know where I might find lodging that didn't involve a cardboard box and smelly neighbors. I also sent Lina a text asking if she knew of a place to stay.

She responded a minute later. *They're kicking you out? That's terrible! I'll ask my boyfriend if he knows of anything.*

A boyfriend? She hadn't mentioned anything about a boyfriend. Then again, it wasn't my business. I just hoped she could help.

Bella swirled the wine in her glass. "Tomorrow, I'll do some snooping. Maybe I can track down Bigglesworth and find out what he's up to."

"Be careful," I said. "That thing is dangerous."

"I know." She shrugged. "But the best offense is a good defense."

I felt an eyebrow rise. "I think you reversed it."

"Did I?" She smiled. "Well, you know what I mean."

Bella watching my back promised to be an interesting experience.

I met Lina for lunch on Sunday. She looked even more tired than the last time I'd seen her. I almost told her to take it easy, but decided I wasn't her dad, and kept my mouth shut.

"Justin, I think I found the perfect place for you," she said after giving me a hug.

"Awesome!" I said. "It's not under a sewage grate, is it?"

She laughed. "No. Follow me."

We left the castle and walked between the dormitories, off campus, and down a road lined with what looked like mansions of various designs, some large as a condo complex, and others no larger than a couple of single family homes linked together.

"What is this place?" I asked.

"Greek Row."

"As in fraternities and sororities?"

She nodded. "Yes, and filled with complete snobs. There's a house out here that has been empty for a long time. I've heard it was haunted, or cursed."

"When was the last time anyone lived in it?" I asked.

She tapped a finger to her chin. "I think a fraternity leased it, but my boyfriend told me the university evicted them for holding party that almost got everyone killed a few years ago."

"Too much alcohol?" I asked.

Her face grew serious. "No, they were summoning the dead."

Chapter 28

"A ghost summoning party?" I asked, aghast. "What kind of idiots hold a party like that?"

Lina laughed. "Frat boys, I suppose."

Just thinking of ghosts running loose in an abandoned frat house made my skin crawl. "There aren't any dead things on the loose in this house are there? Maybe I should reconsider a cardboard box."

She made a nonchalant wave with her hand. "I'm sure the house is empty." Lina stopped at a path that wound through dense trees. We walked down the path and through a rusty iron gate hanging open at a lopsided angle. Beyond, crouching like a boogeyman, stood a rectangular, gray-stoned complex straight from a horror movie. Vines and creepers wound up the exterior, but otherwise, it didn't look too much worse for the wear.

I felt as though I were in a black-and-white horror film as we walked to the front door. The wood and black steel bands looked almost new.

"The preservation spell still seems to be working," Lina said. "There might be a few spider nests inside, but I'd be happy to help you clean it up."

I gulped. "Spiders?"

Lina said a word, and the door opened with nary a squeak. Inside, the large foyer opened to hardwood floors shining beneath a light coating of dust, and a tarp-covered table and mirror sat against one wall.

"The university banned the fraternity from campus, evicted them from the house, and interdicted the building, but it only took some drunk students a couple of hours to hack the interdiction spells and get inside." She led me into a large den with a fireplace large enough to spit and roast a cow, walked up to a tarp, pulled it back to reveal a pool table. Another tarp concealed what looked like a foosball table.

"People come here to party?" I asked. That certainly wouldn't be good.

"If they see the house is occupied, they'll stay away," Lina said.

"It could be kind of awkward," I replied, imagining a group of drunken revelers bursting in while I traipsed around the house in my underwear.

Lina led me through rooms, upstairs to bedrooms, down into the basement, and even further underground to a locked iron grate. Apparently, another group of students had put their own interdiction spell on the grate to prevent anyone else from going inside. I conjured a ball of light at the tip of my wand, and held it through the bars, but saw only a staircase leading further down on the other side.

"What's down there?" I asked.

She shrugged. "This is the first time I've been here. Someone said they heard there are old dungeons down there, and they blocked this off to keep students from getting lost or hurting themselves."

A shiver sent goose bumps racing up my back. "Dungeons? Thank god this thing is locked." I rushed back upstairs, two steps at a time, feeling a chill against my back the entire time. I wasn't sure why the thought of dungeons caused such a strong reaction in me, unless it had something to do with my time as a prisoner with Maximus.

Lina rushed up after me. "Are you okay, Justin?" Her large brown eyes filled with concern.

I glanced down the dark stairwell. A chilly sensation ran icy fingers up my arms. "Yeah. Just bad memories, I guess." As we walked back into the main den, I thought about more practical matters. "Will the university evict me if they find out I'm here?"

"I don't know." She led me down a hall, opening doors, and looking inside until she found a room with what looked like a brass bird bath embedded in the floor. Lina picked up a crystalline sphere, and set it inside the indention in the center of the brass construct. The crystal ball flickered on. Lights in the hallway blazed to life, and a background hum reached my ears as power was restored.

"This place doesn't use electricity," she explained. "Like most things here, it's powered by aether from ley lines."

"Cool," I said, unaware that such a thing was even possible.

Lina and I walked back to campus. "You sure look tired," I said, unable to keep my mouth shut about it any longer.

She regarded me with a tired smile. "I have to work hard, Justin."

"To impress Alejandro?" Her older brother was pretty impressive in the Arcane department, at least from what I'd seen when we'd first met.

"No, to prove to myself that I'm good enough." She sighed.

We reached campus. I gave her a hug before we parted ways. "I have faith in you. Just don't make yourself sick, okay?"

She smiled. "I won't." Her eyes lingered on mine for a moment. "Have a good day, Justin."

Since I'd agreed to meet with Vallaena every afternoon but Saturday, I headed for the school. I wanted to see her, but not for practice. Rage boiled my blood as I thought about her talking with Nightliss. As usual, my aunt waited on a bench in the rear gardens. And also as usual, she offered me a sultry smile when I appeared. It took all my willpower not to punch her in the face.

"You told Nightliss about the angel heart cure," I said, a growl rising from my diaphragm. I loomed over her. "She offered her heart—her life—to me."

"Did you take her up on the offer?" Vallaena asked, raising a golden eyebrow. "No, of course you didn't. Even with the fate of our world in the balance, you won't take the ultimate sacrifice even when freely offered."

My fists clenched. "She's dying. You took her will to live, and gave her a reason to die. I warned you not to tell her, Vallaena. And you did it anyway." Anger swelled inside me, but I pushed it away, snuffing out the heat until all that remained was a cold fury. "I want you to leave. We're not going to have these little classes anymore."

A slow wicked smile spread across my aunt's lips. "Oh, but you have no choice. Not if you want to ally yourself with the Daemos."

"I'll find someone else to teach me."

"I think you'll find very few takers."

"Then I suppose I'll just have to let the Daemos fend for themselves," I said, turning and walking away.

"Don't walk away from me, boy," Vallaena said, her voice still calm, but with an undertone of warning.

I kept walking.

"You're throwing everything away for one half-dead Darkling who is of no use to you."

I kept walking.

"You're being an idiot."

I almost said something, but I'd been called worse. I heard footsteps behind me on the stone walkway as I rounded the corner.

"You will not walk away from me," Vallaena suddenly snarled, and blurred in front of me. "You will take your lessons and do as I say if you want to survive."

"Is that a threat?" I asked calmly as my guts froze in place.

"Take it for what you will, boy." Her lips curled into a sneer. "I have put too much time into your education to let you throw it away over your dark little plaything."

My right hand shook. Somehow I maintained control. Pushed it back until only a lake of frozen anger remained. I would not let her bait me into a fight. "Go to hell." With that, I shoved past her.

Vallaena snarled. "You will not ignore me!"

Her iron grip clamped around my bicep, and flung me back down the pathway. Thankfully, I'd anticipated something, mainly thanks to her daily attempts to beat me senseless, and managed to land on my feet with a thud, sliding backwards. I looked up at the sound of clacking on the stone, and saw Vallaena in mid-shift, her skin turning a deep blue, horns sprouting from her forehead, and her muscles swelling. The clacking noise came from six-inch stilettos which looked ready to burst apart as my aunt's feet strained against them.

"Oh, crap," I said. My cold fury turned to bowel-clenching fear. I knew with deep certainty that this wasn't one of her little tests. This was for real, and my enraged aunt was ready to tear my head off and drop-kick it into the forest. I did the only thing I could do, reaching deep inside me for every bit of strength I had. Then I turned and ran like my butt was on fire. One look back told me what I already knew. My aunt was a lot faster in succubus form.

She chanted something in the furious voice of a woman who just found lipstick on her husband's shirt and fully planned to emasculate him in the most horrific way imaginable. Dark pools of liquid seeped through the earth ahead of me. Something struggled in the dark pitch, jerking, straining, snarling as it rose like a monster from a tar pit.

Snarling? Oh crap!

She was summoning hellhounds.

By now, Vallaena was only thirty yards or so behind me. I briefly considered veering for the forest where I might have a chance to lose her in the undergrowth. But I knew the hellhounds would be right behind me. My only other choice was magic. I pulled out my staff, and shook it to full length.

A black shape leapt from the earth. Before I could react, the hellhound clamped its jaws on the staff and wrenched it from my hand. I stumbled, nearly fell, as the sideways jerk fought my forward momentum. I leapt over another hellhound as it freed itself from an oily pool, and lunged for me.

I was out of options. Well, unless I considered apologizing to Vallaena. When I looked back again at her snarling face and flaming eyes, I realized it might be too late even for that.

My demonic essence clawed at my insides. It raged and slammed against my barriers. I could almost hear it in my head, demanding I free it. Demanding I give it a chance to live another day instead of dying painfully, torn to shreds by hellhounds.

Vallaena won't really kill me.

Then again, hell hath no fury like a woman pissed off. And I had just scorned the hell out of a woman who thought her poop didn't stink. Everything she'd done to me during our lessons had usually involved sexual innuendo. The only thing I sensed from her now was pure death.

FREE ME!

I flinched as the words rang in my head. Had I thought that, or was my spirit really talking to me.

DOES IT MATTER?

Actually, no. It didn't.

Instead of opening the cage a crack as I usually did, I broke the cell doors down. A dark presence filled me, spreading through my chest, my arms, my fingers, running down to my legs and toes. There was no anger. No fear. Only the will to survive another day.

I spun in place. Vallaena, flanked by hellhounds, rushed me. As I turned to meet her, my body swelled, muscles coiling like serpents beneath my skin. Deep beneath the surface, I sensed the mindless beast eager to rampage and destroy. But instead of letting it ride the wave of change to the top, I struggled to stay afloat of the roaring tide in my head. Just as I felt myself hitting the place where I would no longer be able to keep the beast at bay, I slammed a barrier of will between it and my reasoning mind.

My clawed hand slapped aside a diving hellhound. I reversed the swing, and backhanded the next black beast, sending it yelping and skidding across grass already shredded from previous practice sessions. And then my aunt was on me. Our arms locked onto each other's shoulders with a thunderous clap. I felt claws digging into my flesh, drawing blood even through the toughened skin. I snarled, and increased the pressure, forcing droplets of blue from her.

She roared, showing fangs on her beautiful but terrifying face. I slammed my head forward, ramming my horns against her nose. She cried out in surprise, and I used the opportunity to end the stalemate and flung her sideways. Vallaena spun through the air, crashing into a tree at the border of the forest. It shuddered, showering the area with acorns.

My warning senses tingled. I spun. Grabbed a hellhound by the throat. Threw it at my stunned aunt. Two more hellhounds came from my side. I slammed the ground with both fists on instinct just before they reached me, shaking the ground, and knocking them off kilter. I gripped each one, and slammed their heads together with a thunderous boom. The two hounds dropped senseless from my hands.

Vallaena struggled to her feet. Saw her hellhounds, and screeched a battle cry that echoed through the forest and probably all the way back to campus. She charged, her body growing even larger, manifesting into full demon form. I knew if I tried to match her, to allow myself to fully manifest, I'd lose control of my consciousness. As it was, the beast inside slammed relentlessly against what little control I had left.

Words Bella had once spoken to me echoed in my head. *It's not always about brute force. It's about using your brains. Use their strength against them.*

Flicking into my incubus sight, I drew in magic, drinking deep from the swirling energy all around me. I crouched, preparing myself to meet Vallaena's hulking shape. The beauty in her features was gone, replaced by raw bestiality. She closed to thirty yards. Twenty. Ten. Five. At the last minute, I dodged to the side, threw out my hands, and pretended I was my favorite neighborhood web-slinger, just like the day I'd saved me and Shelton from sliding into the Gloom.

Strands of webbed energy shot from my hands, wrapping around Vallaena's thick waist as she blurred past, her clawed feet tearing up clods of earth, spraying dirt in my face. Even with her supernatural reflexes, there was no way she could stop her extra mass on a dime with all that momentum. I imagined the strands becoming flexible. They stretched and stretched, slowing her to a crawl. She reached the apex, and stopped. But only for an instant. With my feet entrenched in the ground and muscles bulging, I jerked on the magical web. It snapped back like a giant rubber band.

Vallaena zipped over my head at what seemed like the speed of light, her body a blue blur. I was so shocked by her speed, I nearly forgot to release the magic holding the slingshot together, dissolving it just before her momentum would have pulled me after her like a Chihuahua leashed to a charging car's bumper. She crashed into the forest, cracked through several saplings, and vanished into the gloom. A moment later, I saw the top of a particularly tall tree shudder with impact. The thud echoed like a thunderclap. Spider bats shrieked, flapping away from the commotion.

I winced. *That had to hurt.*

Something roared in the distance, its ravenous bellow echoing from deep within the woods. The tragon. Even with our, um, disagreement, I couldn't let that monstrosity eat my aunt. I ran into the forest, following a trail of broken saplings, uprooted bushes, and finally found Vallaena lying spread-eagled at the base of a huge tree with a demon-shaped divot in its thick trunk. Blue blood streamed down her animalistic face, running down her cheeks and pooling in her huge demon ears.

As I watched, her body began to shrink back to normal. Another roar reached my ears, this one much closer, so without further ado, I picked her up, and ran for the safety of the shield. Once back in the meadow, I placed her on the ground, keeping an eye on the unconscious woman until she returned to normal size, and her blood had turned to a red hue.

Exhaustion heaped atop my back, rolling over me like a wave. I'd pushed myself today, physically and mentally. I'd actually used magic while manifested. The thought thrilled me, but now my body was paying the price. At least I was safe for now.

Pawed feet padded behind me. I turned and stared into the glowing yellow eyes of a hellhound.

Chapter 29

Mustering what energy I could, I directed a growl at the hound. It cowered, whimpered, and rolled onto its back. Raising a demonic eyebrow, I reached over and scratched its belly.

"Good boy," I said, my voice still deep with the demon form.

Its tongue lolled.

I watched the other hellhounds struggle to their feet. I fought to remain in demon form, but my body wasn't having it. My sight blurred and wavered from the strain. Soon I'd lose control to the raging beast trapped behind the thinning wall of my resistance. I would just have to face the hounds without my demonic advantage. Gritting my teeth, I pushed and beat back the beast, stuffing it into its psychic cage. My body shrank back to normal size just as the hellhounds, still somewhat wobbly on their feet, came toward me. They stopped. Sniffed Vallaena, and rolled onto their backs in front of me. Since my aunt hadn't taught me anything about hellhound summoning, I wasn't sure why they were suddenly my best buds, but assumed it had something to do with my kicking their rear ends rather soundly and proving I was the boss of them.

Vallaena moaned. Pressed a hand to her head, and sat up. Her bloodshot blue eyes met mine. "You."

I nodded. "Me."

She pinched the bridge of her nose, head bent as if in silent prayer, though I figured it had more to do with the worst headache of her life. After a full minute or so, she looked back at me. "You defeated me."

"Yep." I tried not to gloat, but the look of disbelief on her face was just too precious to pass up. "Kicked your butt."

Vallaena nodded, face pensive. "I am sorry, Justin. I should never have talked to Nightliss."

I rocked back on my heels with shock. "Did I get hit on the head, or did you really just apologize?"

"I am desperate for you to be healed. If you succumb to the vampling curse, we will all succumb to the Seraphim." She looked up at me. "Do you understand?"

I nodded. "But your behavior is no excuse." I sighed and offered her a hand. She took it, wincing, and I pulled her to her feet. "If you try to manipulate my friends again, I will leave you in a heartbeat."

Her eyes grew large and hopeful. "Does that mean you're not leaving my tutelage?"

I offered her a smile. "That apology just earned you another chance."

"Well, I think you have proven yourself today, nephew." She took my hand in both of hers. "I am proud of you."

I looked at her dirt-smeared, blood-stained face, and wondered how she could feel pride in my beating the snot out of a woman, but decided it *had* been self-defense. "Um, well that's good. Why don't you go home, rest, and get cleaned up?"

She nodded. "I will. Until tomorrow, then?"

"Until tomorrow." I was glad I'd worn workout attire, and swung by the gym to shower and change so people wouldn't wonder how a filthy bum managed to slip onto campus.

I returned to the dorm to find Bella sitting outside on a bench with my suitcase and hers sitting on the ground next to it. "The RA wouldn't allow me to stay any longer," she said. "Even when I offered to bake him cookies."

A snort escaped me. "Well, I have another place. It's probably haunted, but you're gonna love it."

She quirked an eyebrow. "You discover the most interesting places, Justin."

I led her to our new "home". She stopped and stared. Gave me a sideways look.

"Hey," I said, "it has toilets."

Bella grinned. "I suppose that's a start."

We went inside, and walked upstairs to the bedrooms. The preservation spells in the east wing had apparently worn off, or someone had thrown one too many parties, because not only were the bedrooms on that side dusty and moldy, but some of the beds looked like wild animals had clawed them to shreds. The west wing looked much better, and the rooms actually smelled clean, which was amazing if they hadn't been used since the frat boys had lived here. Then again, thinking about the parties this place had seen probably meant the beds could have been used in all sorts of carnal ways.

"Know any cleaning spells?" I asked Bella as I cast dubious glances at the deep blue comforter atop the king-sized bed.

She replied with an apologetic smile. "I'm not much of a housekeeper but I did once live in a fancy mansion like this one." She walked to a rope dangling from the ceiling, pulled it. A moment later, a golem, its wooden body painted to resemble a butler uniform, a ratty old gray wig perched atop its round head, walked inside the room and stopped.

"You rang, sir?" it said in a perfect British accent even though it had no mouth I could see.

"Clean the sheets?" I said.

"Of course, sir," it said, and began stripping the bed with its finely articulated hands and fingers.

"Goodness," Bella said, looking closely at the golem. "This is quite a fine piece of work. I can't believe anyone would simply leave such a useful golem in an abandoned house."

"You think someone else lives here?" I said, alarm ringing in my head.

"Butler, does anyone else live in this house?" Bella asked.

Without looking up from the bed, it said, "No one has lived in this place for over two years, madam."

"How long have you been here?"

"I am not able to divulge that information," it replied, balling the sheets atop the bed. It walked to a closet and pulled large wheeled basket from inside, and stuffed the sheets into it.

"What do you mean, not able?" I asked.

"The information is simply not available to me, sir." The golem gripped the basket and wheeled it toward the door. It stopped just outside, and turned. "Does the master wish anything else before I take this to laundry?"

"Clean the bed sheets in the next room too, please," Bella said, casting a curious look as the faux butler nodded and vanished around the corner.

I looked at Bella. "This place is weird, but heck, if I have a butler, I think I may just like it."

"I agree," she replied with a smile.

I called Cinder and let him know about the new digs, and then thought hard about what I wanted to eat that night. As I weighed the pros and cons of pizza versus Chinese food, the front door swung open, and Lina stepped inside.

"Hello?" she called and spotted me sitting on a freshly cleaned couch in front of the fireplace in the den.

"Hey," I said. "Thanks for helping me find this place."

She offered a tired grin. "It is very cool." She sat next to me. "Are you doing okay? You look really exhausted."

I had to admit I was feeling not just physical hunger, but demonic hunger as well. I'd intended to fill both needs once I decided where I was going to eat normal food. The school dining hall served three meals a day, though I usually missed dinner thanks to my sessions with Vallaena.

"Do you want to feed?" Lina asked.

She looked so pale, so tired, I couldn't believe she'd even offer. "Are you kidding me? You look dead on your feet."

"I am a little tired." A yawn seemed to take her by surprise.

"Maybe you just need a break." I stood. "You feel like Chinese food?"

"Yeah. That sounds great."

"Hey Lina!" Bella called, leaning over the balustrade upstairs. "I wasn't expecting you. Did you come over to play Scrabble?"

"Food first," I said. "You want to come?" I told her where we were going.

"No, just grab me some goat fried rice," the dhampyr called back.

Lina had a flying carpet with her, so we took it down to the town of Queens Gate in the valley below. From the mountain, the town looked like a miniature replica of Victorian London. Brick roads wound through mazes of townhouses along the outer edges, the gas lamps twinkling like stars, while shops and restaurants formed neat squares with water fountains and quaint parks around the middle. A giant clock tower rose from the center of town, faced on either side by impressive, domed buildings I assumed had some function of state.

Once on the ground, the town reminded me of the Grotto, filled with vendors, restaurants, and supernaturals of just about every persuasion. The Chinese restaurant Shelton liked, the Copper Swan, looked exactly like a giant version of its namesake. Lina and I had dinner. We talked about classes, her brother, Alejandro, and her plans for after college.

She sounded a lot like most people my age—clueless about what they wanted to do with the rest of their lives. At least she had time to figure things out. Lina looked so exhausted, I didn't dare feed from the poor girl, and instead took advantage of other female patrons in the vicinity. Thanks to Vallaena's pro tips I was able to do it without drawing any unwanted attention.

I tried to keep up my end of the conversation, but couldn't stop thinking about Nightliss or Mom's imprisonment. *I have to win Ivy's heart somehow*. With her help, we might be able to free Mom. But I hadn't seen Ivy all day. It was hard to win someone's trust when they weren't around.

Lina's phone chimed, snapping me from my thoughts. She glanced at it and smiled.

"Someone you wanted to hear from?" I asked.

She nodded. "My boyfriend. He wants to meet outside in a few minutes." She looked up. "Is that okay with you?"

I shrugged. "Why wouldn't it be?" I'd forgotten about her mysterious boyfriend, but hadn't figured out a way to ask for more info without giving the wrong impression.

Lina pressed a hand to her forehead, and closed her eyes. She seemed even more exhausted than before, and her skin looked a pallid gray.

"Are you okay?" I asked.

"Just really tired," she said. A smile. "I'm fine, Justin."

We split the bill and went outside. People wandered the streets, their modern clothes anachronistic in the vintage setting. The denizens of the Overworld seemed to enjoy keeping things classic as opposed to modern, and I had to admit I liked it. Instead of trolleys or the horseless stagecoaches which frequented the Grotto, people here favored flying carpets or the shiny rocket boards I'd seen at the Science Academy.

As Lina and I walked toward the sidewalk, I nearly collided with someone. I looked up and was about to apologize when I saw the arrogant face looking back at me with disdain. William Vanderbilt's eyes flared with recognition, and his lip curled into a sneer.

I was just about to steer around him and tell Lina all about how much of a jackass he was, when she gave him a hug and pecked him on the lips. She turned to me and said, "Justin, I'd like you to meet my boyfriend, Billy."

Chapter 30

Billy, flanked by two other guys, stared at me with an almost comical look of surprise plain on his face. I felt certain the expression on my face reflected his.

"This guy is your boo?" I asked.

"This guy is your friend?" Billy said at almost the same instant.

We stared at one another again.

"You know each other?" Lina looked back and forth between us.

"He's a bloomer and a techie," Billy said, his surprised expression melding into a sneer. "I don't like you talking to his kind."

Lina's eyes flashed. "You don't tell me who I can talk with, Billy." Her Spanish accent thickened as she set her arms akimbo and said, "You promised me you weren't going to say those sorts of things anymore."

Billy looked at his two friends, one a short, heavyset guy with hair so thick, it looked like porcupine quills, and the other, a slender male with gray slacks, a pink polo, and silky blonde hair combed to the side. The three of them looked like escaped mental patients from a prep-school asylum circa nineteen-eighty.

"Let's get out of here, babe," Billy said, trying to put an arm around Lina's shoulders.

She threw off his hand with her own, and wobbled for a moment before regaining her balance. "You weren't acting like this the other night when we were alone."

I was sorely tempted to chime in with my thoughts on elitism, spoiled blueblood kids, and maybe even give Billy a token punch in the nose, but decided placing myself between Lina's anger and Billy's obstinacy might be a bad thing.

"C'mon, babe, I'm just joking. You know how I am."

Lina's eyes flared. She opened her mouth to speak. And then she dropped to the ground like a lead weight.

Everyone stood stunned as she lay on the ground like a broken doll. I bent down and pressed a hand to her neck. Her pulse felt fine, but, damn it, I was an incubus, not a doctor.

"What did you do to her, you filthy techie?" Billy said.

Someone clamped preternaturally strong hands on my shoulders and jerked me away from Lina. Before I could react, my feet left the ground. I plowed through a group of nearby students and rolled to a painful stop atop the brick road in front of the restaurant. As I climbed to my feet, I saw Porky the porcupine hair guy charging at me much faster than his stocky frame should have allowed. Billy produced an ebony rod about the size and shape of a magic marker, and gave a flick of his wrist. It sprang out lengthwise, and thickened into a staff that shined and glittered like polished coal.

I strafed right just as Porky blew past me like a locomotive. He hit the side of the Copper Swan, ringing it like a giant gong. He had to be seeing cartoon birds and stars circling his head after a hit like that. A flash of azure blue caught my peripheral vision. A bolt of heat seared into my ribs, slamming me hard against the side of the huge copper bird. The breath blasted from my lungs. Jagged bolts of energy pouring from the end of Billy's staff pressed me tight against the side of the restaurant. I couldn't move. Couldn't breathe. Heat from the magical energy washed over me, the temperature just barely beneath my pain threshold. Lina's boyfriend, his lips peeled back with rage, walked toward me.

"Let's see if your technology"—he spat the word like a curse—"can save you, bloomer."

I flailed with my free hands, trying to grab my phone, my practice staff, anything, but the miniature electrical storm washing over my torso prevented my hands from getting close to my pockets. "Lina needs help!" I shouted. "Why the hell are you attacking me?"

"You insulted me," Billy said. "Besides, you're a filthy spawn who attacked my girlfriend."

By now a crowd was gathering. People murmured, pointing. I could make out some individual conversations.

"Did that boy hurt the girl?"

"He started a fight with Billy Vanderbilt?"

"Dude is toast."

I had no choice. I'd have to spawn like Vallaena taught me. *It might be my only chance of breaking free.* I delved deep inside, and began to lower the barriers. Frost dug bone deep into my left leg, frost so cold it felt white hot. Boiling rage and helplessness churned like acid against the barrier holding back my demonic side. Shadows stretched from every unlit corner around me in the shapes of skulls and robed phantoms, their bony claws reaching for me.

Devour. Eat. Drain.

The voices rasped the same words in my head, a constant susurrus of ravenous need.

"Stop it!" I shouted, pressing my hands to the sides of my head. "Go away!"

The demon inside me surged for the crack in its barrier, rising like bile in my throat. I clenched my teeth and fought back. If I spawned now with the vampling curse raging in my blood, I would lose control. Fighting the curse and my demonic counterpart was a battle I'd nearly lost in the forest. I definitely couldn't lose it now.

"Buddy, you'd better let him go," said a familiar voice. "Or so help me god, I will turn you into a pile of rotten cow testicles."

Someone yelped like wounded dog, and the force holding me to the side of the building vanished. I dropped to the ground, landing hard on my knees. Hands pressed to head, and eyes squeezed shut, I rocked back and forth, fighting the tide of nauseating insanity. Fighting the voices as they demanded blood, death, and destruction.

The numbing cold receded bit by bit like ice under lukewarm water until only the usual chill of the curse drifted in my veins like permafrost. It was accelerating. I could feel it. Physical trauma, or magical trauma, or maybe some combination of the two was giving the curse new life despite the potion.

"Get the hell out of here!" someone roared, and I heard more cries of pain and yelps receding into the distance. "Holy farting fairies, kid. You okay?"

I looked up into Harry Shelton's eyes. He looked pissed and mildly confused. "Lina?" I said.

"The healers are here. They're airlifting her to the university." Shelton gripped me under an arm and hauled me to my feet. "The curse almost got you again, didn't it?"

I nodded. "Yeah."

"Well, you haven't done a good job avoiding trauma, that's for sure," he said in a gruff tone.

I raised an eyebrow, and considered him for a moment. "You're back."

He nodded. "Yeah. Don't get all sentimental about it, though."

"What made you change your mind?" I had to fight back a smile.

"I got bored sitting around Meghan's house, okay? The way she and Adam coo all over each other makes me sick. I figured I'd rather face certain death than hang around that love fest. One day was more than enough." He blew out a disgusted breath. "So, besides brawling in the streets and knocking out Colombian girls, what the hell else have you been up to?"

Pushing aside the dread I felt about the curse, I laughed and slapped him on the back. "It's good to have you back."

He scowled. "Like I said, no big deal."

Shelton and I took the lift back to the university, and I showed him the house. Bella came running from her room the moment she heard his voice.

She looked at him, her eyes soft. "I'm glad to see you, Harry."

"Don't even start with the Scrabble," he warned, looking around the cavernous den. "I used to come here for parties back in the day." He shivered. "But I heard this place was haunted."

"Is the mighty Harry Shelton scared?" Bella said, her eyes twinkling.

"Pssht. No, I just think this place has seen better days."

"What made you decide to come back?" she asked.

He shrugged. "Got bored."

"Bored, huh?" Bella blurred down the stairs at supernatural speed and thudded into Shelton, nearly picking him up off the floor with an enthusiastic hug. "You're so adorable when you try to act macho and cool."

He struggled, but was no match for the petite woman and her dhampyric strength. "Woman, put me down."

She giggled and set him back on the floor. "I knew you were a good man." She winked. "Even if you are terrible at Scrabble."

"I hate to break up the good mood," I said, "but Lina collapsed when we were out, Bella." "Oh, goodness, we have to go see her," she said.

It was all piling up in my head. Nightliss, Mom, and now Lina. Despite having Shelton back, the weight on my shoulders felt heavier than ever. How long did Nightliss have? How the hell could I find Ivy?

The three of us visited Lina.

Healer Hutchins, the same woman who'd treated me and MacLean was checking on another patient when we walked in. She saw me and quirked an eyebrow.

Shelton's eyes went a little wide, and he turned to grab a copy of *Arcane Daily* from the scroll rack, unrolling the yellowed parchment as if the juicy centerfold of a cute female Arcane waited somewhere on the page.

The healer approached us, her eyes glancing between me and Bella. "You again. Find anymore unconscious professors in the hallway?"

"Uh, no, actually one of my friends collapsed." I nodded my head at Lina's bed where she lay asleep. "She was looking really tired. I thought it was just from studying too hard."

"I see you've moved to rescuing girls now." An amused smile flickered across her lips. "You're either a knight in shining armor, or you get your kicks from knocking people out and bringing them to me."

I offered her an uneasy smile because I couldn't tell if she was serious or not. "She's been practicing her magic too hard. Is it possible she has magic poisoning?"

Hutchins shook her head. "You remember these children you saw the last time you were in here?" She looked at the beds where the same kids lay, their faces waxen, eyes surrounded by dark bruises.

I looked at Lina and immediately noticed the similarities. "Wait, are you saying Lina has the same thing?" I asked.

"It's possible." The healer crossed an arm over her stomach. "Her cells are absolutely saturated with magic. Unlike magic poisoning which occurs from within, this has happened from an outside source."

Bella pressed a kiss to Lina's forehead. "Poor sweet girl."

Shelton glanced back from his magazine and sighed. He walked to Bella, and put an arm around her shoulders. "I'm sure the kid just overdid it. Heck, I remember a time or two I passed out—"

Healer Hutchins's head snapped toward Shelton. "Well, well, well, if it isn't the incorrigible Harry Shelton."

"You know him?" I asked, realizing that with Shelton's apparent notoriety at the university, it was probably a stupid question.

"Oh, Harry was a regular here in the infirmary." Her eyes narrowed. "And that's not including his victims."

"Victims?" Bella turned a shocked look to Shelton.

"I'm all grown up now," Shelton said with a groan. "Don't we have more important things to discuss?"

Hutchins waved a hand and turned to a filing cabinet. "Of course. I'm not sure there's enough time in one life to discuss everything you've done anyway." She pulled open a drawer on the cabinet. It extended further and further, every inch packed tight with manila folders. She continued to pull the drawer open until it stretched nearly across the room. It seemed the otherwise ordinary-looking filing cabinet should topple over from the weight at any moment, though it never did. Once I finally found a home again, as opposed to living in Shelton's secret hideouts, I decided I could definitely use a sock drawer with an enchantment like that.

Hutchins finally stopped pulling, fingers flicking through the folders. "Ah, here it is." She withdrew a green folder. "I remembered it being color coded because it was so odd." She licked a finger and flipped through the pages until she reached the picture of a boy about middle-school age. His closed eyes were sunken, and he looked as if he hadn't slept for days.

I sucked in a breath. "Holy crap. It looks like the same thing. Did they figure out what was wrong with him?"

She glanced over the pages. Shook her head. "No. They found him in the Burrows after he'd gone missing for two days. His case is why they barred access to those tunnels."

"They used to be dungeons, right?" I asked, remembering what Lina had told me.

Hutchins nodded. "Even though they never found the cause, the administration determined some form of dark magic used for torturing prisoners might still linger there, and decided it was safer to close the place off rather than risk any further harm to students."

I picked up the picture of the boy. Behind it lay the portrait of how he had been before the incident, young, smiling, his rosy cheeks slightly plump. My eyes flicked to Lina. She looked like someone who hadn't slept for two days. The kid in the picture looked like he hadn't slept or eaten for a week. Was this what lay in store for Lina? I was just about to ask the fate of the boy in the picture when I saw the next page. The boy's name was Toby Peterson. Someone else, perhaps a doctor or more likely an uncaring bureaucrat had stamped a big red word across the page beneath Toby's name.

DECEASED.

Chapter 31

After badgering Healer Hutchins with more medical questions, she made it clear Lina might recover. Toby had lain for two days in the Burrows before receiving medical care while Lina had received almost immediate attention. The healer also made something else clear—she didn't know how to treat the condition. And then she kicked us out.

"The girl needs her rest, and I need all my concentration," she said before shutting the door behind us with a sense of finality.

I took a few steps down the hall before dropping onto a bench. I felt at a complete loss for what to do next. "Nightliss is dying, Lina and those kids might be dying, Daelissa is hell-bent on finding the Cyrinthian Rune and reopening the Alabaster Arch, my sister wants to convert me to the dark side and—and..." I gave Shelton and Bella a hopeless look. "I'm so confused. What do I do? Who do I help first?"

"Why, there's no question," Bella said, her eyes full of concern. "We should find out what happened to Lina."

"We can't do anything for Nightliss," Shelton said. "Unless your mom decides to play hero again."

"The Conroys are holding her in an astral prison," I told him.

Shelton gave me a surprised look. "When did you find that out?"

"Ivy told us," Bella said.

"That little bi—brat," Shelton said with some difficulty. "We've got to take her out of the equation."

"Do you suggest killing a little girl?" Bella asked, raising an eyebrow.

"That's exactly what I'm suggesting," Shelton replied, sarcasm heavy in his voice. "Because killing kids is how I roll."

Ivy had nothing to do with Mom's imprisonment, but would she know how or be willing to help me free her? Would I have a better shot at convincing her to save Nightliss? *No chance in hell. She thinks Darklings are evil.* If I couldn't count on Mom or Ivy, I had to concentrate on finding the angel inside of me. Then I could cure Nightliss and hopefully myself.

Bella looked around the empty hall. "Perhaps we shouldn't discuss such things here."

I was about to comment on how empty the place was and how unlikely it was anyone would overhear us, then remembered Billy and his gang, not to mention Bigglesworth. "What's to keep our stalkers from listening to us at our new digs?" I asked.

"We ward the ever-lovin' crap out of it," Shelton said.

Once home, Bella and Shelton chose a large, empty room off the east hallway of the first floor, and plastered protective wards against eavesdropping and intrusion around it. According to Bella, it was a lot easier than warding the entire house.

I was ready to stumble to bed before they finished, but they made me watch in the hopes I might actually learn something. Instead, my mind ran circles around the many issues plaguing my wonderful life.

"I doubt it," Shelton said, his words penetrating the asteroid field of frowny faces circling my brain.

I snapped out of my reverie and became aware of him and Bella staring at me, arms crossed. "Did I miss something?" I asked.

"Only everything we told you about laying wards," Bella replied. She sighed. "I certainly hope you pay better attention in class."

"I can't help it." I jumped out of my chair and threw my hands up. "I feel like everything is on my shoulders, and I don't have a clue what to do."

"I believe I have one part of the solution," Bella said.

"And that is?"

"Obviously, we kidnap your sister," the dhampyr said without missing a beat. "At best, she can heal Nightliss. At worst, we could use her in trade for your mother."

"No," I said, surprised by how quickly the objection sprang to my lips.

They raised eyebrows at me.

"I've been talking to her. Getting to know her," I explained. "Maybe I can get through to her and convince her to help us."

"Why would she help us when she thinks we're the bad guys?" Shelton said.

Bella's eyes softened. "I know she's your sister, Justin, but she's confused. Bad people have fed the girl lies all her life. How do you think you can turn her around in a matter of days?"

I didn't have an easy answer. Hell, I didn't even have a hard answer. If I pushed her too hard, she might bolt. I remembered her reaction to the mention of our father. She'd told me Nightliss wasn't even a person. Just a Darkling. How could I hope to overcome those prejudices in a short time? If Meghan's best estimate held true, I had maybe six days to do something for Nightliss. *How can I win Ivy over or unlock my angel side in so short a time?*

Bella interrupted my thoughts. "Justin, do you remember the drain ward we encountered in the tunnels beneath El Dorado?"

An icy chill ran up my back at the memory. "You mean right after someone bragged we didn't need flashlights because we had Arcanes with their little glow-balls? And someone walked over the ward and it drained everyone of magic? And everything went pitch black? And the shadow people almost ate our souls? That time?"

"Yes."

"Of course, I remember. Just thinking about it makes me wonder how I didn't crap my pants."

Bella gave a grim smile. "Is there a chance you can convince your sister to meet you somewhere private?"

"I have no idea." I narrowed my eyes. "Why?"

"I intend to use a drain ward on your sister."

The obvious smacked me in the face like a large trout. If she had no magic, she was harmless, unless she had demonic strength like me. I hadn't seen any evidence she did. "What does it net us if we do capture her? The minute she has enough magic to help Nightliss, she'll probably kill us all."

Bella nodded. "The best course would be trading her for your mother."

I hated the thought of betraying Ivy. It would ruin any chance of ever reconciling with her, of that I had no doubt. But it might be our only course.

Shelton wrinkled his forehead. "A drain ward powerful enough to take on a normal Arcane is one thing, Bella, but this kid ain't ordinary."

"I'm aware of that, Harry."

He leaned forward on his elbow. "No, I don't think you are. A drain ward of that magnitude would need to be anchored to a ley line. You can't just siphon off that much power without a place for it to go. For that, you'd need to carve the rune in the right place. We're talking about the work of at least two days unless you know of some trick I don't."

I turned to Bella. Her face remained resolute. Unconcerned. "Is that true?" I asked.

She nodded. "Don't you feel the power beneath this place, Harry?"

His forehead wrinkled. "Yeah."

"I suggest we carve the drain ward into the floor here. If Justin brings Ivy here—"

I held up my hands. "Wait a minute. There's no way she'll agree to come here. I know for a fact she won't leave campus with me."

"The drain ward needs to be isolated, Justin," Bella said. "Once the rune is carved and enchanted, it will remain active until triggered."

I leaned my face into my hands, my mind warring between trying to convert Ivy, or betraying her. Was it even betrayal given what she'd done to me, luring me into Maximus's clutches with the fake kidnapping? What if our current brother-sister talks were part of another way to trick me into their arms? If I continued to talk to her, to get to know her, maybe she would trust me just enough to come here, especially if I told her it was haunted, or had elephants.

Looking at the two Arcanes, I sighed. "Let me see what I can do."

"No pressure," Shelton said with a somber look. "Bella, think we can do this within a couple of days?"

She held her chin in a hand for a moment. "I believe so."

Shelton shook his head. "What I don't get is why Ivy would be scared of meeting you alone." Shelton said. "The girl could probably whip your tail with one hand tied behind her back."

I rolled my eyes. "Gee, thanks for highlighting my insecurities."

"Just sayin', man."

In class the next morning, everyone was abuzz with excitement about the upcoming Grand Melee. Sometime during the weekend, nerds from the Science Academy had snuck into the university's stadium and stolen the team mascot—a fire-breathing toy poodle named Inferno whose other notable trait was the ability to say the word "squirrel". I wouldn't have believed it for a moment except when I Moogled it on my phone, I did indeed find videos of Inferno racing across the university campus shouting, "Squirrel" and shooting fire from its mouth at hapless rodents.

In retaliation, a group of Arcanes had tried to kidnap the academy's shiny chrome robot mascot, Cylo, and failed, instead opting to cast a rust spell on it. Since Cylo's armor was rust-proof, gloating techies had posted a video on Overnet—the Overworld version of the internet—explaining how science had beaten magic.

"Better luck next time!" said a group of dweebs who made the members of the chess club at my old high school look like pro athletes.

The camera zoomed out as one of the nerds said, "What do you think of that, Cylo?"

The robot, a flashing red light zipping back and forth where its eyes should have been said, "By your command," in a robotic synth and waved stiffly.

I felt like I'd died and gone to heaven. These were definitely my kind of people.

Despite my distracted mind, I managed to pass a pop quiz in Ms. Crab's Elementary Magic class. Of course, memorization and regurgitation had never been a problem for me. Actually doing magic—well, that was another issue.

After failing miserably to listen to Gaia in Elementary Mediation, I went to my favorite class, Arcane History. Zagg offered me a grin when I came in.

"I haven't heard anything back yet," I told him, returning an apologetic frown.

He shrugged. "I'll be patient. I've waited this long."

I hoped Michael found something useful soon.

As usual, the students fidgeted eagerly in their seats, waiting for Zagg to begin. I'd generally disliked history, it being about the past and all that boring stuff, but I probably could have listened to Zagg talk about it all day.

He sat on his stool and asked the class a few questions about what we'd learned so far. Every lesson remained crystal clear in my mind, no doubt thanks to the man's mastery at telling stories.

"And then Ezzek turned Doombringer into a statue," said a boy in answer to a question about one of the Arcane's battles.

"What happened to Thaumitus when he and the Order of Arcane Supremacy tried to wrestle control of the council from Ezzek, Justin?"

"Ezzek turned him inside out with a vacuum spell and annihilated his buddies." If I'd learned anything about the founding father of the Arcane Council, it was that he didn't mess around when it came to achieving his life goals. Ezzek had been a ruthless old coot. Nothing stood in his way.

"And so the Arcane University was built," Zagg said, rising from his stool and retrieving what looked like a black marble from his desk. He took the shiny sphere and spun it. Although the sphere should have spun for a second before promptly rolling off the table and onto the floor, I knew from experience this particular marble was what the Templars referred to as an all-seeing eye, or ASE for short.

The ASE spun faster and faster, weaving a web of light, the tapestry growing in size and detail until an image of the Queens Gate valley came into focus. A man in flowing white robes and a tall peaked hat pointed at the mountains in the valley with his intricately carved staff. He spoke, but there was no sound. The strong set of his jaw, and the fierce light in his eyes told me this was a man seething with passion. His eyes were such a light blue as to be almost white, and his hair shone nearly as white as his robes.

I had to wonder if maybe Ezzek Moore was the guy all the wizards in books and movies were based on.

Zagg stepped in front of the holographic image as Ezzek led a large group of robed people toward the base of the mountain where the university now stood. "Unfortunately, most of the ASE recordings of Ezzek Moore were damaged in the same battle that claimed his life. His most trusted advisor, and best friend, Alexander Tiberius, managed to salvage the ASEs before they were physically destroyed. Decades later, specialists were able to recover the video, though the audio in most of them was destroyed."

"Wait a minute," I said, "didn't the university founding happen after the fall of the Roman Empire? How old were these people?"

The historian smiled. "Their actual ages were unknown, but historians estimate Tiberius to have been at least three-hundred when the university was founded. As for Moore?" He shrugged. "We have only wild guesses and no exact birth date. The first record of him occurred exactly four-hundred years before the founding of the university."

"I didn't realize Arcanes were immortal."

"Oh, we're not." Zagg pursed his lips. "Arcanes do have much longer lifespans than noms, but Moore's longevity was abnormal. Many thought he possessed a spell granting him immortality. Others believed his mysterious lover, the woman known only as Lissa, had somehow granted him this long life."

I felt my jaw tighten at the mention of Lissa, who, according to MacLean, was none other than Daelissa. Either Zagg didn't know the truth behind Lissa, or he'd chosen not to talk about it, because he usually skimmed over Ezzek's love life. Then again, he probably didn't want to go into those sorts of details for an elementary grade history class.

We continued to watch the video, Zagg skipping ahead to show the construction of the original castle. At one point, Ezzek conjured a giant eagle, and apparently attached the ASE to one of the bird's claws, sending it soaring above the build site. I saw rows of tents where the builders lived, and wooden houses where most of the Arcanes stayed at the time. A building off a winding trail past the torn earth of the construction site caught my eye.

"What's that?" I asked, pointing to the structure.

"That was Ezzek's estate," Zagg replied, pausing the image, and zooming in on the house by putting his fingers on the location and moving them apart. He made a grabbing motion at the image and twisted it, orienting the view from the front of the house.

I felt my mouth drop open. Ezzek's pad was no house. It was a friggin mansion. And it wasn't just any old mansion.

It was the old fraternity house I was living in.

Chapter 32

After class, I corralled Zagg in his classroom, even though my stomach grumbled and complained since it was lunchtime. "What can you tell me about Moore's house?" I asked him.

The historian leaned against his desk, a hand under one chin. "Well, it was built before the university as a place for the Council to live during the campus construction. After completion of the campus, many in the council took teaching positions and quarters inside the castle. The Council of Seven renamed itself to the Arcane Council, and voted Alexander Tiberius as the first Chancellor."

It certainly explained why the place was so huge compared to the other houses on Greek Row. "And it eventually became a fraternity house?" I asked.

"Yep." He adjusted the holographic image floating above his desk to better show the mansion. "In fact, Tiberius founded the first so-called fraternity. Of course, he hadn't intended for the members to turn into a bunch of alcoholic party animals. His original intent, though, was something of a mystery."

Zagg looked at the open door. Walked over and closed it. When he returned, he took out his wand and made a little spinning motion with it. I felt a slight increase in air pressure as an anti-eavesdropping ward dropped into place.

I felt my forehead wrinkle. "Geez, what's with the secrecy?"

"I want to tell you something. But you have to promise not to repeat it to anyone else."

"Pinky swear?" I asked.

He snorted. "You've followed through on your word to me about the other matter. This is for your protection as well as mine."

"I promise to keep it a secret."

He nodded. "Good." Glanced at the closed door once more, and back to me. "Several years ago, one of my students wrote a dissertation—"

"Wait, a dissertation? Isn't that way above elementary level?"

His lips pressed tight. "Let's just say the story I'm about to tell you had political repercussions for my career."

"Oh." I felt bad for asking.

Zagg continued his story. "My former student wrote a dissertation behind the origins and mysteries of the first fraternity. During his research, he came to me several times, very excited about his findings. One night, he showed up, a copy of his dissertation in hand, and scared out of his wits. He told me people were after him. He said the Primus and Chancellor themselves had, through proxies, told him to cease work on his dissertation and find another subject. He told me the dissertation panelists were refusing to assign him a date for review."

"Why would bigwigs care about a paper on fraternities? Were they afraid people would find out they were wild and crazy in college and kick them out of their positions?"

Zagg shook his head. "It wasn't anything so simple. The student left the paper in my office for safekeeping. When I came the next morning, I discovered someone had tripped or disabled the wards on my office, and all that remained of the dissertation was a pile of dust."

"They burned it?"

"No, they transmuted it to dust so it couldn't be magically reconstituted."

"Why didn't they just steal it? Seems kind of dramatic to turn it to dust."

The historian offered a wry smile. "For one thing, if I'd put a tracker on it, I could have found those responsible. I think whoever did it wanted to send a crystal clear message."

I cringed. "Stop writing or end up like this?"

He nodded. "My thoughts exactly. Transmuting paper to dust is no simple matter. Whoever did it was very powerful. I recommended a safer subject for my student. He ended up writing a lame dissertation about the founding of the library instead. Passed with flying colors."

I raised an eyebrow and wrinkled my forehead for good measure. "Uh, so what's the point of telling me all this?"

"Always make a copy."

I laughed.

He smiled and continued. "I was curious to find out why important people would care about the crackpot theories of one doctoral candidate. While his paper read a lot like something bred from the wild fantasies of a kid who reads too many comic books, I was able to confirm many of his findings. At that point I had to admit his paper held water."

I still didn't understand where Zagg was going with this. "Are we still talking about fraternities here?"

"As a matter of fact, we're talking about the very first one on campus. But it was more than a fraternity. It was a secret order."

"Spit it out already," I said in an exasperated tone. "The suspense is killing me."

"Tiberius founded the Illuminati."

"Oh," I said, thinking that should have been my first guess. Unfortunately, I would never make a good detective. "To counter the Templars, right?"

Now it was Zagg's turn to look confused. "What do the Templars have to do with this?" he said, eyes flicking toward the door as if the chancellor and a squad of dissertation panelists might burst through at any moment and throw us in the dungeons.

I wasn't sure what I could tell Zagg. He seemed like a really cool guy now that we'd gotten past the stage where he'd tried to kill me and all, but I still didn't know him that well. On the other hand, what if he could help me find the Cyrinthian Rune? He trusted me with this secret, so maybe I could trust him with some of mine. "I've met a member of the Illuminati."

The historian's eyes flared. "What? Who?"

"Look, I think my secret is bigger than yours."

"Are you bragging about the size of your secret?" he said, raising an eyebrow.

I shrugged. "Not bragging. Just telling you how it is. I want you to promise to keep it to yourself."

He nodded. "I promise."

"Pinky swear?" I held out my pinky.

He blew out a breath and hooked his little finger in mine. "You are one strange man, Justin." A sigh. "Pinky swear."

I gave him the lowdown on my conversation with MacLean, leaving out his name for the time being. I told him about the rune and that the Conroys, Bigglesworth, and worst of all, Daelissa, were willing to kill anyone who got in their way.

Zagg dropped onto his stool, staring blankly at the floor. "Moore's lover, Lissa, was—is a Seraphim? And she created the Templars?" He seemed speechless for several moments. "These facts change everything. This knowledge would rock the very foundation of Overworld history."

I laid a hand on his shoulder. "Look, I'll be more than happy for you to spring the news on the world, but not now. Not while the Conroys and Daelissa are hunting for a relic that could allow them to achieve world domination."

"It sounds so dramatic when you say it that way." He stood. Nodded. "I'm your man. If Moore and Tiberius hid a relic somewhere on campus, I can probably triangulate it with copious amounts of historical research."

"Could you use an assistant?" I asked, the perfect candidate in mind.

"Definitely." He nodded his head toward the spinning ASE. "I've got hundreds of those to go through. Far more than I can do on my own. Who do you have in mind?"

"You met him in the forest the first night we, um, met," I said. "He was the one in the gray suit."

"I remember him. Odd fellow."

"Yeah, well that's because he's a golem. His name is Cinder."

"A golem?" Zagg's eyebrows rose. "He looks so real."

Feeling buoyed by optimism, I added, "If you can even get a general location of the rune, my Illuminati acquaintance can help us find it. He has a special ability for seeing things most of us can't."

Zagg opened his mouth, no doubt to ask me more about this special ability, but seemed to rein himself in. "Sounds good. I'll get back to you as soon as possible."

By the time I reached the cafeteria, lunch was almost over. I stood in the passageway outside the dining hall as a noisy mob of well-fed students poured from within, while my stomach rumbled angrily.

"Hi, Justin," said a familiar voice. I turned and saw Ivy grinning brightly at me, Morgana by her side. She held out a paper bag to me. "Morgana and I saved you some lunch since you were late." She made a tutting sound. "I went through a lot of trouble to sneak away today, and you didn't come.""I enjoyed talking to you," Morgana said to Ivy. She looked tired. I wondered if the other kids had been teasing her.

"Thanks, Ivy," I said, taking the bag. "This is really thoughtful of you." Somehow, I had to separate her from Morgana so I could talk to her about saving Mom.

"Aw, well, Morgana thought of it." She shrugged. "And then we talked about clothes." A look of wonder came over her face. "I really enjoyed it. I never get to choose what to talk about with the grownups."

"We both like purple clothes," Morgana added. "Especially dresses."

"Out of the way, freak," said a burly guy close to my age as he shoved past Morgana, knocking her over.

White hot anger flared in me. Before I could react, Ivy grabbed him by the arm. She obviously didn't have super strength, because the bully dragged her a couple of feet before turning to face her, a sneer on his face. "Get off me you idiot!"

Ivy's face turned to stone. "You will apologize to my friend," she said.

"Make me," he growled, as fur started to sprout from his face. His voice turned mocking, as if speaking to a child. "Or do you need to go get a Conroy to hold your hand, little baby?"

Ivy seemed to muse the question. "I think I'll handle you myself." Without so much as retrieving a wand, she slammed a palm to his chest. Light flashed between her hand and his body. The lycan howled, flew back, and slammed into the wall hard enough to knock loose several portraits.

Murmurs went up from the assembled students.

"I don't like bullies," Ivy said, her lips curling back. She made a slapping motion and sent the lycan tumbling down the hall. Her hand clenched the air and jerked. The lycan slid back toward her. She leaned over his prostrate form. "I'll make sure you never bully anyone again." Ivy raised a fist and made a pounding motion. The granite stone to the left of the student's head cracked, even though her fist never made contact. She made the motion again, and the invisible force pulverized the stone to dust. Teeth bared, her face red with rage, Ivy clasped both hands together and held them over the lycan's head. "Never again!" she screamed.

I blurred forward, caught her arms. "Ivy, don't!" I said. "Please, don't."

She seemed to snap from a trance. Looked up at me. Tears burst into her eyes, and she slumped. "I hate them, Justin. I hate the way they look at me. I hate the things they say about me." She gripped my shirt, looking up at me with tear-stained eyes. "I *hate* them!"

A crowd of students surrounded us. The lycan scrambled to his feet and plowed through them in his haste to escape. I heard someone whispering about how Ivy wasn't normal. Heard another say we were all freaks. Another asked why we were hanging out with a traitor.

I caught Morgana's tear-filled eyes.

"Show's over," I said to the crowd. "Get out of here!"

The crowd dispersed rather quickly, probably concerned Ivy might lose it again and kill them all.

"I don't like bullies either," Morgana said, wiping her face.

I led them down a quiet hall. Ivy took a deep breath and closed her eyes. When she opened them, her face could have been made of ice.

"Are you okay?" I asked.

She smiled brightly. "I'm fine. I guess I need to work on my temper."

"You didn't seem fine. Don't repress your emotions, Ivy. It'll only make things worse when they break free again."

"Oh, that silly boy just made me mad," she said again, bouncing on her toes.

Ivy was pulling a Shelton on me, I realized, except she didn't hide her emotions with a gruff exterior, but fake sunshine. I turned to the other girl. "Are you okay, Morgana?"

She nodded.

"Do they bully you a lot?"

She looked away from me, her protective shell coming up.

"I was bullied a lot in school, too," I said. "I know what it's like."

Her eyes widened. "You were?"

"Football players beat him up," Ivy said in hushed voice. "Big mean boys."

"That's terrible," Morgana said. "Did—did your parents…" she trailed off as if unable to finish the sentence.

"Did my parents what?" I sighed. Morgana and Ivy were going to drive me crazy if they kept repressing everything. "My parents split up," I said. "My mom is an Arcane, and my dad, well, he's a Daemos."

"He's not our dad, Justin," Ivy said in a fierce voice. "It's a lie, a lie, a lie!"

Morgana and I gave her an uneasy look.

"Unless you know for sure who our dad is, can we just pretend he is?" I said, exasperated. "I mean, it's really cool if you think about it. We're the best of both worlds."

Ivy pursed her lips, and narrowed her eyes at me. "It's cool to be half evil?"

"No, but it means we have the super powers of both sides. Magic and super strength."

"I don't know…" she trailed off, eyes losing focus. "I'm not super strong."

"But wouldn't it be cool if you could pick up bullies without magic?" I asked, wondering if I might have my foot in the door on her dislike of our father.

"I suppose." She toed the floor. "Whatever. We'll pretend he's our father so Morgana doesn't get confused."

I fought back a smile. She'd given me an inch. I wondered if I could take it a mile.

"I guess my problems aren't as bad as yours," Morgana said. "I mean, at least my parents love each other, even if they are traitors."

I stared at her for a moment. "Traitors?"

"Traitors?" Ivy said an instant later. "What did they do? Tell me!"

Morgana nodded, a tear breaking free from an eyelash to spill down her cheek. "They were spying for the Red Syndicate. They're in jail now."

"I'm so sorry, Morgana." I touched her shoulder, unsure how to console her.

She flung herself against me, thin arms clinging tight around my waist, head pressed to my stomach, her body shaking with sobs. I wasn't sure what to do, so I just hugged her back, wondering if this was what it felt like to be a parent consoling a hurt child.

Ivy touched Morgana's hand. "Everyone treats you bad because of what your parents did?"

Morgana nodded. "But I know my parents aren't bad people. I just know it."

My sister's eyes met mine. "I know how that feels." She seemed on the verge of saying something, when her eyes went wide. "Oh, no. I'm really late." She looked around frantically. "They'll be looking for me. Oh, no!"

"Wait!" I said. "I need to talk to you about—"

"No time, no more time," she said in a slightly crazed voice. "I can run. Maybe blink." She stood on tiptoe and kissed me on the cheek. "Take care of Morgana, brother. She's one of us." With that, she literally blinked away, appearing at the end of the hall, about a hundred feet away. Blew me a kiss, and vanished again.

"Your sister is so cool," Morgana said in an awed voice.

Son of a— I sighed, looking back at Morgana. "Are you going to be okay?"

She shook her head. "I can't even stay in my dorm room. The girls make fun of me. I sneak out so I don't have to be near them. You're my only friend now. My other friend got sick, and I don't know if she'll be okay again."

"What happened to your parents?" I asked.

"A man came for them," she said. "They ran away and left me with my aunt. They told me they'd be back, and they loved me. But the mean man, he wouldn't give up. He found them and arrested them."

"Who was this man?" I asked.

She trembled. "I don't remember his first name, just his last." She gave me a hopeful look. "Can you make him give my parents back?"

"I don't know. But I have friends in the Templars who might be able to help."

Her eyes brightened hope. "Please, do."

"Give me the name of the man, and I'll have my friends ask him where they are," I said.

She put a finger to her chin, narrowing her eyes in thought. "I think his name was Shelton."

Chapter 33

I shoved Shelton against the wall. "How many lives have you ruined?" I shouted. I snarled, released him, and paced across the warded room where we'd discussed our battle plans the night before.

Bella watched from a seat near the door, her eyes concerned, but made no move to interfere.

"I wasn't trying to ruin lives, damn it!" Shelton punched the wall, and winced. "I was making a living." He shrugged even as he favored his knuckles. "I brought criminals to justice. Nothing wrong with that."

"How many people did you kidnap?" I asked, a burning coal of outrage simmering in my stomach. "How many mothers and fathers and siblings and girlfriends, did you take away from their loved ones?"

"I didn't kidnap anyone, Justin. I apprehended lawbreakers. Fugitives."

"Justin, these people committed crimes," Bella said, her voice soft. "Harry didn't do anything wrong."

I ran a hand through my hair. Sighed, and stared blankly at the floor for a moment. Maybe I was being unreasonable. Maybe knowing Morgana and identifying with her situation was eating me up inside. Now I was taking out my frustrations on a friend. "Was the evidence solid?" I asked in a lowered voice.

"I'm a bounty hunter, damn it," Shelton said, "not a detective. Looking for evidence isn't my job."

"Does the Overworld convict them by a jury trial?" I asked.

He nodded. "Yeah, the tribunal does." He cleared his throat. "Although, I don't think Zagg's girl has gone to trial yet. Neither have Morgana's parents."

"They've been in prison all this time without a trial?" Bella asked, concern on her face.

"Again, not my job," Shelton said. "Who the hell do you think I am, the Primus?" He threw up his hands. "Holy friggin cow patties, people. Maybe you're confusing me with, oh, I dunno, God?"

"Who else have you arrested that I should know about?" I asked. "Before I stumble across another poor broken little child whose parents were taken away by the notorious Harry Shelton."

"Gee, it sounds so much better when you put it like that," Shelton said, his voice dripping with sarcasm. "I didn't intentionally arrest people for kicks and giggles. My contact—" he stopped mid-sentence, mouth open. His face blanched, and he tried to speak again, his mouth apparently warring with his brain for control. After several seconds of fighting, he dropped into a chair. "Crap. Who am I kidding?"

"What is it, Harry?" Bella asked, rising from her chair as if ready to fly to him if need be.

"I'm such a liar." He swallowed hard. "I can't do this anymore."

I was sorely tempted to pile on in agreement with that assessment, but kept my mouth shut by sheer willpower.

Shelton finally continued after another long pause. "Aerianas." His throat sounded dry. His voice cracked.

The name sounded terrible familiar. And then it hit me. Vallaena had said that name, confronting Shelton with it, and threatening to expose him several months ago right after I'd first met her. So much had been going on at the time—hellhounds trying to kill me, Aunt Vallaena trying to assign herself as my protector, and Underborn, evil assassin that he was, trying to kill my father. Ah, the good old days.

I turned back to Shelton. "So? Who is she?"

Shelton took a long time to answer, his face buried in his hands. Finally he said, "I was in love with her."

My mouth dropped open. Harry Shelton, romantic? *Inconceivable.*

He continued. "When I first started the bounty hunter business, I was pretty bad at it. So I tailed other hunters, watching how they did things, and eventually fell into a partnership with an old-timer named Hooch. He was amazing." Shelton sat up, his eyes filling with something like affection or respect. "I spent two years with him, learning the ropes and steadily improving. Then Hooch got a tip and a lead on a big fish. The holy friggin grail of fugitives."

"Who?" Bella asked, leaning on the edge of her seat.

"Vadaemos Slade."

My skin went cold at the name. "I didn't realize you ever went after him."

His jaw went tight. "Yeah. We did." Shelton shook his head like a dog shedding water. "We were ambushed. Somehow, that slimy pile of butt droppings knew we were coming. Some kind of demon spawn creatures sucked Hooch's soul out of his mouth. Turned him into a dried husk of skin right in front of me. I ran. Holy hell, did I run. Used every spell in the book to get myself out of there. But when I looked back at it later—much later—I knew for a certainty escape from those things should have been impossible. Something or someone held them back, and let me go."

"What makes you think that?" I asked.

His eyes focused on me. "You had to be there. Those things were lightning fast, man. Hooch was one of the trickiest Arcanes I have ever known. He wasn't the most powerful, but he made up for it by being crazy like a fox. He always warded himself, and had a shield spell ready to turn on in a heartbeat. His precautions saved our hides more times than I can count. Those spawn went through his shield like it was thin air. Poor bastard didn't have a chance. And there were enough of them to take us both down at the same time. But they didn't."

I pursed my lips. "Sounds like the same creatures that ambushed the Templars and Daemos at Thunder Rock."

"They make hellhounds look like puppies." Shelton shuddered. "Anyway, I took a break from the business. It wasn't a good time for me. And then I met Aerianas." An almost dreamy look overcame his face. "She came to me, and asked me to help her find a fugitive who'd killed a little boy's parents. I didn't usually do freelance for individuals, but she was so smoking hot I couldn't resist. So, I did the job, and my prize was her."

"Slut," Bella said under her breath.

Shelton didn't seem to hear her. "She told me she knew people in the tribunal court, and could tell me about contracts before they went public so I could get a head start. She told me I was the best, and it would be a shame if I stopped bounty hunting." He sighed. "That's how I got Zagg's girlfriend, and Morgana's parents."

"I imagine they were easy targets," I said.

His forehead pinched. "Are you kidding me? Zagg and his pals hid his girlfriend, Kayla, so well it took me a month to track her down. Morgana's parents, the Findelays, were hiding in the Swiss Alps. They triggered an avalanche that nearly took me out." He looked skyward, as if wondering how he'd survived. "But Hooch taught me well, and I always got my man."

"Didn't he teach you to question things?" I asked. "To find out why you were hunting people?"

Shelton showed a rueful grin. "He tried. Hooch was a different breed of bounty hunter. He always demanded proof before a hunt. Even after he caught his targets, he'd question them like he was the sheriff. He once told me a friend of his had been wrongly accused, and he never wanted to take in an innocent person."

"I guess those lessons didn't stick with you," I said, and I couldn't help the disapproving note in my voice.

"Guess not. I didn't care about that stuff. I just wanted the money and the glory." He looked away.

"What do you mean?" Bella asked.

"One of the jobs Aerianas landed me involved apprehending an Arcane accused of selling magic to noms. I took him in, got my payout, and when I went back to the guy's house to recover supplies I'd dropped during the bust, I just happened to stumble across evidence that completely exonerated him. I—" Shelton blinked. "I decided it wasn't my job to do anything about it. So I just let it lie."

"Harry!" Bella looked aghast.

"I didn't want Aerianas to get in trouble. I was young and stupid. I was so blindly in love with her, I would have—I did anything she asked."

"You kept doing jobs even though you had suspicions." I said in an accusing voice.

He nodded. "But my conscience really started bugging me."

I raised both eyebrows.

Shelton held up his hands defensively. "Yeah, yeah. I actually have a little cricket that nags the hell out of me when I'm doing something bad." He exhaled a long sigh. "I secretly checked out the evidence against the next few targets Aerianas tipped me off about. Each case looked like a complete slam dunk. If Hooch ever taught me anything, it's that if the evidence looks too neat, it's probably a load of bull."

I threw in a guess. "Those people were set up."

He nodded. "I decided to dig a little deeper." A look of remorse or perhaps regret pinched his face. "It didn't take me long to figure out what tied most of them together, once I knew what to look for." He drew in a deep breath as if steeling himself, and looked at us. "My father."

I glanced at Bella. She looked just as confused as I felt. "Care to elaborate?"

"Daddy dearest, also known as the Arcanus Primus, was pushing his pet project, the Gloom Initiative back at that time."

Bella nodded. "I remember. It was very controversial, costing millions of tinsel. They wanted to explore the Gloom and see if it could be used for transportation like the Obsidian Arch network."

"Or see if it had anything to do with the way the arches worked, or find new creatures living there, and blah, blah, blah." Shelton grunted. "The opposition claimed it would cost lives, and possibly allow undesirable entities to enter our world."

"Like the minders?" I said.

He nodded. "Yeah, creepy critters like that."

"These people opposed your father, and he framed them for clear passage of the initiative?"

"Yes, again." Shelton twiddled his thumbs, gazing at them forlornly. "And I still kept right on bagging and tagging the poor bastards. I just couldn't force myself to leave Aerianas. I knew she had something to do with it, but I turned a blind eye. I wanted her so bad, I could hardly stand it, and the thought of losing her drove me crazy."

I wanted to blame Shelton for his misdeeds. Really I did. But I knew how love, real or imagined, could make anyone do stupid things. All I had to do was think back a few months to remember how idiotic I'd acted for Katie Johnson. "How long ago did all this happen?"

"It went on for about a year, and ended just before I met you." He didn't look up from the floor. "Look, I ain't perfect. I was kind of a jackass when I went to school here, and I didn't change much once I graduated. But I didn't go out of my way to intentionally hurt people."

"What was it that drove you out of Colombia when we went after Maximus?" I asked.

"Murderous relatives of someone I'd apprehended for—" He paused a moment. "For Aerianas. For my adoptive father." His lips curled in rage. "Sager used me to catch and kill my real parents. Then he used me again to put away his political enemies." Shelton bolted from his chair. Turned, and kicked it. As the chair skidded across the floor, he whipped out his wand, and with an angry word sent a bolt of white-hot energy into the defenseless object. Wood splintered, spraying across the room. He shouted again, and shards of light intercepted the splinters, reducing them to ash before they hit the floor.

"*Madre de dios*," Bella said under her breath. "Now I understand."

I, of course, was far more impressed with the display of wizardry than anything else, so it took a moment for her words to sink in. Shelton's soul was scarred. He'd been used by his father. Used by the woman he loved. No wonder he walled off his emotions. No wonder he never let anyone see the real him, his emotions, insecurities, and worst of all, the sense that nobody in this world really loved him. He had no family. How could I complain about my situation after knowing what Shelton had been through?

Shelton stood before the falling ash, his back to us, shoulders heaving. I couldn't let the questioning stop now. I still had to understand one more thing.

"Shelton—Harry. What did Meghan mean when she told me you worked with the spawn who killed her family?" I felt my chest tighten. "Is that true?"

He shook his head without turning to face me. "No. The Daemos who did that, as you well know, was Vadaemos. What happened to her parents was long before my time."

I felt myself relax, and saw Bella, hand to heart, breathe a sigh of relief.

Shelton turned to me, his eyes rimmed with red, face screwed up in pain. "She was almost right. I didn't work with Vadaemos, but I did work with someone close to him."

"Aerianas?" I said, taking a logical guess.

He nodded.

"How did she know Vadaemos?"

Shelton let out a shuddering sigh. "Aerianas is his daughter."

Chapter 34

"Holy macaroni," I muttered.

"Now it makes even more sense," Bella said, eyes lighting up. "Was she using her succubus powers on you, Harry?" The hopeful look on her face made my heart ache.

Shelton gave a grudging nod. "Yeah. Later, when I confronted her, she told me she really loved me, but was afraid I hated her." His lips curled up in an angry snarl. "She did something to me. Infected me with her succubus powers. To this day, I still think about her. I still miss her. Worst of all, it feels like I still love her, even though I know with every inch of my black heart I don't. I hate her for what she did to me. I hate myself for what I did to those people." He threw his wand across the room where it clattered against a bookshelf. "I don't want any of these feelings piled on my shoulders, man. I just want to forget them. I want the past to stay in the past and to leave me the hell alone."

"Oh, Harry," Bella said, walking toward him.

He threw out the palms of his hands. "No, Bella. I can't. Do you understand why? I'm a sack of maggots."

I stood rooted in place, stunned by what I was seeing. I could count on one hand the number of times I'd seen Shelton lower his gruff exterior and admit to having a genuine feeling. Yet, here he stood, naked and exposed. I didn't know what to feel. Part of me felt embarrassed to witness it. Another part wanted to help him, and didn't know how. It occurred to me that this time of crisis was a very bad time for him to have a mental breakdown, but I could lay the blame for that squarely on my shoulders. I'd pushed him into this. I'd demanded the truth. Now I had it.

And the truth might hurt us all.

Bella stood feet away from Shelton, tears pooling in her eyes. Her lower lip quivered. "I know you're a good man, Harry Shelton. I've seen your golden heart shine many times." Her voice lowered to a whisper. "It always gives me hope."

"Hope?" He said the word with a scoffing laugh. "Hope to feel like crap for the rest of my life?"

She took a hesitant step toward him. "Hope that maybe a brighter light can outshine the darkness around your heart."

"Nothing can fix me, damn it." A tear trickled down his cheek. He scraped it away with an angry swipe of his hand. "And what makes you think I'm worth fixing?"

Bella took his hand in both of hers, and smiled at him as tears sparkled like diamonds on her cheeks. "I have faith in you. I have hope." She kissed his hand. "Maybe it's silly of me. Maybe all these decades of life haven't taught me anything. But you make me feel young again. Being around you makes me appreciate life after all the darkness and terrible deeds I've seen."

"Me?" he said in a tiny voice filled with confused wonder.

She laughed and cried at the same time. "Yes, you. Can't you see why, you silly man?" Bella leaned up and kissed him. "The reason I know you're not an evil person is because I could never love someone like that." Her eyes met his and held them. "Harry, I love you."

My heart thudded, and I felt my own eyes watering up as I witnessed Shelton's stunned look. As I watched him touch the lip Bella had kissed. And it made me miss Elyssa so much I could hardly stand it.

Harry Shelton, gruff, uncaring, and a royal pain in the ass of good manners, took Bella in his arms and gave her a kiss that made the petite dhampyr melt into his arms.

I turned and ran from the room, closing the door behind me, heart pounding with a mixture of pain and joy.

I pulled out my phone and texted Elyssa. *I love you and miss you.* I didn't expect a response. I just had to send it, to let her know she was on my mind. Because things were getting uglier by the minute on this side of the world.

Shelton had thrown back the covers, revealing true evil and corruption. His father had framed innocent people. But his revelations about Aerianas's parentage also meant there may have been a connection between Vadaemos and Shelton's father, Jarrod Sager.

I felt certain Vadaemos had lured Hooch into that deadly ambush, and allowed Shelton to escape. Then he'd sent his daughter to manipulate my friend. Using my arcphone to create a holographic display on the table in the den, I told Nookli to display several names: Jarrod Sager, Vadaemos Slade, the Conroys, and Daelissa. Vadaemos had helped Daelissa at one point, until she'd turned everyone against him by framing him for the massacre at Thunder Rock. Vadaemos, in turn, had worked from the shadows for years, until he'd been driven to hide in El Dorado where Elyssa, Bella, and several others including me had eventually cornered and captured him. Daelissa had later tried to free him, resulting in the death of Elyssa's brother Jack.

If Vadaemos had worked for Daelissa, did that connect Sager to Daelissa? Why would Vadaemos, a narcissistic Daemos, help Sager? Did it have anything to do with the Gloom project?

My diagram helped me understand why Vadaemos and Sager used Shelton instead of someone else. Simply by looking at Shelton's track record, they knew he wouldn't question evidence. They knew he was young, driven by money and glory. Shelton possessed excellent bloodhound skills. He also unknowingly offered himself as a scapegoat, and a way to distance Sager from his targets. Most people might see Shelton's actions as those of a man trying to protect his father, should the truth about their innocence come to light.

Sager knew his political enemies could stop him, and stop his pet project. By isolating them in prison, he maintained control. I had to find out more about the Gloom Initiative and why it was so important to him. It meant I had no choice but to ask Shelton to investigate his father. He might be the only person who could wrestle the truth from him. In the meantime, I had other errands to run.

I called Michael, and told him what I'd found out about Shelton's past.

"Figures," he said. "I knew the evidence looked too tight."

"Can you disprove it?"

"I don't need to. I just need to find who planted the evidence."

"You're the man with the plan," I said.

"Yes." He hung up.

My phone buzzed. A text message from Elyssa. My heart leapt.

I can't stop thinking about you. The trial is dragging on, but I think I'm near the end. Are you okay? I love you. MUAH!

I tapped back a message. *MUAH, baby! I'm fine, but lots to talk about. Please call the minute you can after the trial. Love you!*

My spirits soared just hearing from her. It felt so strange to have gone so long without seeing her, without kissing her, or telling her how much I loved her. She'd probably kill me once she found out the recent dangers I'd faced. But I wasn't about to ruin her chances at finishing the trial.

My thoughts returned to the conversation with Michael. I felt a strong urge to tell Zagg the good news, but realized there wasn't really any to tell, not yet. Sure, I could tell him someone planted the evidence. Tell him Shelton knew it was planted and arrested his girlfriend anyway. Zagg would probably round up the gang again to kill Shelton if I told him that. Since I didn't know when or if Michael would find the person who planted the evidence, I couldn't give Zagg false hope. Somehow, I had to bring the stack of lies crashing to the ground, even if it meant taking down the Primus himself. I made myself a to-do list on the phone, tacking "Take down the Arcanus Primus" at the bottom. My primary objective of "Make Ivy love me or unlock my inner angel" remained unchecked. "Save Nightliss" and "Save myself" depended wholly on the first.

As I entered first period the next day, Morgana looked up at me with big innocent eyes, and smiled. I took my seat next to her, and grinned back.

"Thank you again for standing up for me, Justin," she said. "I means ever so much to me."

"No problem," I said, feeling a little choked up. Though her words made me feel good, I also felt guilty. I had information indicating her parents might be innocent. Shouldn't I at least tell her that much? Or would it cause her more pain to know?

The poor girl looked so exhausted. I had to at least find out where she was sleeping. She couldn't go on like this.

After Elementary Meditation class, in which Belinda made us stand on our heads against a wall until I was dizzy, I rushed to Zagg's classroom, hopeful he might have some news for me.

"Justin," he said, smiling broadly.

"Any luck?" I asked.

He chuckled. "We've barely begun, though I gotta say that golem of yours is amazing." He tilted his head. "How did you make him?"

"I didn't," I said, avoiding further details. "He's helpful?"

"More than helpful. He's downright curious about everything, and has been cataloguing my old scrolls for me. I showed him how to record stuff onto an ASE so we can index and search it more easily."

"Why not just give in and use an arctablet?"

"Look, I know it's lame, but if the administration found out I was using gadgets like that, I might end up out of a job."

I shrugged. "Get a job at the academy. At least they're forward thinking."

He shuddered. "All they think about is the future. They hate the past."

"They don't teach history there?"

"Of course they do, but it's almost all about technology. There aren't any awesome wizard battles, or castles, or damsels in distress." He grimaced like he'd just swallowed a toilet-flavored roach. "It's a bunch of dry, boring, science stuff." Zagg clapped a hand on my shoulder as students began filling the room. "Don't worry. The ASEs are amazing archival tools, and they're based on old magic."

I nodded, feeling a little placated, and took my seat. Morgana gave me a curious look.

"Do you want to be a history teacher someday?" she asked. "You spend a lot of time talking to the professor."

I chuckled. "No, I'm just interested in particular bits of history."

After class, we went to lunch, and took our usual table. I saw wolf-boy enter the dining hall. He took one wide-eyed look at us, and skirted the edge of the dining hall to avoid coming anywhere near us, even though Ivy wasn't present.

A golem delivered our food—some kind of beef in a rich white sauce with a side of mushrooms and asparagus. I made a note to avoid the bathrooms after this, because the odor of stinky asparagus pee promised to be epic after lunch.

I looked at Morgana. Her head lay on the table, and she seemed to be asleep. Her complexion so pallid, the rings under her eyes so dark—I drew in a sharp breath as a sudden realization hit me like a knife. "Morgana!" I smoothed her hair out of the way, and felt for a pulse in her neck. It felt strong.

She moaned. Looked up at me. "Lunchtime?" she said in a slurred voice.

"Morgana, who was your other friend? The one you said got sick."

A tired smiled crept across her face. "So sweet. She was our RA, Lina." She sighed. "She showed me a secret place to go when I wanted to be alone. I didn't tell her, but I stole a mattress and blankets and started sleeping down there."

My heart felt like it stopped beating. I scooped Morgana into my arms and blurred from the lunchroom, never slowing until I reached Healer Hutchins's office. "She needs help!" I said.

The healer bolted out of her chair, a wide-eyed look on her face. "What is it with you?" she said, directing me toward the back room without pause, and had me place the girl on a bed.

"Morgana? Are you still awake?" I asked.

The girl nodded, smiling faintly. She made a choking sound, gasping for air. Her eyes went wide and terrified. She looked at me, as a final breath rattled from her throat.

And then she lay still.

Chapter 35

"Morgana!" I screamed, feeling hot tears burn my eyes.

"Out of my way," Hutchins said, shoving me so hard, I almost fell down. She took out a wand, ran it up and down the girl's body. The tip glowed bright, and she pressed it against the girl's ribs. Morgana's body lurched, back arching hard before dropping back. She drew in a long shuddering breath, rasping like sandpaper on wood for several seconds, before settling into a shallow, but steady rhythm. I wiped tears from my eyes, my heart pounding against my chest with fear and pain.

Hutchins turned to me. "She'll be okay."

"I think she has the same thing Lina does," I said without preamble. "She's been secretly sleeping in the Burrows, probably near where Lina was going. Something down there must have poisoned them."

"And them," Hutchins said, waving a hand around the room.

I followed the course of her hand, suddenly taking notice of five more sleeping forms, their sunken eyes and pallid skin tone all the evidence I needed to convince me.

"What happened?"

"They found the open entrance to the Burrows, and had been playing hide and seek down there, apparently for several weeks." She sighed. "None of them woke up yesterday morning, and their resident administrators brought them in."

I ground my teeth. This was turning into some sort of epidemic. "If I found the source, do you think you can fix this?"

Hutchins wrinkled her face, eyebrows pinching. "If you bring it up here you might poison the entire school." She shook her head. "Young man, whatever is doing this is obviously dangerous. If the former administrators couldn't find it, what makes you think you can?"

I knew the answer almost immediately. "Trust me."

Her lips pressed together with disapproval. "More than likely you'll just add yourself to the tally."

"Is Lina any better or"—I took in a deep breath—"worse?"

"About the same. I take it as good news, however, that she hasn't worsened."

I nodded, the sliver of hope prying away the dread trying to clamp itself to my heart. "Thanks, Miss Hutchins."

I called my secret weapon as I made a beeline for the library where he was hopefully still hiding.

"You're still alive and ticking, eh?" MacLean said, voice thick with Scottish brogue.

"Sort of." I told him why I needed his help.

After a long pause, he sighed. "Truth be told, I'm going stir crazy hiding in these tunnels. It might be nice to get out for a while." Another pause. "Where do you want to meet?"

I chose a nearby hallway, told him, and headed that way after ending the call.

I'd just reached the area, when I felt the hairs on the back of my neck stiffen. Trying to act casual, I slipped from the stream of students in the corridor, and took a seat on a bench near a window overlooking a wide plaza with the statue of a person in robes raising their hands overhead.

Pulling off my shoe and making a show of emptying it of a bothersome rock, I glanced around the hall. Students, most of them clumped into groups as they made their way to other classes, walked and talked. I spotted a group of nerdy Arcanes levitating a toad down the hall and a clique of pretty girls changing each other's hair color with the touch of their wands. I imagined I could sit and people watch all day if I didn't have to worry about my friends dropping dead from bizarre magical poisoning.

Whatever had tickled my sixth sense, however, was nowhere to be seen.

I stood. Stretched. And felt the tingle again. My eyes jerked toward the source, but found only three girls across the hall talking, their faces animated, but the words of their conversation lost to me in the general hubbub. I took one last look around, and was about to move on, when something drew my eyes back to the girls. They were still talking—all at the same time, their expressions vacant.

Wading through the crowd, I made my way toward the girls. They looked at me in unison, and a shiver ran down my spine at the eerie looks in their eyes. As one, they turned, and skipped down the hallway, taking the first turn. I paused for a moment, weighing the stupidity of following them, decided it was quite likely a trap, and followed anyway.

Since I wasn't a complete moron, I sent MacLean a text message, telling him something was off, and to be careful when approaching, then told Nookli to update him on my coordinates.

The first turn took me down a side corridor with only a smattering of students. The girls looked at me as they entered a door midway down. Another shiver ran down my spine. *This is stupid. This is stupid!* But I kept going. Peering in, I saw the girls holding hands in the front of an empty classroom. They smiled. I looked up and down the hallway, wary of a sneak attack, but nothing jumped from the shadows.

"How'd you figure it out?" the girls asked simultaneously.

I didn't know what I'd figured out, but decided to play along anyway. "Because of creepy stuff like the way you just talked."

They smiled, their expressions perfectly mirroring each other with flawless timing. Their figures softened, faces drooping like melting wax. I gasped, a gagging sound escaping my throat as the girls melted into a soupy mass that reformed into a single figure.

"Guess I need to work on that, eh, mate?" Bigglesworth assumed the shape of a man with a slight paunch, chubby face, and skin the color of biscuit dough. He looked a lot like the first time I'd seen him.

I wasn't sure if I should run away or hold my ground. The last fight with the Flark hadn't remotely gone my way. Magic didn't affect him, and I couldn't punch him to death since his skin would literally eat me alive. Fire had worked. Maybe I could heat the room like an oven and turn him to ash. It would have been a wonderful idea if I actually had a clue as to how I might pull off such a feat.

Instead, I glanced up and down the hall, spotting only a couple of students heading down the hall toward the main hall. "Why are you following me?"

"Well, mate, it seems you've been talking to young Miss Ivy."

"She's my sister."

"True." The Flark offered a greasy grin. "But we can't have you bending her impressionable mind now, can we?"

My jaw went tight. "You're one to talk. Your masters have been brainwashing her all her life." I clenched my fists, frustrated I couldn't do anything to whisk her away from them. Frustrated I couldn't hurt this bastard.

My senses shrieked. I spun just as the two students in the hallway lunged for me. Pain raced across my skin like acid. I instinctively jerked, but their limbs stretched like rubber, clinging to me no matter how I struggled. Bigglesworth slithered across the room, his lower half like a huge snake. His hand merged with one of my captor's shoulders, and the truth snapped on like a light bulb. These students were part of Bigglesworth too. The pain abruptly ceased, and I sagged with relief.

The Flark laughed. "I lied earlier, mate. I don't need to work on this sort of thing at all."

And I'd taken the bait.

I tried to concentrate on a spell, when agony seared across my skin.

"Now, now, none of that." His body melded into the two fake students until only he remained. "You know those little magic tricks don't work on me."

"What do you want?" I gasped. The flood of pain cut off again, and ecstasy warmed my body at its absence.

He chuckled. "Frankly, I'd enjoy torturing you for a few centuries, eating you a little at a time. Unfortunately, I ain't got the luxury."

"Because your Seraphim mistress has you on a tight schedule?" I asked. "I know Flarks come from the angel realm. I know you don't really serve the Conroys."

Bigglesworth pursed his blanched lips. "Seems you're a mite smarter than I reckoned." He leaned into my face. "I serve no one but my mistress. The bloody Conroys are human garbage we're using in the meantime."

"You like Ivy," I said, finding it hard to hold my head up. His touch had poisoned me somehow, or short-circuited my brain.

"She's Seraphim," he said with an amused look.

"So am I."

He snickered. "You're a bloody Darkling lover is what you are. You're worse than garbage." A sigh. "Too bad I can't savor this. I ain't had a Seraphim in ages."

The thought of him eating my essence, using my body like a squeeze bottle full of glowing mayonnaise, sent a shudder of revulsion through me. Magic might not work, but I had something else to rely on. As if the mere thought of manifesting into my half demon form was a welcome mat, the pulsing cold of the vampling virus sent an icy blast through my lower body.

I had to hold back the monster. If it broke loose here in the middle of the school, the results would be catastrophic.

Bigglesworth's hands melted over my arms, his goopy flesh flowing across me like animated slime. I couldn't do magic. I couldn't move. I had one choice left. I had to release the monster in me. But the pain made it impossible. It cut off all reasoning. The Flark's flesh covered my mouth, my nose. I couldn't breathe. Couldn't think. All I could do, a part of me realized, was die.

The pain abruptly stopped. Bigglesworth's form writhed against me. Bubbling shrieks of agony screeched from dozens of tiny mouths all along his skin as he fell off me, and thudded on the floor like a wad of pizza dough. I stumbled backward, catching myself on the door frame, and turned to see Maclean in the doorway, his face a mask of fury as he held a rod against Bigglesworth's quivering mass.

"Get out of here," MacLean said. "This won't stop the bloody monster for long."

I didn't need urging, and raced past the wildly flailing creature.

MacLean grunted, impaling the rubbery blob. "That'll keep him for a bit."

"Can we kill him?" I asked.

The Scot grabbed my arm and dragged me after him. "If I knew how to do that, do you think I'd be running my bloody arse off?"

We ran through the maze of corridors for several minutes before MacLean made me stop, and looked me up and down for any sign of stray bits of the shape shifter.

I thought back to the incident. "How did you do that to him? I didn't think magic worked."

MacLean laughed. "That wasn't magic, lad. It was straight-up technology."

"It looked like a wand."

"Aye. It's called a cattle prod." He chuckled.

I felt my eyebrows rise. "A dinky old cattle prod stopped that thing? How did you know it would?"

"Research, lad. I've been stuck in the walls of the library for a bloody fortnight." He groaned. "Apparently, those nasty buggers conduct electricity almost as good as copper. Too bad it doesn't kill them."

After glancing up and down the hallway for any signs of suspicious children or extremely pissed off balls of dough, I decided it might be safe to return to the matter at hand. "Are you still okay with helping me in the Burrows?"

He snorted. "Might as well, since the Flark is temporarily taken care of."

I waved him onward. "After you."

MacLean led the way down a familiar flight of stairs until we reached the iron door guarding the tunnels where Bigglesworth had tortured MacLean. The big man didn't so much as glance down the hall toward the room, instead turned left and pointed out the iron grate with the hole I'd noticed the last time.

"What are we looking for?" the Scot asked, sending a globe of light into the passage.

"No idea. Whatever it is, I figure your Dark Sight should be able to pick it out."

We walked through the pitch black, the light sphere casting creepy shadows along the tunnel walls, eventually reaching a banded iron door. I pushed it open, the hinges squeaking ever so slightly, and light spilled into the corridor. Magic lanterns, similar to the ones I'd seen in other parts of the castle, lined the walls, their yellow glow offering a welcome respite from the smothering darkness of the previous passage.

MacLean snuffed his light, and we proceeded. Rusted gates, guard stations with levers to control the gates, shackles, and small cells with windowless doors offered a silent history of the dungeon. Unlike the winding corridors in the university complex above, the passages here formed a grid of stone-lined tunnels.

The tall Scot, a strained look on his face, said very little, but swept every crevice with his gaze, even going so far as to stop and look over each cell. I kept track of our progress with my phone, marking off passages as we went. As we reached the dead end of the final passage, MacLean squeezed his eyes shut, pinched the bridge of his nose.

"I've got a bloody headache," he said. "And not a thing to show for it."

Disappointment deposited a heavy load into my chest. "I was so sure you'd be able to see something."

He shook his head. "Sorry, lad. Didn't see a thing—well, except for a few nasty stains of magic here and there left from a particularly brutal execution or torture."

"Are you sure those couldn't have been the cause of the sickness?"

"Unlikely," he said, dismissing it with a shake of his head.

I sighed, and looked at the map I'd made. "I never saw anything like a gauntlet room either. Lina told me she'd been using one down here."

"A gauntlet room?" MacLean raised an eyebrow. "There's nothing down here but prison cells and guard stations."

I nodded. "And did you see any mattresses down here? Because Morgana told me she brought hers down." Biting my lower lip, I headed back up the passage toward the central section. "We must have missed something."

The big Scot blew out a breath, but kept pace even as he rubbed his temples. "Are you sure this is the right place?"

"Positive."

I stopped at the first guard station we came to, examining the small box of a room where one person could turn a wheel with chains wrapped around it to raise and lower the portcullis which blocked the only exit out of the section we were in. I tinkered with it, but rust held the portcullis in place, and it showed no signs of someone having opened it. We stepped into the original section of the dungeons, the central hub, and made our way toward one of the annexes. I suddenly wished I'd invited Zagg along.

"You look like you just tasted haggis for the first time, lad." MacLean squatted on a stone bench near a guard station. "I'm sorry, but I think we've done about all we can at this point."

I pulled out my phone and stared at it. "That's odd," I said, noting I had a signal. "We must be a mile underground, and I still have four bars."

"Aye, because we're right next to ley lines." He rubbed his forehead. "Or didn't you know that's how these phones work?"

"I didn't know." But it sure was handy. I called Cinder. He answered on the third ring. "Justin?"

"I'm in the Burrows," I said without preamble. "And I'm looking for a gauntlet room."

"I believe that would be Zagg's area of expertise. Please hold."

The sound of someone's fingers brushing across the phone preceded Zagg's confused voice. "Justin? Where are you?"

"Down in the Burrows."

"Why are you down there?" the historian asked, his voice full of concern. "That place is really dangerous."

"Well, there are these really sick kids, and…"

He sighed. "Give me a moment." I heard him say something indistinct which may or may not have included swear words, and Cinder replied in his calm voice. "Cinder is grabbing an ASE for me."

"I'll wait." As if I had a choice.

"Who are you talking to?" MacLean asked.

"Professor Zagg. He's a historian, and I hope he knows something about this place we don't."

"Aye, I know the man."

"There is a gauntlet room down there," Zagg said a moment later. "I remembered archiving a diagram of the Burrows a few years ago when I began my project to convert old texts to ASE format." He paused. "Which section are you in—no wait, better yet, have your phone send me coordinates."

"Nookli, send my coordinates to Cinder's phone."

"I will find all Indian restaurants and make the reservation, Justin," my phone replied after a moment.

I groaned, and repeated myself twice more until the phone did what I wanted while MacLean looked on with an amused expression.

Zagg made some thoughtful noises of his own as he did whatever he was doing on the other end, and then said, "Ah. You'll need to go to the guard station in the central hub, and head right. You can't miss it."

Obviously we had.

I jogged to the station, and looked right. A blank wall greeted me. "Zagg, there's nothing but a wall here."

"Unless the diagram is wrong, you should be standing at a door leading into another series of passages where the prison guards bunked."

MacLean furrowed his brow, staring at the wall for a moment before letting out a groan. "A bloody illusion." He regarded it for a moment longer. "And it's a recent enchantment."

I looked at the floor and noticed shoe scuffs and disturbed dust which cut off abruptly at the wall. *I'm a horrible detective.* I tentatively touched the wall, and felt only thin air. Poking my head through revealed an open door and another lit corridor. I went through with MacLean right behind, his eyes focused intently on our surroundings. We hadn't gone more than a few steps when I found the gauntlet room on the right. I turned to make a comment to MacLean when I saw him staring down the corridor.

He stalked down the hallway, muttering under his breath.

"What is it?" I asked, jogging to catch up.

"Bloody hell," he said, and stopped at the end. He touched the blank wall. Unlike the previous one, this one appeared real. He kicked at the stones, but they didn't budge.

I gripped his arm. "What are you doing?"

"There's something on the other side of the wall. It's pulsing like a bloody star."

He didn't need to say another word. I pressed a foot to the wall, and shoved, putting all my strength into it. Without warning, the wall caved in, and I almost tumbled in after it. A large slab of stone narrowly missed my head, and a cloud of dust sent MacLean and I coughing and backing away. When the dust cleared, a tunnel, this one obviously hewn from the mountain, lurked on the other side.

MacLean jogged down the narrow tunnel, as if drawn like a magnet. The illumination from the previous area dimmed to nothing, but light flickered from somewhere ahead, blindingly white one minute before dimming to ultraviolet. The Scot abruptly stopped, and I plowed into his back, rocking him forward on his feet.

"That's it," he said, pointing after he regained his balance, stepping forward into a wide chamber with walls of polished obsidian.

An Alabaster Arch sat in the center.

Chapter 36

The center of the arch crackled with a malevolent pulsar of energy which phased from white to ultraviolet as if a kid were playing with a sliding light switch on a wall. It hummed with the promise of death should anyone touch it, and teased the hairs on my arms with static.

The room wasn't very tall, perhaps thirty feet, and probably as wide and as long as a four-car garage. Not daring to take another step closer to the malfunctioning arch, I magnified my vision, examining its physical properties. I noticed something so odd, it took a couple of repetitions before I felt sure it wasn't my eyes playing tricks. As the white spectrum of light brightened, alabaster veins twined through the obsidian material of the arch, snaking through the material until it looked very similar to the Alabaster Arch I'd seen beneath Thunder Rock. But when the white light waned, the white veins faded until only black obsidian remained during the full power of the ultraviolet spectrum.

I scratched my head, still staring at the odd transformation. One minute it looked like an alabaster arch, the next pure obsidian. "What in the world is going on with the colors?"

MacLean looked just as confused. "It's like the blasted thing can't make up its mind."

I held my phone up to an ear to ask Zagg a question, and heard nothing but static. "I think it's interfering with my phone."

"If this thing is what made your friends sick," the Scot said, "I don't want to stand near the bloody thing a second longer than I have to."

The almost constant pull of static on my clothes and arms was enough to make me wonder what horrible things this pulsar was doing to my internal organs, though I realized with a wry chuckle, it couldn't be much worse than what the vampling curse was already doing. Before I turned, I noticed a doorway on the opposite side of the room. I tried to make a video with my phone, but my phone had other ideas.

"Where do you think that goes?" I asked, pointing toward the mysterious exit. I ran to it, and peered into a small room with a sturdy metal door. Thick bands of steel ran through grooves, holding it shut. It looked formidable, even for my supernatural powers.

MacLean shrugged. "I don't know, and right now, I don't bloody care. I'm getting out of here, and not returning without a magic hazard suit on."

I backed away from the arch, turned, and jogged after MacLean. After we passed through the broken wall, he looked around the room.

"Did you notice how the lamps in here grow brighter during each pulse?" he said.

They did indeed seem to brighten and darken in time with the light from the arch. "I don't understand how magic could make people sick like that."

"Aye, I don't know either. You could stand in the middle of a ley line and not get sick." He shrugged. "I don't know who to even ask about it."

"Maybe an arch operator?"

He snorted. "Those bloody imbeciles know how to push buttons, and that's about it."

"They were working on an arch for the Conroys. They can't be that stupid."

"Well, true. But do you really want one of them poking around down here?" His gaze met mine. "What if this thing could be used as a weapon, or to open a gateway to the angel realm? Then we'd be in a bloody mess, wouldn't we?"

I couldn't argue with him there. "We need to make sure nobody else comes down here."

"No argument there, lad."

We made our way back to the main dungeon, and headed back through the hole in the grate. Once outside, MacLean snapped his staff to full length, and whipped up an illusion barrier, that matched the corridor wall, solid to the touch.

He snapped the staff back down to the size of a small rod, and slid it into a pocket in his pants. "That'll do for the time being."

"We'll have to go back down there and study it," I said. "We have to find out why it made people sick." I tried to call Zagg, but my phone still wasn't responding very well. After a restart, it seemed to function normally once more, but by then, we were already topside. "Let's talk to Zagg."

MacLean looked up and down the hall, eyes darting nervously. "What about the bloody Flark?"

"Do you really think he'll try to kidnap you with witnesses everywhere?"

"Even if he doesn't, what if he follows me to my hideout?" Worry creased the corners of his eyes.

"We need to figure out a permanent solution to our Bigglesworth problem," I said with a growl. "There's got to be some way to burn his bacon."

MacLean chuckled. "True, or there'd be a lot more of the nasty buggers running around." He regarded me with a serious expression for a moment before nodding. "Fine. Let's go talk to Zagg. I'm probably safer with you lot than going bloody insane in the secret chambers behind the library walls."

"I even have a place for you to stay," I said, thinking of all the rooms going to waste at my haunted mansion.

We found Zagg and Cinder in the historian's office. I saw Cinder fiddling with one of the marble-sized ASEs and a scroll of parchment.

Zagg looked up when we entered the room, relief evident on his face. "Man, I was wondering what happened to you down there. Some kind of static burst nearly blew up Cinder's phone." He did a double-take at the big Scot. "Hello, Professor MacLean. Um, why did you bring him in on this, Justin?"

I figured MacLean wouldn't want me spilling his secret affiliation, or his gift. "He's familiar with the dungeons."

"I was dragged into this bloody mess by one of the Conroy's minions," MacLean said. "Justin helped me out, so I'm helping him."

"The static burst was disconcerting," Cinder said, his voice devoid of inflection as usual. "I suspected you might have been annihilated, but Professor Zagg convinced me it was likely a malfunction."

"Thankfully, just a malfunction," I said. "But the cause of it…" I whistled. "I don't even know what to think." I was grateful for Cinder changing the subject, even if the golem hadn't intended to.

MacLean and I told them the details, drawing sounds of amazement from the historian. He consulted the diagrams, but found nothing indicating a room of any sort where the arch sat.

"Maybe it was a getaway portal," Zagg suggested. "After all, the Illuminati were very secretive."

"Not so bloody much anymore," MacLean said in a disgusted voice.

Zagg's eyes widened. "You know something about the Illuminati?"

The big Scot's mouth opened a fraction, the expression on his face clearly indicating he felt like a moron for having opened his big mouth. "They're in movies…and stuff," he said. "Now, about that portal—"

"You're the Illuminati Justin knows," Zagg said, eyes narrowed.

I didn't want Zagg's personal interests to interfere with the matter at hand, so I jumped back into the conversation. "There are people possibly dying right this very minute because of that arch. Do you think Healer Hutchins might be able to help?"

"How?" MacLean said. "She'd just look at it and be as confused as the rest of us."

"We can't just sit here." I huffed out a breath.

"This is a rather vexing problem," Cinder said, never looking up from his work with the ASE and the scroll. "I would suggest a team meeting. Perhaps our cumulative processing abilities will solve the problem." He looked up at me, gray eyes never blinking, and said, "It is time for a brainstorm."

I grinned. "Gold star for your first successful use of an idiom."

"Thank you, Justin. I will proudly display my gold star." Cinder simulated a stiff smile, showing a few too many teeth, though not enough to frighten small children, and turned back to his work with the scrolls and ASE.

I figured Shelton and Bella would probably be finished doing…whatever. I really didn't want to think about where their kissing had led. I called, and told them to expect a group.

"I'll order pizza," Shelton said.

I'd kind of wanted chicken wings, but didn't complain about it.

I arrived with my ever-growing entourage, made introductions. MacLean and Shelton exchanged grips.

"Been too long since we attacked Greek Row with spider bats," MacLean said with a broad grin.

A smile broke Shelton's sober face. "Yeah. Those were the days."

I grabbed a slice of pizza and nommed it in a matter of seconds. As I was grabbing seconds, I heard a disturbance and turned to see Zagg, one hand gripping Shelton's collar, the other cocked back threateningly.

"Whoa!" I said, blurring over to hold Zagg's arm. "What's going on?"

"Let him," Shelton said, face dull and impassive. "I deserve it."

"You're damned right you deserve it, you bastard!" Zagg shouted, straining uselessly against my grip. He pushed Shelton away, jerked his arm from mine. "Did you know about this, Justin?"

Crap. Shelton must have told him about the evidence planting. "I just found out today."

"And you were going to tell me when?" His angry face melted into a hurt expression. "I trusted you, man!"

"I did what I promised, Zagg. Nothing has changed. I didn't want to tell you because I knew this"—I waved my hand between him and Shelton—"would happen. There are other important matters at stake here, damn it." I struck a fist into my palm. "Kids are dying, the Conroys are trying to let the Seraphim into our world, and we don't have time for a personal conflict to destroy everything!" I was shouting at the top of my lungs by the end, as frustration and desperation swelled in an insurmountable tide. "What in the hell do I have to do to get everyone to cooperate?" I threw up my hands. Stormed away.

"Justin, wait," said Zagg in a contrite voice. "Please."

I stopped. Turned. "What do you want? I'm trying to make a dramatic exit to prove my point."

Zagg lowered his head. "I'm sorry I let my temper get the best of me. I'll wait to deal with this jackass"—he thumbed Shelton's direction—"after we save the world. Okay?"

I took a deep breath. It failed to clear the knot in my stomach and the pressure in my chest, but the frustration faded, leaving behind its partner in crime, desperation, to remind me how hopeless our task seemed.

"Looks like a fun lot," MacLean said, taking a big bite of pepperoni pizza. "I think I'm going to enjoy this."

I moved the group to the planning room. A large conference table stretched part of the length, giving it a polished look, even though we were down to three chairs thanks to Shelton's earlier outburst. I called Meghan on my phone since she was a healer, and might have some idea as to how we could treat those suffering like Lina. Once everyone was assembled, I filled in the gang on my and MacLean's little adventure.

Meghan, her pint-sized holographic image hovering above my phone, pursed her lips in thought and said nothing for a long moment after I finished. "I remember something very similar to this happening some years ago, but the cause was much different."

All heads turned to her.

"Go on," I said.

"A Templar was pursuing a lurker through its warrens deep underground and stumbled into a leyworm nest." She grimaced. "Even baby leyworms are quite large."

"Tell me about it," I grumbled, remembering the one I'd freed from Dash Armstrong's lair. He'd been using the leyworm to power an arch and all sorts of other crazy equipment.

"The baby apparently thought he was food and swallowed him," Meghan continued saying. "And then threw him back up."

"How the hell did he survive the teeth in that thing?" I asked, thinking of the jagged shard-like teeth I'd seen in the full-grown creatures. The term "worm" was a misnomer despite the outward appearance of the giant beasts. Technically, they were dragons of some sort, sans legs.

"His Nightingale armor protected him from anything too grievous," she said. "But while he was inside, he was exposed to raw aether."

"Raw aether?" I said. "Um, isn't it all raw until we use it?"

She shook her head. "The aether carried by ley lines might make your hair stand on end, but it certainly won't harm you. The worse that could happen is you get sick if you draw in too much. Leyworms, on the other hand, are named so because they have a peculiar relationship with ley lines."

"They eat the aether," Bella said.

Meghan shrugged. "I don't think they eat it, exactly. We know the creatures eat flesh and even stone."

"All part of a well-balanced diet," Shelton said.

"My point is," Meghan said, giving him a flat look, "the quality of the aether inside a leyworm is quite different than what we usually use for magic. It soaked into the Templar's body, giving him something akin to radiation poisoning."

"Were you able to treat him?" I asked.

She nodded. "The solution was simple, but it took time to set up." Her image vanished, replaced by the image of an intricate rune carved into stone.

"A drain ward," Bella said, clapping her hands together. "How simple and exquisite!"

"Thank you," Meghan said. "Diagnosing the man's precise issue took time, but once I studied it from every angle, I decided a drain ward might be the only way to leech the magic from his body." Her body appeared in the hologram again. "Due to the sheer volume of aether, however, I had to anchor the ward in a ley line, or the siphoned energy would simply form an invisible but harmful cloud."

"Exactly right," Bella said. "I am working on such a ward myself."

Meghan raised an eyebrow. "You planned to use one for the children?"

"Not exactly," I said. "We were planning to trap Ivy with it."

"Ah." The healer touched her chin with a hand, as if in thought. "Adam and I will come to the university. It sounds like you need all the help you can get, Justin."

"Would you, really?" I asked, my hopes lifting.

"Of course."

"Justin, I believe I have made a startling discovery," Cinder said.

"That you're a robot?" Shelton said with a snort.

The golem gazed at Shelton for a long moment with a bland expression. "Ah, you were attempting humor. Unfortunately, I am not familiar enough with the concept to know if your attempt was funny or not." He looked at me. "Was it Justin?"

I burst into a laugh. "No, but you are."

"Tis a sad world when a ruddy golem is funnier than a human," MacLean said, chuckling.

Shelton blew out a breath. "Whatever."

"What is this startling discovery?" I asked Cinder.

The golem retrieved an ASE and spun it on the table. Beams of light crisscrossed each other in a patchwork of colors until a three-dimensional image of the university filled a large portion of the table. "While I was cataloging some of the old ASE videos Zagg gave me, I realized the audio portion was damaged."

"Yeah, that's the way most of the old ones are," Zagg said.

"Despite this damage, I was able to read the lips of those speaking, so long as I had a clear view," Cinder said. "I believe this video was not meant for public consumption." He tapped the air, and the video flickered on, showing a group of men in a very familiar room as they carried on an animated conversation.

"Isn't that this room?" Bella said, looking at the wood paneling on the walls.

"Well, at least we're doing something right," Shelton said.

I shushed them. "What are they saying?" I asked Cinder.

He paused the playback, pressed his hands together in the center, and spread his hands. The three-dimensional image spread like a long poster, flattening to reveal a panoramic view of the entire room. It was rather disconcerting to watch since the men sitting around the table now all seemed to be looking directly at me instead of each other.

"I will speak for each person in turn," the golem said, and resumed playback.

"She will find it otherwise," Cinder said in time with Ezzek Moore, the founder of the Arcane Council, though I noticed Moore's lips didn't quite synch with Cinder's, like the bad dubbing of a kung fu movie.

Alexander Tiberius shook his head. "No, there's a way to hide it. Tell him, Sydow." His gaze went to a creepy-looking man with short black hair, apparently another of the original Arcane Council.

Sydow glanced to the left, presumably at Moore, though the flattened perspective made it hard to tell. "We hide it in between. Neither here, nor there."

Moore held up a hand palm out. "Say nothing more. She is brilliant, and more powerful than I could have believed. She knows we have it, and could be listening."

"You're being paranoid again, old man," said Tiberius.

"Perhaps," Moore said with a nod. "But there is no reason to chance it." He turned to Sydow. "Do what you think best. Either it works, or she will have what she wants, and god help us all." He bowed his head, eyes closed. "My journey is almost to its end, and I do not wish to leave behind a legacy of death and destruction."

"Oh, stop with the theatrics," Tiberius said, rolling his eyes. "One can hardly blame you for sleeping with—"

Cinder abruptly broke off. "From this point, the council meeting devolves into Tiberius bragging about the concubines he once had during the Roman Empire, and Ezzek Moore sighing a lot. I do not think it contributes to the discussion at hand."

Zagg bolted to his feet, face lit with wonder, and said, "I know where the Cyrinthian Rune is."

Chapter 37

Huh?" I asked, feeling like a complete buffoon.

MacLean slapped a palm against his forehead. "Of bloody course. That would explain it."

My head snapped to him. "Explain what?" I said, feeling like an English major in a calculus class.

"The rune is between realms where Daelissa can't find it," Zagg said. "It's caught in a loop 'neither here, nor there'."

"You're making even less sense now," I said, my mind desperately scrambling to reach the same answer everyone else apparently had.

"Ah," Bella said. "How very obvious and clever"

Shelton's mouth stretched into a knowing grin.

"I see the direction the logic is leading," Cinder added. "I was, however, converting their speech from Latin to English, so it is possible I lost something in the translation."

"What did you figure out?" I shouted above the din of all the stupid know-it-alls.

Zagg raised an eyebrow. "Huh? Oh, the rune. It's in the arch you and MacLean found."

Neither here, nor there. "Oh," I said, dragging out the word for several seconds to indicate just how idiotic I felt.

"It's so bloody powerful, it's poisoning anyone who gets near it," MacLean added.

Bella gave him a concerned look. "Does that mean it's dangerous to handle?"

"I do not believe so," Cinder said. "I also restored the damaged video in several other council meeting videos which occurred chronologically after the one we just viewed. There is no mention of aether radiation in any of them, nor mention of hazards associated with handling the rune."

I chomped on a slice of pizza with more savagery than necessary, and chewed it for a moment. "Maybe it wasn't dangerous at first. Maybe centuries of being inside the arch caused a reaction."

"Possibly," Zagg said.

"We should go get the bloody thing right now," MacLean said.

I almost choked on my pizza. "Are you kidding? That thing needs to stay where it is. I say we close the wall back up, and interdict the place so it never sees the light of day."

"There may be a problem with your solution," Cinder said.

I met the golem's emotionless gaze. "I'm all ears."

His eyes wandered across my body for a moment before he said, "Ah. Another idiom. Perhaps you could define this one so I may file it away—"

"What's the problem with my solution?" I asked, raising an eyebrow.

Cinder's eyebrow rose slightly, though whether he was mimicking me, or expressing genuine emotion, I couldn't tell. "When one enters an arch, it is much like looking through a telescope at a far-off location, and quickly traversing the space between through the telescope."

I nodded. "Good description. What's your point?"

"In truth, you are actually speeding at tremendous velocity through a traversion tunnel. If the other arch were sealed off somehow, you would reach the end, and ricochet back toward your origin."

"I wouldn't splat against the other end?"

He shook his head stiffly. "The magical properties of the tunnel would simply reverse your course, while slightly increasing velocity to your trajectory."

I nodded, feeling a bit more in my element with the magical equivalent of physics. "So they put the rune in an arch, and sealed up both ends to trap it. All these centuries it's been bouncing back and forth at higher and higher speeds."

"Indeed," Cinder replied. "I believe this is the cause of the anomaly you witnessed. The pulsing colors change depending on the location of the rune within the tunnel. The closer to this arch it is, the whiter the light." He took out his phone, and brought up a holographic display, showing a tiny dot bouncing along a curved traversion tunnel.

"That's why it looks like an Alabaster Arch during a white phase?" I asked.

"Yes." Cinder zoomed on one arch, and told his phone to simulate the effect. "The attenuation of the rune could cause this."

"Because it was meant to power an Alabaster Arch, it's somehow affecting the properties of this normal arch, morphing its attributes," I said, hoping my brain had finally come to a conclusion on its own.

"Precisely." He made a few adjustments, and sped up the simulation running on his phone. The brilliant pulsars at either end grew larger and suddenly burst into miniature supernovas, the light blotting out everything else.

"Holy goat turds in a picnic basket," Shelton said in a hushed voice. "We're on a countdown to boom, aren't we?"

"I believe so," Cinder said. "One moment, please." He ran the simulation several more times while the rest of us watched the same explosion happen over and over again. "Using the brightest moment of the anomaly at this end, I am able to calculate the speed of the rune. With that information, I am also able to calculate the distance between points, and approximate the location of the other arch."

"I could've done that," I mumbled under my breath. What had been wrong with my mind lately? I wondered if the vampling curse was affecting it, too.

"Where's the other arch?" Bella asked.

"Although I have the distance, I can only approximate the location." He shrugged, the motion a jerky up-down motion. "The distance would place it in either Antarctica, or the North Pole."

"Well, ain't Santa got a nice gift for us this year," Shelton said with a roll of his eyes.

Bella elbowed him.

I turned back to Cinder. "Any idea how bad the explosion will be?"

"The physical damage might be enough to collapse the dungeons, and cause the university campus to cave in," he said.

I imagined kids falling into bottomless chasms as the ground collapsed beneath their feet.

Cinder continued. "There would likely, however, be a more severe side effect."

"Worse than destroying the school?" Shelton with an incredulous look.

"Indeed." Cinder adjusted a setting to simulate a wave of energy. "The physical concussion would be limited to the dungeons. The wave of corrupted aether, however, would travel through physical barriers, and irradiate all of Queens Gate before imploding back upon itself."

"So everyone else would get sick like those kids in the healing ward," I said.

The golem tilted his head slightly. "I'm afraid it would be worse than that, Justin. This implosion would likely rival that of the Grand Nexus destruction. The implosion would drain everyone of light soul essence."

Gasps went up around the table.

"It would turn us all to husks?" I asked. I imagined the brightest minds in the Overworld reduced to soul-hungry shadow people and cherubs. I briefly wondered what kind of husk I would become.

"It is also possible the explosion would open a rift into the Gloom large enough to allow anything living inside to come here, and vice versa." Cinder stared blankly for a second. "I cannot be sure."

I asked the next dreaded question. "How long do we have?"

"That answer is much simpler," the golem replied. "We have until this Saturday at one-thirteen in the afternoon."

"Wait a minute," Shelton said. "That's the day of the Grand Melee."

"Isn't the Grand Melee on the anniversary of the university's completion?" I said, one of Zagg's history lessons coming to mind.

The historian nodded. "It was to commemorate the occasion. Alexander Tiberius started the tradition, perhaps because he missed the gladiator battles from his Roman days."

"In other words, the school is going to blow up on its anniversary," I said.

"Delicious irony," Shelton said, as if he were really happy about it.

Bella elbowed him, eliciting a wince.

Knowing what we were facing at least removed the uncertainty. Or maybe it just increased it even more as another *what if* occurred to me. "If we unseal the arch at this end, will the rune explode on impact? I mean, that thing's travelling at an ungodly speed by now, and the last thing we need is it pounding into the ground like a meteor."

Cinder's calm gaze rested on me. "Once an object emerges from a traversion tunnel, it realigns with its original speed. I do not believe an explosion will be the outcome."

"But this thing's been bouncing around for centuries," Shelton said. "What if it doesn't stop and plows to earth like a meteor?"

"It doesn't matter," I said. "We can't just let the arch explode."

"And if you release it and it explodes anyway?" he said.

"We should warn the populace," Bella said. "Make them evacuate Queens Gate."

"I agree," Meghan said.

Zagg wrinkled his forehead and raked the room with a look usually reserved for mental patients. "Evacuate? Haven't you noticed the tent city going up in the meadow near the stadium? We're talking about thousands of people from both universities, the city of Queens Gate, and thousands of people arriving via the arch for the Grand Melee." He scrunched his forehead, as if painfully calculating. "They'd have to blockade the arch and start an immediate evacuation. That could take weeks."

"What if the Primus orders it?" Shelton said, face grim.

"We have"—Meghan consulted something on her end—"five days until the Melee. Is it enough time?"

"Not even close," Zagg said.

Bella gave us a resolute stare. "We must try."

"Do. Or do not. There is no try," Shelton said.

"Is the Primus on campus?" Meghan asked. "I don't know how we'll speak to the man, otherwise. He's notoriously hard to reach."

"Of course he'll be on campus," Zagg said. "It's the Grand Melee. The entire Arcane Council will be in their usual club seating."

Shelton sighed. "Don't worry about contacting the Primus. I got it covered."

"You?" Meghan said, scorn very clear in her voice. "Why should we trust you with such a task?"

The question seemed to take something out of Shelton. He looked away from the holographic image of the healer and muttered something.

"I'm sorry, but I didn't hear that," Meghan said.

Bella touched Shelton's arm, and whispered to him. He nodded. Took a breath, and steeled himself, spine going straight. "Jarrod Sager, the Arcanus Primus, is my adoptive father."

In the rush of things, I'd forgotten not everyone knew Shelton's secret. I felt like I knew almost too much about the man now. Part of me liked the gruff Shelton. The one who never let anyone in. He might falter at the beginning, but he'd proven time and time again that he could come through in the clutch. I just hoped Bella wouldn't turn him into a pansy.

"Your father?" Meghan said, face aghast. "But how—"

"Long story," Shelton said. "Save it for another time." He squared his jaw. "I'll talk to him and make him understand."

"Make sure he keeps the reason on the down-low," I said. "If the Conroys get wind of this—"

"The Primus must know about the rune," Zagg said. "I'm sure he'll come up with some other excuse about why we're evacuating."

I suddenly saw two big glowing neon dots in my mind's eye. One said "Cyrinthan Rune", and the other, "Gloom Initiative". Slowly, carefully, I drew a line between the two dots. The connection made so much sense, it was all I could do not to jump up and shout, "Yatta!" at the top of my lungs. Turning to Shelton, I said, "Did you ever find out what the Gloom Initiative was really all about?"

His eyebrows arched at the sudden change in direction. "Wasn't it for finding alternative travel options to the arches?"

Here goes, I thought, and opened my big mouth. "If the Primus is on the council, and the council is supposed to know about the rune, then maybe they already know about the danger presented by the arch. What if the Gloom Initiative was really about finding another way to hide the rune from Daelissa?"

"Justin, that is a brilliant observation," Cinder said, speaking in the unemotional tone one might use to discuss toilet paper. "I suggest we warn the Primus about the imminent destruction of Queens Gate just in case he is unaware of the short time left."

Shelton stood, and headed for the door. "No sense wasting any time. I'll do it now."

"Don't you need to call him first?" Bella asked.

"Nah. I know exactly where he'll be. It's the same place he always stayed when I was going to school here." Shelton opened the door.

I stood, pushing my chair back, and joined him. "I'm coming, too."

He shrugged. "Knock yourself out."

"Adam and I will leave for Queens Gate immediately," Meghan said, and her image winked out.

"Cinder and I should stay and study more of these archival videos," Zagg said. "There might be something vital we're missing."

"I suppose I'll stay and help," Bella added. "Although a game of Scrabble would really take my mind off things right now."

"I bloody love Scrabble," MacLean said. He directed a questioning eyebrow at Zagg. "You wouldn't have happened across a way to kill a Flark in all your historical studies, eh?"

Shelton stepped through the door, and I followed. We walked down the path without a word, the only sound that of our feet scuffing the yellow brick road with a pair of brilliant full moons lighting the shadowy landscape around us. I almost opened my mouth to make a comment about something, but one look at Shelton told me all I needed to know. He looked pensive. Worried. Talking to his father wouldn't be pleasant. The man had used his adopted son in the most unimaginable ways possible, first to catch Shelton's supposedly evil parents, and then to take out political opponents. Sager deserved a punch right in the throat. And maybe a broomstick up his rear end.

Somewhere in the distance, a lycan howled at the full moon. Afterward, all went silent except the incessant chirp of insects.

"I'm sorry about earlier," Shelton said, the statement surprising me both for the sincerity in his voice, and the shock of broken silence.

"Uh, sure. Poop happens, I guess."

He snorted. "Yeah. It sure does." Shelton checked the time on his phone. "The old man likes to stay in the Fairy Garden Estate."

I felt my forehead pinch. "What kind of man stays in a fairy house?"

"Bunch of women named these gardens if you ask me," Shelton said with a laugh. "Don't even get me started on the Unicorn Garden." He motioned me to follow him down a path I hadn't taken before which curved through the rear garden, past the meadow where Vallaena and I practiced, and around the imposing stadium. The path bordered the forest where the tragon lurked, and up to an iron gate flanked by tall stone walls.

I stopped in shock and stared at the landscape through the iron bars of the gate. A crystalline pond sat in the middle of a glade. A shaft of pure moonlight shined on the water, where a group of figures splashed each other, laughing and giggling. The yellow brick road continued past the pond and into a dense forest. Lights of every color glittered in the trees, like thousands of tiny light bugs.

"Holy farting fairies," I said, borrowing one of Shelton's scatological phrases. "This looks amazing. Are those really fairies?"

"Geez, kid. How many times I gotta tell you there ain't no such thing?" He pushed through the unlocked iron gate.

"Whatevs," I said, and followed him down the path.

As we drew closer to the pond, the figures abruptly stopped splashing, and the shaft of moonlight faded. Shelton pulled his staff from a pocket and snapped it to full length. I realized I hadn't brought one, and felt naked even though my magic wasn't much to brag about.

The barest pat of dripping water was all the warning we had before two wet figures appeared in front of us. Wood groaned and creaked, and my jaw almost bounced off the ground as several trees tore themselves from the ground and surrounded us.

A beautiful and very naked woman stood next to a heinously naked man, their eyes full of suspicion. I forced my eyes north of the border, desperate not to see man junk of any kind.

"What is your business?" the woman asked in a pure melodic voice.

"We're here on official business to see the Primus." Shelton said.

"Lies!" said the man, his voice every bit as pure and musical as the woman's. "Take them," he said, presumably to the trees.

Giggles bubbled from every direction, and girls, naked but for leaves and foliage draped over their generous curves, appeared from behind the trees, their eyes sparkling with mischief. One gripped my bicep, and suddenly, my feet rooted themselves to the ground. I tried to move, but even my supernatural strength wasn't enough to uproot them.

A savage snarl peeled the man's lips from his teeth. "Get rid of them."

Chapter 38

I hardly had a chance to yelp in surprise at the sudden development. "Why are you going to kill us?" I asked, still straining without results against the force holding my feet to the ground.

The angry man looked confused. "I said nothing about killing you, fool. They will escort you from the garden."

Shelton growled and stopped struggling against his own captors. "Fine. You want the truth? I'm here on unofficial business. The Primus is my absentee asshole father, and I have to warn him about a nuclear friggin meltdown about to blow everyone in Queens Gate to hell. You happy now?"

The man's face flashed to surprise, and then alarm. "He speaks the truth."

"Children, release them," the woman said.

The girls slid their hands away, and the pressure holding my feet to the earth vanished. I almost stumbled backwards as the girls danced back behind the looming trees.

"You may pass, wizard," the woman said, smiling.

Shelton brushed at his sleeves, grumbling something about dryads, and stomped down the path. I hurried to keep pace.

"What was that about?" I asked.

"Security. You think the Primus would stay out here without guards?"

I looked around at the dense forest. Giggles echoed from the dark spaces between the trees. I switched to night vision. Hundreds of glowing eyes flickered on and met my gaze. My heart screamed and cowered behind my guts. I very quickly switched night vision off. "Uh, Shelton? We're being watched."

He snorted. "Try not to think about it. We've been cleared by the Lady of the Pond."

"Is she related to the Lady of the Lake?"

He shrugged. "Might be cousins. I dunno." Shelton's gaze took in the thick woods to either side of us. "Just don't go off the path. You're not supposed to do that."

Tiny flashes of light sparkled in the dark, but did nothing to reveal the lurkers in the woods. My hearing picked up the faint pitter-patter of countless feet pacing through the trees on a course parallel to ours. More feminine giggles echoed from either sides of the path. I knew women were dangerous, but these chicks were downright creepy. After a few more minutes, we finally emerged from the forest. The path continued through a wide green lawn with bushes grown into all sorts of fantastic shapes and sizes. I didn't have time to take it all in before Shelton marched up to the front door and yanked on a string attached to a bell.

A brass golem immediately opened the door, its neat black and white suit indicating without a doubt it was a butler. "He is expecting you," the golem said, waving us into the foyer without another word of explanation. "Would you like a drink while you wait? Tea, perhaps?"

"Nah," Shelton said, following the brass construct into a slightly larger room with benches and chairs. It reminded me of a doctor's waiting room. He dropped into a seat, and grabbed an *Arcane Daily* scroll off the table. The butler performed a concise bow, and wandered off.

"Did the lady tell him we were coming?" I asked.

"Yup." Shelton unrolled the parchment, looking for all the world like a man doing some light bathroom reading, just without the accompanying odor.

A brass golem in a French maid outfit wandered through, dusting the furniture, and singing in an admittedly pretty voice.

After a good fifteen minutes, during which I felt certain the Primus was probably drumming his fingers on a table, and making us wait in the name of bureaucracy, the butler returned. "Right this way, good sirs."

We followed it down a wood-paneled hallway lined with lush red carpet, and into an office furnished with intricately carved bookshelves, tables, and a huge desk. Jarrod Sager sat behind the desk, and motioned to two red leather chairs facing him.

"Please sit."

"If that will be all, sir?" the butler asked.

"Yes, thank you," the Primus replied.

Shelton regarded the chair for a few seconds, as if deciding whether he wanted to spite his old man by not sitting. A shake of his head accompanied an audible sigh, and he dropped into the seat. "Let me start by saying I don't want to be here." Sager opened his mouth to respond, but Shelton shut him up with a backhanded wave. "I don't want to hear it," he growled. "If it weren't important, I wouldn't have come."

"I understand," Sager said, his voice sounding a little strained. "However, there are proper channels to go through for *official* business." He put an emphasis on the word.

"Yeah? Well, this can't wait." He nodded to me. "Go ahead and tell him."

My mouth wouldn't work for a moment, frankly because I'd expected Shelton to tell him. My brain also couldn't decide what to say first, and decided a question might be in order. "What is the Gloom Initiative?"

Sager's eyes darted between me and Shelton. "I'm sure if you went to the library and looked over newspaper archives, you could answer that question."

Shelton leaned forward. "We don't want to hear the crap you fed to the masses. We know there was more to it, or you wouldn't have used me to find and arrest people who opposed you."

His father's eyes flared. "I believe I've heard enough of this nonsense. You should go. Now."

"I ain't leaving until you tell me," Shelton said, standing, his hand clenching and unclenching by his side. "Because I ain't too happy about it. In fact, all that crap with Aerianas broke something inside me. Maybe my sanity. Maybe I'll just take out that anger on you right here and now."

Sager stood, a worried look on his face. "Leave this instant!"

"Not without saying what I came here to say, you lying sack of gerbil droppings!" Shelton thundered. "You used me to railroad people into prison without a trial for that stupid Gloom Initiative.

Well, guess what? You don't even have to tell us what it's for. We know it's so you can hide the friggin Cyrinthian Rune from Daelissa. We know about the arch holding the rune, and we know it's about to blow Queens Gate to kingdom come. That's why you wanted your project to succeed, so you could hide it." He stood panting, as if it had cost him strength to force the words from his mouth, and then said one more thing in a calm sad voice. "That's the reason you tooled your son and threw him away when you were done."

Sager face-palmed, and dropped into his chair. "Damn it, son." He groaned. "You're right. I fed the public a lie—or at least the truth blended with a lie. The project was twofold. It was publicly commissioned to find alternate travel methods to the arch network. However, the secret objective was to open a rift between here and the Seraphim realm. Only after the initiative was underway did I think it could be used to hide the rune, provided I could find it."

"The Seraphim realm?" Shelton said, his expression growing confused.

I didn't need to have detective skills to realize in a split instant what Sager's words meant. Sager and Vadaemos hadn't worked together exclusively. They'd been working for someone else all along. I grabbed Shelton's arm. "We've got to go now!"

"You're working for Daelissa?" Shelton said, his confusion turning to a look of pure horror. "But the Conroys are her frigging lapdogs, and you hate them!"

His father sighed. "I had no choice."

"You always have a choice, you stupid bastard!" Shelton lunged. I caught him by the arm before he could land a punch. He strained against me. "What did they do? Promise you'd get to remain Primus so long as you did what they said? Or did they just give you money? Is that how they got you in their pocket?"

Sager's eyes dropped to the floor. "No."

Shelton fought against me like a wild animal. "Then why?"

His father looked up, eyes sad, and full of an emotion I could easily identify with. Regret. "They promised not to kill you."

Shelton's eyes went wide, the struggle to break free suddenly forgotten. "You're lying."

"I'm not." Sager stood. "Daelissa killed your brother, Martin, as an example. I couldn't risk losing you. That's why I've always been so distant. I hoped they would leave you alone."

Shelton sagged. "No," he said in a weak voice. "You're lying."

"We need to go," I said. "He's working for *them*."

"Justin is right," Sager said. "You need to go. I won't breathe a word of this to anyone."

As if we can believe him.

His forehead wrinkled. "I honestly didn't know where the rune was. Either Ezzek Moore decided not to pass on the information, or the knowledge was lost. Is it really about to explode?"

I nodded. "We have to stop it, or everyone here could die. You need to order an evacuation."

Sager cursed. "How long do we have?"

"Until this Saturday."

"Impossible. There are simply too many people here for the Grand Melee." He stood and paced. "The logistics are completely wrong."

"Even if everyone doesn't make it, some will."

He looked up, fingers moving as if running calculations, all the while shaking his head. "It probably won't save everyone, but I'll deliver an emergency evacuation order immediately."

"We plan to remove the rune from the arch," I said in a confident voice. Then, in a slightly less confident tone I told him, "There's a chance it *might* explode and turn everyone into shadow creatures the second it comes from the arch."

Sager gave a wry laugh. "Wonderful. Not only will I be remembered for a war with the vampires, but for the annihilation of the university and Queens Gate."

My mind took a trip down memory lane, back to the beginning of this mess. "Did the Conroys repair the smaller arches so they could take them into Thunder Rock?"

Sager's gaze snapped to me. "How do you know so much?" His eyes moved to Shelton, and understanding lit. "Ah, yes. Harry is an excellent detective." He nodded. "The plan is to send a team to take the Alabaster Arch back to the Grand Nexus, wherever it may be. From what I've gleaned, Daelissa's memory was damaged from the Desecration. She can't remember where it is."

"Have they already taken the Alabaster Arch?" I asked.

He shook his head. "Too many Seraphim husks in the way, not to mention several Flark husks."

I shuddered at the thought of the infantile cherubs, all that remained of angels caught in the blast of the Grand Nexus when the Cyrinthian Rune was removed from it. "Flark husks?" I said.

Sager's lip curled with disgust. "The things look like animated oil."

I flashed back to the cold water beneath Thunder Rock. To swimming for escape until a black tentacle took me into the underground caverns filled with husks. Had that thing been a Flark husk? I shook my head clean of the disturbing memory. "Can't Daelissa get rid of the husks?"

"Ah, but she can't." A slow smile spread across his face. "If she gets anywhere close to one of those things, she can hardly stand up. They don't even have to touch her."

Maximus had kept a captive husk in his Colombian hideout. I wondered if it was to keep Daelissa away, or for some other nefarious purpose. "She has a weakness," I said, feeling suddenly confident. "But why does it affect her and not—" I almost said "me" before stopping myself. I was part angel, but the husks hadn't affected me in the same way. Was it thanks to my Daemos side, or something else?

"And not what?" Sager asked.

"Never mind." Questioning Shelton's father for hours on end was a temptation we couldn't afford.

"Son." Sager turned to Shelton, a hint of pain in his voice. "You need to get out of here. Daelissa will find out I've told you this. It's impossible to hide things from her. You don't know the torment she's put me through over the years. But I want you to know that I—" He broke off, voice overcome with emotion. "I failed Martin. I was arrogant. I thought I could bluster my way out of any situation. When Daelissa told me she would kill someone I cared about if I didn't do as she said, I thought I would call her bluff." Pain flashed through his face, and a single tear gathered in his eye. He pounded the desk with both fists, eyes filled with torment and rage.

At least I knew where the Shelton temper came from.

Sager sagged. "I tried so hard," he said in a weak, tired voice. "God knows I tried." His defeated eyes met Shelton's. "Whatever happens, I want you to know I tried to keep you safe. They made me use you. But the queen bitch from hell always knew I'd do whatever it took to protect you."

"I'm just your adopted son," Shelton said in a low voice. "You used me to lure my real parents. Don't even pretend you care about me."

"It wasn't me who used you to capture them," Sager said. "Someone on the council found out who you really were, and betrayed your secret. I didn't know until it was too late."

"Stop trying to cover your ass," Shelton growled.

"I'm not." The pain in Sager's eyes looked genuine. "No matter what you think, Harry, you're my son. You're family. I wish I'd had the strength to fight Daelissa, but I didn't. I did what I could to protect you. Martin loved you as only a brother could. I wish I could have been more of a father, but Daelissa took the choice from me."

A war seemed to rage behind Shelton's disbelieving eyes. His lips compressed to thin white lines, and I couldn't tell if he was suppressing anger or some other emotion. He finally spoke. "Did you have anything to do with Meghan Andretti's father or Adam Nosti's parents?"

Sager shook his head. "Daelissa tried to make them work for her, but they wouldn't. She had them killed." He opened a desk drawer and, after fiddling around with something, popped open a hidden compartment, and removed an ASE. "Take this. It's the least I can do."

"What is it?" Shelton asked.

Sager winced. "My confession."

Shelton pocketed it. "And you're trusting me with this? What makes you think I won't ruin your career over this?"

His father looked down. "If you do, I probably deserve it."

"Why are the Conroys helping Daelissa?" I asked. "Don't they realize what will happen if the Seraphim return?"

"I have no idea." Sager's eyebrows pinched. "Jeremiah Conroy has never cared about political office or power, so far as I know. But he is absolutely obsessed with helping Daelissa."

Shelton heaved a great sigh, and came around the desk to his father's side. He placed a hand on the man's shoulder, face grim. "For what it's worth, I believe you." The tension eased in his body, shoulders loosening. "And—" he paused for a long moment, the next words obviously very hard for him to say. "I forgive you."

Sager's face tightened for an instant before smoothing. He stood, and held out his hand. Shelton took it. "I'm proud to be your father, Harry."

The double doors to the office burst open, and a lone figure stood in the richly appointed hallway, his hands coming together in a very slow clap. "How lovely," Bigglesworth said. "Nothing like a family reunion to bring a tear to me eye."

"You," I said, hate boiling up from my stomach. I didn't waste a moment, uncaging my demon just enough to manifest to the point where I could barely keep control. My body swelled, clothes stretching and tearing. Tears of pain sizzled in my eyes as horns erupted from my forehead, curling upward until they brushed the chandeliers.

"My, my, look how big you've grown," Bigglesworth said. "Guess it means there's more for me." His stomach swelled grotesquely until it hung like a fleshy sac from his body. "I'm gonna have to let me belt out a notch."

Two streams of white-hot energy sizzled through the air, and splashed harmlessly off the Flark. I turned and saw Shelton and Sager both holding staffs out, confused looks on their faces.

"He's immune to direct magic," I said. "But you can hurt him indirectly."

"Good luck with that," Bigglesworth said with a derisive giggle. His body stretched and snapped like a rubber band. His swollen stomach detached, a glob flying and smacking onto Sager's face.

The Primus tripped backward, falling onto his desk, hands grappling with the fleshy substance, muffled screams coming from within.

"Dad!" Shelton yelled. He grabbed the suffocating mass, and cried out, jerking his hands away.

"His skin burns you," I told him, my voice unnaturally deep. I didn't know what else to do, and didn't have a chance to think before Bigglesworth flung himself at me like a slingshot. I dodged, and the Flark smacked against a bookshelf, sticking to it like a glob of wet toilet paper. A leering face formed in the spherical mass. It sprang with terrifying speed at my face again.

I reached up and jerked the chandeliers, tearing them from the ceiling in cloud of plaster dust and sparks. I swung them. Smacked Bigglesworth. His booger-like form splatted all over the light fixture. I turned to the huge fireplace on the far wall. Focusing my anger, I launched a fireball at the wood inside. The logs burst into flame, and I hurled the chandelier into the fire.

Horrific screeches came from the creature as it fought to disentangle itself from the baubles and gems of the chandeliers while fire roared around it.

I turned back to Shelton. A constant roar of pain ripped from his lungs as he tried vainly to free his father from the deadly mass on his face. Sager's eyes were wide and his face dark red. He grabbed Shelton's hands, and gave him a look full of regret, pleading, and so much more I couldn't identify all within a fleeting moment. He pulled his son's hands free of the blob, and shook his head.

I remembered MacLean's cattle prod, and wished I'd gotten one. My eyes locked on the wires dangling from the ceiling where the chandelier had been. I tugged on them, pulling more slack from the ceiling. "Hold him higher!" I yelled.

Shelton tilted his struggling father's torso higher. Wasting no time, I pressed the bare wires into the squirming white mass suffocating Sager. Nothing happened. My eyes flicked to the other chandelier in the office, and I saw with horror the light was off. I must have short-circuited the outlet. I remembered what Lina had told me about these places using aether—magic—to power the utilities. And magic didn't affect Flarks.

I roared with frustration. "I'm sorry," I said, my deep demonic voice sounding surprisingly sad.

Dark purple mottled Sager's face. His eyes flashed wide. A final spasm clenched his muscles, and he went limp.

Jarrod Sager, the Arcanus Primus and Shelton's father, was dead.

Chapter 39

"No!" Shelton roared, face suffused with absolute fury.

"Oh, is he dead? So sorry," said Bigglesworth, now free of the fire but slightly smaller than he had been before. He cavorted from one foot to the other. "Now it's your turn, boy."

Shelton whirled, grabbed his father's staff in his other hand, and slammed both of them against the floor at the same time, bellowing a word that ignited the ends of both staffs with seething orange light. He offered the Flark a smile that might have terrified any mortal. "Go to hell, you sorry sack of pus." He aimed the staffs at the creature.

"You can't hurt me, mate," Bigglesworth said, leering.

"Wanna bet?" Shelton flicked the aim of the staffs high and low, and shouted a word. Shafts of rippling light plowed into the ceiling and floor. The room exploded and a blast of heat slammed against me. The last thing I saw was a blue-tinged shield spring to life around Shelton before I felt my huge body smash through a window, fly through open air, and after a brief second of terror, smack into the earth outside. One of my horns caught in the dirt and flipped me hard onto my back.

I pushed myself up, shaking my head, and saw Shelton on the ground nearby, unscathed from what I could tell. He still had both staffs in hand, and planted them into the ground. Two roiling suns of death the size of his head formed atop the staffs. He aimed the staffs at the house, roaring, and unleashed them. They dropped off the ends of the staffs, rolling like boulders, and charring everything in their path. Whatever they burned only seemed to fuel them, and each inferno grew larger. They plowed through the house like meteors, rolling through the structure and razing it to the ground.

"Shelton, there might be other people in there!" I said. Even as I shouted, I saw golems leaving the house, their clothes burning from brass bodies.

The house blazed like a funeral pyre, not only for Jarrod Sager, but also—or so I hoped—for Bigglesworth. I watched the house burn in amazed silence, stunned by the raw power exhibited by Shelton. The Arcane dropped to his knees, slumping forward until his forehead met the ground. I rushed to him. He moaned, eyes drooping like a man after a hard night of drinking. I could only imagine the amount of power he'd thrown into those spells of his. He had to be beyond exhausted.

I snapped the two staffs back to compact size, pocketed them, and slung Shelton over my back. My night vision flickered on, and I saw glowing eyes regarding me from the forest. A shudder ran down my spine at the sight, but I had to go back through the nightmare forest to leave this place. The brilliant fire from the house did little to illuminate whatever horrors waited inside that place.

"Murder!" someone shouted, and I turned to see the man and lady of the pond emerge from a pond on this side of the woods.

I looked around, as if they were talking to someone else, saw no one else to blame, and turned back to face them. "It wasn't us!" I shouted, my voice still demonic. "It was Bigglesworth."

"We saw the wizard destroy the house with our own eyes!" the woman said.

"But he tells the truth," the man replied.

"He is Daemos. They can hide the truth," the woman replied.

The man nodded. "Ever are you right, my love. Children, take them."

I looked around desperately, but the forest surrounded the house and its grassy lawn on all sides. Trees uprooted and lumbered toward us from all directions, scantily clad girls dancing by their sides.

I jumped back from one of the dryads as she tried to touch me. If they rooted me to the ground, Shelton and I were done for. "I'll burn you, I said. Just like the house. Stay away!"

"You can't burn all of them," the man said, eyes growing hard.

"We didn't kill Sager! It was a Flark."

The man shook his head. "You are good at forging the truth, Daemos. But there are no more Flarks. They died with their masters when the Grand Nexus was destroyed."

"Their masters? The angels?"

"They all came from that hinterland, demon, but they are all dead."

"I'm not lying," I said, backing away from the closest dryads.

A feminine giggle sounded, and a warm hand touched my arm. My feet planted themselves in the earth and wouldn't move. I turned to see a dryad behind me, a warm smile on her pretty face. Something in me snapped. I bellowed a demonic roar, and tried to lift a leg. Muscles bunched beneath my blue skin. The sound of ripping and tearing roots came from beneath my foot. A clod of earth the size of a small boulder tore free from the ground. I tried to shake it loose, but whatever magic the dryad wielded made it immovable.

The dryad cried out in surprise, and more of them rushed me, hands outstretched.

I roared and tore another chunk of earth free with my other foot. I took a wobbling step atop the thick clot of dirt and roots. It was like walking on platform shoes only a hooker could be proud of. On the upside, the dirt put me about three feet higher off the ground. The other dryads had to leap to reach me. I had another problem. Carrying around so much extra weight sucked my energy dry.

Icy tendrils spread up my leg, creeping into my stomach. The uncontrollable beast inside me raged in syncopation with the vampling curse. I was running out of strength. Running out of sanity. I tried to shake loose the dryad still touching my shoulder, but she was as rooted to me as the ground beneath my feet. She squealed with either delight or terror as I ran.

Just as I teetered on sanity's edge, instinct showed me the way. I needed energy, and what was I surrounded by? Women! I just hoped they were the right kind of women. I flicked into incubus mode. Glorious feminine halos glowed bright above the dryads, like welcoming beacons. Without thought, my essence lashed out in all directions, hooking into their energy, and drawing hard. The dryads sighed, their eyes glowing bright with lust and desire. One of them sprang atop the clod of dirt under my left foot, and ran her fingers up my back. This time, her touch didn't slow me, although it aroused another completely unwelcome awakening in my body. The other dryads tried to repeat the success of the first, hands groping.

That was when the glowing eyes in the forest came.

Although I'd been curious as to what the eyes belonged to, I hadn't actually wanted to find out. Leaves burst into the air as men with bark-like skin roared, and rushed me. And then I realized the men weren't actually coming from the foliage, they were the trees themselves, shifting into humanlike form. They apparently didn't appreciate their women lusting all over me.

Suffused with excess energy, I concentrated, and redirected the flow of my tendrils through the dryads and into the—uh—whatever someone would call a male dryad. The affected dryads turned as one, and flung themselves at the men. The original dryad who'd rooted me to the ground let her hand fall away from my body. The clods of dirt lost cohesion, and I stumbled down piles of earth, nearly face-planting, or worse, horn-planting into the ground.

The area teemed in chaos, some dryads and dude-ads making out, while others chased me as the man and lady of the pond looked on in horror and fury. I didn't waste another minute, and jetted for the exit. As other dryads came at me, I lashed out with my incubus powers and sent them into the arms of the nearest dude-ads. I hoped they didn't have boyfriends, or there was going to be some serious 'splaining to do later from the explosion of infidelity I'd unleashed on them.

"Oh, god, the trees," Shelton said in a drunken voice. "Not again." And then he slumped, unconscious, against my back.

The iron gates were closed when I reached them. I leapt, trying not to imagine my tender bits being impaled upon the pointy top of the gate as I sailed overhead. I landed with a bone-jarring thud, and heard Shelton oof out a breath. As I ran, I saw figures piling over the gates behind me, glowing eyes burning bright.

"Oh, crap, not the friggin trees," I said. I didn't know what to do except keep running all the way back to the mansion. I felt a buzzing in my pocket, and reached my right hand across to my left pocket to pull out my phone. "Hello?"

"Oh, dear, who is this?" asked Bella.

"Justin."

"What's wrong with your voice?"

"I manifested," I said, huffing and puffing as I ran. "Things didn't go well and I'm running like mad with a bunch of dryad men chasing me."

"That's horrible!"

"No duh, Sherlock! Where are you? I need help."

"I'm at the mansion testing the drain rune," she said. "So be careful when you come in. It's in the center of that large dining hall in the west wing."

"Just grab your staff and be ready. I'll lead them inside, and maybe you can block the door." I checked behind me for pursuit, but the winding path behind me revealed nothing. "I'll be there in a couple of minutes."

"I'll be ready, Justin."

But as I sped through the paths, I realized that I no longer heard the sounds of pursuit. Even so, I didn't slow. I regarded every bush and tree along the path with suspicion as I ran, but none came alive.

I reached the mansion, and stopped outside the door, eyes scanning the surroundings with my blue-tinted night vision. I heard nothing.

Shelton jerked. "Huh? What the—why am I looking at someone's blue-tinted rear end?"

I felt a flush of embarrassment warm my face. My pants had managed to stay on even in their torn state, but I vaguely remembered a dude-ad or dryad trying to rip them off. I set Shelton down. He wobbled, but managed to stay on his feet.

"Oh, man." He sighed. "I feel like I passed out and hit my head on a toilet."

"We're home now."

He made a pained noise. "Dad."

I didn't know what to say, so I opened the door and went inside. He followed after a long moment, head hanging low. I stopped, gathered my willpower, and forced my demon spirit back down to its depths, my body shrinking as it did. When I was back to normal size, I regarded my ruined clothes, and sighed. I really needed to switch to yoga pants or something, because I was going to be broke from buying normal clothes if this kept up. And I wasn't about to strip naked just to change.

Bella was waiting on us, I remembered, so I walked down the hallway with Shelton into the room she'd mentioned. The petite dhampyr leapt from behind a divan ninja-style, staff at the ready. Then she saw it was us, and motioned us over. "Watch out in the middle," she hissed, pointing at a rune carved in the stone floor.

"We're not being followed," I said, hoping I was right. "I think they gave up."

She sighed. "Thank goodness."

Shelton walked across the room to her, and I did the same, except my target was the divan she'd been hiding behind, and dropped into the seat.

"Harry, are you okay?" she said.

"Peachy," he replied in his trademark gruff tone.

"What did we decide about your tough guy act when something is really bothering you?"

He sighed. "Not in front of other people, okay?"

"What a lovely home you have here," said a familiar cockney voice. "I do believe it needs a bit of polish, though."

I looked up at the Flark and shook my head in disbelief. "How—how the hell are you alive?"

"You son of a bitch!" Shelton roared. He pulled out his wand, and flicked it. His face screwed up with pain, and he cried out, holding his head.

"Overdid it a bit, did we?" Bigglesworth said, leering. "What a bloody shame. Since I never got to enjoy the all-you-can-eat buffet earlier, I suppose this little morsel"—he winked at Bella—"will do just fine."

Bella pushed Shelton into a couch against the wall, and walked straight toward the Flark. "Go ahead and try, you big hunk of snot."

"No, Bella!" I said.

But it was too late. The Flark grinned, and slithered toward her with blinding speed, its arms and fingers stretching grotesquely, reaching for her. Inches from her face, Bigglesworth's eyes suddenly went wide. He froze, and a horrific screech tore at my ears.

"What is this?" he screamed. "What is this?"

He stretched, trying desperately to spring away, but his rubbery flesh slowed, stiffening, and hardening from the feet up. His mouth stretched inhumanly wide with another scream, and then with shocking abruptness, his shriek cut off.

Bella looked the creature up and down. She nodded. "I hoped this would work."

"What worked?" I asked, completely shocked, aghast, dumbfounded, and unable to move. My heart felt frozen with the pain I'd expected upon seeing dear, sweet Bella devoured by the abominable Bigglesworth.

"The drain ward," she said in a matter-of-fact tone. "He's immune to magic directed at him, but that's because his entire being *is* magic."

"Uh-huh," I said, feeling particularly dimwitted. "But isn't a drain ward magic?"

"It's more like a magic vacuum." She shrugged. "I took a chance, but saw no alternative. I had to goad him into stepping on it."

"He could have just flung part of himself at you." I glanced back at Shelton, his face a mask of horror as he struggled futilely to push himself off the couch. "That's how he killed Sager."

"Your father, Harry?" Bella's face filled with sadness, and she went to him with open arms. "I'm so sorry." She kissed his cheek. "So very sorry."

"I'm fine," Shelton grumbled, but he didn't try to push her away.

Someone cleared their throat from the doorway. I looked up to see Meghan Andretti, and her boyfriend, Adam Nosti standing there. They stared with abject horror at Bella and Shelton.

"It terrifies me, too," I admitted, and waved them inside.

Their attention turned to the Bigglesworth statue in the middle of the room.

"Oh, and that was a Flark. Bella figured out how to kill it."

Meghan opened her mouth. Closed it and looked at Adam.

Adam shrugged. "Never a boring moment with Justin around."

"Oh, god," she said. "I knew it would be like this."

"I have something," Shelton said in a weak voice. "Let me go, woman." He grinned at Bella as she pulled him easily to his feet then limped across the room.

"What's wrong with him?" Meghan asked. She seemed to struggle internally before taking out her wand and scanning him with it. Her eyes went wide. "You almost burned yourself out. What in the world were you doing?"

"Holy cow," Adam said, looking at the numbers hovering in the air before Meghan. "I haven't seen magical output like that—well, ever."

Shelton waved away her wand and pulled the ASE his father had given him from inside a pocket. He put it on the floor, and spun it. When the image materialized, it showed an array of frozen images, each one of Jarrod Sager with a different label beneath his face. One in particular, however stood out, its name: "The Confession of Jarrod Sager."

Chapter 40

"Search for Andretti," Shelton said.

The ASE responded, one image expanding to fill the holographic projection, and fast-forwarding through several seconds of video before stopping.

"Play," Shelton said.

"Andretti was the leader of rebellious Arcanes, and Daelissa could not let him survive," Jarrod Sager said in a grim voice. "The angel knew Vadaemos was hungry for souls, and allowed him to concoct a plan to take Andretti's soul. But as with such things, he had to have the man's permission before he could devour him whole. My sources discovered the plot, and attempted to dissolve it, but the trap was well laid, and Andretti refused to let his sister die if he could save her. The rebellion died with him. Andretti's wife attempted to carry the torch, but a summoned demon killed her. I suspect Methuselah behind that plot." He sighed. "This is Jarrod Sager, Arcanus Primus, and I approve this message."

The playback ended.

Meghan said nothing as tears glistened on her cheeks. Adam hugged her, but she looked numb to his caress.

"I'm so sorry," Shelton said, his voice still sounding puny, but sincere. He turned back to the ASE. "Search Nosti."

The ASE rolled through images like a stack of cards, and stopped on another video. Shelton told this one to play, and we all stared, wondering what we would find out.

"...Nostis only by sheer luck."

"Pause," Shelton said. "Rewind to start."

The ASE followed his commands, and resumed, Sager's ghostly image narrating the tale. "I found out about the Nostis only by sheer luck. Maximus was Daelissa's newest plaything, and she wanted me to help him set up shop in Atlanta. I refused—" He choked up, covering his face for a moment. "They killed Martin." He took deep breaths as tears rolled down his cheeks. "My son." He trembled. "I had to protect Harry, no matter the cost, so I did as she asked." Sager wiped tears from his eyes. "I overheard Maximus discussing the Nostis as I showed him various places to locate his base of operations, so I asked my sources to look into them."

The Primus took a drink of amber liquid and seemed to gather his resolve. "The Nostis were part of the Illuminati. The order is nothing more than a splintered mess of power-hungry people who have long abandoned our original mission. But the Nostis somehow held true. I met with them in secret and told them to beware Daelissa and her plots. She knew of them, but at the time, I had no idea why they were important.

"Phillip Nosti thanked me and told me he could not, for the safety of all, reveal what made him so important. However, he said that should anything happen to him, to tell his son, Adam these exact words: *In the heart of my mundane beaver, butterflies mysterious lie.*" Sager shook his head. "I have no idea what it meant." He shook his head. "Unfortunately, after Philip's murder, his son and daughter vanished. I believe they've gone underground, but my people have had no luck finding him. Not only do I need to deliver his father's words, but also tell him that Maximus personally killed his parents for Daelissa. She was unable to pry answers from their minds, and they refused her to the very end. Maximus staged their murder as a mugging." The man took a deep breath, and looked back out at us. "I'm Jarrod Sager, and I approve this message."

Adam stared at the image, jaw tight, eyes full of rage, and it was Meghan's turn to comfort him. He threw off her arm and stalked across the room, pacing back and forth. "That son of a bitch, Maximus. I'm going to kill him."

"He's locked away," Meghan said. "The man was stripped of his vampirism by Justin, and he's powerless. Killing him would be a mercy. Letting him live is pure torture to a narcissist like him."

Her boyfriend rubbed his jaw, other hand clenching tight at his side. After a long moment, he nodded. "You're right. The bastard is suffering, and that's worse than death."

"What the hell did that nonsense about beavers mean?" Shelton asked.

Adam barked a humorless laugh. "My dad and I used to concoct code ciphers and say stupid things that only we could understand. My mom would roll her eyes at us when we'd sit at the breakfast table and spout nonsense back and forth."

"A code?" I asked.

He nodded. "Yeah, give me a minute." His eyes went unfocused for a moment before he nodded. "I think 'heart of my mundane beaver' means 'middle of my magical wood.' 'Butterflies mysterious' would mean 'answers why.'

Even translated, the words didn't make a lot of sense, so I said them aloud. "In the middle of my magical wood, lie answers why." My detective skills must have been maturing, because it made a little sense.

"Magical wood—wouldn't that mean like a staff or wand?" I said.

"That's what I was thinking," Bella said. "Inside his staff, perhaps?"

Adam pulled a compact staff from his back pocket, and snapped it out to full length. "This was my dad's staff." He rotated it, looking at the intricate carvings up and down its length. Then he smiled sadly, and pointed to one of the runes carved. It was that of a beaver. With trembling fingers, Adam pressed the carving. For a moment, nothing happened. The end of the staff flickered to light, brightening as the shape of a man's face formed.

"Dad?" Adam said, reaching tentative fingers toward the image, and pulling them back.

The nebulous image spoke. "Adam or Felicia, if you are seeing this, it means something has happened to us, and Jarrod Sager or one of our other contacts has given you the code to unlock this message. Your mother and I were handed down a task from a long line of predecessors to keep safe a secret so vital, if the wrong people were to possess it, it could mean the end of life here as we know it."

The ghostly image paused, as if collecting its thoughts. "There is too much information to compress into this message, so I will keep it short. Thousands of years ago, a race of beings we call Seraphim, or angels, entered our mortal realm. The Seraphim are divided into two factions—Brightlings and Darklings. Although the distinctions have to do with the spectrum of soul essence they feed from, there are other nuances we have yet to understand. The Brightlings enslaved humans. Used them as toys in war games. They fed from them, leeching their light, making the Brightlings even more powerful than when they'd first arrived."

Phillip Nosti's expression darkened. "The Brightlings also blessed their devoted human followers with gifts"—his voice filled with scorn at the word—"granting them immortality at a price—drinking blood, aversion to sunlight, and the vampling curse should they try to pass on their immortality."

"Vampires," Adam murmured.

"The Darklings, long oppressed by the Brightlings, sought escape to this world, and sparked a rebellion. But feeding on humans for so long made the Brightlings too strong. Demons recognized the threat the Seraphim posed to their realm should they dominate the mortals, and gave birth to the original demon spawn. The first Arcane, Moses, and the Darklings reluctantly allied with the Daemos. Even with their combined might, the Brightlings were nearly impossible to kill. The Darklings recommended an all-out assault on the only thing allowing access to our world—the Grand Nexus. Despite horrendous loss of life, they were able to remove a key component of the nexus, the Cyrinthian Rune, disabling it. Parting the rune caused a tremendous shockwave that drained the light from anyone in the blast radius, including those within range of any Alabaster Arches linked to the Grand Nexus." Philip Nosti shook his head sadly. "This left behind husks of humans, Seraphim, and Flarks—dark creatures that drain the light from the living."

The apparition flickered like a television image with a bad signal. "Moses kept the rune hidden, passing it down to generations of Arcanes, until it ended up in the hands of Ezzek Moore. He founded the Illuminati and discovered a better means for concealing the rune. Though the Illuminati long since splintered into dysfunctional cells, we have carried this burden and must pass it on to you. Should the Brightlings find the rune, they will reactivate the Grand Nexus and unleash Armageddon on this world. I have left detailed records for you. Go to the place your mother and I met, and let the staff guide you from there.

"We love you, Adam and Felicia. Please do not seek vengeance on our behalf, but work toward the greater good."

The image winked out, and the glow faded.

"Moses?" I said, wondering if it was the same guy who'd parted the Red Sea.

"Demons made Daemos?" Bella said.

Nosti's briefing had opened a king-sized can of worms.

Shelton took out his father's staff and regarded it for a moment before walking up to the statuesque remains of Bigglesworth. With a roar, he swung it like a bat, shattering the grotesquely deformed head of the dead Flark. "Rot in hell," he muttered, and left the room.

The next day, I went by the infirmary with Meghan, and explained our idea for healing those sickened by the rune with the use of drain wards to Healer Hutchins, leaving unmentioned, of course, the cause of the illness. I hoped Meghan's idea would work, but wanted to have a backup plan just in case it didn't. There was only one other person I could think of who might be able to help, but I had to find her first.

I grabbed an *Arcane Daily* scroll from the healer's office before I left, expecting to see Jarrod Sager's death as the top headline. Instead, it was something about the Grand Melee drawing record crowds.

"What the hell?" I asked myself.

In each class, I couldn't stop looking at Morgana's empty spot. The other kids seemed to notice it as well, their eyes wandering to me as if I might have information. I did my best to ignore them. Zagg had taken a leave of absence to study the rune. I should have skipped out on classes, but following my usual routine was more important than ever. With Bigglesworth dead, I didn't want to act unusual or guilty. If I did, Ivy might know something was up, and she was my backup solution to the aether poisoning. I just hoped she was at lunch today.

After sitting through a horrifically boring lecture where Zagg's backup read straight from the textbook, I went to the dining hall. I sat down, and took lunch, waiting, and hoping to see my sister. She never showed.

As I was trudging to my next class, someone tugged on my shirt. I spun, startled, and saw Ivy smiling innocently up at me.

"Can we get ice cream?" she asked without preamble.

A profound sense of relief swept through me. "Of course."

"I heard about Morgana," she said, eyes sad as we walked toward the gelato shop.

I steeled myself, hoping, praying she would say yes to my next question. "Would you like to stop and visit her before we get ice cream?"

Ivy's forehead pinched. She nodded. "Yes."

Healer Hutchins was out. A golem was attending the clinic, so Ivy and I walked straight in. My sister gasped when she saw the little girl, her face pallid, dark rings beneath her eyes.

"What's wrong with her?" Ivy asked.

"Some kind of magic poisoning," I said. "They don't know how to heal her."

"Oh no." Ivy touched Morgana's hand. "I like her. I—I think she was my first real friend." She looked up at me. "I like Mr. Bigglesworth, but he's a grownup like the others. He told me what to do a lot. I like friends who aren't bossy." Tears pooled in Ivy's eyes. She looked up at me, lips trembling. "Do you think she'll die, Justin? I don't want her to."

I hugged my sister. Her arms wrapped tight around me as she sobbed. After a moment, I pulled away, holding her by her shoulders. "Ivy, you're so talented and strong, you might be able to heal her." I motioned to the other children in the ward. "You might be able to heal all of them."

She wiped away tears, her face growing horrified at the sight of more children suffering from the same condition as Morgana. "This is terrible, Justin. What's making them sick? Please tell me it's not something you did, something evil."

I shook my vehemently. "No, I promise. Why would I want you to help them if I did it?"

She regarded me for a long moment, her red eyes harboring suspicion. Finally, that suspicion faded. A nod. "I'll try."

Chapter 41

A desperate breath I'd been unconsciously holding escaped. "Oh, thank you, Ivy. Thank you!"

Brow furrowed in concentration, Ivy laid a hand on Morgana's chest. Pale white light glowed between her hand and the sick girl. Minutes ticked by at a snail's pace, but I didn't dare move or ask Ivy anything which might distract her. Sweat glistened on my sister's face. Her eyes crinkled, and her face blanched even as dark bruises appeared beneath her eyes.

Ivy let out a little whimper and crumpled.

I cried out in dismay even as my lightning reflexes caught her before she hit the floor. "Ivy? Oh god, are you okay?" I touched her cheek. Rubbed her sweat-dampened hair from her face. She moaned, eyelids fluttering. The purple smudges beneath her eyes faded, and her skin took on a normal flushed hue.

Blue eyes blinked open, unfocused. Ivy looked at me, confusion on her face. "Justin? What happened?"

"You fainted," I said. "Your face started to look like Morgana's."

She groaned. "I feel sick. I think I'm going to—" With that, she threw up all over me.

For some reason, I wasn't grossed out. I didn't even yell, or jump away. Instead, I turned her over so she could empty herself out on the floor. When she was done, I felt horrible. Had she infected herself with aether poisoning? Was I responsible for making her sick, too?

"Ivy, are you okay?"

She wiped her mouth. Looked with disgust at her dress, at the floor. "I'm going to be in big trouble," she whispered, sounding frightened.

I helped her to her feet, grabbed some washcloths from a nearby sink. "I won't let you get in trouble," I said, dampening a cloth, and handing it to her to clean up.

"I ruined my dress," she said. "Bigmomma's gonna have a spell when she sees it."

"Haven't you thrown up before?" I asked.

She nodded. "When I was first learning magic. But I haven't done it for a long time." She smirked at me. Took a cloth and stood on her tiptoes to dab at my face. "I got it all over you." A giggle escaped.

I couldn't help but smile. "Are you feeling okay now?"

She nodded. A sad look clouded over her smile as she looked back to Morgana's still form. "I couldn't help her. I don't know how." Her lower lip trembled, and tears spilled from her eyes. "I don't like feeling like this, Justin. She's sick, and she might die. I have all these powers, but I don't know how to save her."

I touched her shoulder. Squeezed it gently. "I know the feeling. To have all sorts of abilities, but no matter what I do, I can't save the ones I love."

Her tear-stained eyes looked at me. "I feel that way about you, brother. I want to save you from the dark."

"I want to save you from the light," I said.

"No matter how hard I try to convince you, you won't believe me," she said.

Despite all the battles I'd fought. The times I'd been captured, tortured, and otherwise molested. I'd never felt so helpless as I did now. Ivy was so close, but still a million miles away.

The clinic golem walked up to us. "I noticed you regurgitated. Here are some sanitary spells to clean up the mess." It handed us tiny scrolls.

We opened them, and the cleaning spells sparkled around our clothes, removing the puke the washcloths hadn't gotten. After saying our goodbyes to Morgana, we went into the hallway.

"Still feel like ice cream?" I asked.

Ivy nodded. "I feel super hungry now."

"Will they notice you're gone again?"

She shrugged. "They're busy looking for Mr. Bigglesworth. He never reported back yesterday. I think he went"—she shuddered—"on a feeding binge again. He can be so gross."

We got ice cream, but the shop was so crowded, we decided to walk outside. I looked toward the road leading to the mansion and wondered if I could convince her to go there. Bella told me since the drain ward was already carved, she was able to reset it last night. That meant it was ready.

"You ever walk along Greek Row?" I asked Ivy.

She shook her head. "No, Bigmomma won't let me go near that pit of Satan spawn—at least that's what she calls it. I've always wanted to see what was so bad."

I winked. "I'll take you up there. If you want, I'll even take you inside one of the houses."

Her mouth formed an "O." "Really?" She looked around with a conspiratorial look. "Are they really awful? Full of drunk naked boys and girls who worship demons?"

I wondered what in the world Eliza Conroy had been telling the poor girl. "No, it's not bad. They just like to party and act stupid."

"Well," Ivy said, still licking her gelato. "I guess maybe you could show me. It'll be our secret, okay?"

I smiled. "Cross my heart."

We walked along the road, passing drunk fraternity boys and girls, some of them swerving on brooms as security golems chased them down for intoxicated flying. The closer we drew to the mansion, the more my heart pounded. I wasn't sure I could do this. Ivy seemed to trust me. She was walking with me, talking and having fun like siblings should. Why would I ruin that?

What if she trusts me enough to help me?

The question lingered in my mind. I saw the driveway to the mansion coming up on the right. Cinder stood outside watching the revelers, his face mimicking expressions. He glanced over, eyes locking onto Ivy. Without another word, he walked back toward the mansion, probably to tell the others to be ready to spring the trap.

Sweat broke out on my forehead. If I did this, I would ruin any chance of my sister ever trusting me again. It would be a complete betrayal. She would hate me. I pause at the end of the driveway. Ivy looked down the road.

"Oh, that's a spooky looking house," she said. "I think I remember hearing it was haunted or something. Bigdaddy said he used to live there a long, long time ago."

"What?" I said, my mind distracted. "Was he in a fraternity?"

"Can we go inside?" she said, finishing off her cone. "Pretty please? He's never taken me inside, and I want to see where he lived."

I took a hesitant step down the driveway.

"You look scared," Ivy said.

My heart thudded. My guts clenched. *This feels wrong.* So, so wrong. But I had to do it. We could trade Ivy for Mom, save Nightliss and me, and maybe even those sick kids if Meghan's plan failed. But I felt so close to making a breakthrough with Ivy. I felt as if I'd won some small battle for her trust, and that I might be able to win the war if I just didn't betray her.

We closed to within twenty feet of the door. I froze in place unable to take another step.

"Are you okay?" Ivy asked.

I couldn't answer her. *I think I'm going to throw up.* One way or the other, I had to make a decision. Whatever I decided could determine the fate of everything. Betray my sister, or try to win her heart, and pray I did it in enough time to save my friends.

"Justin?" she asked.

I flicked my gaze to her. "Let's not go in," I said. "I don't like haunted houses."

"But, I've never seen one. Please, please, please?" She clasped her hands together and gave me such a sad look, I felt even worse than before.

"Oh, crap," I said, widening my eyes. "I saw security golems in the windows. We gotta go or we'll get in trouble."

She gasped. "But I can't run in these shoes." She looked down at the ruby-red slippers she wore.

"I'll carry you," I said, scooping her up in my arms, and running at top speed down the driveway back to the main road.

She squealed with delight the whole way. "Again! Again!" she said as I set her down.

I laughed. "Maybe later."

"You're so fast," she said, giggling. "And that was so much fun." A little sigh escaped. "I really like having you as my brother."

My eyes misted. I wiped them. "I like having you as my sister," I said.

She touched my hand. "Maybe you're not so bad after all. Maybe…" she trailed off, eyes lost in thought. "Maybe you're right about some things."

"Sometimes you have to stop listening to what other people say and listen to your heart," I said.

"Do you still want me to meet with Nightliss?" she asked, a shudder working through her shoulders.

"Yes. She's very sick, Ivy. Daelissa did something to her, and I think she's going to die."

A troubled look crossed my sister's face. She looked at the ground for a moment. "If she's sick, she couldn't hurt me, could she?"

I shook my head. "But you might be able to help her."

"Why would I do that?" Ivy said, looking at me with horror.

"Because she's my friend, and I love her. I don't want her to die, just like you don't want Morgana to die." I got down on my knees. "Please, Ivy. Can you help her?"

Her mouth dropped open a fraction and she just stared at me. "I don't know if she's brainwashed you. I don't know if she's done things to make you love her, and your feelings are fake." She looked down again, shuffling a foot on the pavement. "Do you love me, Justin?"

I couldn't stop the tears from trickling down my face. "Yes, Ivy. I love you. I would never want to put you in danger. Do you believe that?"

She wrapped her arms tight around me, squeezing desperately hard. "I love you too. I know you've been through bad things, and evil people have tried to take advantage of you. But my heart tells me to help you."

"You'll come see her?" I asked.

"No. But if you bring her to the healer's office, I'll help her there." She put her arms akimbo. "If she tries anything bad, I'll have to hurt her, okay?"

I nodded. "I understand."

Her gaze wandered to the ground again, and a sad look pinched her brow. "I'm really sorry about what I did to you. About tricking you with Maximus. They told me it was the only way to save the world."

I took her hand and squeezed it. "I forgive you," I said.

She grinned. "This is a perfect day."

"It is," I said.

Something slammed into my back. Ground and sky tumbled in my vision until I came to a stop, dazed and warm blood trickling across my lips. I sat up in time to see Jeremiah Conroy, eyes blazing with anger, his staff aglow, coming right for me. Students scattered out of the way like scared rabbits.

"Please, Bigdaddy, no!" Ivy said.

Jeremiah flicked his staff, and an invisible force hauled me up by the front of my shirt. He glared at me. "I told you not to talk to him, girl."

"But—"

"Did you know he intended to lead you into a trap?" Jeremiah said. "That at this very moment, there are people waiting to ensnare you inside the mansion right down the road?"

"The haunted one?" she said.

His lips curled with anger. "The very same."

Ivy's blue eyes, clouded with disbelief met mine. "How do you know, Bigdaddy?"

"I used to live there, girl. I have ears everywhere."

Does he know about the rune? Dread welled in my chest.

Ivy looked at me, as disbelief morphed to denial. "It's not true, is it, Justin? Please, tell me it's not true."

I thought about lying. I thought about playing dumb. But what if Jeremiah really knew somehow? And how had he managed to overhear it even with the wards? "I planned it a long time ago," I said. "But I decided not to do it, Ivy. I changed my mind."

"You lied to me!" she shouted. "You told me"—her voice grew very quiet—"you told me you loved me." Tears poured from her eyes.

Jeremiah hugged her with one arm, keeping his other with the staff pointed at me. "It's okay child. I told you he was dangerous. You need to listen to me."

Ivy bawled, burying her face in his robes.

Her "grandfather" scowled at me, and released her. He came closer, and whispered in my ear. "I have no quarrel with you personally, boy. But you are interfering in my plans, and I will not have it. There is more going on here than you could possibly understand."

I tried to speak, but my vocal chords suddenly locked up.

He shook his head. "Not another word, do you understand? Now, leave Ivy alone, and stay out of my way, or I will finish you off. Nod if you understand."

I wanted to glare at him. I wanted to tell him he'd already tried to kill me and failed. I wanted to remind him there were hundreds of eyes on us at this very moment, and killing me would be a mistake. But I saw Ivy crying, and all I wanted to do was cry, too. She probably hated me now. And I'd been so close—so damned close to—" My vision blurred with tears. I nodded.

"Good boy," Jeremiah said. He flicked his wrist, and the lights went out.

Chapter 42

"Justin?" said a calm voice. "Are you alive?"

My eyes flinched open and found a serious gray face looking at me. "Cinder?"

He nodded. "We waited for some time in the house. I feared something had happened to you, and found you passed out here."

I looked around, and saw I was lying on the lawn of a fraternity house. Several other prone figures lay nearby, empty cups and alcohol bottles still grasped in their hands. "How long before you found me?"

"From the time we thought you were entering the house until now, it has been an hour." He held out a hand. I took it, and Cinder hauled me to my feet.

I felt a bit groggy, but otherwise none the worse for the wear. "Let's go to the house," I said. Bitter anger and sadness filled my heart as I thought back to Ivy's face. *She was going to help me!* I fought back depression. Jeremiah Conroy was always one step ahead of us. Even if he had lived in the mansion before, how could he have gotten past the eavesdropping wards?

The minute we stepped inside the house, Shelton stormed from the planning room, muttering. He looked up and saw me. "What the hell happened with Ivy?"

"Jeremiah Conroy," I said.

His jaw tightened. "Dammit. Nothing's going right today." He motioned me inside the planning room where a silver plate covered the rune, presumably to keep someone from accidentally triggering it. An image of the arch floated above the table. Shelton turned around. "Bella and I scoured the arch for wards. We found only one, but it's a doozy."

"Can you remove the ward?" I asked, wondering how much worse my day would get.

Shelton rolled his eyes. "And risk killing ourselves? Hell no."

"What do we do?" I asked. "Just evacuate the place and let it blow?"

"I don't think that's an option anymore," Shelton said. "In case you hadn't noticed, there's been no news about Dad's death. There's also been no evacuation order."

I couldn't stop thinking about Ivy or the look in her eyes when Jeremiah told her about my betrayal. Fury superheated my blood when I pictured him. I wanted to kill the old bastard for ruining everything. For ruining the fledgling relationship with my sister.

"You okay, buddy?" Shelton asked, looking at me with some concern.

"I had her, Shelton. She was going to help me. She was going to heal Nightliss." I dropped into a chair, my breaths ragged as I fought back the tears. "She told me she loved me."

"Ivy?" he said, eyes disbelieving. "But she thinks you're evil."

"We connected somehow," I said, fitting my fingers together. "We connected." I couldn't hold it off anymore. Couldn't fight off the pain. "I've got to go," I said, and raced from the room.

A figure emerged from the foyer as I crossed the den. Dirt covered Elyssa from head to toe. She looked tired and unkempt, and I detected a slight odor coming from her dirty Templar armor. She smiled at me, and it was the most beautiful sight I'd ever seen.

We met in the center of the room. My lips pressed tight to hers. She let out a little moan, I emitted a little groan, and my worries seemed to melt away.

Sometime later, we lay in bed together, smiling at each other.

"I missed you so much," I said, pushing negative thoughts of Ivy away.

"I didn't even wait around for the ending ceremony," Elyssa said. "I was in the middle of nowhere, but I got to the closest arch and took it straight here." She smiled. "Nobody wanted to stand near me on the shuttle."

I laughed. "You were a bit ripe."

She kissed me again. "I couldn't stop thinking about you. I couldn't stop thinking about how meaningless everything would be without you, and how stupid it was of me to leave you for the Cho'kai."

"I wanted you to do it," I said. "You're strong and independent, and I love that about you."

"If Meghan hadn't given you that potion, I never would have gone," she said, looking with dismay at the dark veins in my leg. "It's still spreading, Justin. Are you sure the potion is working?"

"Yes. But getting the crap beaten out of me daily hasn't helped."

She made a cute growling noise. "I'm not gonna let that happen anymore." She kissed me. "You need to tell me everything."

So, I did.

She was visibly upset by the time I finished. "Oh, Justin, I'm so sorry about Ivy." She wiped away tears, even as her teeth clenched with anger. "I'm going to personally beat the crap out of Jeremiah Conroy."

I couldn't help but chuckle. "The world might end, Queens Gate might blow up, but you're the most upset about Ivy?"

"You have a chance to connect with your sister." Her anger melted to sadness. "I'll never have that chance with Jack again."

I could only imagine her pain at losing her brother during our fight with Vadaemos. I hugged her tight and said nothing. It seemed like one of those moments where there really was nothing to say.

When we came downstairs, Shelton jumped up from a chair in the den where he and Bella were playing Scrabble. "I figured it out," he said, excitement in his eyes. "I know how we can defuse the ward."

"How?" I asked, caught off guard by this happy version of my usually grumpy friend. Apparently Bella had improved his bedside manner.

"Your incubus sight," he said. "You can see magic, right? That means you can see the ward, and we can figure out how to get rid of it."

I snapped my fingers. "Brilliant plan."

"First thing tomorrow," he said.

"Why wait?" I asked. "We need to act now."

"Are you kidding me? I nearly burned myself out fighting Bigglesworth yesterday. I'm exhausted." His eyes looked me over. "And I know you're not up to snuff yet either. What if something else unexpected happens?"

I sagged. He was right. We needed to be fresh for this. "You're right."

He tilted his head to the side. "You okay—I mean emotionally and all? I know it was rough with your sister."

Meghan and Adam came through the front door. Meghan looked exhausted. "Making drain wards is a lot harder than I remembered," she said, sinking into a chair as Adam massaged her shoulders. She caught Shelton's troubled gaze. "Is something the matter?"

I told her about Ivy.

"Do you think there's a chance you can convince her to help?" Meghan asked after I finished.

"By now, I'm sure Jeremiah has filled her with lies," I said. "Ivy probably hates my guts."

Meghan thought for a moment. "If there's a chance Ivy will help, I need to know. I'll have to bring Nightliss here because it doesn't sound like Ivy will go to her."

"Don't forget this place is about to go boom," Shelton said.

"I haven't," Meghan replied, eyes hard. "As you well know, Nightliss will probably die one way or the other." She made an angry wave with her hand. "I also need to evacuate the children. For that I'll need to spend most of my time planning." Her eyes found me. "Should I bring Nightliss or not?"

Meghan's words echoed in my head. *She'll probably die one way or the other.* Really, we had no choice. "Bring her," I said.

"Okay." Meghan's shoulders straightened. "I need an evacuation plan for the children. It won't be easy."

"I can help with that," Elyssa said.

"That would be very helpful," Meghan replied. "Thank you."

Thursday already. My head felt like a big alarm clock attached to sticks of dynamite, relentlessly ticking down to detonation. Elyssa went with Meghan while I made like a ninja and slipped down to the Burrows. Thoughts of Ivy plagued me. How I'd failed Nightliss. How

I'd failed to convince Ivy to help me rescue Mom. The countdown on my own life still ticked away. I squeezed my eyes shut. Took a deep breath. Willed it all away.

It's not working.

"Hello, Justin," Cinder said when he saw me at the bottom of the stairs where he and Zagg had created something of a makeshift workshop. "We are examining several texts I discovered after repairing flaws in damaged ASEs. It is possible Ezzek Moore left instructions regarding the rune should an emergency arise."

"More like a bunch of meaningless personal diaries," Zagg said, sighing deeply. "Most of this is so dry, I don't understand why he even kept a log."

"I am also uncertain why Moore kept a log detailing laundry day," Cinder added, turning his serious face toward me. "He also recorded his favorite location to take lunch, and his frequent conversations with someone he refers to as the Lady of the Pond."

I shuddered. "Yeah. I've met her. Weird woman."

"Isn't this kind of a bad place to be reading?" I asked, nodding my head toward the entrance where the dungeons started. "Because of the magical radiation, I mean."

Zagg poked a thumb toward a line on the floor. "Bella put up a shield ward. She and Meghan said the malaether can't go through it."

"Malaether?"

"Yeah. That's what they're calling the corrupted aether. Mal as in bad."

I imagined a seething cauldron of malaether hovering like a poisonous cloud on the other side of the shield. I hoped Meghan would be able to use drain wards to heal the sick students.

"Ready to get to work?" Shelton asked as he and Bella came down the stairs.

I nodded confidently, but the nervous clenching in my stomach offered a sobering reminder that even if I could see the ward guarding the arch shield, we might not be able to do anything about it. I followed the two Arcanes through the dungeon, past the gauntlet room Lina had used, and toward the pulsating, glowing orb of death in the room with the arch.

"How long do I have before I keel over?" I asked, my skin tingling as if it were already mutating from the malaether.

"It takes several days of this much exposure to sicken most people," Bella said. "Your supernatural healing might protect you."

"I'm using a shield," Shelton said, his voice sounding a bit muffled. Tiny sparks erupted around him like bugs in a zapper.

I regarded the arch for a moment, closed my eyes, and extended my essence as if searching for prey. When I opened my eyes, I saw a glowing shield stretched tight across the arch, except for a noticeable bulge, like a dent in stressed metal, where the brilliant sphere of malaether sparkled.

What really caught my attention was a strange black lump floating in front of the shield, tethered to the ground by a thin black strand. Though a thick layer of dust covered the floor beneath it, I saw traces of glowing lines. I wandered closer to the balloon-shaped oddity. Careful to avoid the glowing lines, I stepped to within a few feet, and peered at it.

The black mass quivered.

I shrieked like a girl and jump back about twenty feet.

"What is it?" Shelton asked.

I described what I saw.

"A guardian ward," Bella said, her voice almost a whisper. "This will be even harder than I thought."

Regaining some courage, I walked back up to the tumor-like mass. "Hello?" I said, the greeting more of a question than statement.

A glistening white eye with a blood-red iris blinked open. The middle of the orb split, open in a display of serrated teeth. A low growl vibrated against my eardrums.

"Uh, what's that noise?" Shelton said.

"Perhaps you shouldn't talk to it," Bella said, backing toward the door along with Shelton. "Justin, come away from there at once."

I stared at the eye monster, suddenly feeling angry. Why was it growling at me?

How dare it show me disrespect.

I blinked, suddenly wondering where in the world that last thought had come from. *Disrespect? Why would I think that?* I took a breath, and regarded the thing as it continued to snarl. One of my tendrils wandered close to it, as if drawn there like a magnet. I jerked it back before I touched the disgusting thing. The demon part of my soul clawed against my control, as if suddenly driven insane, like a caged dog foaming at the mouth as it tried to kill a cat on the other side.

Somehow, my inner beast recognized this guardian. But how and why?

The answer came to me an instant later. To confirm my suspicions, I closed my eyes and switched off my incubus sight. When I opened my eyes, I looked at the area where the dust covered the floor. Not daring to take another step closer, I stared at the floor right about where the giant eyeball hovered, its growl only now fading away. I wasn't about to walk into that area.

"If you sent a stiff breeze in here, would it trigger the guardian?" I asked.

"I don't think so," Bella said from the other side of the hole in the wall.

"I need you to clear that dirt." I pointed it out.

The dhampyr took a nervous breath. Nodded. "Stand to the side."

I backed away from the center, and watched.

Bella took out a slender wand, and moved it in a whirling motion, faster and faster as she chanted under her breath. Her voice grew louder, and then as if blowing a kiss, she blew air the length of her wand, her cheeks puffing out like a little girl blowing bubbles.

A blast of air nearly knocked me off my feet as it rushed past, clearing away dust and debris. Even though it didn't clear the floor completely, it was enough. A twisting shape of spirals and other odd geometric shapes caught the light from the room. Etched into the floor and lined with a silvery metallic substance, the rune confirmed what I'd suspected. I'd seen designs like this in one of my mom's books when I was a nosy kid. It looked somewhat similar to the one I'd seen as a child when gray men had placed a chunk of plywood studded with nails in an intricate pattern beneath Sandy Andretti's house and powered it with electrical generators.

This rune looked simpler than the one I'd seen as a child. Whether that meant anything, I didn't know. What I did know was this: the giant eyeball was a demon.

Chapter 43

"A demon?" Shelton said, face aghast as I told them about my discovery.

"Now I know why my demon side was so pissed off." I shook my head. "It didn't like being growled at by another demon."

"We are so very screwed," Shelton said.

We crossed the line where Bella's shield guarded the tunnel from malaether. Zagg and Cinder looked up from their work.

Shelton jabbed a thumb my way. "One of Justin's long-lost cousins is guarding the freaking shield."

"This is very fortunate," Cinder said. "If one of your family members is guarding it, they may be more likely to give us access."

Shelton rolled his eyes. "No, you walking bucket of bolts. It's a full-fledged demon. Looks like Moore and the gang inscribed a summoning rune, and gave a demon eternal guard duty."

"Your description of me is rather inaccurate," Cinder said, looking at his body. "I am not a bucket—"

"A demon?" Zagg said, eyes wide. "There's no way we can get past the shield and a demon in a week." He pounded the table where the ASE spun, shook his head. "Damn it. It's all been for nothing, hasn't it? This place and everyone in it is—they're all going to die, and there's nothing we can do to stop it."

Bella gave him a helpless look. "I'm sorry, but this is beyond me. Beyond any of us."

Zagg shook his head. "No. I won't let them die. We need to force an evacuation. Not everyone will escape, but I'm going to give them a chance."

"How?" Shelton said. "If you run around telling everyone this place is gonna blow, you'll look like a raving lunatic."

"And let the Conroys know about the rune," Bella said.

"So what?" Zagg threw up his arms. "They won't be able to get to it, not with a demon guarding it. Let them blow up with the place. At least then Daelissa will never get her hands on it." He headed toward the stairs. "I don't know how I'll do it. If I have to make up something, I will."

Cinder turned his steady gaze to me. "Justin, what is the demon's name?"

"His name?" I said, imagining both eyebrows arching like mirrored question marks. "How should I know that?"

"You are part demon. Can you not communicate with him?"

I almost replied with a sarcastic remark, but suddenly remembered the demon in Sandy Andretti's basement. It had burst from the summoning rune through her floorboards, and then bitten her leg off. I'd found her outside bleeding to death. I'd run inside the house and seen my mother barely holding the demon, a giant, green, shark-like monster with tiny red eyes all over its snout. It had spoken to me in a deep guttural voice. I'd spoken in that same voice before while a demon. The strange tongue wasn't Cyrinthian, although it felt similar in the way it rolled off the tongue.

Could I remember how to speak that language again? Or was the knowledge buried too deep inside me?

Zagg froze on the stairs. He turned and looked at Cinder. "Your question made me think of something." He stopped the spinning ASE on his table, sorted through a bowl of them, and plucked one out. After it spun up, Zagg opened a document and scrolled through it until he reached a passage. "Listen to this. 'We spoke of the inconsequential before wandering back to the solemn duty. I knew my time for small talk would soon be ending. The Lady understood as she always did, and said she would miss our conversations. I knew the infernal name would remain safe with her until the proper time.'"

"Infernal name," I said. "A demon name. We have to talk to the Lady of the Pond!"

"Wait," Zagg said. "I don't know why this didn't stick out before. I guess I was zoning out. There's more you should hear." He traced the Latin words with his fingers, and resumed translating. "'Safer subjects followed, but then the Lady turned to the subject of children. I am no lover of the infantile. The rigors of raising youth holds no appeal for me, although my friends assure me once I have a child, my feelings will change. However, if the foreseeances remain true, I will have a child, though not of my own loins. She will be the harbinger of the Return. She will also signal the time of action. Though, in truth, I dread this child, it will be her child that holds the key to revenge or our destruction.'"

I watched Zagg for a moment before realizing he was done reading. "Um, so Moore was gonna have kids?"

"How very odd," Bella said, fingers resting thoughtfully on her chin. "Didn't Moore die childless?"

Zagg nodded. "He died not long after this. There is no record of him having adopted a child."

I shrugged. "Maybe he did and kept it a secret," I said. "It doesn't matter. The Lady of the Pond knows the name of the guardian."

"She *might* know the name," Shelton said. "Don't get your hopes up."

"Fine." I headed toward the stairs. "I'm going to have a talk with her."

"Lead the way," Shelton said.

Bella, Shelton, and I made our way topside, taking back hallways to avoid students the best we could. Knowing Bigglesworth was dead was certainly a heavy weight off my back, but I wasn't about to let my guard down.

I reached the gates to the Fairy Garden, took a deep breath, and headed toward the pond with a confident stride. Shelton and Bella stayed back to cover my retreat, should one be necessary.

The Lady of the Pond and her annoying boyfriend leapt from the aforementioned body of water to greet me.

"You are persistent," the woman said. "And do not listen to the wisdom of women."

"I want to listen to your wisdom," I replied, and then shot a glare at her man, as if daring him to question the truth of that.

"He speaks the truth," the man said.

"It's a good thing your lady here isn't the truth detector," I told him. "Because you'd probably be in trouble all the time."

The woman laughed. Her man gave me a surly look and cracked his knuckles.

"I do not need his abilities to divine the truth of what he says," the lady said. "I also know I have no need to worry about him. He is ever honest when he tarries with the dryads of the woods. But he is male, and nature demands he spread his seed."

I waved my hands, and grimace. "Gross. That's way TMI." The last thing I wanted to imagine was this guy—*oh never mind.* "What I came here to ask is in regard to Ezzek Moore."

The lady's eyes went from smiling, to granite. "Then we have nothing to discuss."

"The infernal name," I said. "I need it, or everyone here will die."

"He speaks the truth," the man said in his rumbling voice.

I rolled my eyes, but refrained from commenting on how annoying he was. "There's a demon guarding the arch with the Cyrinthian Rune in it. The arch is ready to explode by the end of the week, and it'll take this entire place with it."

The man opened his mouth to speak, but the lady interrupted. "That you know of these things is very troubling." She made a motion, and trees sprouted from the ground in a tight circle around us. "Very troubling."

I backed away, eyes searching the circle, but the trees were too thick to break without manifesting into demon form, packed too tightly squeeze through, and too tall to jump. "Does that mean you're going to have to kill me?"

She stared at me for a long moment, as if trying to search me out. "My dear friend, Ezzek, told me any person other than the child must never possess this information. I do not wish to kill you, but I will hold you prisoner."

"That didn't work out so well last time," I reminded her.

"We will hold you beneath the waters," she said, looking at the black waters of the pond.

I thought of being dragged into those depths and gulped. I'd sprout demon claws and climb over these trees if I had to before I'd allow her to take me in the pond. Besides, I just knew she and her man probably peed in the water all the time. "I know you two spoke of children," I said, grasping at straws. "He didn't like them. He knew he was going to have a child someday though, even if she wasn't biologically his."

The lady tilted her head and regarded me for a moment. "How do you know these things?"

I took a calming breath before I spoke. "Ezzek is dead. Whatever plans he had for the rune perished with him. I'm trying to save lives by temporarily freeing the rune, but I promise to put it right back. Unfortunately, there's a demon guardian there, and I need its name so it won't bite my head off."

"He speaks the truth," the man said, still frowning at me, most likely about my earlier comment.

Some people just can't handle the truth.

The lady looked from the man to me, eyes uncertain. "The intended one is female. You are not her. I made a promise I cannot break, young man."

Could she mean Ivy? I couldn't let Jeremiah use her to get the rune. "How do you know it's a female child? Did Ezzek specifically tell you that the only person you could give this information to would be a girl?"

She remained silent for a moment before answering. "No. He expected a female, but his promise only stated that the child would give me a sign."

"What kind of sign?"

"He told me I would know it when I saw it."

I groaned. "That's stupid! The fate of the world hinges on this rune, and he decides to be all enigmatic?"

"He speaks the truth," the man said, his voice calm.

The woman looked at him, and laughed. "I told Ezzek he was being rather foolish, but he always did have a flair for the dramatic."

"Maybe it's sign enough that I know about the rune, and that I'm telling you the truth regarding my intentions." I sighed. "Because I got nothing else, really."

"I am truly sorry," the Lady said. "But it is not enough."

Men with bark for skin burst from the ground all around me. They looked angry, probably for the debacle I'd caused with their women. Before I could react, they gripped me. Dragged me toward the water. I struggled, but collectively, they were stronger than me.

"No!" I shouted. "You have to listen to me! You have to—" My legs turned to jelly as intense cold swept from one and down the other. I felt ice tendrils crawling up my waist. The bark men seemed to sense something was off, and dropped me, disgust in their faces. I pulled up my shirt and watched in horror as the veins blackened and pulsed.

"What is this?" the lady said in alarm.

I tried to speak, but agony tore through me like frostbite. I felt consciousness fading, and with it, control. My demon half took the chance and surged for freedom. Skull-splitting pain erupted on my forehead as horns sprouted.

"No!" I cried out.

The cold surged again, creeping from my lower body, toward my stomach, and grasping for my chest. The faintest whisper of cold seemed to sear the bottom of my heart. And then a burst of fire radiated out from my core. I heard a scream tear from my throat as the heat and the cold ravaged my senses until my consciousness dangled by a thread. I heaved a breath, and saw blood dribbled on the ground beneath me. Fire burned through my shoulders, and I screamed again. The world blinked black for an instant, and all sensation faded. I heard my panting breaths. Felt the pounding of my heart. My lower body burned with cold. Somehow, I stood.

The lady and her man stared at me, mouths hanging open. I pressed a hand to my head, and felt the curving horns. My hands and skin seemed normal, however.

"What's wrong?" I asked, my voice sounding a bit slurred. "You've seen me manifest before."

"This is the sign," the lady said, eyes wide with wonder. She motioned at the pond, and a sheet of water rose like a giant mirror.

I looked at the shimmering image for a long moment before realizing it was me. Ebony horns curled upward from my head, even though my skin remained a normal pink hue. I suddenly knew they weren't the cause of her wonder. Ultraviolet flames billowed behind me, dark light smoking off them like frozen mist. I flinched with surprise, and the flames unfurled from my back. The darkly burning shapes on my back weren't flames.

They were wings.

Chapter 44

Wings? I have wings?

"Ah!" I shouted, spinning in circles like a dog chasing its tail so I could see the wings without the aid of a mirror. I felt them burning deep in my shoulder blades, like hot knives. And yet, the pain didn't reach agonizing levels. Maybe it was because I was so used to pain by now, thanks to the vampling curse dominating my lower half, or maybe I was just in shock. As if growing horns wasn't painful enough, I now had to deal with wings stabbing through my back.

"You must be the one," the lady said.

I stopped chasing my wings, and looked at her. "I am so done with this crap." Pulling at the waistband of my jeans, I watched as black veins writhed through my waist. Lifting my shirt revealed the full extent of the curse. A single dark talon speared through my abdomen straight toward the left side of my chest where my heart pumped furiously. I didn't have much longer. For all I knew, this week might be my last.

A loud *poof* startled me, and my wings vanished, leaving behind dark smoky smudges in the air.

The lady took my hands, and smiled. "You are the one. True, you are not a female." She looked me up and down as she said this, smiling. "But my old friend could not have known such a thing so far in advance." She leaned toward me, her lips brushing my ear, and whispered a word. Even though the word was filled with consonants, sounding like the noise someone would make after a steamroller just ran over their foot, the demonic part of me understood it on the first try, burning it into my mind.

More than just a word, it evoked an image in my head—a symbol that was neither Cyrinthian, nor human in origin. The symbol bore an uncanny resemblance to the symbol in the floor beneath the eye demon. I knew without a doubt if I uncovered the rest of that rune, it would look identical.

"Thank you," I said, my voice a whisper. "I will try to make things right before"—I suddenly had a terrible premonition—"before the end."

"He speaks the truth," the man said, and gripped my forearm, pressing my hand to his forearm. "May the peace of the world go with you."

The pain in my lower body receded, leaving behind a delicious numbness. It felt so wonderful, I almost twirled like a little princess in a fairy tale and pranced around from the sheer joy of not feeling pain. The huge trees around me abruptly uprooted, and lumbered into the forest to join their brethren, while dozens of dryads sang and danced after them.

"I have only removed the pain," the man said. "Not cured the curse."

The Lady of the Pond kissed my cheek. "You will do well."

Shelton and Bella stood twenty yards away, eyes wide as the giant trees strolled away. Bella's staff glowed purple, while a sun-like inferno spun atop Shelton's. I was glad they'd held their fire. Things could have gotten ugly.

I turned from the two pond people without another word, offered a weak smile to my friends, and we departed.

"So, what happened in there?" Shelton asked as I gave purpose to my stride to get back to the arch.

"I don't know, exactly," I said, savoring the pain-free movement of my legs, and the absence of the ever-present cold ache below my waistline. "I had an episode."

"An episode?" Bella said, keeping stride despite her short legs, and regarding me with narrowed eyes. "You're moving differently."

"The man did something to me. Helped me, I guess."

Bella's brow furrowed. "Helped you? How?"

"What happened?" Shelton said again. "Saying you had an episode doesn't explain jack."

I stopped. Bella skidded to a halt, Shelton beside her. "Maybe I should explain it to everyone all at once." I gave them my best pleading look. "Okay?"

They looked at each other, worry obvious in their eyes. As one, they turned back to me and nodded. We proceeded without conversation toward the university and the Burrows, though I could sense Bella's worry. I wasn't sure if it was due to my incubus super powers, or just a gut feeling. I didn't want to worry them, but I also didn't feel like explaining everything twenty times.

We passed the east garden, entered the hallways, and proceeded down the stairwell when a faint noise caught my ears. Bella seemed to hear it too. We turned, and saw a flicker of blonde hair pull back behind the turn in the landing. A blue eye peeked around the corner followed by a sigh. Vallaena stepped out, face placid, and not an ounce of shame to show for stalking us.

"When you missed your lessons, I waited, and saw you pass the garden without stopping." She arched an eyebrow. "Naturally, I was curious, since you all have such determined looks on your faces."

I was fishing in my mind for some excuse, when the stomping of feet up the stairs caused us all to turn and look as MacLean, Cinder, and Zagg, faces worried—well, except for Cinder—rushing up the stairs.

"Justin!" Zagg said, breathing hard. "We can't get back into the chamber. There's a shield blocking it—a powerful one. We must have tripped a ward."

"Impossible," Shelton said. "Bella and I went over every square inch of that place and didn't see any other wards."

"What do you mean you can't get through?" I said.

"We tried blasting it down. We tried blasting the walls, but it's like the shield forms a bubble around the area." Zagg shook his head. "What are we going to do?"

"Who the bloody hell is that?" MacLean said, pointing up the stairs at Vallaena. "She's a fair sight on the eyes, that one is." He gave her a toothy smile, and flourished a bow.

"Oh, for crying out loud," I said, having completely forgotten our unwanted guest in the confusion.

"I do not blame you for your secrecy," Vallaena said, a smirk plain on her face. "But it appears I know enough that it would do no harm to tell me more."

"Actually, you know next to nothing," I said. "I'm sorry, but I don't trust you farther than I can throw you."

"As I recall, you threw me quite a distance during practice the other day." Another smirk.

I groaned. "Everybody back to the house."

"I am coming as well," Vallaena said.

"I'd be happy to escort you, lass," MacLean said, still grinning.

The Daemas regarded him with a haughty look. "I can manage on my own."

"You're not coming to the house," I told my dear aunt.

She turned her gaze on me. "And you will stop me forcefully?"

I sank to the stairs, ran my hands through my hair. I had the demon name. All I had to do was get in there and speak it, and we could secure the rune. Victory was so close I could taste it. This shield was no coincidence. It had Daelissa or one of her cohorts written all over it. But why? If they knew where the rune was, why hadn't they tried to take it? Did they know about the guardian? What if Jeremiah really had ears in the mansion?

Too many questions. Too many problems. Too little time.

I didn't know if Vallaena would complicate matters, but I knew without a doubt she'd eventually find out about the rune by hook or by crook. At the moment, I just didn't have an ounce of fight left in me. I just wanted to curl up in bed next to Elyssa and forget all about this mess.

But I couldn't.

My legs pushed me to my feet. Despite the strange lack of sensation, I had no trouble controlling them. I mustered some willpower and headed up the stairs. My gaggle of friends followed me, mumbling to themselves. I heard Zagg asking Bella if I was okay. I heard her tell him I was under a lot of stress. I almost turned around and told them I was crazy—or nearly so. I no longer felt qualified to lead them into whatever the hell lay ahead.

I called Elyssa, and told her I was about to deliver a major briefing. She and Meghan showed up about the time the rest of us reached the mansion. In the meeting room, I dropped into a seat at the far end of the table, and waited, slumped and defeated. Only minutes ago, I'd been so happy. So confident. How were we going to get through that damned shield?

Once everyone was situated, including Vallaena, I told them about my encounter with the Lady of the Pond. Mention of my wings drew gasps from all corners of the room. When I pulled up my shirt and showed them the reach of the vampling curse, Bella broke into tears. Vallaena's lips curled, though whether from disgust or fear, I couldn't tell.

Elyssa went pale, her finger tracing the line up my chest.

I spoke before she could, addressing everyone. "So, I guess what this all means is nothing," I said. "I have the word to get us past the guardian, but the new shield is going to keep us from getting in."

Shelton and Bella traded looks. Zagg consulted with Cinder. MacLean stared at Vallaena who pointedly ignored him and glared at me.

Zagg turned from Cinder and gave me a shake of his head. "The new shield is tethered somewhere inside the chamber. I've been thinking about it, and there's no possible way someone could have just thrown it up in an instant. The enchantment evidently was already in place and just waiting for someone to trigger it."

"There were no wards," Shelton said. "We would have found them."

"It didn't have to be a ward," Zagg replied. "Just an enchantment that needed a word of activation."

"By whom?" I asked. "Ezzek Moore and his gang are dead."

Zagg's eyes flared for an instant, and he flicked his gaze to MacLean. "By the Illuminati." He bolted upright. "You were there. You showed up just minutes before it appeared."

MacLean shoved his chair back and rose. "That's a load of rubbish. If that was the bloody case, why didn't I do it sooner?"

"It's the only answer," Shelton said, adding his two cents. "The freaking Illuminati."

"I didn't do it!" MacLean shouted. "Why would I want to keep us from fixing the bloody thing if it could destroy all of Queens Gate?"

"Wait," I said, holding up a hand. All eyes turned to me. "Will that shield protect the rest of us when the rune goes nuclear?" A spark of hope smoldered in my heart.

Zagg shook his head. "I don't think so. If anything, it might compress the blast and cause it to be even bigger."

"Bigger?" I said, shaking my head in confusion. "How's that?"

The historian clenched a fist. "If you hold a firecracker tight in your hand, it could blow your hand off. If you hold it in the palm of your hand"—he opened his hand—"it'll hurt when it explodes, but it won't destroy your hand."

"Holy crap in a donut box," Shelton said, eyes distant. "He's right. If that thing explodes inside the shield, it could create a shockwave that might take out more than Queens Gate. It might collapse the way station cave and cause half of London to sink into the ground."

"Technically, the explosion will be more concentrated," Cinder said. "I do not think half of London would be destroyed. Perhaps only a quarter of it."

"Okay, I get it," I said, waving my hands in surrender. "We're screwed. There's no way inside the shield, and nothing short of a big explosion can take it out."

"That's not technically true," Vallaena said in a quiet voice.

The room went absolutely still.

"And?" I said, implying ellipses at the end of the word.

"It is possible we could summon a hellhound on the other side of the shield."

"What good would that do us?" I imagined the poor dog running in circles on the other side, and drooling on the floor.

She pursed her lips. "If you give me the demon name, I may be able to summon a hellhound on the other side of the barrier and imprint the name on it. It could then morph into human shape, and speak the demon name."

"Are you certain?" I asked.

"Of course not, but we can try."

I tried to speak the demon name, but my tongue got in the way. I saw the name emblazoned in my thoughts, the intricate pattern and the associated sounds clear as day, but I couldn't form them with my lips.

"I can't say it," I said. I tried again, and made a horrible gurgling noise.

"The name has been sealed to you," she said. "You can only send it to the demon, or imprint it on your own summoned demon."

"You're saying I can imprint it on a hellhound, but I can't give you the name to do that?"

"That is exactly what I'm saying." She frowned. "It means I have no choice but to teach you how to summon a hellhound."

"I don't like the sound of that," Elyssa muttered, giving me a worried look.

I didn't like it any better than she did.

Chapter 45

"Summon a hellhound?" I regarded Vallaena warily. I checked the date and time on my phone. "We have two days until kabloom." I projected a huge holographic timer above the table with my phone. "Forty-eight hours, people. That's it. This is our last chance." If raising a hellhound was the answer, then, by god, I would learn how to do so.

Adam exchanged a knowing look with Shelton.

I raised an eyebrow. "You have any other bright ideas, Adam?"

He shrugged. "Even if you banish the guardian, we still need to get inside the barrier, and lower the shield on the arch." He nodded at Shelton. "Remember how we used to lower the forest shield to let out spider bats?"

"Shelton's only mentioned it a dozen times," I said.

"You think we can decode the cipher spell on this shield?" Shelton said, ignoring my jibe.

"Anything is possible," Adam said.

Shelton shrugged. "You're the genius."

"What about the other end of the arch?" Bella said. "Did we ever find out where it is?"

Zagg shook his head. "No. We didn't think it was important. Besides, what's to guarantee a similar shield isn't around the chamber on that end?"

After the meeting, we had a somber meal of pizza. I still craved chicken wings and wondered if I'd get to have them again before the vampling curse took me.

"I don't like this," Elyssa said as I changed into workout clothes for my hellhound lessons with Vallaena. "Summoning demons of any kind is risky."

"Banishing the guardian isn't something I'm looking forward to either," I replied.

She ran a finger up my skin, her eyes troubled by the darkness in my veins. "How much longer, do you think?" she asked, her voice a whisper.

I shook my head slowly. "I don't know, baby. But, I'm glad you're here, no matter what happens." I'd taken more of the potion, what little Meghan had left, but it seemed to have lost its potency.

Elyssa squeezed her eyes tight, but tears leaked out. "I've got to find your sister. I've got to convince her—"

"You can't, babe." I stroked her hair. "It's too late for that."

"It's never too late," she said, violet eyes blazing with determination. "While you're off practicing, I'm going to find her."

"Please don't," I whispered. "It's too dangerous. Jeremiah—"

"Can suck the business end of my sword, Justin." She pressed a finger over my lips. "Life isn't worth living without you. I don't care what the risk is. I will find her and even ask nicely."

I sighed. I knew it was useless talking to her when she got all determined like this. I just had to hope she didn't get anywhere near Ivy.

Vallaena led me to our usual practice place and started the lessons.

"Do you know what it feels like to summon your inner demon spirit?" she asked.

"Yeah, like opening a cage, and unleashing a monster."

She nodded. "An apt description for a male. It is different for females, but that is of no concern. When you reach for your inner demon, you are bringing that side of you from the demon plane into your body."

I crinkled my forehead. "But it's always there, isn't it? A part of me."

"Yes and no. Your mortal soul and demon spirit are tethered in both planes simultaneously." She held her hand flat. "This is the barrier between our worlds. There is always a slight crack in the barrier which allows your soul to remain whole. If this barrier were to close completely, your soul would be severed, and your body would lose access to your incubus abilities. Even though your body has certain supernatural qualities, you would become almost mortal."

I shuddered. "Someone could do that to me?"

She shook her head. "Not that I am aware of. This is not something we share outside our race for obvious reasons, however. A skilled Arcane summoner could possibly contrive an exploit, and we do not wish that to happen."

I nodded. "Our secret is safe." I shuddered again. "That's freaky."

"Using this same split in the barrier, we can also summon other creatures from the demon plane and project the opening just about anywhere in our line of sight."

"But if the crack in the barrier is inside us, how can you project the opening somewhere else?"

She pursed her lips. "The barrier is not physical. It does not recognize the boundaries of this world. I honestly do not know why it works as it does, but just accept if you look at an area and focus on whatever you are summoning, it will emerge there."

"Like those black oily lakes," I said, thinking back to how the hellhounds she'd summoned against me came into being.

"Yes. They use whatever materials are available to form their physical shell."

"What if I do it in concrete?"

She blinked. "They will still emerge as flesh, not concrete. Although hellhounds will conform to the original shape you give them, their spirits differ. Some will be larger or smaller, and they each have different personalities."

"I could give them horns?"

Vallaena simply stared at me for a long moment. "Was I mistaken in my understanding that this place is in imminent danger, and yet you are asking insignificant questions which serve only to waste time?"

I looked away from her, a bit ashamed. "Sorry. It's how I cope with imminent death."

"I understand." She placed an arm on my shoulder. "I am proud of you, nephew. You are a brave, capable Daemos, and I have full confidence you will not allow us all to die."

A sad laugh burst from my throat. "Thank you, my dear, sweet aunt."

She laughed. "Perhaps your humor is something of a balm. I must admit I am rather nervous."

I gave her a pained look. "I really wish you hadn't just told me that."

"While you were preparing for our lessons, I went with the MacLean character down to the shielded area. I was able to summon a hellhound on the other side of the barrier."

I felt my eyes widen. "That's great! That means the plan will work, right?"

She returned an uncertain look. "Provided you can imprint the demon name on the hellhound, yes."

I rubbed my hands together, buoyed by sudden optimism. "Let's get to work."

She nodded. "To summon from the demon plane, you must first be able to sense it. Bring forth your incubus senses, but redirect them inside and through you rather than out."

I did as she said, closing my eyes, and allowing my demonic essence to emerge. Rather than extend my tendrils to the outside world, I sent them flowing inside me. Unfortunately, all they did was go through my body, and come out the other side. I kept practicing, and listening to Vallaena explain how it felt to stop thinking of them as physical projections, and how I could turn them inside out which would project my senses through the barrier, and into the demon realm.

Over the next few hours, I did just that. The problem was, seeing past my own self was pretty difficult. My demon side was a complete asshole, and just when I thought I'd managed to turn my sense inside out, he would make a break for the opening, and try to manifest me into a killer beast.

"Argh!" I shouted, pounding a fist into my palm, as the demon played spoiler yet again. "I can't do it. My freaking demon side won't let me."

"The demon side is part of you," she said. "You must make it do as you wish."

"Easier said than done." I took a deep breath. Gritted my teeth, closed my eyes, and directed my senses inward again. For some reason, swallowing helped me invert my senses. I did so, and felt the strange sensation of seeing inside myself. I sensed like I never had before, the other presence inside me, almost like a split personality. That side of me had no sense of responsibility. It wanted everything. It was ravenous for food, sex, anything, and it didn't give a damn how it fulfilled itself. It was like a spoiled child.

The moment I sensed this part of me again, it was as if we were looking at each other face-to-face. I could practically see a slow greedy smile spread across a cruel face as it darted for control.

Stop! I roared inside my head. *I am the boss of you, and you will stop!*

Almost like a choker leash on an unruly dog, my demon side jerked back. An image formed in my mind, gathering solidity and clarity, and formed into a black void. I stood in the void, the darkness beneath my feet solid as stone flooring. Despite the pitch, the area around me was illuminated in a dim white light. A figure emerged from the darkness. He was my height and build. And he looked—I gasped. He looked identical to me. Well, except for the long spiraling horns sprouting from his forehead.

"You are not the boss of me," he said, his voice just like mine, but more guttural and deep.

"Yes I am," I said, my voice sounding tiny.

He strode closer, seeming to tower over me despite our similar heights. Fear gripped me, and I backed up a step. As I did, he seemed to grow taller. "I am in control," he said. "Mine."

"No." I tried to yell at him, but my throat locked up, and I trembled.

His lips peeled back from serrated teeth, and black claws grew from his hands. His body swelled a little, gaining height. "You are weak. I am strong. I will take what is mine as it should be."

What the hell was happening to me? I clenched my fists, but they felt so weak, as if I were in a nightmare, and if I tried to punch him, nothing would happen. He would knock me out in one punch.

"Yes," he said, muscles bulking on his shoulders, his arms, his claws growing longer. "I knew you were weak. I am the boss of you. I will take everything. Nothing will stand in my way. Your people will be mine. Your life will be mine."

"No!" I said, my shout sounding muffled and pathetic. "You will destroy everything!"

"I do what I want. It is all mine." His eyes glowed bright, and he smiled. "Elyssa will be mine." His eyes turned to slits, and a forked tongue licked across his blue lips. "She will be delicious."

Rage burned hot inside me. *No. Not Elyssa. He can't have her.* "You will not touch her," I said.

"I will have her," he said, his greedy smile widening.

A volcanic blast of pure rage ignited my soul. I launched myself at him. "Never!" I roared. My hand locked around his throat.

He roared back and gripped my arms, pulling my hands off his neck. "You are weak!"

Clawed hands dug into my flesh. Blood welled, and pain shot up my arms. His grip tightened, and I felt my bones cracking from his grip.

If he wins, everyone will die. If he defeats me, Elyssa is his.

No. I couldn't let it happen. We could still stop it. Vallaena's plan was crazy, but it offered something I thought we had lost after the latest disaster. It gave all of us something we could hold onto and draw strength from.

Hope.

"We," I said, pushing my hands toward his neck. "Will"—I clenched my teeth so hard I could feel them cracking—"win!" I believed we had a chance. I believed this plan could work. And most of all, I believed this stupid bastard wasn't about to have his way with the love of my life.

Fear suddenly lit in his eyes. Without warning, strength seemed to flee from him, and flowed into me. I gripped his throat and throttled him. I picked him up by the neck and held him above the ground, choking the life out of him.

"Who's the boss?" I roared, my voice echoing in the void.

He gave me a furious look, and snarled.

I squeezed harder. Blue blood ran between my fingers, trickled down my arm. He thrashed like a wild animal, clawing at me, but his attempts did nothing to harm me.

"Who's your boss, you effing moron?" I shook him like a rag doll. "Submit to me or I will crush you to pulp."

"You cannot kill me," he said. Tears of blood streaked from the corners of his eyes. "I am part of you."

"Then I will keep you in torment," I said, taking my other hand, and gripping one of his horns. I pulled the horn, and he screamed in pure agony.

"Stop!" he cried.

"Who's the boss?" I said in a low growl.

All the fight went out of him. He sagged. "You are," he said in a whimper.

"I didn't hear you."

He looked at me, expression bleak, like a child denied candy on Halloween. "You are the boss of me."

I grunted. Set him down. "Good."

The void shattered, and suddenly I was looking into Vallaena's blue eyes. "Ah!" I shouted, startled.

"What happened?" she asked.

"I had a discussion with my inner self."

She cocked her head like a curious dog. "You talked to yourself?"

"I took control."

She cocked her head like a curious puppy. "How troubling, and yet interesting. Very well, try to sense the other side now."

I repeated my swallowing ritual, and felt my senses turn inward. This time, my demonic side surrendered, and the world suddenly felt a whole lot bigger. I sensed beings—countless beings. Some brushed past my senses without stopping. Some were so minute as to be almost unnoticeable. Others felt strangely human. I let my senses drift, and felt something truly gargantuan pass by. I felt like a dingy in the wake of a cruise ship at its passing, and felt my physical body stagger.

"You have just sensed a very powerful being," Vallaena said. "They will usually pay you no mind, Justin, but you must take care not to draw their attention. Without their name, you would be as easy to squash to them as an ant."

"I can see that," I said in a weak voice, still keeping my eyes shut so I wouldn't ruin my concentration. "How do I know which ones are hellhounds?"

"Remain passive. You will eventually gain a sense of what is what. This is the part that takes time."

I did as she asked, eyes closed in concentration, my senses extended into the demon world. I sensed all kinds of things. Some sent cold chills down my spines, their presence like insatiable hunger. Vallaena told me they were crawlers—creatures which devoured the essence of mortals until they were nothing but brittle husks. I remembered Shelton's story about Hooch, and hoped I didn't find any more of the creatures.

"Does everything live in the same place" I asked her some time later. "So many seem to pass by whatever spot I'm sensing."

"Although you think you are remaining still, your senses are actually moving. The demon plane operates much differently than here."

"Well, my feet really hurt," I said. I'd remained standing for much of the duration since it was hard to sit down while maintaining my connection to the spirit world.

I suddenly felt something approaching. It grew closer. I wished I could actually see the demon plane, but apparently that wasn't possible, according to Vallaena. I felt a bit exposed, like a man sticking his arm down a tree stump to feel inside at the risk of being stung by an alien scorpion creature with poison that would drive him mad and make him beg for death.

The presence stopped. It actually seemed to sniff my presence and then stopped nearby.

"Um, I think I found a dog," I said, and described the sensation. I hoped it didn't try to sniff my demonic butt.

"Yes," Vallaena said, her hand gripping mine. "Now, envelop it with your senses, open your eyes, and will it to manifest before you."

It sounded easy enough, so I did as she asked. The being in the demon world seemed to sense something was up, and tried to make a run for it, but I—for lack of a better word—lassoed it with my tendril, opened my eyes, and thought, *Manifest.*

The ground turned murky black. The presence in my senses began to slip away. As it did, a form took shape in the oily pool, struggling to free itself. It squirmed, and fought, and a tarred shape took form. A head pushed free of the muck, followed by a body.

Trembling legs quivered and unglued from the earth. To my utter amazement, a hellhound stepped forth.

Vallaena looked at the hellhound as it wagged its tail and ran circles around me. She burst into genuine laughter, picked up my hellhound, and kissed it on the nose. "It's so cute!" she said, sounding like a little girl.

I buried my face in a palm. Just great. My first hellhound wasn't big and scary. In fact, it might have trouble scaring a cat.

Great job, Justin.

My first hellhound looked like a freaking miniature poodle.

Chapter 46

"What went wrong?" I asked Vallaena, watching as my admittedly adorable little hellhound licked her nose, and wagged its tail.

"What did you imagine when you ordered it to manifest?" she said.

I thought back to that instant and remembered an image of my former best friend's dog flashing into my head. Except his dog was big. Why mine turned out so tiny was a mystery. I told her this, and she shrugged.

"The spirit you pulled forth might also be young. There are many factors which can affect it." She kissed the hound on the nose again, and set him down. "In any case, you must now banish it."

My hellhound looked up at me with huge adoring eyes, his little tail wagging. "But—but I can't. He's too cute."

She sighed, tapping her fingers on her leg, and nodded. "I agree. Summon another hound, but try not to make it cute so you can banish it without emotional trauma."

I went back through the process, and found a similar presence to the first, though this felt a little different. It actually felt as though it was more intelligent, older. I pulled it through, and ended up with a dog the size of a Doberman. It didn't wag its tail, but just stood there looking at me, as if waiting on a command.

"Sit," I said.

It looked at Vallaena, back to me, and remained standing.

"Some of them require training," she said. "Although this is definitely a much older spirit. He would be a fine hellhound."

"And I have to banish him."

She nodded. "You need to learn how." She walked to the newly minted hellhound, and petted it. It grudgingly gave its tail a wag or two, as if it found the whole process somewhat degrading. "Using your Daemos senses, grip its spirit, and imagine the manifestation portal swallowing it whole."

I tried as she said, but had trouble grasping the soul. It felt slick. When I explained this, she told me that since it was in a physical shell, it would be harder to grasp, but to continue trying. Thankfully, the new hellhound didn't seem to mind, and sat on its haunches while I tried to banish it back to hell. I finally managed to latch into the creature's soul. How exactly, I did it, I wasn't quite sure. It was like trying to latch a suction cup on a porous surface, and finally finding the exact area where it can grip.

Willing the manifestation to reverse itself was easy after that, and the oily pool swallowed the hellhound whole. The baby hellhound whimpered as the other one sank into the earth without so much as a bark, and huddled at my legs.

"It's okay," I cooed, picking—I checked between its legs—*him* up and petting him. He seemed to take comfort.

"How sweet," Vallaena said, her voice weary. "Now, let us keep practicing."

By midnight, I'd repeated the process numerous times. Every hellhound was different. Some were mean and had to be restrained. Some were full of energy and wanted to race after every squirrel they saw. Others were calm and stoic like the second one.

Most of them didn't come through fully trained, and that was the hard part. Vallaena explained that if I manifested one who refused my orders, the plan would fail.

"When I manifested the hellhound inside the shield," she said as we walked back to the mansion, "it took a great deal of energy. I was so tired, it took all I had to banish it."

"So I might only have one try at this," I said.

She offered a grim nod.

I was beyond exhausted, so trying tonight was out of the question. That left tomorrow, and a short window on Saturday. We were cutting it too close.

Once home, I set the puppy on the floor. He raced around sniffing everything, tail wagging like mad.

"How cute!" Bella said when she saw him, and knelt down to pet him.

He made a little growling noise, and backed away. Even if he was a puppy, he was still a hellhound. One bite from those little teeth, and it wouldn't be good for Bella. My felycan friend, Stacey, had almost died from hellhound bites, and I'd almost died saving her.

"Behave," I told him in a stern voice. "She's my friend."

He looked at me, looked at Bella, and wagged his tail, little black tongue lolling.

Bella wasted no time petting and doting on him. He snuggled up to her, and licked her.

"His breath is a bit sulfurous, but he's still adorable." Her head tilted a bit. "Wait, is he a hellhound?"

I nodded. "My first."

She giggled. "You are too cute sometimes. What's his name?"

I gave her a blank stare. "I don't know, and I'm too tired to think of one now. I'm going to bed." I glanced around. "Is Elyssa here?"

"She's upstairs, I believe. She said she tried to text you but you never answered."

I pulled out my phone and saw two missed texts. I groaned. I'd probably been sensing the demon plane when her messages came through.

I ran upstairs and found her in bed reading a book. She leapt up and embraced me in a tight hug.

"How did practice go?" she asked. I heard yipping and growling behind me. Elyssa's eyes darted toward the floor and went wide with adoration. "He's adorable!"

The puppy seemed to love Elyssa right away, licking her nose and wagging its tail.

"A hellhound?" she asked, surprised.

"My first," I said.

She laughed. "You're so cute."

"Any luck finding Ivy?" I asked.

She shook her head. "It's possible Jeremiah pulled her off campus for the time being. I've got plenty more places to search and people to question."

"It's good to have you back," I said, and kissed her. The puppy licked our noses, obviously wanting in on the action.

I awoke with a jolt the next morning. *Friday.* Doomsday was tomorrow. My old friend, dread, seeped into my stomach, making it hard to feel hungry for breakfast. Elyssa kissed me goodbye and left in search of my sister while the puppy licked my nose, as if to tell me everything would be okay. I let him stay at the mansion with Bella since I didn't want him tagging along.

The university was positively seething with even more supernaturals than the day before as Vallaena and I headed back to the usual practice spot. There were no classes that day due to the Grand Melee celebrations. Robots and golems of every shape and size walked down the path from the ferry station as teams from the Science Academy and Arcane University showed off their latest creations.

Most of the robots and golems I saw were competing in the light- and middle-weight competitions. A huge flying saucer ferried robots the size of small buildings into the stadium. The fights with the giant golems and robots were the ones everyone was talking about.

Vallaena and I had to wend our way out of the east garden through tents that had sprung up overnight as people camped the grounds outside the east garden. Keg parties filled with frat boys and sorority girls sprouted like weeds among the campsites. Most tents flew flags announcing their loyalty to the various teams from each school, or simply to the academy or university.

We walked to the edge of the forest before Vallaena decided we were far enough from the crowds. I heard a trumpeting roar. The ground shook, and a group of guys burst from the woods an instant before the tragon slammed its snout against the shield, jaws snapping, and plumes of fire bursting from its maw.

The boys laughed and taunted the creature as it threw itself against the shield.

"Idiots," I said. I peered closer and recognized Billy and his friends from the night Lina had collapsed. A part of me hoped the tragon managed to bite off an arm or two.

"College boys," Vallaena said, shaking her head. She led me further away from the commotion until a bend in the forest hid the crowds from us.

"Why don't we go straight down to the barrier now?" I asked her, eager to summon a hellhound.

"You need to learn how to imprint the demon name on them," she said. "Summoning hellhounds here will not drain much energy. As I said yesterday, you may have only one chance to manifest one on the other side of the shield."

"How do I imprint the name?" I asked.

"First, you must find a worthy vessel," she replied.

For once, I remained silent, and waited for her to explain.

"The hellhound must be older, more mature. You've learned how to differentiate them by now."

I nodded.

"When you find them, you must picture the demon name the moment you bring through the hellhound." She tapped her forehead. "This will imprint the name. Then you must force your control over the hound, and command it to shift into human shape."

"Do I picture it doing that, or tell it?" I asked.

"I find a verbal command along with a visual image of the form to work the best. For example, I will say, 'shift', to the beast, and imagine the form I wish it to take."

"Sounds easy enough," I said.

It wasn't. I summoned a mature hellhound on my third try, but failed to imprint the demon name during manifestation. Thankfully, I could do this with a mental command, though it was much, much harder than during the summoning. Forcing the hound to do my bidding and shift took some time, but wasn't nearly as hard as I'd imagined it. While I was far from being the hellhound whisperer, I felt good about my chances.

After banishing my successful hellhound, I turned to Vallaena. "I'm ready. Let's do this."

She looked me over. "I believe it would be best if you had lunch and rested for a few hours. I know you don't feel tired now, but manifesting it on the other side of the shield will require a great deal of concentration and effort."

I sighed, but decided she was probably right. "Okay. We'll try tonight."

The rows of tents outside the stadium had thickened since our earlier passing. We ended up walking around the entire tent city to reach the other side so we could follow the road to the mansion. Greek Row was packed to the gills with parties, cookouts, and revelers of all ages acting like morons. A group of drunk guys staggered over and wolf whistled at Vallaena. She arched an eyebrow and grew horns. They screamed and ran.

Shelton greeted us with a worried look the minute we entered the mansion. I saw another figure emerge from the planning room behind him. The figure was large, obviously masculine, and a figure I knew well—Elyssa's brother, Michael.

"I got the proof," he said without preamble. "Found the person who planted the evidence, and made them confess. A judge is already reviewing the records, and the accused will probably be freed within a few weeks."

"That's great!" I said, walking to him. "Does Zagg know?"

Shelton shook his head. "He and Cinder are trying to figure a way through the shield. I just came up here to grab some lunch and found him waiting." He jabbed a thumb at Michael.

I almost asked him how he knew where we were, but decided it would be a stupid question.

"I have more intel," Michael said, crossing his arms and leaning back against the wall. "Unfortunately, it's not actionable enough to trigger a Templar response."

"What is it?" I asked.

"I followed the trail of crumbs from the guy who planted the evidence, up the food chain, and found the ringleader of the operation." He pulled out his phone, and displayed the image of a middle-aged man in robes. "This guy told me the Arcanus Primus himself was involved."

Shelton sighed. "It's true, to an extent." He told Michael about the events in the Fairy Gardens.

Michael hardly batted an eyelash at the death and destruction. "I think I know why Daelissa covered up his death," he said when Shelton finished.

"How could you know that?" I asked, wondering if I'd missed something vital.

"The ringleader had records. He'd contacted several golem experts, trying to figure out how to bypass the protective spells on a golem and reprogram it without killing the spark." Michael pursed his lips. "I thought he was trying to rig the Grand Melee to win bets. But given the Daelissa angle, I knew there had to be more. He didn't know the answers, so I took all the data to a golem expert."

"What did they have to say?" I asked.

"He dug through the golem modification spells, and told me that if they worked, they'd make a golem change its targeting parameters." Michael took out his phone, and produced a holographic image with a group of older men standing as if for a group photo. I recognized Jarrod Sager in the center.

"Holy ass clowns," Shelton said. "It's the Arcane Council."

Michael nodded. "This spell will make the golem target these people. There's a shield in place that protects the spectators, and the council has even more protection. I assume someone on the inside will drop the shields." He flicked to another image, a series of runes making up a spell. "After the carnage, the golem will self-destruct, but leave enough evidence to trace a trail back to the Red Syndicate, leaving the vampires with the blame for the slaughter."

"But, they're about to sign a peace accord," I said.

Shelton made a popping noise with his lips. "Didn't I tell you Daelissa wouldn't like that? She wants the Arcanes and vampires to go to war."

"Why can't the Templars act on this?" I said.

Michael grunted. "I explained what I'd found to Commander Borathen. He told me he has to receive permission from the Arcane Council to act. Even though he marked his request as urgent, the council is too busy with the Grand Melee to pay attention. Everyone I've spoken to has blown me off—told me I'm paranoid."

"This was her end game all along," I said. "Kill the Arcane Council. Blame the vampires. Create chaos. She doesn't know where the rune is yet, so everything happening here is for another reason."

"Didn't Phillip Nosti's recording say the vampires were once allied with the Seraphim?" Shelton said. "Sounds like she wants the vampires to be on the outs with the Arcanes so she can convince them to fight for her instead."

I opened my mouth to say something else, when my vision blurred. I thought for a moment the vampling curse might be raising its ugly head again, but this felt somehow different.

"Justin, you okay?" I heard someone ask, as though far away down a tunnel.

I opened my mouth to reply when I saw something which looked remarkably like a stone floor rushing to meet my face.

Chapter 47

"He's coming around," said a familiar voice. I opened my eyes and saw Meghan Andretti looking back at me. "Justin, can you hear me?"

"Are you okay, baby?" Elyssa appeared from my other side.

I blinked. "What happened?" I looked around and saw I was in my bedroom. Shelton and several others crowded through the doorway.

I nodded. I felt groggy, but otherwise not too bad.

"I believe he has overtaxed himself in the past few days," Vallaena said. "Yesterday's activities and the strain of the vampling curse have been too much."

"Not to mention today's," I muttered.

Vallaena's eyes met mine. "Justin, you slept all night. It is Saturday morning."

Meghan gave me a worried look, and added. "The Grand Melee starts in two hours."

The end is nigh! I leapt to my feet, and almost fell down from a wave of dizziness. "We've got to go, now!"

Shelton gripped my arm and helped me stay upright. "Hold on, cowboy. What makes you think you're in shape to do anything?"

"He's right," Elyssa said. "You've done too much."

A sardonic laugh erupted from my throat. "It doesn't matter how I feel. All that matters is we get this done." I pounded a fist into my palm to punctuate the last three words. I turned to Vallaena. "You ready?"

Her chin lifted, and she looked at me like a proud mother—or maybe like a mad scientist who just brought a monster to life with a bolt of lightning. "I am."

Elyssa sighed. "You're crazy, but I love you." She pecked my cheek. "Let's do this."

I heard a yipping noise, and saw the puppy hellhound at me feet, jumping up and down. I picked him up and petted him. "If anything happens to me, please take care of the hellhound, Vallaena."

Meghan's lip curled in disgust. "I was petting a baby hellhound? But he's so cute!"

"I will," Vallaena said.

I sighed. "I'm not looking forward to walking across campus."

"Oh, yeah," Shelton said with a smirk. "Guess you don't know what your girlfriend did."

I grabbed a protein bar from the pantry and gave Elyssa a concerned look. "What did you do?"

She smiled. "I happened to find a tunnel connecting this place with the arch."

"A what?"

"The doorway behind the arch," Shelton said. "It leads to here. We cut through the iron grate in the cellar and followed it down to that iron door. Didn't take me long to burn off the locks."

I gave Elyssa a smile. "You're amazing."

"I know," she said with a smirk.

My mind unscrambled as the protein bar kicked in, and I formed a plan. "In addition to getting the rune, we also need to stop the giant golems from killing the Arcane Council." My gaze found Michael standing at the edge of the room. Elyssa seemed to avoid looking at him. "Michael, can you convince the council not to go to the Grand Melee? Maybe evac them to an undisclosed location?"

He nodded. "I'll take care of it."

I turned to Zagg. You're well known here. "I need you to find out which golems are affected. Maybe you can get through to the operators and convince them to double-check."

"I'm on it," the professor said.

I looked at Shelton and Adam. "Please tell me you have good news."

Adam grinned. "Once Elyssa found the alternate route, we went down and ran our shield-hole generator. It's running through thousands of magic cipher combinations. We think this barrier is similar to the forest shield in design, otherwise we'd have no chance of opening a hole."

"How long will it take?" I asked.

"That, we don't know," he said with a frown. "But we also discovered the demon guardian is bound to the shield over the arch. If you banish it, the arch shield will lower, release the rune, and we'll have all the time in the world."

Profound relief swept over me. We could do this.

We took the stairs to the cellar, went through a hole Shelton had made in the grate, and followed more stairs down to a tunnel. At the end, I saw the slagged remains of the steel door that had blocked me the other day, propped against the wall. Through the doorway pulsed the star of malaether.

An arcphone sat near the door, the holographic images of runes and spell code dancing in the air above as it probed the shield for weakness. A row of six slots floated at the top. Cyrinthian symbols filled three of the slots.

"Halfway through to making a hole," Shelton said, his voice tense.

I felt Elyssa's hand tighten on my arm. She kissed my cheek. "You can do this. I know you can."

Just having her there meant the world to me. I looked to Vallaena. "I'm ready."

"Wait for the right demon spirit, Justin," she said. "Remember, you will probably have only one chance at this. Manifesting across a magical barrier will tire you more than you can imagine."

I managed a weak smile. "I got this."

I opened my incubus senses, and felt the tendrils of essence extend from me. Then I swallowed, my physical trigger to direct them inward. My own soul halo glowed before me for an instant before I felt the twisting sensation of my tendrils flipping inside-out as they pressed through the barrier between this world and my second astral address, the demon plane. I waited. Hundreds of spirits passed me, some tiny, some huge. Several times, I sense the presence of a good candidate for hound-doggery, but they sensed me and escaped before I could draw them in.

How long I sat there, I couldn't say, but finally, a presence came into range. It felt very much like most of the ones I'd summoned, albeit more mature. I ensnared it with my tendrils, gripping the soul before it could whisk away. Opening my eyes, I focused on the area just on the other side of the shield.

Manifest!

A dark pool formed in the floor much like the ones I'd summoned through outside. Suddenly, the weight of the world fell on my shoulders. It felt as though all my energy was being drained at once. I staggered, fighting to keep my concentration on the manifestation.

"The name, Justin," Vallaena whispered. "Remember the name."

My face went tight with strain, and I felt sweat pouring down my forehead. I almost fell.

"I've got you," Elyssa said. "I'm here."

Her voice bolstered me. Lent me strength. I sent the demon name to the forming hellhound. The dark form struggled free of the primordial matter, standing unsteadily on four legs, and looked at me with yellow eyes. Through the connection I sensed the demon name burning in its mind.

Shift, I thought to my minion, and imagined a shape.

The hellhound twisted, smoothly morphing into a familiar and naked shape, though it was missing vital components south of the waistline.

"Is that Shelton?" someone murmured.

"Where's his—"

"Shut up," Shelton said with a groan.

I told the hellhound—using mind waves, of course—to give the demon the name. It turned toward the cancerous growth in the floor. The demon's eye and mouth were closed, leaving a seamless black tumor connected by a thin strand to the summoning rune beneath it. The moment the hellhound stepped closer, the eye blinked open. The creature rotated toward it, horrific mouth peeling open in a toothy snarl.

The guardian's name blazed into my mind and the hellhound's at the same time, the pattern of the summoning rune somehow translating into sounds, twisting my mouth and that of the hellhound's into unnatural shapes as we spoke a string of consonants usually reserved for Scandinavians.

The demon's maw flickered, the teeth vanished. An eye stared back. It blinked once, twice, and the demon melted into the floor until nothing remained but the glowing light from the shield.

The shield over the arch flickered like a failing florescent bulb, then solidified.

I groaned.

It flickered again, slower, and slower. Then blipped out of existence. An instant later, a small sphere shot from the arch. It hovered in the air, rotating inches from the malaether. The thrum of deadly energy lessened, fading as the tiny sphere sucked it in until it vanished with a blink. The orb hovered for a moment more, dropped onto the floor, bounced once, and rolled to a stop.

Silence.

I looked around the small room at the tense faces. "I think we did it," I said. "We did it!"

Cheers erupted. Elyssa hugged me tight, smooching all across my face. Relief swept through me, and my legs dissolved to jelly. Vallaena had been right about the strain. I was beyond exhausted.

I told the hellhound to shift back to doggy form since nobody wanted to look at a naked, emasculated version of Shelton, and told it what a good doggy it was. The hellhound growled, sending me a message loud and clear that he felt degraded by such treatment, and curled himself on the floor around the rune.

"Once we get through the shield, we can put it back in the arch, or find another hiding spot," Shelton said as he high-fived Adam.

My phone rang. I answered.

"Justin, this is Michael. We've got problems."

The Grand Melee. "Did you warn the Arcane Council?"

"Security won't let me anywhere near them. Security golems barred Zagg from entering. "We're not getting anywhere, and the main event will be starting in thirty minutes."

Across the room on the other side of the arch, figures appeared, one of them in a top hat. He waved his staff and a hole appeared in the shield. Jeremiah Conroy stepped inside the room, and tipped his hat to us.

I looked at Shelton, at the arcphone. "We need a hole, Shelton, now!"

"I can't make it go any faster," he said, kneeling to look at the symbols floating above it. Five of the six slots glowed green. The last one flipped through symbols faster than I could read them.

Ivy entered the room behind Jeremiah. She gave me a sad look.

"I didn't betray you," I shouted. "I couldn't go through with it, Ivy. Please believe that I love you, and would never hurt you."

Her lower lip trembled. "You lied to me, Justin. Bigdaddy was right about you."

"No, he's not," I said, praying Shelton's spell breaker finished in time.

The hellhound burst from its position, hackles raised, lips peeled back in a snarl. Jeremiah gave an almost contemptuous wave of his staff, and sent the beast slamming hard against the wall with a yelp. Another wave, and the Cyrinthian Rune floated to him and landed neatly his outstretched palm. He clenched it. "It's too early, but it'll have to do." He regarded me for a moment. Sighed. "You have done more to muddle my plans than a rabid coon hound, boy. I told you to stay out of my business, but you won't listen."

"Guess you would have gotten away with it if not for us meddling kids," I said, my voice low and angry.

"Oh, but I have, boy. I have."

"You've twisted my little sister," I shouted, anger pouring from me. "You've warped her into your little child soldier." I looked at Ivy. "Don't listen to his lies. He's just using you. You're more powerful than he could ever hope to be."

"I listened to your lies, Justin," she said, tears welling. "You hurt me." She shook her head, wiping at her eyes.

"Let's go, child," Jeremiah said, patting her on the shoulder. "We have a mission to finish."

"Like killing the Arcane Council?" I said. "You're insane! Daelissa will use you and enslave everyone." I banged futilely on the shield. "She'll kill you!"

Jeremiah grunted. "Forget us, boy. Forget Foreseeance four, three, one, one. It's over. I promise you, I have only good intentions"—he revealed the rune in his hand—"for this."

I pounded on the shield. "You're going to doom us all!"

He chuckled, and it sounded downright evil. "You don't know the whole story, but someday you will." Jeremiah turned and walked away. Ivy gave me one last glance, and left with him.

Shelton's arcphone chimed. Thc shield peeled away in the middle, leaving a hole. I rushed through without any plan but to tackle Jeremiah and take the rune back. He flicked his staff, and the shield on the other side closed. I rammed it with my shoulder, over and over, as if brute force might break through. Exhaustion claimed my strength. I slumped against the shield, panting and could only watch as Ivy and Jeremiah disappeared around the corner.

Elyssa knelt by my side. "We have to stop the golems from killing the council," she said.

"How in the hell are we gonna stop a monster golem?" Shelton said.

That was a damned good question. "When do the giants fight?" I asked.

"Any time now," he said.

"Can we take the golem down with magic?" I asked. "Or is there a kill switch?"

Everyone exchanged uneasy glances. Shelton answered. "Once those things go in the ring, they're autonomous. But the controllers should have a kill switch."

"Michael told me Zagg was detained by security. That means we'll have to go down there and do it ourselves."

"I don't know if we can break through all those security golems," Shelton said uneasily.

I remembered the size of those golems in the practice field. How could I possibly take something like that down? The answer was obvious.

"MacLean, you go to the operators. Get to them by hook or crook and hit that kill switch."

"Aye," he said and raced back up the stairs.

"I'll go with him," Adam said and left.

"Elyssa, can you do whatever it takes to evacuate the council? I don't care if you have to carry them out over your shoulder."

"I'm coming with you," she said.

I gripped her shoulders. "Please, I need you to do that. Shelton and Bella will have my back."

She opened her mouth to speak.

"We don't have time, Elyssa. Please."

She kissed me hard. Looked at the others. "Don't let anything happen to him." With that, she blurred away.

"Shelton, Bella," I said. "Let's go."

"I will come with you, Justin," Vallaena said.

"Are we going to be running?" Shelton asked. "You know I can't keep up with supes."

"I will carry you," Vallaena said.

Bella arched an eyebrow. "He's my boyfriend. I'll carry him."

"Uh," Shelton said, an instant before Bella slung him over a shoulder.

"Follow me," I said.

"I'm gonna lose my lunch," Shelton shouted.

We blurred through empty hallways, emerged outside, and headed toward the stadium. Cheers erupted as an announcer called out names. The tremor-inducing thud of giant feet pounded the earth from within. It sounded like the fighters were already on the field. I went past the stadium, toward the forest, and stopped at the edge.

"How do the stadium doors open?" I asked Shelton.

"There's a gatekeeper," he replied, face bright red, though definitely not from exertion. He gave Bella a pleading look. "Can you put me down, now?"

Bella looked at me. I nodded, and she set him on his feet.

"Vallaena," I said. "Do whatever it takes, but get the gate open. Can you do that?"

She nodded and flitted back the way we'd come.

"You still know how to open the forest shield?" I asked Shelton, remembering the spider bat pranks he'd told me about.

He gave me an uneasy quirk of an eyebrow. "Yeah. Why?"

I turned to the petite dhampyr. "Bella, I need you to camouflage yourselves from smell and sight."

"Whatever for?" she asked. "I don't like the sound of this, Justin."

"Yeah," Shelton added. "'Cause spider bats don't attack humans." His face went pale. "Whoa, wait a blasted minute."

I put a hand on his shoulder. "I'm going to bring the guest of honor to the fight."

"This is a bad idea, man."

"It's a terrible idea," I agreed. "But we need to bring out the big guns to take down the golem."

"What are you talking about?" Bella asked, her violet eyes wide with concern.

Shelton groaned, and stabbed his thumb at me. "Genius here is about to let loose the mother of all predators."

I needed something huge and powerful to fight the golem. My answer?

The tragon.

Chapter 48

Releasing the tragon from its forest prison might rank near the top of the stupidest things I'd ever done, but since Michael and Zagg had failed their tasks, I had no choice. I sent text messages to them, just in case, before I went through with this insanity.

I waited impatiently for several seconds before Zagg replied.

Security let me go, but I don't know if I can get to the operators.

Michael responded a split second later.

Still no go. Taking alternate approach.

MacLean and Adam didn't reply.

I held back a string of expletives, and clapped my hands together. "This is crazy. This is crazy. This is crazy!"

The looks I received from the others only confirmed that.

"Get ready," I told them. "I'm going in." Without another word, I raced into the forest. Thorns and branches snagged my clothes, making fast progress difficult. "Here traggy, traggy!" I called. "Come and get me you big ugly thing!"

I picked up a large branch, and thwacked a tree, shaking leaves, and upsetting a flock of spider bats. They shrieked and flew away.

"Come get me!" I yelled.

I heard a grunt. A low groan. Loud snuffling. The trees fifty yards away parted, and a scaly, red snout poked through the foliage. It snorted, rustling leaves and sending a thin column of smoke drifting skyward. Two beady eyes appeared seconds later. The tragon glared at me for a moment, tilting its head as if amazed anyone could be so epically stupid as to yell at it. It roared, and flames licked the trees nearby, stopping well short of me, but heating the air enough to make my eyes water.

Limbs crackled and broke, and the beast lunged. I yelped, and raced back the way I'd come. A tree branch slapped me in the face, and I stumbled through a patch of thorns, which tore at my shirt. Somehow, I managed to keep my feet. I saw Shelton and Bella ahead. "Now!" I shouted.

Eyes wide, Bella raised her staff. She and Shelton flickered from sight. I ran toward the invisible shield, hoping Shelton knew what he was doing. I looked behind me as I blasted out of the woods and into the open field, a spray of dead leaves flying in my wake, and a thorny vine at least ten feet long dragging from the tail of my shirt. The tragon skidded to a halt just short of the treeline, angry eyes glaring at me. Apparently, it remembered the shield.

I jumped up and down. "Come on, you idiot. Come and get me!"

It took a slow step forward. Leaned down. Opened its mouth and roared. Flames shot into the clearing. The creature tilted its head. Took another step forward, tiny wings on its back flapping with agitation, and gingerly poked its nose about where the shield usually stopped it.

I picked up a clod of dirt and flung it. It smacked into the center of the tragon's forehead. The monster reared back, opened its massive muzzle, and roared. With blinding speed, it sprang like a reptilian kangaroo, flying through the air and landing only yards away from me. The ground trembled beneath me and earth sprayed in my face with the tremendous aftershock. I stumbled, somehow recovered, shrieked, spun, and ran, all within the space of a split second. The tent city loomed, forcing me to dodge through narrow alleys, jump stakes and ropes, and avoid coolers, beer bottles, and other garbage littering the grounds. The tragon, meanwhile, simply tore through everything in its way, crumpling tents, and crushing anything so unlucky as to sit between its feet and the ground. I prayed nobody was inside any of the tents, but there wasn't much I could do about it.

The moment I passed the final row of tents, I veered left, and ran along the stadium wall. A roar went up from the crowd, and thunderous applause echoed from within. Jubilation abruptly morphed into screams and sounds of panic. I heard the announcer shouting something as the screams grew louder. I looked up, and saw flying carpets streaming from landing zones high up in the back of the stadium, some of them with people clinging desperately to the side. Swarms of spider bats, frightened by the commotion in the forest collided with fleeing super-humanity, resulting in even more hysteria.

I was too late.

Unfortunately, with a gazillion-ton dinosaur-slash-dragon hot on my heels, I couldn't exactly stop. The portcullis loomed on my left. If I hadn't been breathless, I would've breathed a sigh of relief upon seeing it open. At least Vallaena had done her job.

I pivoted on a dime to veer beneath the portcullis. Unfortunately, someone had spilled ice cream on the walkway. My foot skidded on it. All sense of traction vanished. My feet flew sideways, and my shoulder slammed into stone.

The tragon leapt, tiny wings flapping, and a clawed foot smashed into the walkway, two of the creature's three toes landing to either side of my body. Ebony talons screeched against the stone, digging gouges. I looked up in time to see jaws the size of a monster truck rushing toward me. I dove, and hit the walkway as the tragon's mouth chomped empty air where my body had been a split second earlier. My feet skidded on the spilled food, found a clean spot, and I lurched forward on all fours beneath the portcullis. I heard a whooshing noise. Monstrous teeth clacked together so hard, a rush of warm air puffed against my backside. By then, I'd managed to get upright, despite my legs feeling like overcooked spaghetti.

Giant claws pounded the earth behind me. I ran through a massive tunnel, and emerged an instant later into the stadium. Across the wide space, a four-armed robot five stories high grappled with an equally giant stone golem. Parts of the stadium near the melee looked blackened and charred, especially the enclosed club seating area where Zagg had indicated the Arcane Council usually sat.

The robot smashed the head of the golem with one huge fist. Red lasers speared from the metal monster's eyes, burning molten gouges in the golem's stony body while its other hand held the stone giant's head motionless. The robot's other two arms gripped the golem's, holding it immobile. It looked like the robot had the upper hand, but had the golem already killed the council?

I magnified my vision, and saw the charred remains of two corpses behind melted glass. On the opposite side of the room, a gaggle of gray-haired men in robes beat frantically on the door. One of them pulled out a staff, and shook it, but it apparently wasn't working, because nothing happened.

The hand the robot held over the golem's face glowed cherry red. A white beam burst from bubbling metal, melting it to a nub. Now free, the stone giant turned its head, showing a single giant eye glowing white as the moon. Light speared from the eye, hitting the robot in the face, turning the metal lava red. The robot threw up another hand to shield its face, but it was too late. Its head sagged in the middle, drooping like a wet paper bag, and melted away in a stream of molten metal. The mega-bot's arms went limp, and it listed to the side, metal groaning like a ship running aground on rocks. In slow motion, it fell to the side, crashing to earth, sending a wave of grass and mud spraying in every direction. The ground buckled beneath my feet, nearly costing me my life as I stumbled away from tragon jaws.

The Cyclops golem rotated back to the panicked council members in the club box, its single eye glowing with unholy light.

A relatively miniscule beam of light speared from somewhere in the crowd, and I saw Zagg, staff outstretched direct the energy at the golem's eye. The automaton flinched as though a mosquito had bitten it. It let out a gravelly roar. Turned its baleful gaze toward the section of seating where Zagg stood, now bare of spectators. Scores of flying carpets circled the stadium far overhead, including a large one with a news crew.

The white beam erupted from the golem's eye, ripping up seating, and leaving a massive swath of black ash as it ripped toward Zagg. The historian threw up his arms in a futile gesture, and the beam of light washed over him.

"No!" I screamed.

The tragon, scant yards behind me, roared, and sent a blast of heat washing over my skin.

I reached the golem. Looked behind me and saw the tragon's eyes alight on the giant. One of the golem's giant feet rotated toward this new threat, nearly crushing me. I went down on my back, sliding on the slick grass beneath the lifted foot. I watched, helpless as the bottom of the foot traveled earthward. A hoarse cry erupted from my throat. The foot slammed to earth an instant after I cleared the ground beneath it. The shockwave lifted me off the ground, and sent me tumbling through the air. I thudded face-first into mud, sliding for several feet before coming to a stop.

Clearing muck from my face, I rolled onto my back just as the tragon leapt, claws extended for its new enemy.

The golem rumbled in protest, and grappled with the giant dinosaur creature which nearly matched it in height. The baleful eye glowed, and I feared the tragon was about to meet its match, but the huge reptile roared, blasting a gout of fire so hot it melted the ridge of stone just above the golem's eye. Lava washed across the deadly orb.

I glanced back at the club seating, and saw Michael rip through the door with his sword, freeing the council. The golem seemed to sense its primary targets' escape attempt. It rotated its head, and fired a blast at the fleeing Arcanes, but the molten stone across its eye blocked all but a tiny sliver of the death beam. The tragon's jaws clamped around the golem's head, gouging huge divots from it, and causing the giant to stumble backwards. It crashed against the stadium wall, sending chunks of rock raining down on the field.

The tragon and stone golem circled each other like two predators waiting for the other to make a mistake. The golem's eye burst into light, and the beam speared for the tragon. The tragon opened its jaws and blasted an inferno of ruby-red flames. The rippling energy met in the middle, swirling into a sphere of red and white. I watched, mesmerized at the sight, unable to move. I hadn't seen anything so awesome since watching a movie where pirates with laser swords fought ninjas.

The two creatures seemed evenly matched as the ball of energy boiled unmoving between the two. Any little change in energy would shift the battle. I raced forward, drawing deeply on the magic around me, and heard the whoosh of flames ignite in my hands. Two fireballs, each the size of my head, swirled in my palms. I raised my hands, palms up, and clapped the two fireballs together into one large mass. Rotating my hands around the energy like a kid would do with putty, I focused more and more energy, willing it to grow larger.

Out of the corner of my eye, I saw the glowing ball of energy between the two combatants shift closer to the tragon. Despite its immense power, it was still flesh and blood. The golem was essentially a machine—tireless so long as it had energy to draw on.

The ball of energy in my hands grew wide as my body, and heat washed over me like a desert. My knees grew weak, and I knew I was beyond my limit. I aimed the shot, and, turning my palms straight out, willing the inferno to speed forward. It struck the ground, rolling and bouncing, burning a charred furrow through grass, boiling steam up from mud. It bounced one final time, and hit the golem in its pinky toe, melting through stone like a hot knife through butter. It sliced away the remaining toes. The golem might be powerful, but without a functional foot, it didn't matter how strong it was. The creature shifted to the side, its damaged foot crumbling. In an instant, the stalemate ended. The massive ball of coalesced death between the tragon and the falling golem streaked toward the stone giant, engulfing its upper body. Lava streamed down the sides of the golem. The bright ball of energy faded, revealing a molten mountain of rock, which crumbled as it toppled sideways. Boulder-sized chunks of rock rumbled and bounced, massive chunks of shrapnel with deadly speed.

I zipped side-to-side, dodging the big pieces, but small bits of sharp rock tore into me. Something big slammed into my chest, and I flew backwards. A boulder thudded to earth, just missing my leg. A large rock plowed a furrow near my head. Thankfully, the boulder near my feet shielded me from the rest of the shockwave. I tried to stand, but agony lanced up my leg. I cried out, clutching at the spot where a bone jutted from the blackened skin around my shin.

Whatever blessing the man from the pond had given me seemed to be wearing off, because my lower body started to hurt like hell. I pressed the bone back into the skin, screaming non-stop, hoping the healing process would start. Usually my skin knitted itself together within minutes after an injury. The curse-infected skin wasn't healing, just as it hadn't the scrape from days ago.

As if sensing that I'd just thought of it, shards of cold pierced my veins, running up my legs, and curling towards my heart. My body locked in a spasm. I couldn't move my muscles. I couldn't speak. All I could do cry in ragged agony.

Something thudded. Giant nostrils sniffed the air, and the tragon loomed behind a boulder several yards away.

I bit my tongue until I tasted blood in my mouth hoping to quell my scream.

The tragon's red eyes lit on me, the pupils narrowing to slits. It huffed, jaws opening and closing almost as if it were laughing.

I felt another wave of cold rush up me, like the arctic ocean tide trying to claim the beach. I was able to move my head just barely, and watched as throbbing black veins crept up my chest, visible through my shredded shirt. I knew, with certainty, I was going to die. Whether the curse or the tragon killed me first was the only question.

The tragon leapt.

I looked up as the sinuous, majestic reptile, ebony talons extended, soared in a parabolic arc that would land right on top of me and squash me like a rotten watermelon.

You have to admit, this is a pretty badass way to die.

As brutal deaths went, this one wasn't so awful. This was something people could brag about at my funeral. I felt a grin tug at the corners of my lips as I waited for the end.

The impact rattled my bones. My broken leg twisted. Before I could scream, darkness consumed the light.

Chapter 49

A massive roar pulled me from the dark. I looked up to see the tragon spinning in circles as a figure in black ran up the bony spines on its back like a ladder, and gripped the stubby wings. The tragon blasted fire, and slammed against boulders, trying in vain to shake the intruder.

The figure aimed a fist at the back of the tragon for several seconds. The creature staggered, beady eyes blinking. Its right leg folded, and the creature crashed to earth. I watched in amazement as the dark figure ran off the end of the tragon's snout, and leapt at the last minute as debris from the monster's crash to earth hid them both from view.

I tried to move. Tried to call out. I was so tired. So cold. A silhouette dashed from the cloud of debris and raced to me. A hand touched the neck of the dark Nightingale armor of a Templar, causing the material to peel back from the face and vanish. Raven hair spilled out. Violet eyes filled with tears at the sight of me. Elyssa dropped to her knees and pillowed my head on them.

"Elyssa," I said, feeling hot liquid forming at the corners of my eyes. My voice sounded hoarse. I felt the muddy earth against my back.

"I'm here, baby. I'm here." Large tears dripped from the tip of her nose, and splashed on my lips.

I sputtered.

"I'm sorry," she sobbed. "Oh, god, I'm sorry I wasn't there in time." She held my hand to her face, and I saw my mottled, blackened skin. I knew Elyssa had only postponed my grisly demise, though this one wouldn't be quite as cool sounding as, "Justin fought a tragon, but the tragon won, and clawed his guts out like spaghetti." Then again, turning into a blood-sucking zombie also sounded sort of cool, just not as glamorous.

"I will always love you," I said.

She pressed her lips to mine, sobbing, peppering me with kisses. "I will always love you, Justin."

I decided I didn't want to be remembered this way. "Will you please tell everyone the tragon killed me, and not the vampling curse?"

"I'm not going to let you die," she said, but the hope was gone from her voice.

Darkness gathered around the edges of the world. Shadowy shapes flickered in my peripheral vision. Fanged skulls strained at the fabric of darkness, trying to tear away.

Drink. Devour. Kill.

The voices urged me to kill with violent whispers. But I knew that would never happen.

"When the time comes, you know how to end this," I said, feeling a tear trickle down the side of my face. "I want it to be you. Please."

She squeezed her eyes shut. Nodded. Her arms squeezed me as sobs shook her body. My arms felt numb. They wouldn't respond when I tried to hug her one last time.

Just when I need a hug the most.

"Is—is he dead?" said a small girlish voice.

Elyssa looked up, her red-rimmed eyes wide. "No."

Ivy's pretty face filled my vision. I vaguely felt pressure on my hand. "I know you tried to trick me, Justin." She sniffled. "I know you don't like Bigdaddy or my family, but—but I don't like this. I saw what you did. How you saved those people."

"You're my sister, Ivy," I croaked. "I only wanted to save you."

"I thought about it a lot," she said. "You could have kidnapped me. We almost went inside the house. But you changed your mind. You decided not to." Tears gathered in her eyes. "You really do love me, don't you?"

"Yes." I tried to reach for her, but my body was done responding to my wants or needs. I tried to say more, but a wave of dizziness tried to claim my remaining consciousness.

A sparkling tear fell from her eye, and splashed on my cheek.

I tried to say something witty about girls drowning me in tears, but arctic cold swept up my neck and into my throat. I heard Elyssa gasp.

"Get away from him, child," said the voice of Jeremiah Conroy, but I couldn't turn my head to see. What I did see was Elyssa frozen in place. Her eyes widened, but she didn't seem to be able to use her mouth, or move.

"He's my brother!" Ivy yelled. "My only brother! I won't let him die."

"He will only cause you harm, child." His voice turned pleading. "Let him go. Otherwise, the world will suffer. We stand at the precipice of light and dark, child."

"But, he's my brother," she said, choking back sobs.

"Your brother stands against everything we have taught you. If you do this, if you make this choice, you could destroy everything we have worked for." I heard a foot splash in water. "The fate of the world could rest in this decision, Ivy. Will you choose this demon boy, or your family?"

I heard Ivy sobbing quietly. Several long seconds passed, and then I heard her whisper. "I choose family," she said.

"That's my girl," Jeremiah said. "That's my good girl."

I felt pressure on my chest, and heat scorched through my veins, seeming to light every molecule of my body on fire.

"*Justin*," Ivy said in a furious voice, "is family."

My mouth suddenly responded to the agony in every fiber of my being. I cried out, my voice hoarse and raw.

"There will be consequences for this, girl," Jeremiah said in a low angry voice. "I promise you will not like them."

Ivy leaned into view, her face screwed up with worry. "I love you, Justin." She kissed my cheek.

"Nightliss," I whispered in a hoarse voice. "In…healer's…" I couldn't get out another word.

My sister's lower lip trembled as she drew away from me. She vanished from view, and I heard feet splashing away. A moment later, Elyssa gasped and grabbed my hand.

She's holding my hand, and I can feel it!

Strength rushed into my body. I sat up, and watched as blackened skin and veins returned to a normal pink hue. The jutting bone in my shin snapped back inside with a painful *pop*. My gorge rose, and I lurched onto all fours, gagging as something bulged up my esophagus. Slime slithered up my throat, and the world went black for a moment as I puked like a sorority girl on a Friday night.

When I opened my eyes, I saw a vile black slug-like mass the size of a python squirming on the ground. A circular mouth lined with the kind of latching teeth someone might see in a leech opened, and made sucking sounds. A gout of fire streaked toward it, boiling the awful thing. It screeched, writhed, and shriveled down to ash.

"What the hell was that?" Shelton roared. "What was it? Holy—oh god, I think I want to puke."

I rose unsteadily to my feet, and looked around. Neither Jeremiah Conroy nor my sister were anywhere in sight. "Ivy?" I said.

"They're gone," Elyssa replied. "Took off on a flying carpet. If we hurry we can catch them."

"And do what?" I said, beyond exhausted. Jeremiah was too strong for me to handle. Besides, there was only one thing I wanted at that moment. A kiss. I grabbed Elyssa around her slim waist, and pulled her tight. My other hand caressed her jawline, and pushed a lock of stray hair behind her ear. "I love you," I said, gave her a kiss to remember.

"He's alive?" said a familiar voice somewhere into the second minute of the epic kiss I was giving Elyssa. I looked to see Zagg, a little singed, but otherwise no worse for the wear, standing next to Cinder.

"I thought you died!" I said, and, letting go of Elyssa for a moment, gripped the historian in a bear hug. "How—"

"I threw up a shield at the last minute. And the tragon redirected the death beam just before it burned through my defenses."

A hulking figure in black emerged from behind a pile of rubble. I looked at Michael, and nodded. He nodded back. He'd taken care of his end of the bargain, now I had a chance to do the same for him. I took Elyssa aside, and told her everything Michael had done.

"He wants your forgiveness," I said.

She regarded me with a sad smile. "It's not forgiveness he needs from me," she said. "It's trust. He broke that trust the day he worked for Underborn. I can't just forget that. He has to earn it back."

"Everything he did, it was to make sure you were safe. He thought he had control from inside Underborn's circle and miscalculated. Underborn outsmarted him and used you anyway." I sighed. "Then he rubbed it in your face, bringing Michael along with him to show you he can manipulate anyone. If you don't forgive your brother and trust him again, Underborn wins."

She laughed. "So I trust my brother, or the bad guys win, huh?"

"That's about it."

Her eyes grew pensive, and she stared at the ground for several moments before a slow nod moved her head. "He'll have to make me some promises. He can't just go around trying to protect me in secret. I'm a big girl now. And he'll have to welcome you into the family with open arms."

I grimaced. "Just don't make him kiss me, okay?"

She giggled. "You are too much sometimes."

I kissed her. "And I can never get enough of you."

"We have a lot of catching up to do," she said, and nibbled on my ear. "So much catching up."

The low, sexy tone of her voice sent shivers of anticipation up my back, while other parts of my body perked up. "I can't wait."

My heart went still, as I remembered a friend still in need. *Nightliss.* I had no time to waste.

I saw a discarded flying carpet lying on the ground near the stands. "We need to go, now," I told Elyssa, and turned to the others. "I'm going to the infirmary."

Before they could respond, I grabbed Elyssa's hand, and ran for the carpet.

"Do you think Ivy will help her?" Elyssa asked.

"I don't know." I just prayed she would.

I zoomed low to the ground, beneath the portcullis, and veered down the stone path to the entrance of the school. The carpet was a much nicer one than the ones from the library and had some zip to it. I took it inside the school, whooshing through empty corridors, and dodging around corners. Within minutes, we reached the healer's office.

I jumped off, stumbled, and went down on my knees. My legs were still tired from the beating I'd put them through, apparently. Elyssa pulled me to my feet, and we went inside. The place was a beehive of activity, with golems loading sick children onto flying carpet gurneys, and pushing them down the hallway.

Meghan appeared at the end of the hall, directing traffic. She spotted us and raced over. "Is everything okay? Adam told me you stopped the arch from exploding."

"That's true," I said. "And we stopped the council massacre by giant golems."

"Then why do you look so upset?"

"Where's Nightliss?" I asked.

She pointed inside the office. I raced inside without another word, weaved through the procession of golems and gurneys, until I reached the ward.

Ivy looked up as I entered, her hand on Nightliss's chest. White light glowed beneath her hand. "This feels like a terrible mistake," she said.

"Where's Jeremiah?"

"I told him I was going to help your friend." She frowned. "I thought he would be furious, but he just looked at me and said, 'You and those you love will have to live with your choices.'"

"That's it?" I asked, completely confused.

Ivy's brow furrowed in concentration. The light between her hand and Nightliss's chest flashed bright. "This is a terrible curse," Ivy said, lifting her hand.

Filmy white fluid oozed from Nightliss's pores. Every inch of skin emitted the milky substance. The angel's back arched. She screamed. Ivy swirled her hand over the angel's body as the sickly white poured from Nightliss's skin, her mouth, her nostrils, and even her ears. One last drop hung reluctantly to the tip of her nose before drifting up into the swirling mass now hovering beneath Ivy's hand.

Sweat formed on Ivy's brow. She took her other hand, placed it on the opposite side of the mass, and spoke a word. The substance crystallized with an icy crackling sound. She directed the orb to float and land in a biohazard disposal container.

Nightliss coughed.

Ivy looked at Elyssa. "You're very pretty."

"Thanks," Elyssa said, her a confused look on her face. "You're very pretty, too."

Ivy grinned, but it faded quickly. "I don't like making these kinds of choices, Justin. It's scary. Grownups usually tell me what to do." She looked at Nightliss. "I mean, what if she's really evil, and you're lying to me?"

I embraced my little sister, and kissed her on the cheek. "I'm not lying, and I want you to trust me. Will you stay with me, and not go back to the Conroys?"

Her eyes went wide with horror. "No, I can't do that. Mom is there, even if she is in an astral prison, and I love my grandparents. Please, don't make me make that choice."

They're not your grandparents! I resisted the urge to emphasize the point and simply nodded. "You can visit me any time, okay?"

She smiled. "Maybe I will." She stood on tiptoes and gave me a kiss. "Goodbye." With that, she *blinked* away, vanishing in a cloud of shadows.

"Whoa," Elyssa said, mouth hanging open. "Did she just teleport out of here?"

"Sort of," I said, my attention elsewhere at that moment.

"She did it," said Meghan, who'd apparently been standing in the back of the room, her voice soft with wonder. "Leave the room, please. I need to feed her." She opened a cabinet, and withdrew a mason jar filled with glowing white soul essence. I'd seen her feed it to the angel before, and did as she wished so my demonic side wouldn't try to hog it.

Moments later, the healer stepped out. "She's exhausted, but her skin, her muscles are already filling out again."

"Do you have any chocolate?" I heard a weak voice ask within the room.

"Are you kidding me?" Meghan said, laughing. "I have tons of chocolate!" She vanished somewhere and returned with an armful of dark chocolate bars.

"Can I go in?" I asked.

She nodded. "I think Nightliss would like that very much."

The angel was sitting up. Her face still looked gaunt, but her olive coloring was back. Elyssa approached her, trepidation in every step. Nightliss smiled and held out a shaking hand. Elyssa smiled back and took it. I wondered if that meant Elyssa trusted Nightliss, or if she was just playing nice.

For now, I decided, it didn't matter. We had a brief moment of peace, and I intended to enjoy it. It wouldn't be long before the real storm arrived.

Chapter 50

A week passed. Nightliss grew stronger. The rest of us licked our wounds and regained our sanity. The university canceled classes while they investigated the rampaging stone golem. The golem had killed two members of the Arcane Council by the time Michael was able to free the others.

Zagg's girlfriend, Kayla would be released from prison within a few days, along with all of the other people wrongly imprisoned due to Jarrod Sager and Daelissa's plot. Zagg could hardly contain himself. He was even being nice to Shelton for a change, but I wasn't sure how long that would last.

I called a meeting and invited everyone, including those friends of mine who hadn't been involved in the latest adventures of Justin Slade. Felicia, Adam's sister, appeared, a new boyfriend in tow.

"Justin!" she said, wrapping her arms around me, and giving me a firm kiss on the cheek. "This is Larry."

Larry looked human. I shook his hand and smiled. He didn't seem troubled by the company I was keeping, however. "Are you a nom?" I asked him.

He nodded. "I'm in the Overworld rehab program." A shrug. "I was attacked by vampires, but Felly here saved me and kicked their asses."

She smiled. "I turned over a new leaf, Justin. I want you to be proud of me."

I couldn't help but smile. "I am proud of you," I said. "But, if you take pride in yourself, that's even more important." Bella had told me that once. I hoped she didn't mind me stealing it from her so I could sound wiser than the typical eighteen-year-old.

Felicia leaned close. "He's such a nerd, but he's so good to me."

"Aren't you tempted to drink his blood?" I asked.

She gave me a sheepish smile. "I am, but I'm on the wagon. The Templars have a great blood bag program as an alternative to drinking live." She grimaced. "It doesn't taste very good, but it keeps the hunger at bay." She looked back at her date. "Larry's been begging me to introduce him to Cinder. Do you know where he is?"

I glanced around and spotted the golem sitting in a corner, mimicking the expressions MacLean made as he told Zagg a story. "There he is," I said, and pointed him out. Larry looked a little disturbed as Cinder's eyebrows waggled above a maniacal grin.

"Thanks!" Felicia kissed my cheek again, took Larry by the hand, and led him to meet the golem.

A hand rested on my shoulder. I looked back to see Adam Nosti, Felicia's brother, a grin plastered on his face. "Isn't it amazing?" he said. "She's a different person, man."

I nodded. "I'm really happy to see her coming along so well."

"You've done so much for us—" Adam looked away for a moment as emotion overwhelmed his voice. "You helped us find out who killed our parents and why." He took a deep breath. "If you ever need anything, we're here for you. Meghan, too."

I didn't know what else to say, so I simply said, "Thanks. Maybe we can all survive to enjoy happier times."

He laughed. "True. Guess we'd better be glad for the time we have before the crap hits the fan."

Nightliss appeared in the doorway alongside Katie Johnson, and a hush fell over the group. The angel smiled. Her cheekbones still showed a little, but the glow was returning to her skin. I excused myself from Adam and greeted the two women.

"Justin!" Katie nearly cracked my back with a hug. "I'm so sorry I missed out on everything. I didn't even find out until Nightliss told me."

I laughed. "You're starting college, right?"

She nodded. "Yeah. I was hoping to attend Arcane University, but they don't admit noms." She made a sad face. "Anyway, I'll give you some alone time with Nightliss." She looked across the room and waved at Meghan. "I've got some catching up to do."

"You're looking better," I said to Nightliss after Katie left.

"Thanks to you," the angel replied, her voice still sounding a bit weak.

"Thanks to my sister," I said back.

The angel nodded. "She is a puzzling girl." Her dark eyes softened. "We will save her, from the Conroys, Justin. Your mother too. I promise."

"Baby steps," I said with a grin. I pulled a chair from the table. "Have a seat. I'm going to start."

She touched my hand for a moment, eyes welling with tears. Nightliss wiped them away, and nodded, taking the proffered seat.

I clapped my hands to get everyone's attention. Shelton and Bella entered the room, their faces blushed, and clothes looking a bit rumpled. They looked at each other and laughed, like two kids. I hadn't seen Shelton look so happy before, though he seemed to realize his slipup and reigned in his smile before too many people noticed he wasn't being his usual grumpy self. He had a reputation to uphold, after all.

It took me a while to go from beginning to end of the story. Larry's eyes went round as saucers, and my super hearing overheard his whispered questions to Felicia. "Is this guy for real?"

That guy was gonna need balls of steel to hang with this crowd.

"If Jeremiah Conroy gave the rune to Daelissa, why haven't we heard reports of angels storming the world?" Ryland asked. He stood with his felycan girlfriend, Stacey, who regarded me with her trademark sensual smile.

"Maybe they're still preparing," I said.

"It is unlikely they will invade immediately," Cinder said. "They require time to return the Alabaster Arch to full functionality."

"Daelissa might want to visit her home for a while, too," Zagg said. "From what you said, all this time in the mortal realm was slowly driving her crazy. Maybe she needs some downtime before marching in an army of Seraphim."

"She's unpredictable," Bella added. "Let's hope whatever she's doing will give us enough time to stop her."

"I've got something to add," MacLean said, his voice rising above the hubbub. "But I don't think you'll like it."

"Can't be much worse than Daelissa having the rune," Shelton said.

MacLean ignored him. "It concerns Foreseeance Four, Three, One, One."

I felt my eyebrows rise. "You said it could happen this year."

He nodded. "In fact, I think we already witnessed it."

Murmurs went up around the room as people exchanged worried looks.

"Maybe I'm bloody crazy," the big Scot said, "but I'll break it down." He took out his arcphone and displayed the entire text for everyone to see in a holograph hovering over the table.

In the year of plague comes the Unmaking or the Remaking. The half-damned will make a choice. Each will ally with a harbinger. Should the light prevail, all will be cast in shadow. But should one light the flame in the dark, the shadow may not rise. With either choice comes the end.

After giving everyone a minute to read it, he said, "The widespread outbreaks of the vampling curse make this the year of plague. The half-damned refers to either Justin or Ivy, according to most popular translations. Each one is allied with a harbinger—Ivy with Daelissa, and Justin with Nightliss."

Alarm lit Nightliss's face at this.

"Then it all boils down to the choice," MacLean said. "The only one specifically mentioned is lighting the flame in the dark. I think the flame was lit."

"Well, that's good, ain't it?" Shelton said, looking at Bella as though for confirmation.

The big Scot tilted his head side-to-side. "The only problem is, Ivy is the one who made the choice."

Alarmed conversations erupted. I felt shocked. What choice was he talking about? I didn't remember any flames being lit. The scene remained vivid in my mind, maybe because my death had been so close. I remembered Ivy's argument with Jeremiah. The burst of heat running through my body when she healed me. The nasty black slug I'd barfed. The answer suddenly hit me.

"When Ivy healed me, it burned through me like fire," I said. "She made the choice to save me, and lit a fire in the darkness within me—the vampling curse."

MacLean gave me a proud smile. "Exactly, lad. You told me Jeremiah warned her about the choice. Told her it could cost them everything."

I leaned back, trying to understand what this meant. "You're saying the Foreseeance has come to pass, but wasn't I supposed to have a choice as well?"

He nodded. "According to another corollary foreseeance, two choices would be made. I believe when you decided not to betray her, you made your choice, and that one led to her saving you."

"Hang on a minute," Shelton said, looking as confused as I felt. "If the bad guys made the choice, but lighting the flame means the shadow may not rise, then where the hell is this train headed? Did we come out ahead, or are we doomed?"

MacLean shook his head slowly, eyes serious. "I'd like to think it means we came out ahead. But I don't know for sure."

I looked at Bella. "You've had a foreseeance about me before. What do you think of MacLean's interpretation?"

She gave me a shrug. "I think he's right. I don't know if it's for better or worse. There are other related foreseeances, which say we're doomed. There's also the one which says you have to unite the splintered alliance to stand a chance against the angels." Bella bit her lower lip. "Maybe Foreseeance Four, Three, One, One has come to pass, but this isn't over."

That was one thing I knew for certain.

"There's one other thing I don't understand," Shelton said. "How did Jeremiah Conroy get the drop on us when we were getting the runes? How did he find where it was? How did he drop the shield? It was like he already knew everything, and just waltzed over us to get it right on cue."

Those were questions I'd been asking myself. Bigglesworth had died before he could have told the Conroys anything.

"Remember what he said when he got the rune?" Zagg said. "Something about not having much longer, and miscalculating. And then he said something about it being too early, but it would have to do."

I nodded. "Yeah, you're right. I didn't think about it until just now. But if he knew about the arch and the rune, why wait all this time? Why not go get it? And why would Bigglesworth torture MacLean for the information if they already knew?"

"Remember, lad," MacLean said. "Flarks serve the Seraphim. If Jeremiah knew the location, he didn't tell the Flark."

"In other words, Jeremiah Conroy is in this for himself," Shelton said. "I'll bet he wants to control Daelissa, but hasn't figure out how to yet."

"And we probably did him a favor by killing Bigglesworth," Bella said.

Silence settled on the assembly as we digested these unsettling new revelations. Just when I thought we had answers, we were right back to square one.

"Well, thanks for coming," I said at last. "Lunch is being served in the main hall."

The room cleared in seconds.

Elyssa took my hand and squeezed it. She and I had been doing a lot of catching up the past week. I turned my head and smiled. "I'm going to visit a friend," I said. "Want to come?"

"Another girlfriend?" she said in a joking tone. "You seem to pick up new ones all the time."

I nodded. "She's really pretty, too. Don't get jelly, okay?"

Elyssa laughed. "I know I don't have to be jealous."

"Because you'll ninja kick me in the face if I get out of line?"

She tangled her arms around my neck and heated my lips with a kiss. When she pulled away, leaving us both a bit breathless, she smiled. "No. Before I met you, I didn't know what real magic was." She touched my lips with her fingers, and pressed them to her heart. "That's what we have, Justin. I've fallen in love with you twice. I'd do anything for you."

"I'd take a bullet for you," I said.

She smiled. "I think you already did that once."

"You took a tragon for me," I added.

We laughed. I took my girlfriend's hand, and we made our way across campus.

When I reached the infirmary, Morgana jumped from her bed and ran to me, clamping her thin arms around my waist. Tears streamed from her eyes as she looked up at me. Her parents stood from their chairs, smiles lighting their faces. Meghan's drain runes had done the trick, sucking the malaether from the stricken bodies and allowing them to recover.

"Thank you for making our family whole again," Morgana's mother said.

"Michael did it," I said. "All I did was ask him to look into it."

The Findelays still looked tired and undernourished from their time in prison, but the joy in their eyes overpowered everything else.

"Can Justin be my big brother?" Morgana asked, both of her hands clamped around mine. "His family left him."

I choked up and looked away as hot moisture built in my eyes.

"I think that's a question Justin needs to answer," Morgana's mother said, an apologetic look on her face.

I knelt next to the girl, and kissed her on the cheek. "I would love to be your honorary big brother," I said.

Morgana squee'd and hugged me around the neck so tight I almost choked.

Lina appeared at the entrance to the room. She looked much better than the last time I'd visited her a couple of days ago. "Mind if I borrow your new brother?" she asked Morgana.

The girl smiled. "Sure. My parents are taking me out for ice cream anyways. Do you all want to come?"

I thought back to the times I'd had ice cream with Ivy and felt a twinge of sadness. I hadn't heard from her since the last time I'd seen her. I hoped and prayed she was okay, and not imprisoned along with our mother for helping me.

"Justin?" Morgana said, snapping me from my reverie.

I smiled. "Heck yeah, I'd love some ice cream!" I made a concerned face. "I don't know if Elyssa can have any, though. She's got to watch her weight for the Templars."

Elyssa punched me in the shoulder. "Maybe you do need a ninja kick in the face," she said, grinning.

Lina led us into the hallway, and gave us both hugs. "I'm ready to help you in whatever way I can," she said.

"The odds of us stopping Daelissa are looking pretty bleak," I replied. My voice sounded tired.

"You're wrong, Justin," Lina said, her voice stern. "A week ago, the healers thought I would die. They thought all of us with aether poisoning would die. A week ago, that little girl, Morgana, thought her parents would never get out of prison. She thought she was doomed to be alone in this world." Lina wiped away a tear. "Don't you understand, Justin? You make the impossible possible. You give us the one thing that keeps us going and makes us strong."

"And what would that be?" I asked, since all it seemed I did was give people around me multiple opportunities to die in spectacular ways.

"Hope."

The word triggered a cascade of emotions. My mother had left me. My father was marrying another woman. Ivy loved me, but she was still with the Conroys. And still, I persisted. Still, I fought against incredible odds and powerful enemies. Why did I continue to hope? What gave me that inner drive to keep going?

I met Elyssa's eyes, and, in an instant, I knew.

Love.

I loved my girlfriend. I loved my crazy friends. They were my adopted family. And knowing they returned that love, knowing there were people in this world who cared for more than power or money or world domination—it gave me hope.

A sudden smile lit my face as I thought of having ice cream with my newly adopted little sister. One day I would have my family back. I would have my sister back. And then I would treat them all to ice cream, even if I had to mug someone to afford it.

Morgana and her parents entered the hallway.

"Are you ready, Justin?" the little girl asked, eyes glittering with excitement.

I took her hand in one of mine, and Elyssa's in the other. "Let's go."

####

Section A
MEET THE AUTHOR

John Corwin has been making stuff up all his life. As a child he would tell his sisters he was an alien clone of himself and would eat tree bark to prove it.

In middle school, John started writing for realz. He wrote short stories about Fargo McGronsky, a young boy with anger management issues whose dog, Noodles, had been hit by a car. The violent stories were met with loud acclaim from classmates and a great gnashing of teeth by his English teacher.

Years later, after college and successful stints as a plastic food wrap repairman and a toe model for GQ, John once again decided to put his overactive imagination to paper for the world to share and became an author.

Connect with John Corwin online:

Facebook: http://www.facebook.com/johnhcorwinauthor

Blog http://johncorwin.blogspot.com/

Twitter: http://twitter.com/#!/John_Corwin

www.ingramcontent.com/pod-product-compliance
Lightning Source LLC
LaVergne TN
LVHW050922080826
845145LV00001B/180

* 9 7 8 0 9 8 5 0 1 8 1 5 3 *